Praise for *Courageous Lady*, Book #1 of the "Lady" series:

"A very good look at Native Americans and their spiritual beliefs . . . I could feel that I was in Alaska with Leigh, and her interaction with other people and especially the animals of Alaska. Highly recommended."

> — Shirley A. Sampier, "Coyote Woman"
> Dexter, MI

"...It combines romance, adventure, and intrigue all at once. A must read for romance readers and historians!"

> —LeAnne G. Wilson
> Alexandria, VA

"I recommend this book to any lovers of Jim Harrison's Northridge novels, since this has a similarly sympathetic ear to Native American concerns."

> —T. Parker Flangan
> Clayton, MO

"I now believe that my life can change if I simply have the courage to act. A great read, it demonstrates a spiritual depth lacking in the modern world. BRAVO."

> —Hellmut Oskar Klensch
> Salt Lake City, UT

Intrepid Lady

Intrepid Lady: Novel #2

A woman's Alaskan quest for Native
American spirituality

Mark Allen North

Fresh Ink Group
Roanoke

Intrepid Lady: Novel #2
A woman's Alaskan quest for Native American spirituality

Fresh Ink Group
An Imprint of:
The Fresh Ink Group, LLC
PO Box 525
Roanoke, TX 76262
Email: info@FreshInkGroup.com
www.FreshInkGroup.com

Edition 1.0	2008
Edition 2.0	2013
Edition 3.0	2016

Book design by Ann E. Stewart

Cover design by Stephen Geez/Fresh Ink Group

Inspired by the artwork of Frank Minnick

Cataloging-in-Publication Recommendations: General Fiction; Multi-cultural (Fiction); Contemporary Women (Fiction); Cultural Heritage (Fiction); Action & Adventure (Fiction); Mythology (Fiction); Alaska; Alaskan Wilderness; Tlingit Culture; Native American; Wilderness Survival; Women's Fiction

Library of Congress Control Number: 2013930978

ISBN-13: 978-1-936442 13-3

For Milton Duane Redick

and

Irene L. Parker-Redick,

two of my best friends, my brother and sister-in-law

Acknowledgements

Writing *Courageous Lady*, *Intrepid Lady*, and the last installment, *Valiant Lady*, would not have been possible without a great deal of help. Leigh's experiences could not have reached this form without the contributions of many people. In many ways, both obvious and obscure, it is a collaborative work.

I want to express my gratitude to the people who helped develop the "Lady Series" along the way: Dave and Becky Halverstadt, Shirley Sampier, Gay Lynn Redick-Cookson, Tom Redick, Denium Roman, Anne Arnold, Betsy and Bill Ince, Carol and Chuck Jennings, Dave and Kay Wagner, Chuck and Non Rycenga, Pam and Bill Gnodtke, Glenn Bongard, Lyman Jones, Janet Curio, Ian Lamb, Robert Tiran, Scott Detloff, and Henry Phillips. Whether through financial or literary support, they all saved me from the more obvious forms of embarrassment when I used words to express my thoughts.

I am particularly thankful to Leonard Gasco (full-blooded Odawa Indian elder) for his counsel on Native American customs and traditions.

For her inspiration, I thank Madeline Kiser.

Thanks to George Parker for his faithful support.

Many thanks to Francis S. Minnick, whose artwork inspired the covers for all three books.

For his contribution of many storyline ideas, scientific insight, financial support, marketing ideas, and counsel, I thank Big Brother Milton Duane Redick. He's my best friend and supporter.

Heartfelt thanks go to Ann Stewart and Stephen Geez of Fresh Ink Group for the file creation, book design, and cover design.

Ultra-thanks go to my agent and ever-present advocate, LeAnne Redick-Wilson, who managed and coordinated publication with Fresh Ink Group—I couldn't do this without her help.

Of special note, I acknowledge my friend, David Duyst, Sr., whose constructive criticism was always welcome and whose creative ideas enhanced the story throughout.

Finally, thanks to my confidant and teacher, Stephen Geez, for his invaluable editorial opinions. He's a mentor, author, and patient artisan of words who contributed immeasurably to the book's readability.

I beg readers' forgiveness for any errors in the text, and for omitting any helpful people I have overlooked.

Author's Note

It has been an extremely rewarding endeavor writing *Intrepid Lady*, the second book in the trilogy that follows *Courageous Lady*, released in 2006. The series chronicles Leigh West's many and varied adventures in Alaska. Its penning served as a release of love lost, a finding of new consciousness, a restored life. As a result of this cleansing, personal feelings are interwoven in the design of the story.

Native Americans tell many tales about the relationship between animals and human beings; these stories are found in various tribes and languages throughout the North. The versions expressed may differ from others collected by scholars and folklorists. The seed that grew into a secondary story of animals interacting with humans developed from a combination of many traditions involving ravens, owls, wolves, bears, and, yes, even mice. Many are coastal legends from Southeastern Alaska, and the others come from the northern interior. This novel is not meant to displace or contradict any of the scholarly work that has been done by authors prior to my efforts. However, rest assured, characters and events of the episodes are products of my imagination. Captivating Alaska, of course, remains very real.

The cities of Juneau, Skagway, and Yakutat; the Lynn Canal; and the majestic Tongass National Forest are easily found on a map. The proud and distinguished Tlingit Tribe, around which much of the storyline revolves, is present in Southeastern Alaska, as are their neighbors, the Haida and Tsimshian Tribes. Native American beliefs about the Natural World and its Creator, their god, "the hero with a thousand faces," strengthen their commitment to preserve Earth Mother and Father Sky as the backbone of tribal unions to deter white man's intrusion into their land, including his "taking" policies. The landscape in and around Leigh's hut on the meadow is fictional.

Prologue

Satellite images of Alaska on the far reaches of the North American continent show the southwest portion of the state like a skinny irregular tail dangling from a large kite, an afterthought of the mapmakers. They certainly didn't arbitrarily intend to take this sliver of land from the Canadians; it must have been based on political logic. Indeed that appears to have been the case in 1728 as the Russians sailed south from the hostile Bering Straits to the more temperate south. They established fishing and fur trading posts at Juneau at the northernmost part of the archipelago, Sitka, centrally located on the Pacific, and Ketchikan, the most southerly at its terminus.

After 139 years of overharvesting fur-bearing animals, lumber, and fish, plus the declining profits and increased native Tlingit hostilities, the Czar saw the colony as a burden. In 1867 he sold Alaska (alayeksa, Great Land named by the Aleuts) to the United States for $72 million. Considering it a foolish investment at the time the doubters soon changed their tune. Three years later, gold was discovered in the Yukon, and America's frontier expanded in Alaska.

Many changes have occurred in environmental practices since prospectors, miners, meat hunters, and lumbering and fishing interests despoiled the tranquil Alexander Archipelago.

In the early 1900s President Teddy Roosevelt declared most of the islands a forest reserve, and set aside the Tongass National Forest, named after the Tlingit Tribe settled in the northern area. World War II altered man's altruistic beliefs in the forest reserve, and Congress allowed for large-scale timber harvesting in 1947. Despite protests from all three tribal groups along the coast—the Tlingits, Haida, and Tsimshian—their claims of treaty violations were ignored. Their traditional subsistence hunting and fishing practices were ravaged by the wanton *taking policies* of contract industries from the lower forty-eight.

This constant abuse of the land and its people continued through the 1970s until the Native American (First Citizens) objections were finally heard and the U.S. Courts ruled in favor of the 1971 Alaska Native Claims Settlement Act, giving the Natives a role in the state's economic future.

The first book in the Lady Trilogy, *Courageous Lady* chronicled Leigh West's spiritual odyssey living in Alaska's wilderness. Surviving the terrors of man, beast, and nature, she gained a new perspective on life while writing about her experiences.

She achieved contentment through romantic relationships, first with a local bush-pilot, then with a Native American Tlingit shaman. She loses both. She faltered emotionally, but steeled herself, determined to survive. Bolstered by beliefs learned from the Tlingits, she welcomed the comforting presence of Manitou, the Natives' deity.

Her most striking mystic encounters involved witnessing the personification of ravens, owls, wolves, and others; and at times found herself unable to distinguish between the animate and inanimate. She adopted an abandoned wolf cub, then returned to camp and discovered an intruder, the brother of her late Tlingit lover. They bonded in their grief, but tragedy shattered her again.

A rogue white wolf befriended her, presented Leigh with her cub, and a fatherly British DNR officer came to her assistance. Undaunted, she found comfort with the three wolves. They led her to a Tlingit Chief, Chi Mukwa "Big Bear," who invited her to stay with the tribe's Raven Clan where she became an adopted member and given her own spiritual name, "Runs with Wolves." She and Chi Mukwa decided to live together when the clan chose to abandon the subsistence lifestyle and move to local towns for work. As winter's snow threatened the landscape, her soul still felt naked, and she wondered if she would be able to write her story while sharing her life with a man.

The second book, *Intrepid Lady*, follows the relationship of Leigh and Big Bear, two independent souls with thorns in their romantic bed of roses. As a Conservation Officer with the Alaska DNR in Glacier Bay National Park, Big Bear reports to his old friend, British Subject Joe Bloom, and juggles the rivalries of the "three-legged-stool" of fishery, lumber, and tourism industries. Bear loves working in the forest and along the wave-mauled beaches, developing his knowledge of and appreciation for nature's role in the web of life.

Leigh "Runs with Wolves" explores the forest, while her wolves protect her from predators. Keeping a journal, she documents the changes starting to impact the Alaskan environment and the lifestyles of its inhabitants.

Big Bear learns to fly fixed-wing aircraft, allowing for more aggressive interdiction options and for monitoring animal habitat among calving glaciers, budding flora and birthing fauna. Leigh often travels with him, leaving Wind Spirit, the orphan boy, in charge of the camp.

With permission from the Raven Clan, Leigh and Big Bear recite their nuptial vows and adopt Wind Spirit and Raven Maiden in a moving, spiritual ceremony by starlit night. Many of the tribal members join them on the meadow to sanctify the event. With a heartfelt emotional plea to the clan, Leigh urges the resplendent assemblage to drop by their hut at any time to enjoy the beauty of the Tongass. Wind Spirit becomes a DNR intern working with Joe and Bear. He also becomes romantically attracted to Raven Maiden.

The new family explores the far reaches of Gitchie Manitou's Kin(g)dom and the beauty of the national park with the excitement that two 16-year-olds add to their exploits. They also invite Chinodin "Big Wind," Big Bear's son in Skagway, to visit the forest and share in his extended family.

Join Leigh and her people as she and the last Tlingits of the Raven Clan struggle to survive the Alaskan wilderness.

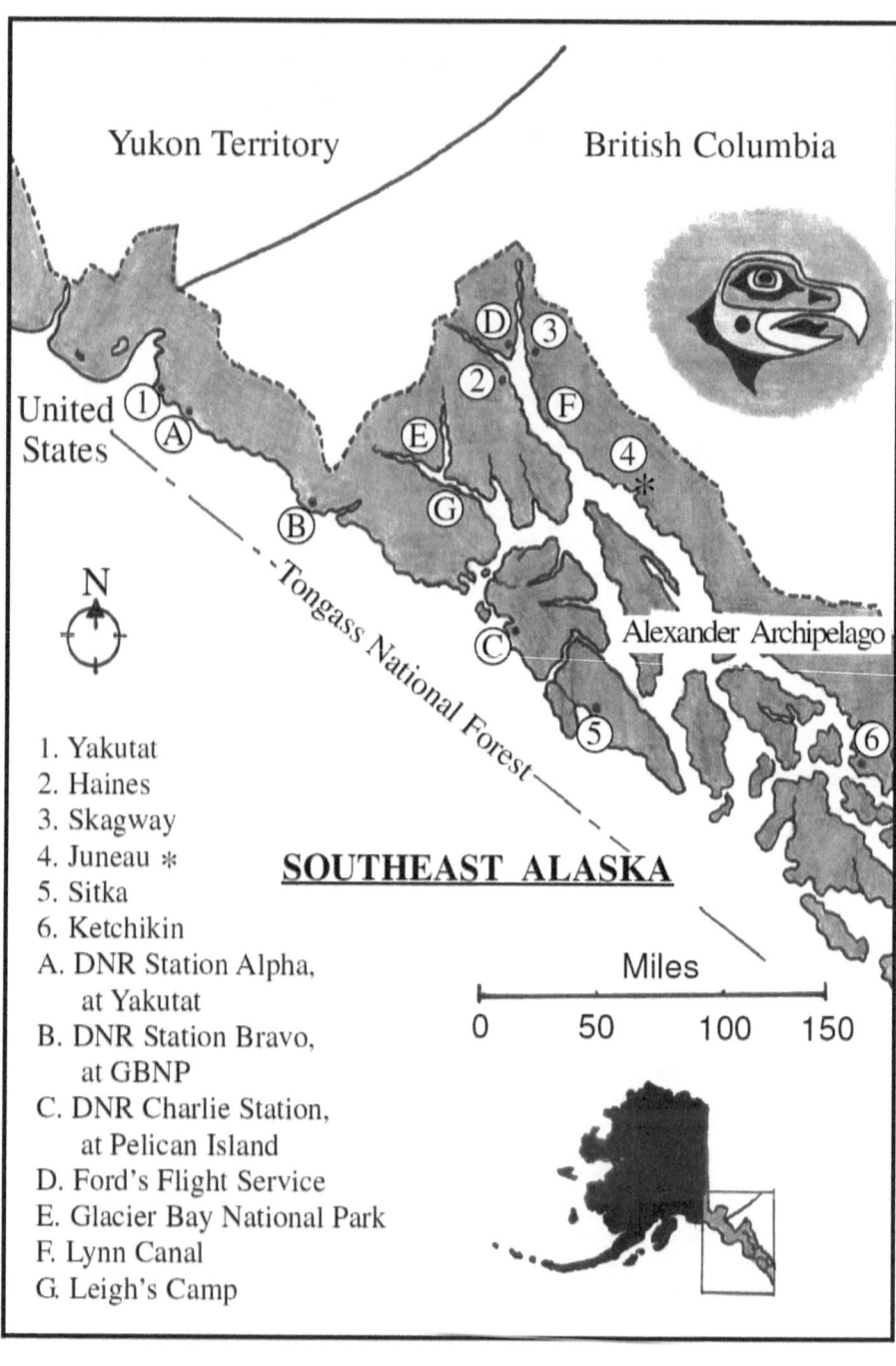

Yukon Territory

British Columbia

United States

Alexander Archipelago

N

Tongass National Forest

D
3
2
F
E
4
*
G
C
5
6

1. Yakutat
2. Haines
3. Skagway
4. Juneau *
5. Sitka
6. Ketchikin
A. DNR Station Alpha,
   at Yakutat
B. DNR Station Bravo,
   at GBNP
C. DNR Charlie Station,
   at Pelican Island
D. Ford's Flight Service
E. Glacier Bay National Park
F. Lynn Canal
G. Leigh's Camp

SOUTHEAST ALASKA

Miles

0   50   100   150

Chapter 1

Reverie

Chi Mukwa stepped outside the hut at midnight, then gestured for Leigh to follow. Their rifles at the ready, they crept across the meadow to the bank of the Bitterroot River.

The moonlight music of the forest creatures hushed as the gurgling river maneuvered peacefully in its passage to the sea. Then it appeared to brood in silence. Flashes of mischief sparkled as the water's eddies turned to freshly bubbling rapids of foamy white brilliance. Forgiving, the river not only provided nourishment, cleaning, and conveyance, but its beauty inspired. Native Indians knew very well how to conserve Mother Nature's watery gift, the powerful bounty for winged, finned, four- and two-legged animals in her kin(g)dom. Her credo lived in their hearts:

"If we give life that gave life, life will give again."

Lying prone next to the water, they watched across the meadow to the north as the unwelcome fog rolled across the plateau and down the slope. Out of the boiling sky to the west, a lance of lightning speared the ether, exploding with a flash of light so brilliant it saturated the air with the smell of ozone. So savage, so beautiful, so timeless, the burn would be like steel piercing flesh. The explosions continued to pound the western sky as the storm's main force moved farther off to the west.

He glanced at her wet hair hanging in deep-red ropes over her shoulders. Her aquamarine eyes swum with emotions from the task at hand. He imagined holding her close, her body pressed intimately to his, the heat from it seeping through his sodden shirt and into his bones . . . but it was not to be, at least not now. Still, he could dream.

Looking toward the meadow at the foot of the plateau, he felt his emotion sinking as the fog's thickening presence closed in around them. Damn the fog. He could feel it, hear it, even taste it. *Why us? Why tonight?*

Being downwind from the hut and the game trails along the plateau's slope gave them some security to the front, but less to the rear. The fog kept rolling onto the meadow, slowly obliterating their view.

This was the third night they had settled into the undergrowth by the river, awaiting the arrival of the unwelcome intruder to their homestead, most likely a bear coming closer and closer. A bear would certainly kill the horse, Old Gal, and the wolves . . . then attack Leigh.

Chi Mukwa watched her earnestly and scans the meadow. He reflected on his first month with Leigh. Yes, there had been many changes: his new job in the DNR, the personal adjustments of living with Leigh instead of his wife and son in the Tlingit, Raven Clan camp, and of course the celibacy.

Leigh's "rules of the house (hut)" were clear: she was to keep her distance from him, and he from her. He was used to having his way; a life of abstinence was not his style. For reasons he hoped to discover soon, she had not shared her bed. Her porcelain psyche had so far proven impenetrable.

The fog now completely masked the meadow.

"What's that?" Chi Mukwa whispered, glancing toward the hut.

"Damn," she whispered, "it's Old Gal chomping on corn I gave her last night. She's chewing loud enough to be heard beyond the meadow; no wonder we've had a bruin visitor. As nice as she is to have around, her life is in danger, stabled in that small lean-to and temporary corral. Too bad, I like her. Maybe we should give her to your son to keep in Skagway.

"Maybe . . ." Chi Mukwa mumbled, not really agreeing. Old Gal was his horse, a working partner on certain DNR assignments.

Silence.

Chi Mukwa whispered, "You know, we can just stop giving her whole corn at night. That's probably what attracts our bruin visitor."

She turned to give him 'that look.' She got the point: it was his horse, and morning feeding would be no problem.

Startling both, a huge blue heron took flight. The elegant bird lurched from the shallows into fog-laden ether, voiceless as she cut through the dense vapor stroking her massive wings against the masking blanket of moisture.

Silence.

Another waggle followed as a startled family of muskrats swam through the cattails' furry brown spikes along the shoreline. More invisible denizens of the night scuttled to the protection of their bankside homes. The human intruders were upsetting the natural order of things, for these critters truly owned the night and deserve to be left alone.

"I feel like telling our animal friends it's not our choice to be here," he whispered. "Say, look to the rear, over the river into the swamp. The dense air is vaporizing into a misty mask as the temperature drops; this transformation used to be called 'toxic miasma' by superstitious old-timers. They thought it caused disease and certain death, so they never ventured into it. Thank goodness these myths have been disproven through sound science and reasonable thought. Still, I wouldn't walk through that misty swamp at night. Would you?"

"Hell no," she said quietly. "I don't even like this bruin stake-out, but I think your plan will work. At least it's worth a try."

The fog swirled around them until all he could see was her face.

Silence.

*   *   *

Moonlight suddenly slashed through the mist to reveal a whip-poor-will flying silently between them. It abruptly climbed, banked, and dove on an unsuspecting insect with an acrobatic display rivaling aircraft agility during dogfights in WWII.

"Stay in focus, Leigh," she whispered to herself. "Listen for the grizz. That's your full time job tonight."

She heard whispering sounds filtering through the trees, but decided they were just the storm's winds polishing the air, ready to explode in front of the numbing nimbus tempest. Could it be Chinde, the death voice of the Wailing Wind?

Leigh, stop it. Your imagination is getting carried away by the storm's violent fury.

Many visions on the meadow played through Leigh's head as the storm's lightning blazed its radiance across the meadow. Was that a shadow or an animal? Was that a bush or a bear? She would swear that bush moved. Every illusion nature had at her command was adding to the visual fiction on the meadow. She was embarrassed several times thinking she had seen a bear stalking toward them. She remained silent, later finding that the bear was a dense bush in its wind-blown rhythmic sway. Her Manner was more than genial, but it couldn't disguise her impatience with fools, and she didn't want to be one in front of Chi Mukwa.

She looked at him with the same admiration, the same resolve, as the last thirty days, a dear friend; but she had to keep her distance even though he had already captured her heart. Yes, she would love to feel his arms around her every night, but she had vowed to herself to be more cautious in affairs of the heart. She had been hurt in the lower forty-eight, then traveled to Alaska as the survivor of an emotional train wreck of disquieted love, of an unfaithful lover. Even though the pain lingered, she responded to new relationships with the hope that new love would repair her broken heart.

Her decision to wrap her heart and desire around several men in Alaska had brought short-term gains but long-term disastrous consequences. Through no fault of their union, each relationship ended tragically, driving her to seek the salve of love to heal her wounds. They were all single, beautiful men of the North, each with the admirable traits of rugged Alaskan landscape, whether Native American or a local Bush Pilot. Their love did work, but only temporarily.

Christ! Three men taken from my arms, from my heart in six months. That's too much for any normal woman to endure. Everyone, no matter who, has emotional limits. I've reached mine. Yes, I want to love Chi Mukwa, but he's not like the others. He's still married. Out of respect for Morning Star I will not violate their bond, even though the separation straining their relationship is at the breaking point. Until he proclaims that his physical and emotional ties with his wife have terminated, I will keep my behavior under control and my love repressed.

I know men. He'll try to weaken my resistance to his desires, but he'll get the point as soon as he probes my emotional needs. I'll reveal my principles. He cannot have it both ways. Oh yes, he'll be upset and try to sweet talk me when his testosterone flares, but it won't work. No, I'm not necessarily looking for a marital relationship, but he will not place his shoes under my bed until he clarifies his intentions.

Look at that hunk.

Yes, he's focused on conquering that nosy bear right now, but without a doubt he wants to conquer me, too. Aaahhh, my kind of man. I can hardly wait to romantically duel with him, to share, to love.

More silence.

*   *   *

"How's it going, Leigh?"

Silence.

"Leigh, are you okay?"

"Oh . . . Ah . . . not good, I have imagined every animal in the Tongass on the meadow at one time or another over the last couple of minutes. That damned lightning illuminates scrub oaks, blueberry bushes, and random pines to appear as an animal. I wish it would either rain or blow by. This alternating wind, rain, lightning and fog is a pain in the butt."

"I agree."

Silence continued.

Fortunately, the storm appeared to be moving off to the west. The wind died down and the meadow became silent.

A calm embraced the region.

Suddenly a thrashing noise echoed across the meadow from the north. A large dark mass moved toward them from the plateau. Its slow, methodical gait indicated a bruin. They knew that rhythm, that lope, that fearsome sound. The bear apparently scented their location.

"Well, dear, it's decision time. This is what we wanted, a confrontation with the animal that's been stalking the hut for the last few weeks, and I think it's exactly what we expected: a silver-tipped grizzly."

"What's our next move?" Leigh asked as she moved to a shooting position.

"As discussed, let's go with Plan A. I'll fire around over its head first, hoping to chase it away. There's no reason to take the life of a nosy bear who stumbles upon the hut and horse in its domain. It just needs a reminder to stay away. As my dad used to say about nosy wildlife bothering domestic animals, just blister its ass with rock salt in a shotgun or throw a thirty caliber across its path. Let's hope it works. For all we know, it could simply be young and curious. Go ahead and rack one into the chamber so that if it does not turn we can both send a message . . . a couple rounds into its shoulders. Remember, don't be shy; the bear isn't."

"Okay, done," Leigh responded nervously as the bear continued to approach their location.

"Leigh, it's probably best to point your rifle toward the sound out there. You'll be able to get a quicker sight. Use your iron sights in the fog. Bears are unpredictable, so be ready if it does not turn."

"Okay, I'm ready."

Silence.

"He must have stopped," Leigh whispered.

Grunt . . . and a wolf-like sound pierced the fog.

"Damn, you're right. The bugger's probably checking for our scent right now. Trying to see how close we are, knowing we're here but not exactly where. This darn fog is troublesome to all three of us."

"Okay, babe, let's assume we've just got a curious, friendly young bear, and if it gets too close to us the darn thing will turn and run due to the confusion of our presence, the fog, and our scent."

"I hope you're right. It's been quiet out there for quite awhile, too damn long for my nerves."

Lightning crashed through the ether, drawing their gaze to the meadow . . . and there it stood: a huge silver-tip grizzly in a veil of fog.

They froze in place.

It seemed like minutes passed as they stared at each other.

Neither moved. Only the moon's glow through the billowing fog outlined the bear.

"Okay, Leigh, that's enough. I'm going to squeeze one off just over its head. You ready?"

"Yeah! I've also got the bear in my sights."

"Good, We'll need all the firepower available if he charges." Tension and fear filled them with anticipation.

Grunt.

Suddenly, lightning crashed across the meadow like a flying torch. No longer standing, the bear had casually moved toward the pair with apparent indifference. Chi Mukwa felt a little relieved. It appeared to be a younger bear on his own for the first time, clumsily exploring the forest. Thankfully, the bear was not going to charge. Trial and error are a part of life for all animals. Nevertheless, the bear had to be scared away from this homestead.

The bear stood again . . . only twenty-feet away.

Ka-Pow!

The round whistled through the air, followed by a shock wave separating the fog.

The meadow exploded *ROOOOAR!* as the thrashing animal turned, whip-sawed, whirled while rending the ground, then spun all the way around and looked at the pair once more.

Ka-Pow!

Another round fractured the air around the bear's head. The insurance shot demonstrated their seriousness and sent the bear to all fours. It leapt to the rear, then ran at a galloping speed across the meadow and up the slope's game trail in a matter of seconds.

The bear appeared to be slowing down, silent now, except for the continued sounds of splintering timber, cracking branches, and tearing terrain. The five-hundred pound mass slowly ploughed through old-growth timber and smaller standing trees. Then it slowed, stopped, and turned back at one-hundred meters. His posturing seemed to indicate that he had just escaped certain death. He seemed to recognize the significant reality of the slipstream of noxious gunpowder lingering in the fog.

*   *   *

Reflecting on the closeness of the two shots, the bear felt it was not a coincidence not being hit. Either of the two persons could have dropped him at thirty-feet. No, it was not accidental that he survived; there was a reason.

Why alive?

Why saved?

Who? The creator? The homesteaders?

Maybe they were trying to just scare him away from the meadow and the unusual scent. Maybe they just wanted to be left alone. He understood. Those people must be reasonable. He was fortunate.

He ambled away knowing the point where the transgressor could easily become the victim. His friends of the meadow could rest well now. He would view them from a distance now.

*   *   *

Leigh strained her eyes and all her senses to determine if the bear was gone.

"Do you think the bear has run off?"

"Most likely. He'll have to decide if this encounter created enmity or, better yet, a learning experience that he cannot stalk or worry our animals without consequences. I hope it's the latter. You know, I've a sense he is a novice on his own, making some bad decisions on his learning curve of what to do and what not to do to survive."

"We, too, are fortunate. Killing a beautiful animal for a mere intrusion is unacceptable to our people, correction—to all people—and certainly to Manitou. All the animals are our brother in the struggle for survival on Mother Earth's sanctuary."

"You are right, Leigh. You've learned your lessons well as a sister in the Tlingit Nation. Gete Wabiska (Old White), our chief, would be proud. I sensed his spirit, his presence, with us tonight. I felt him in my heart as I fired the warning shots. For all I know, Manitou may have shape-shifted to the bear's psyche in order to influence the bear's actions. As with all faiths, some events do not lend themselves to reason, but amity dwells with all of us through faith in the Creator's teachings. To love one another, we live and let live . . . and follow the Red Road as a goal in life."

Getting ready to leave, Leigh marveled at the meadow's absence of color, which reminded her of Ansel Adams, her favorite photographer; he would love the striking contrasts of black to gray to white found in the tableau of the clearing meadow.

*   *   *

Walking back to the hut through the clearing fog, the pair feel relieved, a sangfroid, a calm in having met and solved, they hoped, the challenge of the meadow-stalker. They discussed the dangers experienced as part of wilderness living, but took no unnecessary risk. Only a fool invites trouble. Everyone in the Creator's domain, winged, two- and four-legged, have a place in the survival of the fittest. A few trophy hunters would have harvested the bear, but not being a part of that group, it would have been an aimless death to Chi Mukwa. Subsistence hunting was okay; harvesting for the table did fit into the Creator's plan, if you thanked Him by asking for his blessing, the gift of one of his animals.

"You'll do very well with the DNR, my friend. Joe has mentioned how you are a natural for conservation work. Your credibility in management decisions will finally offer minority representation for your people and out-of-state hunting interests. It's about time."

"Thank you, I'll do my best. Are you aware I'll be training for several weeks in Juneau, and after some field time go back to learn to fly the DNR's fixed-wing and rotary aircraft?"

"Sounds exciting, I know you'll be first-rate as a pilot," Leigh said smiling. "You'll bring reality and proportion to game laws for those who have no sense of the big picture of game management. If necessary, your drill-bit eyes would say it clearly to those who disagree with your long-term plans over myopic, self-serving political idealists," she teased.

"True, I remember only too well how the wilderness life was summarized to me in an old African Proverb that my grandfather Golden Bear gave me as a gift:

"Every morning in Africa, a gazelle wakes up.
"It knows it must run faster than the fastest lion
 or it will be killed.

"Every morning a lion wakes up.
"It knows it must outrun the slowest gazelle
or it will starve to death.

"It doesn't matter whether you are a lion or a gazelle.

"When the sun comes up, you better start running.

"How 'bout that gal? I was only ten when the chief gave me the assignment. It's the first maxim I've memorized."

"That's beautiful, and an expression of the ultimate truth, my dear."

"Did you hear that?" Chi Mukwa looked toward the hut, hearing the wolves howling in concert, if not in rhythm, with the whinny of the horse. I suppose they're wondering why we're both stamping around the meadow in the middle of the night during a storm. Little do they know our night-time vigil and contact with the four-legged bruin may have saved their lives."

Leigh led the mare from the lean-to and walked her to calm her, to let her know the meadow noise was over and the area had returned to normal.

"Yep," she said, "she's a good old gal, let's make her a better enclosure. One that's more secure from rogue wolves or bears."

"Right you are my friend," he acknowledged. "Now, how 'bout me working on a big breakfast for you after lying with me all night?"

She seemed to get the play on words, but did not respond.

The wolves exploded to the meadow, and started backtracking the pair's footprints to where they had lain during the night. He rustled some grub while Leigh ran with the wolves.

He thought, What shapes a man's life? Heredity? Environment? Friendships? Or is it some unknown influence? It appears a woman may soon be shaping mine . . .

Chapter 2

Reflection

The early-morning ride along the Bitterroot was in response to Joe's request to
investigate an illegal fish net about ten miles downstream from the meadow. Old
Gal was all ears and frisky as Chi Mukwa rode the mare along several meandering
game trails. Both were excited to be on their first assignment. He loaded the large
saddlebags earlier with enough equipment and supplies for a week in the forest.

Voices of the forest surrounded the pair as they penetrated Nature's sanctuary. The sounds were small and faint at times, many of which were unusual, weak,
and subtle, requiring fine tuning to hear. In all men there remains much of the
primitive, and after a short time in the forest a man's senses begin to be more

intense. He must listen, he must wait, he must give himself time to get the wavelength of the forest; then he becomes aware of the creatures around him, and becomes one of them.

Chi Mukwa lived in the Alaska wilderness long enough that his ears had become alert. He was in his element—the Creator's province. This trip would serve as nostrum for his soul. He had a lot of family decisions to resolve . . . soon.

The mountains, too, were neither quiet nor still. A mountain lives at an infinitely slow pace, but it stirs, it creaks, it grows, it comes apart in a slowness barely noticed by man.

Still preoccupied with his living arrangements in the hut, he thought of his desire to have Leigh at his side; it grew on him daily. The longing as he watched her face asleep on the pillow beside his bed, to see her eyes open in the morning, near, yes, but not next to her, just watching and waiting for her to wake up, to share themselves.

He understood the differences they had, her insistence in it being acceptable to live together, but not to share their love. Morning Star was his problem and he would address its resolution sooner or later in fairness to her and their son. Fair to his wife . . . no. But who ever said affairs of the heart are fair. He knew one thing for certain, it would he unconscionable to appear in a life so completely enamored by a woman like Leigh, then not act on it and let her slip away.

He could not permit that to happen. Then, again, he supposed it was too much to expect a normal life out here, but where you are in life is a journey, always a journey, always a change in direction. No man knows how it will end—or when. Nevertheless, he was steadfast in his determination to grab this brass ring named Leigh, sooner than later.

However, his feelings for early Tlingit cultural rules and lifestyles, formed over the centuries, would not be violated. They would guide his decisions in respect of Tribal Law. Tlingits always live according to their needs, and now he was living according to his, which required blending in with the white man's culture. His marriage to Morning Star was based on Tlingit cultural principles, not the civil laws of Alaska, so his task was simply to face the facts and gain enough confidence to face her, to tell her that he was doing the right thing for him, for Morning Star, and for their son. The decision will come very soon.

His loneliness was more apparent than ever riding through the Tongass without Leigh.

*   *   *

The game trail became too narrow, so they turned toward the river to follow its more open passage.

Old Gal's ear perked up and her nostrils flared.

"What's that, Old Gal? Is the wind picking up through the valley?"

The sound came from the south side of the river. Old Gal heard it, whinnied softly, and threw her head around so abruptly she stumbled. Ears up, she looked to the south with nostrils flaring for a stronger scent.

"What is it, Gal?" he exclaimed turning in the saddle and scanning the southerly landscape.

Old Gal stomped and dug the earth with her hoof, then started to dance in place while looking squarely across the water.

"Hold it, Gal. It's okay, settle down, girl."

Then he sees it, sees what is threatening her . . . she has cause for alarm.

At about twenty feet, in an old half-dead pine, lay an elegant mountain lion with its huge black-tipped tail swinging like a metronome keeping time to Gal's prancing. He removed his Winchester from its scabbard.

The golden-gray to reddish-yellow fur glistened in the early morning sun as the cat repositioned to attack profile, fangs flared. It uttered a low, guttural cry and hissing whispers.

He thought it rather strange for the cat to hold her position once discovered, for they are very reclusive animals who avoid intruders. Then he discovered why. It was a magnificent sight, rarely seen by man.

In a jumbled mass of large boulders and rocks at the base of the pine, four little spotted lion cubs romped, darted, leaped, and rolled. Their color flowed across the rocks like colorful frolicking Monarch butterflies. One of them stood out as larger, maybe the boss, as the remaining three fought as if their lives depended on conquest of each other.

Old Gal settled down a little, but remained very alert, ramrod stiff, while continuing to paw the ground. For good reason, lions are one of the worst enemies of a horse. They generally pounce on an animal's back from a tree. The prey is down before it knows what hit it as the cat's fangs plunge into the equine's throat.

Caw—Caw—Caw.

A majestic raven landed on the top of a neighboring tree and looked to the scene below. It cried again to ensure its presence was known..

The lion family all looked upward to the sound of the raven.

The lion uttered a subtle low pitched cry like murmur, that changed the scene dramatically as all four cubs scrambled over each other running to the entrance of the hidden den.

Calm returned to the opposite bank, save for the hiss of the lion as it descended the tree, never losing sight of the intruders. Reaching the rocks at the tree's base, she slinked away, turning toward the pair several times to give the twosome a few last loud hisses before disappearing into the rock-strewn bank with its long tail swaying to and fro.

"I'm proud of you, Gal," he whispered. "You not only alerted me to our stumbling onto a lion's den, but you behaved in a protective yet graceful manner. You have proven yourself in very dire circumstances by not bolting, not being violent, but rather standing your ground, good girl." He slowly dismounted, replacing his rifle and patting her head while leading her slowly down the trail.

Walking her to a safer location, he reflected on the learning experience by the outcrop of boulders moving down the trail. Lions are generally found at higher elevations, and also in larger rocky areas clear of all vegetation. He'd make a note of this change for future trips. He was pleased to see a family, which could indicate an increase in the breeding population in the lower sections of the forest. He had not seen a lion in years, so he hoped all four cubs would make it to breeding age and find mates in the area. He felt good to know they're doing well.

To ensure he could relocate the den, he recorded its GPS coordinates down to the degree, minute, and seconds in his log book. He'd share the good news with his fellow workers. Later, when traveling alone, he would check back periodically to record progress of the cubs' growth with minimal intervention so their mom would not feel threatened and move them.

"How you doing Gal? Okay?" Stopping on the trail, he held her head and muzzle while patting her neck. "Looks like we're both back to normal, babe. I, too, wouldn't like to have an encounter like that again. We are either lucky or appear to be more threatening than I'm aware. Do you think our raven friend affected this meeting? Or maybe it was just us—or both. We never know for certain when Manitou acts on our behalf. Never will. So let's keep the faith. The creator is always with us in potentially dangerous encounters with menacing two- and four-legged confrontations and, likewise with the uncontrolled fury of nature. The raven has always been a messenger and a protector from the gods. I'm going to believe he was this time, too."

Walking along the game trail was easier then riding with the overhanging branches restricting their passage, and it gave his butt and her back a little rest. After an hour, Old Gal seemed to be over the stress of the encounter. That face-to-face meeting was resolved so peacefully showed how every one of the Creator's subjects carries on without conflict.

Stopping a moment, Old Gal drank while Chi Mukwa stood in the river for a clear satellite view to determine their location with his GPS unit. With its topographical map of the area and his knowledge of the forest, he knew within a few meters their true location.

"All filled up, babe? By my calculations, we're about two miles upstream from the suspected netting operations. It's about ten o'clock, so let's keep moving. With any luck we'll be on site by noon."

Still dismounted, they continued to follow the game trails along the river. He sensed the spirit of the wind speaking to him in its softness, especially as he became more alert by moving in on their goal. The wind had become a sound of its own, and that sound could be different among rocks, pines, streams or mountains. Small animals scampered as they walked making only faint rustlings, easily recognized by his and the horse's trained ears. A fall of timber is natural; displaced by the wind or loosened by the alternating heat of the day and cold of the night, a limb may break, a trickle of leaves may follow, then silence . . . or is this subtle noise, that of man?

Was it the wind or the noise of the tenders poaching? With first assignment jitters, he was uncertain of his judgment as a Specialist, not as himself. He knew what had to be done, but would his judgment conform with DNR policies? Who knows? He'd have to just go for it and hope for the best. Judgment, there's a ten-dollar word, he thought. Compromise. Compromise is the cornerstone of civilization for both Native (First Citizens), and Anglo (White Europeans), just as politics is the art of conflict resolution. Thank god spiritual beliefs are pluralistic in the modern world, and yes, many reasonable men do not, cannot, and hopefully never will think totally alike. Reasonable people must yield to compromise to avoid conflict, yet be willing to defend their beliefs, but above all know when a conciliatory resolution is warranted.

He murmured, "I will be ready. Regardless of regulations, I value my neck. It will be the poachers' decision to come along peacefully or be at war with Alaska's laws. I enforce the people's rules of behavior. They are not by my hand." As he moved through the underbrush by the river bank, he sensed something ahead. The river's bank had been disturbed recently by a man or two in boots. How long ago was difficult to judge, but, for sure, in the last few days. He was now more aware of his and others' footfalls, which sounded different than stones or leaves dislodging or falling to the wishes of gravity, as they tumble, and race to rest.

Strange sounds seemed more abundant as they approached the suspected site. Was it him, or his overtuned receptors, or were there others further downstream? Was it him and the horse, or the scoundrels who grab for the easy low hanging fruit.

One distant sound occurring more frequently as global warming continues was the crashing sound of claving glaciers, primarily those on Glacier Bay National Park to the northwest. At one time it was music to the ears of local inhabitants, but now a fearful indication of faster than expected recession, and possible disappearance. He thought of all the changes taking place in his life, some good, some bad . . .

Isn't life just that? A combination of good and bad? How do you manage the two is the measure of comfort with what the Creator has dealt.

At an oxbow, the river formed a perfect 'U' shape, void of young trees or brush. Maybe the area was scrubbed clear by the torrent of ice and water during spring thaw. He spotted a ramshackle camp from their upstream location.

Old Gal raised her head first and came to a dead stop, pulling Chi Mukwa's arm to full extension.

"Whoa, girl. What's up? Steady now. What do you see?"

Carefully climbing a hillock, he discovered a depressing scene, typical of law-breakers, a make-shift, transitory illegal fish camp exactly at the GPS coordinates relayed by headquarters.

"Damn girl, look at all those ravens perched in trees around the site. They know an easy meal when they see it near a fish weir. There must be fish offal all over the place. You're not going to like this gal, but I've got to halter and tie you to a tree while I investigate. Chomp some of this grass while I swing around the other side of the camp. It looks vacant, but I've got to be sure. I'll see you in about an hour."

He retrieved his Winchester from the saddle scabbard. Silently racking a round into the chamber, he waded across the river with his boots and rifle over-head. Climbing the bank, he paused and booted, then slowly circled the camp, looking for the violators, and returned to the forging point and then stealthily crawled toward the camp. The ravens became silent stares. The wind seemed to change pitch, direction and intensity. He'd felt this before. The spirit of the wind was with him as the tension quickened his heartbeat, flushed his face, and warned him to be prepared.

His heart took a leap as a red fox almost scampered over his legs in a fright-ened escape from the offal. All the varmints, two- and four-legged had departed. The camp was a mess. A tarp hung between four trees, providing some shelter from Autumn's onslaught. A large temporary fish-cleaning station with a hole for entrails to drop directly into the water hugged the edge of the river. A kitchen fly was stretched between four trees next to the fire pit ringed with boulders. A large black kettle hung on an iron cross arm. Cooking pans littered the area. A half-butchered deer hung from a yard arm in a tree with a sheet partially covering the raw meat. Plastic containers were stacked near the cleaning station.

It was an active camp, no question about that. So much stench permeated the area that it stunk to high heavens. Rotting offal less than a couple days old, lay about the camp and river bank, a sodden, sloppy, swill of fish guts. Several new mounds of horse manure indicated they were using a team to haul the illegal catch, most likely to the coast.

Several evergreen branches covered these items, a feeble attempt to block their activities from aircraft surveillance. A weir stretched across the narrowest section of the river. Vertical rods allowed small fish to pass but kept the larger ten- to twenty-pounders captive in a swirl of corralled anger, a maelstrom that indicated the poacher(s) had not returned to dip the fish in days. Maybe for recreation or to try for hitting it big, a sluice type flume at the edge of the river served to capture or pan for gold, even though gold had not been successfully panned from the Bitterroot in a hundred years.

The ravens cried, flapped their wings, and flew away as if to signal their vacation from the area while man was present.

Not wanting to leave a scent in case the violators had a dog, he did not enter the camp, but rather departed through the river to plan a course of action.

"Hi Gal. They have been here and are due to return soon, so let's make our battle plan. You missed nothing by staying back. We've got 'em red-handed as soon as they return. Now I can affect change as a CO, where before I was powerless. A judge will find them culpable if we do our job right and through my testimony as an officer of the court, and photos from my good old Nikon. What do ya think, Gal? They must be a few fries short of a Happy Meal. We'll go to a spot downwind for a good view of the camp and the trail leading in, then wait. How long, I don't know, but I'd guess no more than twenty-four hours. Come on, Gal, daylight's a burning. Yep, you're going to get wet, but that's no problem; the river's only five feet deep."

They moved across the river together and settled behind a knoll about thirty meters to the south of the camp. He tied Old Gal with a shorter grazing line, then lowered himself onto a pile of cedar boughs. He was determined to close down this operation.

The Whispering Wind sounded again as it thrust through the oak trees, rattling the unyielding leaves of fall. Was it whispering to him? Was the Spirit announcing, joining, combining forces in this sensitive mission at the river side, or was it his imagination? Could it be the first of the katabatic wind of winter? It seemed likely as the temperature dropped.

They waited with the only sounds being the wind and splashing captive fish. At 1500 hours, he called headquarters with a status report.

Thunder clouds started to form in the north, and wind velocity increased. "That's strange. Here comes a raven from the west."

It circled and perched above the camp and cried once, then flapped its wings as near silence returned to the river side. The only background sounds were the subtle swoosh, swoosh, of captive fish and the wind's increasing speed.

Silence.

Then it happened. Suddenly, two horses with riders appeared on the trail from the west. Chi Mukwa carefully raised his head to get a better view as the riders approached the camp.

He drew in a deep breath— "Oh" —as the riders' identities were revealed. It was his old nemeses, the drunken, no good, Haida Indians, Yellow Knife and Red Dog, whom he'd confronted while they were stealing totem poles from the old Tlingit Long House, less than a year ago.

His thumb found the open hammer of the Winchester and pulled it back to the firing position.

"They appear to be drunk again, this is going to be interesting."

Chapter 3

Reconciliation

It may be that some little root of the Sacred Tree still lives. Nourish it then, that it may leaf and bloom and fill with singing birds. Hear me not for myself, but for my people; I am old. Hear me that they may once more go back into the sacred hoop and find the Good Red Road, the shielding tree.

—Black Elk, Holy Man and Medicine Man

The alien-looking creature trudged across the meadow at daybreak. Barely visible, it emerged from the miasma suspended above the swamp in a tentative fashion, dragging one leg. Unrecognizable, its face was masked by swamp muck and the shadow cast by the low-angle back-lighting that created a radiating nimbus from the rising sun. Grime clinging in all hollows of its face gave the being a fierce, almost-wild appearance. Its thickened sodden garment hid the body's motion. A cudgel appeared to be its only protective weapon, now being used to help maneuver the weakened body across the meadow. The obliterated face had a pitch black stain streaked with reddish-purple like dried blood similar to a series of tattoos, as if the skin were broken. It was indeed a strange and slightly sinister scene.

Leigh spotted the beast during her morning walk. She considered backing away and slowly returning to the hut to release the wolves for protection. She stepped backwards slowly and turned to increase her pace, then heard a familiar voice.

"Runs with Wolves . . . ahhh, Leigh . . . ahhh, Aunt Leigh . . . it's me, Wind Spirit. Don't go. I need your help. Please. It's me, Wind Spirit, your friend."

She stopped, couldn't believe her eyes, wondered how this creature could be the young orphan from the Raven Clan, the Clan that moved from the forest to Skagway two months ago. How could it be? That's 50 miles from here.

"Wind Spirit, is that you?"

"Yes, Leigh, I need your help. Will you help me?"

Frozen in place, Leigh searched for the answer. It came a moment later with the warmth and caring of a mother's voice. "You know you're always welcome.

Come over here."

He ran to Leigh with wanton abandon like a nervous, long-lost wolf cub who had just found its mother. A bundle of nerves, he cried. She smiled, as he collapsed at her feet.

"Here now, let me take a gander at this mortal in front of me. You certainly look the worse for wear. Where have you been? How did you get here? Just what's going on, young man? You look terrible. Furthermore, your arms are covered with insect bites, skin cuts, and abrasions. Your face is also a mess of bites and contusions. Chi Mukwa would love to see a picture of you. Guess what? That ain't gonna happen. Let's get you cleaned up in the river and get something in your gullet."

She gave him a careful motherly hug to calm him down, providing him some assurance that he was welcome, so he could relax. He had apparently reached his goal—the meadow—an escape from life in the city.

She walked him toward the bench on the river. Having a second look now, she was even more shocked by his injuries. His left pantleg was torn off, his knee-cap sliced open and clogged with muck.

"Get those clothes off so we can see just how bad you've been beat up by the Tongass."

A small rucksack contained a drained canteen, crumbs from a twelve-pack of mixed doughnuts, wrappers from beef jerky, a compass, a hunting knife, and a roughly drawn map showing an approximate route from Skagway to the meadow by way of the old Raven Camp. The first leg from Skagway to the camp was about thirty miles, then twenty miles from there to the meadow—quite a hike, half of it being in the pitch black of night forest, mountains, rivers, lowlands, and swamps. It looked like he experienced the consequences of them all. How he survived his all-day and all-night trek from town was beyond her. A sight for sore eyes, he nevertheless carried himself with a certain air of confidence and the positive attitude of a person on a mission.

In the face of his decrepit state, he still attempted to arrange his clothes properly. He stood erect and carefully folded them while disrobing, never losing his bearing. His pleading to let him stay with her persisted. While he petitioned her over and over again, she gave him the rest of her morning biscuit. He swallowed it whole, like a gulping wolf. Feeling sorry for him, she also gave him the last of her morning coffee, which disappeared in one swallow. He continued to slowly peel his clothes from his filthy, torn, and bruised body. He was a mess. Having seen just about every condition of her fellow man, she had to admit to never having experienced such a shipwreck of flesh. If it wasn't scratched, it was bruised. If it wasn't cut, it was full of deer fly, black fly, and the infamous no-see-ems' bites.

"Take your time, dear. I'm going to grab something for you to eat and be right back. And don't be bashful; take everything off. I've seen everything in other men that you've got . . . more than just a few times. Don't be modest. You know I'm old enough to be your mother. Be right back."

I might as well be talking into the wind. No way he's going to strip in front of me—or likely any woman, for that matter. He still shows the modesty of a boy, but he's man enough now that maybe there's some vanity there, too. It would be nice to think he sees me as still a bit foxy, and that he's worried his body might reveal in painfully obvious ways that this old gal can still excite a young feller.

"Try these biscuits, big fellow. They're covered with butter and jelly. They will hold you for a while; here's some fresh apple cider, too. Eat up, my friend. Wind Spirit, you know the chief will be upset, and likely Chi Mukwa, too. I understand your reluctance to stay in town. Nevertheless, the Raven Clan's decision was unanimous. They all agreed with Gete Wabiska. Now you've put a burden on me. If I take you in, the chief will not only be annoyed at you for disregarding his authority, but with me for welcoming you. Then there's Chi Mukwa's concerns. However, I've been told you're much like him as a youth—independent, headstrong, and assertive. The fruit doesn't fall far from the tree." Leigh softened the reading of the riot act to him.

"Please, please, Runs with Wolves, I know the chief will be upset, but if you and Chi Mukwa agree to take me in, I can serve as a caretaker and hired hand. I can watch your property and wolves while both of you travel, and you when Chi Mukwa is gone with DNR business. You know he'll be gone to Juneau and Anchorage a lot, and I'll be here so you'll not be alone."

He thinks he's got it all figured out, most likely has been rehearsing this little presentation while dragging his body over the Tongass for the last twenty-four hours.

"I'm not sure if you're a fool, or a tough young upstart needing a home so bad that you put your life at risk so that you could find it, but time will tell. Do you realize the chances you took traveling almost fifty miles, half of which were in the pitch-black conditions of the Tongass? Plus, you did it during the salmon run when our four-legged bruin friends are searching for prehibernation grasses, berries, and protein. Yes, you're the latter: bruin dessert.

He chuckled a little, fidgeting nervously while standing near-naked by the river, doing very little talking, but a lot of listening.

"I see you've got most of your clothes off. Are you in one piece?"

"Of course, Aunt Leigh. I mean, Leigh. I'm going to be all right." He flexed his body in several muscle groups as if to show her how fit he was at sixteen years old.

She laughed to herself. *Men! They have to show their prowess when the right audience is available. Oh well, no harm done.* Underneath all the pontificating, he was still scared to death that she'd send him back.

"You're in pretty good shape, young man. Do you feel any sprains or torn muscles?"

"Not that I can feel or detect right now. I'll have to check again in the morning. That's when the joint stiffness sets in."

It sounded like he wanted her to let him stay and work on Chi Mukwa next. It was her call, but Chi Mukwa's opinion would weigh heavily.

"Do you see our friend above?" Leigh asked while bringing a bucket of soapy water and a towel to the bench.

"Oh yeah. The raven joined me at noon yesterday, and has been with me as a beacon, a friend, a guide when the going got rough. I was uncertain of which way to go several times. Even in the dark, the raven called out to let me know the best route to follow. Its cries led me to safe passage more than once. Hi, big fella. How are you? We can finally rest. Thanks," Wind Spirit said. "Do you know Leigh?"

She looked to the arboreal perch, knowing very well the raven knew her and all the denizens in the forest. She had a very close relationship with Manitou and His animal kin(g)dom. The raven's guidance for Wind Spirit was no accident. Manitou appears where needed.

In a sudden leap the raven burst into the air and flew to the opposite end of the meadow. It perched on the lower branch of a weather-beaten spruce and cried in a deep rumbling c-r-o-a-k with variations indicating alarm. She'd heard this cry many times, a call, a warning, an attention-getter for man. One does not ignore this sound. She looked toward the raven to determine what all the fuss was about. Sure enough, there it was. Standing on its hind legs was a large black bear sniffing the air for a fresh scent.

"Jesus, that's all I need. An injured boy and now the bear that, no doubt, followed him here. Do you see it, boy? Your friend from the swamp is paying us a visit. It's probably been tracking you all night."

Wind Spirit exclaimed, "What the hell! What are we going to do? Should I get a rifle? Damn, he's a big bruiser!"

Leigh demurred, in part to calm the boy, and casually walked toward the woodpile. She grabbed a tin bucket and an old tire iron. Then she immediately ran toward the bear, banging, and yelling, "Git, Bear, Git!"

Wind Spirit stood in awe as the bear stared at Leigh for a moment then turned-tail, and ran back into the swamp, crashing through branches and bellowing in retreat. Leigh stood in the center of the meadow a moment, then returned to the boy with a big grin on her face.

"Leigh, you could have been hurt. Wasn't that kinda risky?"

"No, my son, I've chased several black bears away using the same clanging technique. It's effective, don't you think? Then again, if one of our furry guests resists, I throw a round over its head to let 'em know I'm serious. It works. They must tell their bruin family that sometimes the old bat is armed."

"You're something else, Leigh. I'd like to get that chase on film, it's one for the books. Do you know you just called me son?"

"Did I? Slip of the lip. Your real name should be Swamp Rat."

She did not take the slip of the tongue lightly. Was it a Freudian slip, or a wish?

"Oh, what the hell. Jesus. I suppose I can stand you around here for a few days, at least until Chi Mukwa returns. I can use some help, especially in getting ready for winter's whitening. Our list is long, my dear, are you sure about staying with your—as you've a tendency to say—Aunt Leigh? I'm a tough task-master. You can also chase the next black bear away, too."

"Heck yeah. I can do anything you throw at me. I'm a young warrior trained in the tradition of my Tlingit brethren. Just ask Chi Mukwa. He knows. I'm a good guy to have around the hut, the meadow . . . and you."

"Stop. Enough blowing your own horn. Get cleaned up and throw me those clothes. I'll rinse them in the river with a little soap. Now git. You're dirtier than that swamp bear, and blacker, too."

"Okay, but I'll wash my own shorts. I'm too old to run around naked. Here's my clothes. I'll jump in the river and get my Native skin back."

"Ha, off with you, boy. If I were forty years younger, you'd be eager to run around the meadow naked—showing off what you've got to catch the eye of an eligible lady. Go away with you, boy. On with your dance in the river. Don't come back until you're clean as that thunderhead above. 'Tis a beautiful day, my lad. Away with you, Windy. Ha! That's a good nick-name: Windy. That will teach you to call me Aunt Leigh. Yep, Windy, that's your new moniker."

Strange. I just shifted to my British mother's manner of speaking. I think I mimicked her intonation, too. I wonder if it's due to me talking to a young person. Stranger still. Damned if I didn't sound like Brit friend Joe Bloom.

With his modesty in full bloom, he made sure there was a little separation from Leigh along the river bank. He washed and danced in the river's cool current upstream while Leigh beat his clothes on a rock downstream. After a couple of minutes, she decided they were in such bad shape that they were headed for the rag bag. She was not into repairing clothes—or darning socks, for that matter, except for calling them "darn socks" as she threw them in the rag bag.

"Are you through dancing and swimming, boy? You look clean. That's the good news. Now the bad. I just threw away all your clothes. They're uncleanable and beyond repair, something I don't do anywho. So come on over here with your shorts, 'cause that's all you've got anyway. Seriously, I'll get you some of Chi Mukwa's or my clothes later. Come over here. Let's have a look at some of those insect bites and cuts—come on, boy."

Begrudgingly, he sauntered downstream to Leigh by the bench with a little Chi Mukwa/John Wayne chest-out swagger. Some men cannot resist doing so around women, whether a potential mate or not. They just want to look good physically when nearly naked. Some things never change among animals, be it two- or four-legged.

I suppose it's understandable, since after adequate nourishment the drive to reproduce is a close second in the hierarchy of life's goals, whether the animal is domesticated or wild. Windy's posturing seems to support this concept.

"Have a seat on the bench so I can examine some of those injuries I saw under the muck."

He yielded to a normal cadence, leaving the river's edge, and climbed the bank to the bench.

"Egad, boy! You're as punctured as a low-flying duck over a ten-man duck blind. What the hell did you get into? Where did you pick up all that torn flesh?"

"It's nothing, Leigh. It's just the reality of being in the forest, whether in the day or night, wet or dry, when you cannot follow a trail. The biting flies and no-see-ems find you, broken branches seek your flesh, and rocks are your cushions when crawling or running over virgin terrain. Remember, I had to sneak out of town without any protective bear salve or proper clothing. I snuck away from Golden Bear's Lodge while Gete Wabiska was elsewhere. I did not announce my intentions to anyone. Not even my aunt. You know very well if I'd told her she would not let me leave for the meadow."

"I suppose, although we have not talked. I'll have to call Skagway and tell them you're here. I'll do my best to cover your plans. But no promises, hear?"

"Yeah, I hear. You're right. Do the best you can and tell them not to worry and that I'm okay. By the way, thanks, Aunt Leigh."

"Okay, here's the plan. I'll use an astringent to wash and bathe the skin, then apply a salve to reduce itching and put a poultice on your numerous cuts. I'll use my Native Medicines for the remaining treatment. Then I'll have you wear some of my long pants and long-sleeved shirts tied at the bottom and wrists, buttoned to the neck, and three-quarter shoes so you have no chance to scratch, rub, or otherwise disturb your wounds. We'll rinse and replace all treatments every day for three days, rain or shine. Are you ready to go? Let's do it, pal."

"Okay, pat yourself dry with this towel and I'll return in a moment with Native American Medicines and Leigh's home-made cure-all salve. While you're waiting, rotate in the sun like a pig on a rotisserie to get completely dry."

The preparations to treat infection and reduce itching were from the Raven Clan's shamans of old. They formulated many remedies from wild plants in their environment, focusing on roots in the spring before the plants flowered. On the other hand, bark was gathered in winter or in very early spring. Gete Wabiska had taught her the history of Native medicine, and she would continue the education of Windy. It was an obligation of being in the sisterhood of the Tlingits.

She decided quite early in her relationship with the tribe that the Bag Balm her father used in the milking parlor would remain her secret salve. It was used on the cow's teats, and on both mom's and her chapped nipples when nursing. Its outstanding curative powers filtered down to the men who started using it, too.

She murmured, "I better not tell the macho man the background of the Bag Balm salve. He needs only know the excellent results expected."

Having collected a basketful of medicinal needs in the hut, she headed out to her patient and decided to let the wolves out to meet the new boarder.

He saw her coming and hollered. "Hey, Leigh, I'm good to go. I feel like a dancer in a nudist colony. Let's give it a go."

Then he saw the tricolored pack of wolves approaching. He stopped abruptly and jumped on the bench.

Not a moment too soon. With the wolves just a few meters from the bench, Leigh shouted, "Down!" The White and Tough halted and, as usual, the partially trained cub, Jet, looked back at Leigh and continued running toward Windy on the bench. Though smaller, Jet was still a factor to deal with. He had grown like a weed. The fear in Windy's eyes remained as the young black wolf leaped up and joined him on the bench, an aggressive attempt to make friends through his licks. In typical wolf body language, Jet rolled over on his back in submission to the boy.

Leigh caught up with Tough and the White. They were holding their positions about twenty meters from the bench.

"Okay, guys, you can come with me, but you must stay at my side. Heel. Good. Now let's rescue our young brave from Jet's affection. Jet, come here, you rascal. You'd better come. Leave that boy alone. Windy, sit down and hold Jet. He's not going to hurt you."

"Okay, Leigh, but this black furry cub is all wet tongue, sharp claws, and sharp teeth—and all over my body at once. Being almost naked doesn't help. I'm getting beat up again, this time by a miniature bear. Okay, I've finally got a hold on him."

"You'll be okay. Let me bring Tough and the White over. They're anxious to look you over, and lick you over, too. Just stay put and hold on to Jet. Here we come."

Generally cautious, the wolves surprised her by treating Windy as if he were a long-lost friend. They checked him out for a few moments, then frolicked on the river bank, which led them to the river, which led to total immersion of all four: Windy, Tough, the White, and Jet. A blur of wolves and boy romping along the bank and diving into the cattails made it difficult to tell which was which. She smiled, feeling acceptance and warmth for the visitor, the escapee whose needs were not met in Skagway. She also had an idea that Tough may have recognized Windy from when he attended to Tough's broken ribs just a few months ago.

He was so much like Chi Mukwa, neither he nor Windy apparently wanted to leave the open spaces, the forest, the independence that wilderness provides.

"Okay, you guys, play time's over. Come. You, too, Windy. Get out of that water. You've got to dry off all over again."

Apparently there was no problem in habituating the wolves to Windy's presence. He seemed to be accepted as a member of the meadow clan, or Leigh's gang, or the Tongass gang. They had many names.

"Windy, go back in the water and get cleaned up again. Take off those shorts and get 'em clean. If you want to cover yourself when I treat your wounds, fine, but you've got nothing I haven't seen before."

"Come on, Leigh, I'm sixteen, don't you understand?"

"Okay, get over here."

He stepped out of the river, dried again, and walked to Leigh with his shorts in hand covering his privates.

"Finally, the Witch Hazel," she said, applying it liberally to his body, "may have been used before in camp. The formula is from the Raven Clan's elders responsible for recipes from botanicals. You've probably already learned that your elders, centuries ago, were the first plant scientists. It's one of the many known remedies. The clan shared their knowledge as we searched the forest for popular medicines such as hemp, tobacco, papose root, blood root, dogwood, ginseng, sassafras, Indian pipe, and wild ipecac. This astringent will reduce the swelling."

"Okay, if you say so. Where do you find these plants?"

"I'll show you someday. It's found in the moist woodlands, at the bottom of many ravines. We'll go on a botanical search party someday. When we do, I'll show you how to identify the plant, collect it properly, break or crush the smaller twigs with the leaves, add water, and boil the resulting mixture for a couple hours. That's how I prepared the Witch Hazel. Get it? One, two, three, and voila! We won't need a prescription from the drugstore. We did it ourselves.

"You're looking better. How do you feel? Don't answer. I know. You itch, are sore, and want to hit the sack. Well, guess what? That's next."

"I'm better, true, but all my cuts sting a little, and the bites beg to be scratched. Never again will I go into the woods at night without a coating of mint-laced bear grease. Never again."

Leigh retrieved her Bag Palm with its curative powers acclaimed for teats and nipples and other parts of the body. "Sit down so I can apply this properly. You'll be out of action for a while, so get used to being horizontal. I suppose you'll sleep for the next twenty-four hours after your little hike. Now, be still."

She applied two moss poultices with light dressings and wrapped his remaining wounds soaked in Indian pipe (also called corpse plant), noted for reducing inflammations and for its soothing properties. "Okay, put your shorts on and get up. Doctor Leigh's finished." She walked him to the hut, then dressed him from neck to toe with a combination of her and Chi Mukwa's clothes so he could not scratch or displace the poultices, and so the wolves would not be so curious.

He lay on a blanket next to her bed, for a minute or two, without a word. Then, with eyes dropping, he mumbled a quiet, "Thank you, Aunt Leigh," and passed to his Tongass world, to the forest of his dreams.

"Rest, my son. I won't see you until tomorrow, I'm certain. You'll be zonked out for a while. Sleep well, my Native friend."

Leigh sat next to the boy and cast tobacco from her medicine bag to the four corners of the earth, then retrieved her drum and started drumming in a manner to simulate Earth Mother's heartbeat. Played very softly, it can sound like breath, wind, or the running water of a river.

Drum—drum—drum—drum—drum . . . drum.

Vocals followed in a chanting ceremonial fashion as an additional call to the healing powers of the Creator, Manitou. Singing, chanting, or the methodical beat of the drum was certain to help the injured boy. She sang the song learned from, Gete Wabiska to call for healing.

> *Ho! Ye Suns, Moon, Stars, all ye that move in the heavens,*
> *I bid you hear me!*
> *Into your midst has come an injured youth,*
> *Consent ye, I Implore!*
> *Make his healing path smooth, that he may reach manhood.*

> Tlingit healing song.

"Rest well, my son."

She moved to the back porch. Resting with the wolves, she pondered the consequences of this dear boy wandering into her life. Looking down the river to the west, she wondered how Chi Mukwa was faring on his first DNR assignment. She hoped it wasn't a dangerous task.

Here I go again, worrying about one man I love as he heads into danger, and a boy I care for very much, just surviving a similar life-threatening adventure. Dear Leigh, tighten up. Set your anchor for your needs first. Don't keep getting so involved in men's lives . . . .

Caw—Caw—Caw.

A raven perched on the lone pine by the river, and looked down at Leigh. "Welcome, my friend. Thank you for helping the boy."

Chapter 4

Renunciation

From his precarious location across the river, Chi Mukwa watched as the eerie scene unfolded. The two scoundrels came riding out of the shadows of dense undergrowth, of lichen covered boulders, ferns, moss, and decaying timber. As the pair moved to the edge of the campsite, he felt a prickling tension travel up the back of his neck. Since it was his first assignment, it was probably a normal response when dealing with unpredictable low-lifes.

The smell of opportunity was too strong for bottom dwellers to ignore, attracting a procession of drifters, con artists, geeks, bushwhackers, rustlers, and Gypsies. Their inventiveness and tenacity and utter contempt for the wilderness around them would shame their forefathers. They preserved only what was free and immutable—the sunshine, the oceans, and the majestic mountains. Land and sea animals were marked for destruction.

Assured of no immediate threat, he let the Winchester's hammer e-a-s-e silently forward, then lowered the rifle to his side. Although Native American Haida, he could not cut them any slack. Enforcement of gaming laws must be color-blind. He thought a little jail time, about six months, would do both of them good. Furthermore, they gave law abiding Native Americans an undeserved bad name with their illegal schemes. Justice, however rough, would be swift.

*　　*　　*

Yellow Knife was first to ride his grayish yellow buckskin slowly toward the river. He twitched and twisted in the saddle while he scanned the area carefully. Sitting tall on the buckskin his bearing made a positive impression in stark contrast to his apparel. His clothing was filthy and disheveled, a mismatched combination of nondescript ragged shirt and torn pants resembling that of an unkempt sanitation worker. One yellow and one black galosh gave him the look of a ne'er-do-well mucker. In contrast, he wore a bright yellow sash symbolic of a Haida warrior. A pity. He denigrated its symbol of pride and stature. The forest was their protection and, unfortunately, their prison, too.

His luminous gray watery eyes in contrast with his dark red skin radiated an eerie appearance. He continued to survey the disheveled fish camp. As he strained to examine the riverbank, the hollows in his cheeks tended to deepen. Suddenly the buckskin stopped, turned, jerked its head around, and looked across the river. Yellow Knife turned, too. They both stared at the hillock where Chi Mukwa hid. Yellow Knife's sneer seemed to be staring through the earthen knoll as if he knew someone was there. What was assuredly seconds, Chi Mukwa felt as minutes. He murmured, "Oh, oh, I wonder if he sees us or knows this is one of the few hiding places along the bank."

He carefully brought his rifle to the ready position, pulled back the hammer, and froze. Beads of sweat tumbled down his face as the stare-down continued. "Damn, I'd better get ready. He must have seen either Old Gal or me. Dammit!"

Standing in the stirrups, Yellow Knife strained for a better view. Apparently still frustrated, he sat in the saddle and reached for something in his sash. "Here we go. He's probably got a gun. I'll bet he's gonna throw a few rounds this way," he mumbled, drawing a bead on the rascal.

Tension built as he struggled with his sash, then diminished quickly as he took a half-pint of liquor from his waist and raised the bottle to twelve o'clock sky high for a long noisy gulp. He wiped his mouth with his dirty sleeve, then with his dirtier hand, and belched, "Buurrpp!" Just as quickly, he lost interest in the hillock area and reined his horse toward the weir. With his surprisingly clean yellow headband, he was easily spotted as Chi Mukwa tracked his movement around the moss-covered hemlock toward the river. His long, once-blond, but now-graying hair hung crimped and lank. Its oily pewter appearance cascaded off his high ice-edged cheek tones. His eyes not only appeared watery, hut clouded over and weepy like those of a heavy drinker sobering up after an all-nighter. In fairness, he looked like any worn-out vagrant, a beat-up drunk running from the law. Riding all night through an unforgiving forest, sucking on an even more unforgiving bottle, would debase anyone.

Apparently the scans and staring at the hillock were just the typical check and double-check characteristic of lawbreakers on the prowl. The pair probably spent most of their lives looking over their shoulders and covering their tracks. Constant vigilance was part of a scoundrel's untoward lifestyle. Lawlessness was their norm. The expected. The challenge. Their problem was that they had no idea that living within the law was more beneficial to their families, their health, their survival. Together they could always conjure up a rationale for illegal activity against their fellow man, the state, or the feds—especially the feds, through the DNR, who were telling the Haidas when, what, and where they could fish and hunt.

*   *   *

After checking the riverbank, he dismounted, removed the tack, and secured the buckskin to a temporary hitching post by the cleaning station. He got what appeared to be a bag of oats and corn mixture from a weather-tight fish box and fed his horse, now in halter, on the ground. He dumped another pile nearby and looked toward the trail's entrance to camp.

There he was, good old Red Dog, his partner in crime, the usual bottle in one hand and carbine in the other—a sorry sight as the rear-guard providing cover as they reentered the camp.

"Get over here, you Bum. I've dumped some grain for yer horse. Come on. The area is clear. Yahoo! Put that gun and booze away. We've got a lotta work to do. Do ya hear that sound? It's coming from behind the weir. That's the sound of money . . . the sound of five different salmon species quiverin' and a-thrashin' against the weir. They still think they're struggling against the current to spawn like rapids running in reverse. They're pounding like a lover gone mad. They wanna breed. They need to breed. They've been waiting three years for this opportunity. They're frustrated. From what I see, the only visitors to camp were eagles, ravens, and crows who've left their moltin' feathers among the fish guts all over the place. Good thing, there ain't no bear tracks. Let's get humping. I need not tell ya we're the 'keepers' of the Creator's land of big timber, big bears, big birds, and big fish. Salmon is our chore this week, especially Big Red: Sockeye. Let's get a move on before that storm in the north heads our way. Come on. Bring that ice over here."

"Okay, okay, for Christ's sake. You don't have to yell so loud. Someone might hear you. Shut your pie-hole! Ya never know who's in the area. I'm coming," replied Red Dog.

Having held back at trail's end, he entered the campsite while stuffing his bottle of whiskey in his belt and sliding his carbine in its scabbard. He was probably a perennial subservient partner to Yellow Knife, the apparent leader as he started barking instructions at Red Dog. His brownish orange sorrel mare had a rickety travois strapped to its back with a jury-rigged harness of improvised ropes and straps. It wasn't a pretty sight, but the harness/travois seemed to serve its purpose—to haul out illegal salmon filets to illicit buyers. The single large container indicated a load of dry ice as the outgassing cloud of carbon dioxide followed the rickety rig.

Red Dog's appearance was worse than his partner's. His clothes combined a ragged sweatshirt, blackened and torn, and rattier black jeans. He, too, looked like an unkempt bum, sans the typical Haida yellow headband and sash. Nevertheless, some aspects of his ragged appearance mirrored his partner and gave a raunchy impression of a pair of riffraff. His hair was dark, shot with silver, and fell over his face like a waterfall. His features were blocky and eyes a dark brown with bags that magically vanished when he talked. His mouth was tiny. His ears were large, and when yelled at by his partner, he appeared at times to be hapless or baffled. Was he hearing impaired? Dimwitted? Maybe both. His frumpy clothes accented his features and made his short, stocky build resemble a tree stump. His voice sounded like a wounded goose on the run. He not only sounded like, but looked like Wallace Berry in a black dress. Moving closer to the river revealed a sidearm tucked into his waist, and a skinning knife in a scabbard on his belt.

He reined in the sorrel at the edge of the cleaning station. The two unloaded the dry-ice container and disconnected the travois so his horse could feed on the grain by the hitching post.

"We've got lots of work to do. I'd like to be packing out of here by sunset. Traveling at night is still our best bet to sneak back into camp without being observed. So let's hustle. Why don't you start throwing some of the dry ice into those two clean containers by the shelter. Please remember to put your brain in gear this time and use the tongs so you avoid freezer burn."

"Okay. For crying out loud, you treat me like a kid sometimes," grumbled Red Dog.

He stumbled to the tarp-walled shelter and dragged the containers alongside the cleaning station. Using the long-handled blacksmith tongs, he filled both semi-clean containers until the ice covered the bottom. Then be threw a small tarp over the ice to prevent freezer burn to the fillets.

"We'd better hustle. There's only about four inches of ice on the container's bottom. That'll only last about twelve hours when loaded with fillets," Red Dog hollered.

"You're right," Yellow Knife mumbled. "Do you remember the last time we had some tainted salmon due to a lack of enough ice and hiding unexpectedly from the law? The only ones that would eat the fillets were Pistol Pete's sled dogs. Christ, they chew on each other daily, too. I thought they'd survive on anything palatable and live. Let's not do that again. I think a few of his dogs died. It was some sort of bacterial poison called salmonella. So let's be careful. I'll be damned if Pete is still looking for us. If he caught us, it wouldn't be a pretty sight."

"Yeah, I remember. We'd better get with it. My man, you start dipping into the spawning horde. And try to position the dip net near the 'Reds.' The red sockeye always bring more dough whether fresh or smoked. Reds are the favorite of Chomoman from the lower 48. For that matter, Juneau, too."

Red Dog grabbed the three-foot-wide fish net and scooped through the maelstrom of thrashing pink-fleshed mass. He lifted the heavily laden net up to the cleaning station and dumped the flopping angry mass. Luckily, a four-inch edge kept the squirming cold-blooded beauties contained.

"Good, my dog," said Yellow Knife. "Let's get humping and cutting. With any luck we can get five-hundred pounds of fillets in each of the containers. That's about fifty fish in each, or a hundred total."

With fillet knives singing through flesh, they methodically cut the heads off with an aggressive whack. Then, without gutting, they grabbed the tough skin with pliers, and tore it off from the tail fin forward. Flipped, the other side was skinned. Finally, with the journeyman's skill, not unlike a surgeon, the razor-sharp fillet knife separated the fleshy fillet from the skeleton.

The measure of skill was in separating the skeletal bones from the excised fillet. These two were good. Why? They had been working in the canneries along the Lynn Canal for years in their youth. Now, they honed their skills under extreme conditions, making a quick buck—illegally.

Both fillets were removed, rinsed briefly, and thrown into the iced container. Fillets flew like flying fish as the pair worked in silence for about an hour while a third person across the river was documenting their progress with a digital camera.

"My man," Red Dog pleaded, "pass that bottle over here. I'm thirsty. I've got salmonitis of the throat and need to wash it away. Come on, we've been working almost an hour."

Yellow Knife insisted, "No way. If you start drinking, we'll never get done and all I'll have is a 'Doggie in the Bag,' unable to wield a knife effectively. Nope, but you can have all you want to drink when both containers are full and we're on our way. Your horse will make it back to our camp whether you're drunk or sober. Nada. None. Nothing to drink till we've cleared this godforsaken camp. As you know, we've only got one more 'meat' run this year. After this one, you can drink all day for all I care."

"You wanna know something? You're a real pain in the ass. You act as if you're my boss, my guardian, or my 'keeper.' Well, you're not. I should give you a little nick with this knife to put you in line—you're a bitch like my first wife. You cur!"

Yellow Knife mused, *Little does he know I am his keeper in more ways than one. I'm probably the only one that would put up was his harangue. I'll let him blow off some steam; by now I've been called everything in the book. Fact is, he couldn't pour water out of a boot if the instructions were on the heel. He's the classic double digit IQ . .'. a low number at that.*

Without further protest over not having a drink, Red Dog kept dumping fish on the station as their flashing knives extracted the tasty pink from the Sockeye, Chinook, Coho, and Chum. They flew into the container like a stream of pink flesh. The mound of skeletal remains were periodically pushed into the river, adding food to the lower end of the food chain.

*   *   *

He'd seen enough. Chi Mukwa secured his camera and double-checked his rifle as he waded across the river downstream from the camp. After reaching the bank he secured Old Gal and traversed slowly along the shoreline to about twenty feet from the cleaning station. He approached the pair with his rifle at his side so they would not feel threatened. He casually and quietly addressed his fellow Native Americans.

"Gentleman, put your knives down and throw all your sidearms over here. I am Chi Mukwa, Conservation Officer with the Alaska Fish and Game Department. You are under arrest for violating Alaskan fishing rules. Please move to the center of the camp area and sit down. Take your boots and socks off and throw them over here. I don't want you going anywhere right now. Now take all your clothes off and fold them neatly at your feet."

"What? We're not doing that!" said Yellow Knife.

They held fast and leered at him in disbelief, as if to test his resolve.

"Oh yes you are, and do it quickly! Maybe this will encourage you to follow instructions."

Ka-Pow! He threw a round into the tree near where they were sitting.

"Okay! Geez, you don't have to shoot at us," complained Red Dog. "We'll do it; give us a break."

"Hustle then. I'll let you dress when I get this situation and camp cleared up. Don't worry, the only thing that's going to see your bare ass is a she-bear. And she'd probably puke . . . turn and run. I see your rifles by the saddles. Are there any more weapons? No? Okay, let's talk, how 'bout it. Do either of you have anything to say? Is that silence—No? I urge you to say something before you are arraigned. Still silent, okay, so be it. Maybe you'll talk in court."

He called headquarters to report the apprehension and his plans to bring the violators in peacefully. *He hoped.* While signing off, he noticed the buggers trying to inch away to the edge of the clearing near an undergrowth of ferns.

"Hold it you two. Get back where you were sitting. Sit on your hands if the pine cones are uncomfortable."

For emphasis, he raised his rifle and pulled the hammer back.

"Brothers, I also feel like a beheaded and skinned salmon. Can't you see the risk? Don't you understand? This is not eighteen-ninety. Four generations ago you could take as many fish as you needed. But, my brothers, times have changed. There are game laws now so we can preserve the fisheries for future generations. The real crime here is in knowing that all Native American Indians have generous subsistence grants to take up to twenty-five fish daily, at any time, without a license. You both know it's a generous compromise by the state. What you are doing is illegal harvesting of fish for personal profit. In doing so, you embarrass me, your tribal brothers and, more important, yourselves. Now I have to take you in front of the local magistrate with a summons for your arrest and his judgment. Since you've got a long rap sheet, he will not be lenient. You will do some jail time. By the way, wasn't it just a couple months ago I caught you stealing totems from the abandoned Tlingit Camp? Of course you know it was and at that time I told you both to shape up. As I remember you promised to behave and ran away before I brought the hammer down. I see your pledge has not worked out."

Suddenly, both of them had strange expressions on their faces.

"Look behind you!" they both yelled. "It's a Bear, a Black Bear coming across the river!"

He turned. Sure enough, the bear was swimming toward the cleaning station. Since he had his hands full, he told the scoundrels to hold fast and he'd throw a couple rounds at the advancing bear.

Ka-Pow! Ka-Pow! Geysers of water exploded around the bear's head. He waited to see the bear's reaction.

Ka-Pow! He threw another round at the halted bear, and it finally turned.

Ka-Pow! "That should keep the bruin moving, boys," he added, turning. They had disappeared. "I'll be damned. Those sonsofabitches took off, naked as jaybirds."

He turned back to the river a moment to check if the bear kept moving across the water and out of the area. Not seeing it anymore, he turned and ran into the ferns and then down the trail leading out of camp. Sure enough, there they were, bare-assed and all, running over a hillock about 100 yards to the west. He threw a round over their heads to let them know he could have blistered their cheeks. He would not use lethal means anyway; he just wanted them to know he could. Illegal fishing does not merit lethal means for apprehension. To scare them, he let another round go into the western sky. If nothing else, it would make them run faster and take a toll on their bare feet and nakedness.

"Here I go again, stuck with a couple horses, a couple hundred pounds of choice salmon fillets, and two scoundrels escaping by running naked to their camp somewhere in the Tongass. Damn. Why me? This is not going to look too good on my first report. Nevertheless, the weir will be shut down, the illegal sale of fish terminated, and a warrant will be posted for their arrest. The scoundrels probably knew I would not shoot them, not for illegal fishing. No sweat, we'll get 'em sooner or later."

He decided to call headquarters to amend his earlier report, including the escape. He added, "The campsite is fully documented on film, so I will return it to its natural state. I will also bring in two horses and approximately five-hundred pounds of choice salmon fillets, for your direction on their disposition. I will report upon arriving at camp of Runs with Wolves. Nothing further. Chi Mukwa, out."

Chapter 5

Redress

Midnight passed while Chi Mukwa sat by the fire and meditated in the prescribed sitting position—legs crossed, arm aside—as he spoke to Manitou. He petitioned to ask forgiveness and a blessing for his brethren of the three fires. Sadly, his Haida brothers had violated the sacred trust of tribal rules—Nature's law.

> "In the last flicker of day let the wind lift the flames of our fire high.
>
> As air lifted his face to the sky, and night takes the day, I offer light.
>
> We are true to your way and stand for the right.
>
> Truth here is done in this circle of one, I now ask forgiveness for two of our own who have gone astray.
>
> Teach us to care for every rock, tree, and animal in the life's stream.
>
> Carry us with it on midsummer's moonbeam."

He cast tobacco to the cardinal points in the circle of life as an offering to the creator. He gave thanks for his safeguarding during his stressful day and safekeeping for the future. This act of supplication was a humble act of thankfulness not only for him, but for his wayward Haida brothers.

> "Do not fret, my bothers; we tried to carry out trading expeditions and obey the new laws, white man's laws, and still maintain our identity.
>
> "Do not fret, my brothers; we will carry on our traditions individually with pride we had as a Tribe. You will succeed individually; it is in your blood.

"Do not fret, my brothers; change is necessary for our children to survive; they could no longer do so with our old ways.

"They will do well."

Finally:

"My brothers, remember this place and treat it for the lessons learned. It is the resting place of an event that will not repeat itself. Great Spirit, bless the people of the Three Fires as they start a new life."

Chi Mukwa decided to stay in the camp overnight for two reasons: he needed time to completely clean and return the clearing to its original state, and also to guard against the possibility of the two naked warriors returning. He figured they may not have done the wise thing and go home. If not, they'd be a little cold by now, and would use the cover of darkness and approaching rain to snarl back to reclaim their clothes, horses, guns, and booty. That was not going to happen. It would not be a good decision for them. But knowing their double digit mentality, they'd probably try something like that. A better decision for them would be to get back to their camp near town and get some clothes. This would prevent the local dogs from waking up the entire settlement by howling at the unappareled ghost-like bodies sneaking into their camp. They'd be wise to get out of the area. If not, the law would apprehend them quickly. In either case, he would personally track them down. Being Native, their lawlessness reflected on him and the entire Nation of law-abiding brothers.

He collected their weapons and hid them with their tack under a tarp by the horses. He grained all three again and soothed their restlessness with a hands-on talk and a quick rub down. The buckskin and sorrel seemed more relaxed now. Gunshots and the accompanying chaos were probably not a part of their normal routine. They appeared to be more at ease standing with Old Gal; nothing bothered her. In her late teens now, she'd probably seen just about everything. The other two appeared much younger, most likely under ten. He hoped they were not stolen. In any event, the DNR would confiscate not only their horses, but all their weapons and other miscellaneous equipment. The local charities would eat top-of-the-line fillets if he could get them distributed before spoilage. He'd do his best to ensure Earth Mother's wealth was given to the needy in Skagway, Haines, and Klukuan along the Lynn Canal.

He resolved it was going to be a long night without sleep. The first priority was to ice down the fish properly. One container was ninety percent full, so he laid a tarp over the fish and transferred all the ice from the second. After securing the lid tightly to minimize outgassing, he dragged it over to the travois and pushed it onto its rails.

"Dang, it's almost five o'clock. I'd better hustle; it'll be dark in a couple hours. Let's see, the travois will work well in getting the fish back to the meadow, but I've got to determine if there's anything else to save and haul out. The horses can be led easily, but there are many containers, tarps, and tables all over the clearing. Let's see . . . I know. I'll need a fire for security tonight so I'll burn everything I don't need and bury the rest. I'd better get humping," he exclaimed.

A solitary raven croaked, apparently to announce its presence.

"Hello, my fine-feathered friend. What's up?"

He started a fire in the center of the clearing, then waded into the river. The sound of his axe echoed across the river as the weir and its side members buckled and fractured under the blade of the warrior's lethal strokes. He stopped periodically to gather splintered oak and maple portions and throw them on the waiting pyre. Then, as if by a starter's pistol, finned breeders dashed upstream with the vigor of a sailor on a short shore leave. At one point a mass of thirty-pound Chinooks surging forward knocked him down, ass-over- teakettle. Falling into the maelstrom of finned fury was brutal. They jumped over, darted around, and ran into him as they escaped with wanton abandon through the fractured weir. After a short immersion in the scale-and-fin attack, he regained his footing downstream and rinsed the blood from his multiple cuts. He continued tearing off the loose boards, throwing them on the bank. Later he fed the splintered timbers onto the raging fire. With the last section removed, he dragged his exhausted body up the bank and yelled, "Go breed, my friends! Finish your task as the Creator has planned. Breed and be proud that your progeny will soon hatch and return to the mighty Pacific. Charge on, my brothers, and repeat this cycle you've started. Go, my brothers. Find your mate . . . and create new life in your Kin(g)dom. Damn, this feels good. I feel like a father again. Go, guys, go! Do your thing. Lock and load. Fire. Have your last fling. Look at 'em go!"

His eyes followed the racing multitude upstream and, much to his dismay, at about a 100 yards there she was again. Good old she-bear had wandered back to the river to fish. Chasing her away from dinner, earlier, only momentarily delayed her feeding habits. A beautiful and most natural sight, she fished as the salmon raced to their spawning grounds, Nature's food-chain unfolding before his eyes. It was beautiful.

"Hey! Hey, bear! How are you? Are you enjoying your dinner? Be sure to taste the Reds; they're the best. Sorry to throw a few rounds at you earlier today. I had my hands full with a couple rogues from the reservation. They won't harm you anymore this year if I have my way. Enjoy your dinner."

Caw—Caw—Caw.

"Well hello, my feathered friend. Did you hear me talking to our cohort fishing upstream? She's in her glory. Look at her. She strips the skin off first, where most of the fat is located. She's no dummy. She knows what's needed to fatten-up before her hibernation. Ah! Look. A red fox has joined her. He'll dance around like a ballerina, picking up all her leftovers, and be very satisfied, never getting his feet wet. Look, I think that's a surly old solitary wolverine fishing farther upstream. This is a beautiful example of hunger in the face of plenty neutralizing aggressive behavior among animals. Eat hardy, my brothers; the spawning run will be over soon."

As the last couple of confused salmon cleared the containment area, he dragged the last pieces of wood up the bank and into the fire. The river's flow soon cleared the area of dead fish, splintered wood, fish entrails, and miscellaneous debris. Finally, the river bottom looked unclouded again as the current slowly moved sand into the hole evacuated by the thrashing mass of angry fins. Pebbles soon covered a portion of the bottom as Nature took its time to replace the river's natural characteristics.

As the sun slid behind the mountains to the west, long shadows raced across the clearing. The storm moving in from the north would rob him of starlight, so the impending darkness with a new moon meant the fire would be his only radiance for the night's activities. The lone figure's shadow danced across the clearing with the flickering ebb and flow of the fire's intensity.

Burying the miscellaneous metal and plastic containers and equipment required a hole about four-feet square and two-feet deep. This type of digging was not a problem for Chi Mukwa; he embraced the out-of-doors, and this digging put him in direct communication with Earth Mother. Digging into her breast also gave him a chance to speak with her. He chatted about his stressful day and its successful conclusion with the release of her finned brethren and apprehension of the violators. Although still on the run, he gave her assurance that they would be brought to justice. He thanked her for the silent hand of guidance that prevented any bloodshed.

Late evening shadows of the trees, horses, and the lone man cascaded across the river with striking beauty—beauty beyond measure, beauty surpassed only by a woman's bare behind, as Joe Bloom, his boss, would say.

As this portion of the Earth rotated away from the sun, shadows were eclipsed by blackness but for the flickering fire's illumination. It was indeed an eerie scene of fire's yellow on black with a deep gray on the clearing's tree-rimmed border. Anything and everything could be hiding in the depths of the forest. While digging, his mind flashed to imagery of threats within the mysterious potential of man and beast on the prowl. He paused several times to scan the silent timber and the trail leading from the west, the river to the east, and the sky, noting the total absence of light at earth's zenith. His mind wandered to mythological imaginary of metaphysical dangers. Layered with these abstract legends was the real-live threat of the return of Yellow Knife or Red Dog. They were probably miles from the clearing by now, but he wasn't certain. Both were desperate men. He had learned to expect the unexpected.

He thought to himself, *One tiny screw-up and I could be lying in this hole. No one could get in here to rescue me. Certain portions of the Tongass are just too remote. This incident was a powerful reminder of how far I have stretched my safety net. I should probably have a partner. On the other hand, to stretch that net is to undergo something that not many people ever experience. To be completely reliant on your own abilities and judgment, without any kind of backup, is quite rare in everyday life—and strangely gratifying for that very reason. Timely rescue here in the Tongass is, for now, impossible. Maybe a twofer would ensure a longer life . . . then I'm not sure. C'est la vie.*

Tired of digging, he wandered over to the horses to see how Old Gal was getting along with the sorrel and buckskin geldings. He stroked them and noted clearly from their lowered heads and dispirited looks that they were all beat from the day's activities. Two were under saddle while one pulled the travois most of the day. They were ready for a good night's rest. As he moved back to finish burying the junk from the clearing a raven croaked again.

"Well, my friend, you're still with me. Welcome. I need some company." The bird croaked again, a deep slow groaning sound.

I wonder what's gotten into the bird. They seldom sound-off at night.

He thought, finally, with a few more shovels the junk will be covered. The sooner the better. He could smell the lightning in the air, and now waited for the clasp of thunder. It would soon be followed by rain. He kept shoveling the last mounds of dirt. As expected, a cleansing rain washed over the clearing. He stopped and leaned on his shovel to rest.

∗   ∗   ∗

"What the hell!"

Suddenly something seized Chi Mukwa in a clinch lock around the shoulders, and in a second he found himself gyrating side to side around the hole, then literally rolling in the dirt and mud. Unfortunately, whoever it was outweighed him by at least twenty pounds. Luckily though, whoever it was smelled as if loaded to the gills, so he was not exceptionally nimble. They wrestled and pummeled each other. Still remembering a few basic survival rules, in two quick motions he was able to twist free and dump the naked assaulter on his ass. The dirt-laden naked one then kicked with both feet, managing to nail Chi Mukwa in the shins and toppled him backwards into the freshly dug hole. The nude jumped in, just missing Chi Mukwa, who had rolled clear. Before the intruder could get up, he grabbed his long hair, rotated his head, and drove an elbow into his nose, then followed it with a fist to the throat. It was over. He stayed down, slobbering from the clobbering like a gut shot deer. He dragged him out of the hole, sprawled him on his chest, then planted a knee in his groin and pinned both arms over his head.

Lowering his face to his, Chi Mukwa said, "Hello, Yellow Fellow."

"Huhhggnn?"

"Do you hear me, you crook?"

Earlier rage had fled his eyes. He struggled to breathe without choking on bloody viscous fluids flooding his airways.

"How are you, Yeller?"

"Wha—uh? Wa—rr! I need wat—r. Can't breee!"

"Yeah, no doubt."

"Heelppp . . . meeee! Waatr!"

Yellow Knife blew bubbles of blood out his nostrils and mouth and pointed to the river. Not wanting a death on his hands, from his own hands, Chi Mukwa ran to the river to get some water in his hat.

Lighting struck as he stumbled down the bank. He dipped his hat in the water and returned to the hole that was nearly Yellow Knife's grave. Yeller now sat on the edge leaning backward to clear his throat. Chi Mukwa poured water from his hat onto his face first, and then into his mouth. Yeller gagged, coughed, and spit, but asked for more. It rained harder now as Chi Mukwa returned to the river for more water. He fell going down the bank, then again climbing back up the slippery slope. He was very nervous about the damage he had done to subdue Yeller. As he walked back, a bolt of lightning illuminated the tableau: the big timber, the fire, the horses, the loaded travois, the shovel in the freshly dug bole . . . and unexpectedly—a bare-assed man running from the clearing and breaking away into the forest.

"I'll be dipped in dung and rolled in flour! I've been tricked. I'm an unlucky good Samaritan . . . dang it! There he goes, caked in dirt and blood. He's gotten away—again. One hell of a CO you are; that's twice in one day," Chi Mukwa groaned.

He dumped the water or his face, rubbed his bruised shins and cut lip, then washed the blood from his nose.

"Now what?"

A raven called out in a mournful croak.

"Yeah, yeah. I should have listened closer to your clue. Okay, so I had blinders on my sixth sense. Don't rub it in. Maybe I can catch that sonabitch. He can't run very fast with that injury to his throat."

He ran across the clearing. When he reached the trail head at the edge he ran another 100 feet and stopped. It was pitch dark, the kind of black he first experienced at fourteen during his vision quest. You could not see your hand in front of your face. He quickly decided he could not find Yellow Knife under these conditions, and would probably run into an ambush . . . shortening his life considerably.

After returning to the clearing, he cleaned up in the river, finished burying the miscellaneous junk, and tied a small tarp between four trees to act as a little rain protection during the night. The canvas fly was strategically located between the fire and the trail's entrance to the clearing. He could also see the horses and the river. He lay some spruce boughs down and leaned against a tree to eat some freeze-dried stew, heated with water from the fire, and a few of Leigh's biscuits. He'd have to stay awake for another six hours. Dawn, at six, couldn't come soon enough. He had no idea whether crazy Yeller would try to re-enter camp with some kooky far-out scheme.

He wondered if Yellow Knife knew the seriousness of assaulting an officer of the law. That's a 5- to 10-year felony. Yep, he would do some jail time when caught.

He lay his Winchester across his lap and scanned the area. His thoughts shifted to Runs with Wolves and her cautiousness in their relationship. An optimist, he expected that they would soon see eye to eye on the future. He would definitely clear up the conflict of still being married to Morning Star. He'd have to, there were no other options if he wanted her love equal to his love for her. Some things are not negotiable. It was now clear, after living with her for a few months, that he loved her. He would file for divorce upon return from this trip.

Caw—Caw—Caw.

"Welcome, my friend; it's been a busy day."

While he daydreamed about his future, a visitor appeared. Old she-bear stood on the bank and roared. She must have swum across the river and didn't like the new layout, which excluded her buffet of river specialties. She wandered into the clearing, looked at the fire, the horses—who whinnied softly—and then at Chi Mukwa. She turned to where the weir had fed her very well over the last few months. She stared at the river. Then she looked at the shadow in the canvas fly. Someone was under there. She sniffed the air. Apparently frustrated, she looked back at where her buffet of salmon delights once resided, and roared. She pawed the ground, looked at the canvas fly again, and walked peacefully away into the night. Maybe she knew she would have to work for her fish from now on.

Maybe the raven told her.

*   *   *

When the rain stopped, Chi Mukwa left the canvas fly to get a drink, chewing on deer jerky. No doubt fresh venison would taste better, but that would have to wait until dinner back in camp. Venison is one of the most delicious and elemental feasts he could imagine, making a deer part of the body.

He lowered himself for a drink of the sparkling clear water. While drinking, he looked up and across the water. A large buck moved out from the trees and stepped to the water's edge, nervously switching his tail. The deer reached down, without fear of Chi Mukwa's presence, and drank . . . as if he were one of them. It was one of the most tranquil moments of his day, thanks to Manitou.

*   *   *

Returning to the clearing, he prepared to meditate. Holding his amulets, he cast tobacco to the cardinal points of the compass:

> "I cast East, warmth, to warm your body,
> South, wisdom, to nourish your mind,
> West, wind, to provide spiritual power,
> North, passion, representing our love.
>
> We thank you, Great Spirit, for this day.
> That we are allowed to live upon
> our Mother Earth.
> For us two-leggeds,
> you give us courage and endurance;
> these strengths are now ours.
> We are blessed
> as we face tomorrow."

Chapter 6

Revenge

Chi Mukwa welcomed dawn as the rising sun chased darkness to the Gulf of Alaska. The colors of sunrise complimented the fire pit's smoldering red embers, not having been stoked since four in the morning. He was not alone; entertainment had enveloped the clearing during his nightly vigil. Several avian visitors were drawn to the fire as the clearing glowed. Earlier in the evening night hawks danced in absolute silence, among the rising ashes of the fire, searching for a meal of tasty insects. They swirled left and right at breakneck speeds, then soared out of sight, only to return in an explosive halt as wings flared to stall an earthly dive.

Around midnight, a red fox appeared with its short, trotting gait and uniquely horizontal tail. The cunning trickster danced in double time toward the pit likely searching for tasty morsels from the cleaning table. He spun, jumped, and pranced as if to raise a salmon from its earthen death. Frustrated, it looked at the figure in the canvas fly, yipped a couple of times, and moved on in a disappointed swagger. Then the vixen stopped, looked back, yipped again as if in disgust, and disappeared into the moss-draped cedar.

Much later, to Chi Mukwa's surprise, the she-bear returned to the clearing in the predawn light. She appeared confused while searching for the now-absent cleaning table.

The restlessness of the horses suggested her presence. The intruder was not a welcome sight for the horses.

She certainly had no immediate need for additional nurture; she had gorged on salmon all afternoon.

"It's okay, broncos, settle down," he yelled to calm the horses.

Frustrated, the she-bear climbed down and then up the river bank as if looking for fish, then stopped and found the solitary figure under the canvas fly. Satisfied for the moment, she plopped down on the river's edge. Gormandized with Reds, she'd worry about harvesting more in the future and, for now, sleep off her recent indulgence.

One thing was certain: the horses would never settle down while a slumbering bear lay on the river hank. They continued to prance and softly whinny in their halters. Their concern, their fear, their flight instinct had exploded. As if inbred, the scent of a carnivore, whether bruin, cat, or wolf had triggered their flight response.

He removed the canvas fly and attended to the horses. He approached the nervous steeds with a soothing tone. "Hold on, my friends, I'll take care of our bruin intruder shortly. Steady now, settle down."

He wanted to be between the bear and the horses before rousing their unwelcome guest. At about thirty feet, with rifle ready, he yelled at the bear in increasing volume. It didn't work. He threw a broken tree limb, another, and another larger one.

"Christ, what did you do, girl? Hibernate right here on the bank? You're apparently more than sleeping; you've passed out."

A little frustrated himself, he wanted to avoid a gunshot at close range. If startled, the bear might turn violent. The sound along with the acrid smell of burnt gunpowder could bring back incidents of hunters' intentions of the past—to kill.

The horses' restlessness continued. They pulled and jerked on their halters and temporary rope-hitching post. The big sorrel started rearing up, flagging the air with its four white socks, then kicking Old Gal in frustration. Conflicted and confused, it pranced in its tie-downs. Its flight instinct was about to go into high gear.

He thought, *It looks like I've very little time to think this over. I have to get this bear out of here. I can't have those horses injuring each other or, worse yet, breaking loose. I need them.*

He felt an emptiness in his heart due to the fruitless attempt to raise the bear. He knew there would be consequences in startling her with the sound of a round plunging into the earth, not to mention the smell. Harsh enough to an awake bear, that sound awakening her from a sound sleep would cause all hell to break loose. The results of his actions could be devastating.

The buckskin reared up, cried out in a blood-curdling whinny, and jerked on his tie-down with such force the larger hitching post rope came untied. Confused, they all started biting and kicking at each other to escape the smell of the sleeping she-bear.

"That's it. I'll throw a round into the dirt, decidedly clear of her head."

Ka-Pow!

The shot echoed down the river into the ravines and against the cliffs beyond, then to his surprise returned as if a series of shots: *ka-pow . . . ka-pow*.

The bear sprang to her feet, roared, looked around, stood on her hind legs, sniffed the air to locate the source of the gun powder's pungent smell, found Chi Mukwa, roared again, then quickly turned and bounded toward the source of the shot. Startled at the bear's violent response, he racked another round in the chamber and fired point blank at the bear's approaching mass.

Ka-Pow!

There was no time to sight perfectly; he shot from the hip.

The round tore flesh away from the bear's right shoulder. It stumbled, re-gained footing, and charged on with another monstrous roar and an altered gait. Blood gushed from the torn flesh.

Ka-Pow!

The second round entered its chest with an explosive eruption of blood as the bear stumbled again, head skiing the ground with its bloody right foreleg banging loose, left leg churning forward. A pathetic sight, she skidded along the ground with her hind legs plowing a half-moon shape as if in her dying move-ments. Not so . . . In a last desperate effort, she leaped toward him to destroy her adversary, to ravage his body—to kill.

Ka-Pow!

The shot ripped open her throat and severed her neck vertebra, but not her forward momentum. Seconds from death, she made her last lurch forward as Chi Mukwa made a quarter turn to escape her thrust. She savagely swiped her left paw across his back with the fury of a well-aimed pitchfork. As he spun in pain, the bear tumbled onto him. Panicked, with the bear on top, he drew his knife and plunged it into the bear's neck. Finally, in her last convulsive act, she opened her jaws and drove her incisors into his shoulder and neck.

Chi Mukwa's heart rate soared, his breathing accelerated, and the pain inten-sified as his back cried out in agony and her teeth imbedded in his neck muscles.

He blacked out . . . lapsing into shock and lying still.

The she-bear's bloody mouth slobbered as the gurgle of death echoed from her lungs. As she died, her jaws relaxed from Chi Mukwa's neck. In shock he did not feel the release, or her dead body on his.

The horses were nowhere to be found.

The sound of death silenced life on the clearing.

The only noise heard was the river's ripples as salmon fought its current to seek new life in their spawning grounds. One life ends as another suffers jeopardy on land . . . and another, in water, was about to begin anew.

*   *   *

Joe Bloom, Chi Mukwa's supervisor, had stopped by Leigh's camp while do-ing a DNR game survey of Glacier Bay National Park. He enjoyed getting out from under his desk in Skagway, and hiking through the Tongass's big timber was his first love. It also gave him a chance to visit Leigh, and maybe Chi Mukwa. With a slight deviation from his route, he could have a *real meal* with Leigh and follow the trail to the weir, too. Luckily, he did visit, and had just enjoyed a great meal with Leigh and met her young Tlingit visitor, Wind Spirit.

They were both aware of Chi Mukwa's transmissions to base summarizing the problems with violators Red Dog and Yellow Knife. Joe thought he might need some help—if for nothing else, to tear down the illicit camp, the weir, and for taking out the salvageable equipment, and maybe even a few fish if they had not spoiled. Then there were the two additional horses.

He was surprised by how large the wolves had grown and how well all three behaved both at dinner and while having a little grog at sunset. Typically, Jet, the younger cub, demanded more attention and, likewise, more discipline. He was a frisky little fellow. The sharp teeth marks on Joe's hands displayed their wrestling matches. Wind Spirit, was also a well-mannered young brave with a lot of curiosity and the verbal skills of an adult. Leigh appreciated the stopover and, even more, plans to follow Chi Mukwa's route to the illegal weir. Both had a feeling there might be more trouble brewing at the weir, having heard his last troublesome transmissions.

Leigh opened another unexpected can of worms, one for which Joe could help. Wind Spirit wanted to go with Joe to meet Chi Mukwa. He wanted to help him as needed, regardless of the troubles with the violators. Being only five miles downstream, it was a reasonable request. Joe leaned toward a yes, no problem. Leigh was more cautious.

As one might expect, Wind Spirit wore her down with his constant pleading, and she relented. After a dozen instructions of what-to-do in a dozen more cases, he hit the sack with plans to leave with Joe at dawn.

Joe carried his large cross-country rucksack that was good for a week in the forest. Windy brought a smaller one since he'd be out no more than one day if things went as planned. Windy's x-factor was convincing both Leigh and Joe that Chi Mukwa would need, beyond question, extra help with the two additional horses. It was Joe who tagged Wind Spirit with "Windy" because it was easier. He also tagged Chi Mukwa (Big Bear) with "Bear" for the same reason. Leigh (Runs with Wolves) did not necessarily accept her shortened name, "Me Bonny Lass." Joe had a way with words, he thought, but not everyone agreed—especially the lovely ladies in Skagway restaurants whom he called "Dearie" as he gave them a little pinch. Unfortunately, he also called Manitou "Da Man."

Joe was still concerned because they had not heard from Chi Mukwa since noon the previous day. That, in itself, was no cause for alarm, he generally did not care to bother anyone at base unless it was absolutely necessary. However, of more concern to Joe was the status of the violators, who were still on the loose—somewhere in the Tongass. Chi Mukwa might be in trouble and unable to use his SAT.

Joe took a reading on his handheld GPS to determine closing distance to the weir's lat/long coordinates. The digital display indicated they'd be at the weir, from their current location, at their current pace, in less than an hour. He tried to reach him again, without success. He felt very uneasy, but did not let on to Windy.

"Joe, here are some good prints of Old Gal headed west. At least no one had been on the trail in the last twenty-four hours. That's a good sign; Dog Face and Old Yeller did not escape in this direction."

"Hey, good names, me man. I was thinking more like Dog Shit and Yellow Pee. 'Tis a sorry lot, are they not? As Natives they can fish to satisfy all their needs . . . but not for profit. In a word—greed. These characters get enough of such truck. It could just as well be illegal game as fish. They may have gotten away from us this time, but we'll get 'em sooner or later. They can run but they cannot hide . . . believe me, I'll find the bloody buggers. If they're still on this planet, I'll hall their ass to the gaol . . . they'll soon slip off that slippery slope."

"Joe, how far now?"

"Well, me boy it looks like we'll be closing in within the hour. If you're getting anxious, 'tis okay by me to pick up the pace. Have at it, me boy, I'll keep up. Away with ye."

A small wind fiddled among the pines. They quickened their step. The trail dipped into a thicker stand of pines, and the sky was no longer visible except directly overhead. Occasionally, through the trees ahead and much lower, they caught glimpses of the river and some rock escarpments.

"Be alert, me boy, Bear reported a family of mountain lions in this area. They're probably over there in that outcropping of rocks. They won't bother us, and we've other fish to fry. Now there's a play on words. We may do that, too. That's part of my survey, me boy. I'll count the lion's den with the cubs that Bear reported. We share data and sightings. This type of survey on the ground, is called ground truth. When complete, I'll do a flyover count and compare the results. That's how we discovered the weir. A conservation officer was doing a fish survey and noticed the salmon were being blocked from appearing upstream. Voila! He found the weir. A later fly-by reported its location to my office, and the rest is history. Pay attention over the next few months and, if you think you'd like to do what Bear does, we could always utilize a good man like you. Think about it. Being Native, you'd have a leg up, since you're from the area."

Joe and Windy kicked around some of the assignments on land, sea, and air in the DNR. The boy was excited that he could be an intern helping a CO until he turned eighteen. The possibilities of helping both Joe or Bear gave him a little more vigor to his step.

Caw—Caw—Caw.

"Look, Joe, there's our feathered friend, the raven. I'll bet it will know where Chi Mukwa is. Hi, our black sentinel of the Tongass. Have you seen Chi Mukwa?"

The bird immediately exploded in flight and flew ahead, croaking again and again as it sped to the west.

"Joe, there's trouble ahead. I can tell by the raven's flight. I know. Let's hustle. We'd better get to the weir as soon as possible. Come on, let's push it!"

"Right you are, me young friend. I read the bird as ye did. Let's push some sod behind. Lead the way, but be careful to keep your eye on this old bloke and not leave him in the brush. Let's vamoose!"

Wind Spirit led the way, but was careful not to get too far ahead of his partner—a partner that had seen everything and experienced life at its fullest, a comrade you'd want as they moved into the lawlessness that lay ahead.

"It looks like the raven has perched in that large spruce. I'll be, we're at the weir.

Caw—Caw—Caw.

"Okay, me boy. What have we got here? Let's move to the edge of the river and have a look into the clearing. Be careful; this bank is slippery from last night's rain. What do ya see, me boy?"

The silence of the clearing radiated an eerie feeling of uneasiness.

Seeing nothing across the river, Joe yelled, "Me man, where the bloody hell are you? Big Bear? Bear, are you there?"

Three horses casually grazed in the center by the fire pit and along the edge of the river. Their halters were partially torn with tie-downs still attached as they dragged them along. Towards the edge of the river a container rested on a travois with a hissing sound. The fire pit looked cold. Puzzled, Joe looked at Windy and back at the clearing.

"Do you bloody well see anything, me boy? Something is amiss. Let's be checking out what's wrong here; this scene is crackers, my boy. Let's be checking on our peeler."

They waded briskly across the river, climbed up the bank, looked around, and spotted what seemed to be a lifeless bear lying on a man's body—a body that looked a lot like Chi Mukwa's. A sudden overpowering terror grasped both of them. They rushed to the motionless mass of blood-soaked black fur.

"It's him, all right. I've a round in the chamber, me boy. Grab that branch and poke that bloody mess. Let's be certain it's dead."

With no response, Wind Spirit cast caution to the wind and pulled the bear out of the way so he could get to Chi Mukwa's bloody torso. Joe knelt down quickly, felt Chi Mukwa's carotid artery, found a healthy pulse, and with joy proclaimed, "He's alive; he lives! Bloody well, his motor's thumping!"

"Great, Joe. What's next? What can I do?"

"Quick now. Get some water from the river. Your hat will do for now. Get along now. Quickly! He's still in shock."

Joe took his first aid kit out of his pack and laid out its contents. His triage assessment was to determine where Chi Mukwa's wounds were first and, if there were any active bleeding, stop the flow. Other than a few puncture wounds on the side of his neck, there were no other visible marks. The visceral area below his rib cage was soft, indicating there was no internal bleeding. He lifted his legs and put a blanket under his legs so they were higher and threw another blanket over his body.

"There you are, me boy, good. Let's have a pop at that water. While I pour, you wipe his face with this gauze. Good. We'll need him clean to see if there are any more wounds. Those neck wounds look like teeth marks, but are not serious. It's like this old she-bear tried to take a chomp and died in the middle of the bite . . . whatever, they're not critical. I'll lift him up to help you strip his shirt off. Never mind, cut it off."

As they raised him to a sitting position, the case for going into shock was revealed. His back had four deep claw marks that tore the flesh partially open for about ten inches. Some of the claws penetrated up to a quarter of an inch.

"Just as I thought: it appears the bear must have been half dead when she gave our boy a swat on the back and bite on the neck. Done by a healthy bear, both would have been fatal. Get my bedroll and lay it down so we can clean these wounds."

"Okay, me boy. We're about to tell this warrior he survived a bear attack. Help me roll him over to a sitting position again. Good, now let's give the bugger a little treat. Hand me those smelling salts. Thanks. Watch this."

He broke open the crystal salts with one snap and placed them under his nose.

"'Tis time to wake up, me boy. Come on now, me laddie. Give me a little blow out. Well, you are alive. Throw that water on him, Windy."

Wind Spirit, with a little reluctance, emptied his entire canteen on Chi Mukwa. That did the trick. Their patient blew bloody water, snorted more with his nose, and coughed up more blood. He shook his head and looked around at his tormentors.

"O-o-o-o-h. What the hell. Wa? What happened? Where am I? Is that you, Joe? Who's the other fellow? What the hell! My back is killing me. Damn, where's the bear?"

He leaned forward in pain, then unexpectedly with Joe resisting, sprang to his feet, saw the bear, grabbed the hilt of his knife, withdrew it, and plunged the knife into the bear repeatedly until collapsing from the trauma of pain in his back.

"There, you sonofabitch; how's that feel?" Chi Mukwa cried out.

"Get over here, you bloke. You're delusional. That bear's been dead a couple of hours now. You put three shots into its body before it fell on you and tried to chomp on your neck. Fortunately, it was only a dying wish; her bite was no longer effective. But, my boy, she gave you a good swat on your back. Get over here and sit down so I can dress those wounds. Infection is your next enemy, and we've got to get a jump on it. A bear's mouth and claws are filthy."

"Wait a minute. What's Wind Spirit doing here?

"Where are the horses?

"Where are the fish?"

Joe, with a smile on his face, yelled, "Will ya just shut up a minute?! Slow down, mate! I'll tell you, but first park your butt, and I'll explain."

As they brought Chi Mukwa up to date on the day's activities a raven perched in the cedar tree above their reunion and offered a subtle croak.

The clearing returned to normal as shadows disappeared with the sun at its zenith.

Chapter 7

Rubicon

Wind Spirit assisted as Joe dressed the claw wounds on Chi Mukwa's back with a strong solution of disinfectant from his rucksack. They had spent at least thirty minutes cleaning foreign debris from his wounds using tweezers and surgical gauze. Windy thought, *His back looks like a bear scrape on a tree to mark its territory, or to sharpen its claws. Unfortunately, the scars will stay with him for life.*

"O-o-o-o-w!" Chi Mukwa's cries echoed down the Bitterroot's cleft to the ridges below. "What did you do? Pull out a claw left in my back? Damn, you guys, take it easy!"

"Me Lad, we'll only be a poking at you a wee bit more. Remember, you've been rolling in the mud while fighting Yellow Knife, and then lying where rotting fish guts reside, not to mention sleeping with a filthy she-bear. Leigh's gonna hear about that. Ha! In short, you were coated with a mess of dirt and who knows what else. If I had me way, I'd run your bod through a sheep dip tank and make sure I'd kill everything living on your hide. But, this will do for now."

Chi Mukwa retorted, "Too bad Hawkeye and Trapper John aren't here to give me some *real* medical support."

"Yeah, me lad, if the truth were to be known, 'tis Margaret "Hot Lips" Hoolihan's fingers ye be wanting on your body. Ye don't fool me; all you Tlingit warriors like your women to dote. Okay, me bloke, you can sit up now."

"Dang, are you guys ever going to finish cleaning up a few little claw marks? You'd think they were deep and long, but they're probably only a few surface scratches."

"Never you mind. Quarter inch tears in the skin are not scratches. You know, you're one lucky Indian. That bear was about to take a bite out of your neck, too. Fortunately, me thinks she died in the middle of the chomp. She had her teeth into your skin, all right; the bruises show as much. It's kinda like a cute incisor pattern like the high school girls claim as a 'hickey' after snuggling. But the bear wasn't sucking . . . That's it, Windy. Let's just assume the old she-bear was giving him a 'hickey.' Who am I to judge what he was doing sleeping with her? Then again, you may have just tasted s-o-o b-a-a-d she spit you out." Joe chuckled, his stories trying to add some humor.

"So that's the way it is. Have you ever thought you're so damn ugly, even a love-struck she-bear wouldn't attack you? You're jealous since she wanted my body. I understand. Who'd want to chew on a limey?" Chi Mukwa chuckled.

"'Tis enough of your blarney. While I finish dressing your so-called scratches, tell this English blue blood how a Tlingit Warrior is going to live down being pinned by a she-bear. Wait. Windy, hand me that bottle of iodine; I've missed treating these tooth marks on the back of his neck. I think her incisor broke the skin here. Thanks. Here, hold the lid, boy."

"O-o-o-w! You bloody buggar, that stings!" Chi Mukwa hollered.

"Ah, that should do it. Pay me nurse on the way out. About one-hundred pounds will do, or a liter of the crown's best whiskey; you decide. I'll not charge you for my good shirt, but suggest you not wrestle with bears for a while, or at least while you're wearing me shirt. I'll want it back, you know. If necessary, I'll get it from Leigh. Now, how the bloody hell did all this come about? Wait. Windy, go dress-out that bear before the flies take over. We can at least get us a bear pelt for all our trouble. I might sleep with it this winter. It'll be warmer than wool, and that old she-bear pelt won't complain about me drinking or harmlessly carousing with a few lady friends. Yes sir, that's a good idea. Windy, do a good job, for I may be shut of women with a good pelt. Yep, at least until a good one comes along . . . and will have me. Now, how the hell did this bear end up on ye?"

Chi Mukwa explained the whole story of his confrontation with Yellow Knife, Red Dog, and the bear. "Apparently the terror of the moment and tremor of the wound turned to bodily collapse, or shock. Isn't that the way you found me, passed out under a blanket of dead bear? It all happened so fast, less than five seconds, I don't know what I could have done any different. When a bear has a mind to attack, it's going to happen. They're not bashful. After all, we're in their territory, their feeding grounds, their home. I'm here of my own free will. She's not. She must survive in a hostile environment bestowed to her by the Creator, Manitou. The Tongass is her home."

"Right you are, me boy. I, too, agree. Her loss is our loss. Nevertheless, your position in the Tongass is also beneficial to all its plants and animals. I'm elated you survived. Yes, hell yes, we need your kind."

They discussed the process of headquarters announcing an all-points bulletin for the arrest of the scoundrels that led to the trauma on the clearing. Joe would take care of the details so Chi Mukwa and Wind Spirit could pack up and return to the meadow. Once there, Chi Mukwa could rest a few weeks until his wounds healed. His worst enemy would be infection. Claw and teeth marks of animals, including humans, are brimming with infectious bacteria. They knew very well about infecting bites, having heard of Joe's experiences in a few bar fights when he was young lad.

Cleaned, bathed with iodine, and loaded with antibiotics his wounds would still require constant attention for weeks. Leigh and Windy would have to take over in changing his dressings.

They had also decided to forgo distribution of the fresh salmon fillets to local social services. He requested Windy to coordinate with Leigh to obtain salt for soaking the fish in a brine bath and smoking the entire catch. That way they could be distributed in a more manageable fashion. They would have to fabricate a temporary smoke house with pin racks, not to mention enlarging the barn and corral for the additional horses. The DNR would pick up the costs for both of these projects since the fish would be welcome protein for social services and the horses would add mobility for various DNR assignments.

Wind Spirit moved to round up the horses, harness the sorrel to the fish-laden travois, then saddle Old Gal for Chi Mukwa, and the buckskin for himself.

While clearing camp, Joe eased up to Windy and whispered, "I didn't want to let on by Chi Mukwa, but you and Leigh have to be very insistent on bed rest for that warrior over there. He's not used to taking orders. You'll be pulling his load now, boy. It'll be a test, but you can do it."

Walking over to the partially sedated warrior, Joe barked at him, "Me boy, I've given you a shot of penicillin and a couple Tylenol; here's a few more to take during the ride. Taking one every two hours should do, and with any luck you'll be to the meadow in six hours. Under no conditions should you dismount, including to pee. You'll find a way to "hold it," literally holding your willy in a "stretch it" to clear the horse. Believe me, I've stretched me willy many a time—in and out of the saddle. Ha! I'll call Leigh right now and fill her in on details and your expected time of arrival."

Windy had rolled the bear's pelt and stacked it on the travois along with both rucksacks. The canvas fly fit snugly to hold things together and hid the pelt, with head attached, from the horses. At that, he covered the entire pelt with ferns and moss to mask the bear's smell from the horses. The caravan was ready to roll.

After reaching the DNR's receiver at Leigh's, Joe talked to Chi Mukwa. "I could not reach her, so I left a text message on your condition and what to expect as you roll in tonight with three horses, five-hundred pounds of fish to smoke, and one she-bear pelt. Sadly, I told her her favorite man, me, would be moving on to the coast. I also threw her kudos on her decision to let Windy come along, since it has been a good experience for all of us and he'll soon be an essential part of your rehabilitation. Now let's get you mounted. It's gonna hurt, so be prepared."

They led Old Gal to a depression in the ground, and both lifted the groaning warrior into the saddle.

"Damn, you guys are devil-may-care, slipshod buggars," Bear cried in pain.

Joe said to Windy, "Ignore him, me boy. He's half out of his mind in hurt."

As they departed, the quiet pastoral feel of the clearing returned. Joe took a picture of the trio's easterly trek to Leigh's meadow. Wind Spirit led on the buckskin with a lead rope to the halter on the sorrel harnessed to the travois. It was indeed an unusual sight. Wind Spirit's responsibilities had certainly been amplified as a result of Chi Mukwa's bear attack. Less than a week ago he was a runaway from the Raven Clan, distressed at the constrained life in town. Now, after a few days with Leigh and Joe, he was trusted to help Chi Mukwa survive the trip back to the meadow.

As they rode into the primitive game trail under the cool shadows of the forest, Joe barked out his last reminder. "Let me know when you arrive, mates. Have Leigh give me a call on the SAT, and have a good trip, me Tlingit Warriors. Joie de vivre!"

As Joe headed west to the Pacific, one thought crossed his mind. Will the lad and Chi Mukwa make it back to the meadows without incident? He thought, *You old bloke, you'd better shut the thoughts of trouble, for you'll not be there to help. Think positive; it's only five miles or about six hours at most. 'Tis no problem. Away with your worry, Joe. The lad will do fine.*

With rucksack repacked and canteen full, Joe surveyed the clearing one last time to ensure it had been returned to its natural state, then left on the same trail used by the scoundrels a mere twelve hours earlier.

He wondered, *Surely those bastards are at their own camp, or dive, by now. I hope so. They are desperate men and liable to do anything to their fellow man. Bear's trick of taking their clothes is a new one on me. I'll have to check if that's allowed in DNR policy. Bloody hell. Who cares? One thing is* certain: the two will not be telling that a CO took their clothes, and they ran home naked. No way . . . Ha!

"'Tis a lovely day after all. Hello, me fine-feathered friend. Nice of you to appear. Could I ask you a favor? Since this old buggar can take care of himself, do you mind helping me friend Bear and Windy on their way to the meadow? You'd be making this old bloke very happy. What say you, me ebony beauty?"

With neither response nor movement, he knew the bird understood his message. Living in the forest for half a hundred gave a naturalist like Joe a sixth sense of comprehension, of understanding with Manitou's creatures. His knowledge of the forest, after experiencing almost every struggle and subsequent harmony had earned him the wisdom of self-assurance. He knew what worked and worked it well.

The bird flew silently to the east.

*   *   *

Leigh sat facing east in a meditation stance. She opened her medicine bag, retrieved tobacco, and cast to the cardinal points, repeating at the four directions:

"I honor your spirit . . ."

She raised her arms, stretched her hands upward, and rotated her eyes to the sky and repeated: "Boozhoo—Manitou, Boozhoo—Manitou, Boozhoo—Manitou." She sat in silence to allow the Creator to hear . . . and prayed:

"I come to you in thanksgiving,
in appreciation of your gifts
of Mother Earth, Father Sky,
and your creatures of land, air, and sea.
I ask your guidance, please help me.
Teach me to understand my place with my fellow man,
Once again, I am involved with another,
show me the way.
I await your sign,
I await your blessing,
I await your concurrence
regarding my affection for Chi Mukwa, Tlingit warrior."

Calm embraced her after she spoke of her concerns to Manitou. Silence overpowered the ether, the meadow, and Leigh as she continued to meditate, asking herself, *Am I capable of unconditional love?*

A raven croaked. Its sudden appearance was strange. It landed very close to Leigh, croaked again, then lurched back to the sky for a hasty return to the west.

"Well, my friend, you didn't stay long. Was your call a message that the Creator heard me, or was it a call to tell me the men are on the way? Which is it? Both? In either case, thank you. I believe your presence was in letting me know you're flying with the caravan, and that they're on the way. Good show, my ebony sentinel."

Joe's message had implied Chi Mukwa's wounds were so bad that he may need total care for a couple weeks. Leigh decided that with the time remaining she might as well do what she could with the materials she had.

"Well, boys," she said to the wolves, "let's clean out all those five-gallon plastic buckets we've got other junk in, and get ready to put those fillets in brine. I may have just enough salt; we'll see. I know we've enough oak and apple kindling for the smoker. Now, let's gather as much extra plywood and boards as we've got over by the woodpile so Wind Spirit can throw up a temporary smoke house. The materials for corral and barn expansion are on Joe. He'll have to air-drop what's needed, along with enough fodder if they stay. As to Chi Mukwa's treatment, I can manage that, if Wind Spirit can handle the rest. I suppose you guys wonder what I'm talking about. Well, I've got news for you: the wolves of the meadow are about to see their predictable daily routine change. It's going to be hectic around here for a couple weeks with the smoker going day and night, plus building on to the barn area. Add two men—one out of commission—and two new horses. Sound interesting? Hope so, 'cause it's gonna happen."

After Leigh did what she could to prepare for smoking the fish and rounding up some good scrap wood, with the wolves trailing her every move, she rested on the river bank and patted the confused wolves who didn't know what all the activity was about.

She slowly rubbed her fingers over the scars administered a few months ago in honor of her dear fallen friends, Ford, Jack, and Steven. They had unveiled to her many incredible life experiences through their feeling, their agape . . . their unconditional love.

The three one-inch scars, like steps on a ladder, represented a permanent symbol of notation, a life time record of honor and remembrance. Joe had told her the story of his Norseman ancestors who honored their ancient warriors with a small break in the skin to mark their comrade's memory. The cut, by one's own blade, was made in a stream so blood would flow to the sea and join previous partners' blood. It flowed to those who had shared in similar life struggles for virtue, propriety, and righteousness.

Relaxing on the bank of the Bitterroot, she was overcome with joy, knowing that her men would soon return. She reflected on the various ways Chi Mukwa and Wind Spirit had entered her life. She thought, *Life is so complex, I know I'm about to be involved with Chi Mukwa. I just know it. I can feel it in my heart, and I know he loves me, too. Another man? Not sure. She rubbed her finger over the three scars on her inner arm again. The others did not fare very well. What to do? Oh well. Amor vincit omnia. Love conquers all things.*

"Come on, gang, I'm feeling just a little too melancholy. Let's jump in the river and clear out the cobwebs and get clean while we're at it," Leigh yelled at the wolves while doffing her clothes. They all leaped playfully into the Bitterroot and tumbled together as if playing water polo.

*   *   *

As the sun moved four fingers from the horizon, the trio of horses plodded along the game trail without incident. The raven had returned after a short absence as it called and flashed among the tops of the spruce forest. An occasional skittering fox paid a visit. A passel of chubby marmots followed noisily, jabbering as though the caravan had disturbed their private domain. Several prancing mulies stopped and stood as if at attention while the horses moved along the trail. Wild creatures seldom see domestic horses, much less a horse pulling a hissing load.

As they passed the point on the trail near the lion's den, every one of the horses raised its head, looked across the river, whinnied, and picked up the pace. Windy calmed them with soothing words of comfort, and they settled down.

He was more or less on his own as they proceeded along the last half of the route. Chi Mukwa had long since dropped the reins and held the pommel of his saddle for stability. Old Gal was on her own to follow her lead at the end of the caravan. He did not respond to Windy's small talk—he was in pain. The progress was somewhat slower than expected due to Chi Mukwa's inability to stand the pain beyond a slow walk. The jostling of a faster walk by the horses was out of the question. The overloaded travois prevented a faster pace anyway. Starting to break apart, it had been patched once by Windy hoping his quick fix would last for the next two miles. He also hoped Leigh had done some preparation for smoking the fish, since the dry ice was almost depleted. She probably had already made provisions.

"Hey, Bear, do you want to stop a moment to pee, drink, or stretch your legs?" Windy yelled over the startled sorrel gelding. He stopped anyway, since the horses took his comment as a command to stop the queue.

"Okay, Windy, I guess so," Bear responded as he started to swing his leg out of the saddle. "It looks like the horses could use a little rest anyway. I think I can get down and stretch my legs and, as Joe would say, my willy, too."

"No! Don't do it, Bear. Wait. You'll hurt yourself. I'll help! Please, Bear, wait!"

Too late.

With Bear's pain-racked clumsy manner, his foot slipped out of the stirrup, his hands slid from the pommel, and he rotated under Old Gal's belly and fell squarely under the startled horse's hooves. She reared, pivoted, and bolted to the rear.

Windy dismounted and ran to Bear, hoping the horse had not stepped on him. "Bear, are you okay? Bear!"

Bear did not respond. He did not move.

"Bear! Bear! Can you hear me?"

Chapter 8

Refuge

With the sun low in the western sky, two fingers from the horizon, Leigh thought she'd better set aside some of the venison stew. The guys in the caravan were going to be a little late. It was hard telling what they might run into. Countless things could delay them on the game trail along the river. Who knew what might be lurking in the shadows this time of year? Many animals scampered about, getting ready for winter hibernation. Countless numbers just ran after each other; it was the breeding season for many. Mulies pranced across the meadow on a daily basis—bucks in rut, does in estrus, both at their peak of sexual excitement. She frequently heard the penetrating clatter and crack of their competition for the right to breed. Night and day the determined bucks battered their antlers violently at each other to claim the territory and its amenable does, ensuring that the strongest and most persistent bred, and optimal progeny prevailed. To Leigh, it was lilting eloquence—a lively song of beauty. The natural tune of life's struggles.

Rummaging through the wood pile for smoker materials, she noticed several mice had started building their winter quarters of spun grasses and leaves. Sadly, she disrupted their efforts and decimated a few squirrel nests and acorn storage chambers, which rattled to the ground.

She paused for a moment to take in the sounds of the forest toward the river trail. She heard the faint rustle of the trees and the distant call of a nocturnal bird, but nothing else. It looked like a wilderness of mirrors, mirrors reflecting mirrors, a forest that never truly revealed itself.

Leigh and the wolves gathered around the bench by the river . . . waiting.

The forest along the river trail by the meadow and along its westerly path was a dense collection of old birches, with peeling bark and tall, slender pines and spruce. Cover along the river was thicker as there was a natural tendency for foliage to be more abundant in the flood plain of the river.

Settling darkness restricted her view of the trail. A heavy canopy of clouds obscured the moon. She tried not to worry. *Wind Spirit can handle the task of bringing his injured brother to the meadow. Joe had called over eight hours ago to say they were on their way, not to be concerned, but it was only a five-hour trip.*

"Okay, my furry friends, I'm going to light this Coleman lantern and hang it on that pine tree so they'll have a target as they move closer along the darkened trail. I suppose it would be sheer folly to head out after them. But what if they need my assistance? They must be only a mile or two away by now."

She resolved to wait another hour before deciding on what to do.

*   *   *

Wind Spirit spoke softly and calmly. Old Gal made a low, grunting noise as he began patting and stroking the animal's neck, withers, and her sleek flanks. In a few minutes the horse began to relax. Her ears lolled to the front, and her lower lip dropped. She had finally settled down after jolting to the river's edge. He adjusted her tack and slowly led her away from the river.

As they returned to the trail, the sorrel and buckskin stopped pawing the ground and prancing in place. Their calm was welcome as he led Old Gal back to her position in the queue.

Her breathing became regular, almost inaudible. He rubbed her gently and groomed her with a towel to put her at ease. He did the same to the other two, tied them to a tree, and moved toward Chi Mukwa.

Earlier, Windy had helped Chi Mukwa lie down carefully to recover from the fall while he chased after Old Gal. Windy had determined that the horse accidentally stepped on him, after being thrown, and that he may have suffered a cracked rib or two. Windy's earlier exam indicated as much as he felt the wound through his bruised skin.

"Bear, how are you feeling? Can you move? Bear?" Windy pleaded as he attended to the unresponsive warrior.

"I'll be okay," Bear moaned. "I just want to lie awhile and move carefully to determine if that hoof bruised, cracked, or broke a few of my ribs. What did you think when you rolled me over and felt my chest?"

"I'm no medicine man," Windy said, "but in my opinion you've cracked a few ribs right under your left arm. I heard the snap. Sorry, Bear, that snap was not a twig. It was you. It's lucky Old Gal didn't come down on your arm, or it would most assuredly be broken. In a way, you were fortunate. At least your chest gives a little. I'll bet as soon as she felt you under her hoof she pulled back. I believe she tried to miss you and, in a startled moment, her hoof glanced off your chest."

"Damn it all, now we've got another problem," Bear groused, "I can barely move, much less get on a horse that's already a little skittish due to my clumsiness. Add the potential of another fall or sudden move to completely break a rib and force it into a lung. Dammit! That ain't good news in a doctor's office much less in the middle of the Tongass, at night, miles from medical help."

"You're right on all counts," Windy agreed. "I've been thinking of another option to get you out of here in one piece by avoiding a saddle on a fidgety mount.

I'll build a travois . . . a wooden ambulance."

"What? You can't do that! It would be hard enough in daylight. Do you realize it will be dark out here in less than an hour? Pitch black! I can't see you chopping wood and tying a travois together for a horse that you are unaware will even permit such a rig. These are not coach horses. Add their skittishness at night. It will never work, my brother. Do you understand? Just leave me; go ahead and come back for me in the daylight. We're only a couple of miles from the meadow. Go ahead. I'll swallow some aspirin and stay here. Get out of here. I'll be okay."

"Maybe, maybe not. You're forgetting one thing."

"What?"

"I'm in charge here, and I've decided to get you out—tonight. You're not going to sleep with four-leggeds tonight. You need medical attention as soon as possible, and Leigh can provide that."

"It looks like I have little sway in this matter. Anyway, I suppose you're right . . . dammit!"

"Yep," Windy said, "as I see it, we've no other option. I've repaired that rickety old travois enough by now to throw one together, even in the dark. What do you think? It only needs to survive for up to two hours over the next three miles or so?"

"Yeah, maybe not even that. Have you enough rope?"

"Yep. By the way, I'll need your belt in a bit so if you can remove it while I'm chopping down a few pines for shafts and cross members."

"Damn, now my pants will probably end up somewhere on the trail."

"Out here, who cares? Just snug 'em up once in a while. Old Gal could care less about your bare ass."

Windy chopped two long four-inch pine shafts for the runners, trimmed the branches, and lashed the twenty-footers to the pommel of the buckskin's saddle. He decided to ride Old Gal, who was still acting a little skittish after the incident with Bear. After cutting a few smaller cross members for the platform, he lashed each end to the shafts to secure the isosceles triangle at its base. The platform's truncated shape was big enough for Bear. He moved to the head of the gelding to check on its stability with the travois in place. He showed nary a care, the good old boy probably had been hitched up in a similar fashion before. Who knew what the Haida scoundrels had rigged to him in the past? The final touch was a layer of spruce boughs laid over the framework to cushion the ride. Double-checking the clearance of the rig to the horse's shanks, he was satisfied. Finally he spoke to each horse in a soft manner while patting its head and stroking its neck, hoping to assure each one that things were under control and they'd be moving out soon. They enjoyed the sugar cubes he shared.

He looked to the fluttering in the treetops to find the raven in a muted presence. "Hello, my friend. It's good to see you are sharing the night with us as we attempt to get our wounded warrior to safety."

Windy returned to Bear with another difficult job: moving him to the litter/travois platform. Bear would be riding on spruce boughs, laid over four stringers, connecting two shafts tied together two feet behind the south end of a horse headed north—hardly a Stryker Bed. It would not be a smooth ride along the game trail with its continuous ladder-like presence of surface roots, much like a series of speed bumps.

"How are you, Bear? Do you think you can make it? The med evac is waiting."

"Funny. It looks more like something Tarzan would use . . . with Jane. Here's my belt. It was a real pain in the ass just getting it off. I'm in worse shape than I thought. By the way, what in the world did you need it for?"

"It's your handhold strap, just like on the subway or a ski-lift. I don't want you bouncing off along the trail and being lost among a wolf pack, especially after I made such a neat throne for you."

"Enough of your marginal humor, m'man. Seriously, I may not have made it without your help. Thanks, my brother."

"No problem, but, as the saying goes: 'We're not out of the woods yet.' We're still fighting skittish horses, darkness, and a bumpy ride on a body that should be immobile—in bed. Let's give it a go. I'll lift your good right side while you try to stand and roll onto the platform."

Wind Spirit leaned over to lift Bear by the arm as he tried to stand on his right leg.

Bear bellowed, "Hoo-eee-ooo," echoing across the river and bouncing back hoo-eee-ooo as his true pain was revealed. He slumped back against the tree and swore.

The cry of pain must have triggered a tawny doe to leap from the darkened shadows of the forest's edge. Kicking up dirt, she pranced by the pair and dove into the river.

Strange, that she should run towards us. What must have triggered her flight? She almost leaped over Old Gal.

"No sweat, Bear, we'll figure something out. I'll build a hoist if necessary. Hang tight, and rest a minute while I figure something out."

*   *   *

Leigh shined her lantern along the trail as darkness robbed its details following the subtle murmur of the Bitterroot's current. An eerie feeling surrounded her as she moved westward to be with her men. Doubts of her decision to trek alone plagued each and every step. She had never been so unsure of her judgment, but having decided, she was resolved to forge on.

Frustrated an hour ago, she secured the wolves and set out just after the sun moved over the horizon to envelop the forest in early evening nautical twilight, (EENT). It was a beautiful afternoon before a cloud bank moved over the river and the day ended with the sun masked as it moved over the horizon. Its subtle rays were barely visible in the western sky.

The lantern served several functions. It announced her presence along the trail to animals to avoid startling them, alerted the men on horseback, and gave her vision to minimize errors in footfalls. The exposed roots were built-in "trippers." She had placed a half-moon reflector on one half of the glass to project the light beam forward. This rearward restriction gave her better vision forward without the blinding glare.

After walking about one hour, she came upon a curious doe parked in the middle of the trail as if frozen in place. Leigh stopped, and a stare-down ensued. It was indeed an eerie sight. Two reflective eyes and a partially illuminated body would not move as she kept looking both directions as if something had sandwiched her. Impatient with the doe's indecision to leave, Leigh moved forward one step. A bloodcurdling scream of hoo-eee-ooo filled the stillness of the night. She froze in place as the doe leaped away in a westerly direction, kicking dirt as she pranced into the darkness.

Leigh sighed. "That's Bear, I've found them! Bear!" she called. "Windy! Is that you? Hold on! I'll be there in a minute."

*   *   *

"Bear," said Windy, "did you hear that? It's Leigh!"

The horses raised their heads and pranced in place as the bobbing lantern light moved toward the queue.

Windy ran to the lead horse, Old Gal, while giving the buckskin and sorrel words of assurance. He held Old Gal's elevated head by the bridle as Leigh approached. Calmed now, the horse lowered her head as Leigh spoke to her. Windy and Leigh embraced briefly and moved slowly to the rear while he explained the current complications with Bear's additional injuries.

"Hi, gal. Nice to see you. What brings you out at such a late hour?"

"Enough of your drivel. What additional damage have you done?" Leigh leaned over with a kiss on the forehead. "I'm upset with you for not letting us know about your fall on the SAT phone."

"Yeah, I knew you'd be ticked, but I thought between Windy and me a few fractured ribs would not slow us down. I was wrong."

"Let's take a look."

She had Bear hold his arms out while she felt under his left side where the contusion was apparent. After causing some pain in her exam she, too, determined a few ribs were cracked.

"You sure know how to mess up a good body, my friend. Luckily, Joe's handiwork on your back is still in place. Lay back; I've got some work to do."

"I'd lay back for you any day, gal; but what the hell are you up to?"

"Never you mind. Here, Windy, hold my coat."

She doffed her coat and removed her shirt to use as a means of binding Bear's chest.

"Now, hold still. And, both of you, don't get any fancy sexy ideas in your head. You've both seen a woman in her bra by now, and in this case it's purely a medical necessity."

Bear, never at a loss for words, said, "Move a little closer while you're wrapping me up. I'd like to check out that frilly red lace. You must have known red is my favorite color."

"Stop it. You should behave in front of Windy."

"Leigh, there's not a chance; he's an unruly sort."

"I noticed, Windy. I've also noticed he's not hurting enough to diminish man's insatiable desire for sexual conquest. Behave, or I'll wrap you tighter."

"Okay, I'll just enjoy the scenery."

"Good. How's your memory? Do you remember me binding Tough in a similar manner, the day he attacked a bear, lost the fight, and barely lived?"

"Indeed, I do. How could I forget? I barely knew you and you did the same doffing of your shirt to bind the wolf, with one exception: the scenery was even better that day—in those days you didn't wear a bra."

"Men! It's your chest we're concerned with, not mine—bare or not!"

The binding of his chest complete, Leigh donned her coat and, with a two-man carry, she and Windy hoisted Bear onto the travois. Thankfully the buckskin held firm, without movement. The good old guy behaved like a classic coach horse.

Windy buckled Bear's belt to the last crossbar as a looped handhold and prepared the queue for movement.

"How do you feel, Bear? Comfy? Are you ready to rock and roll?" Windy teased.

"I'm not sure about the R&R, but yes, let's get this show on the road."

"Leigh, you lead the buckskin, and I'll lead the sorrel while up on Old Gal. Okay? I'll carry the lantern."

"Yep, let's go before Bear breaks something else."

"I heard that," Bear replied as the caravan headed easterly toward the meadow. It was midnight as the raven's croak indicated his joining the team.

"Welcome, my friend," Windy said. "Did you wonder if we'd ever make it?"

*   *   *

After an uneventful trail ride to the meadow, Leigh walked Bear to the hut while Windy took care of the horses with a simple tie-down with a chain so they could graze. Upon checking that the fish would make it one more day—with luck—he threw a tarp over the container.

Windy returned to the hut to find Bear sleeping fully clothed, any plans to change his dressings on hold. Windy told Leigh he would prefer sleeping outside near the horses to ensure their safety. He had noticed her preparation for salting down the fish in brine, and that she had set aside materials for the smoker and enlargement of the barn and corral. He was pleased, so pleased he gave her a kiss as he left with his bedroll and a smile of gratitude.

*   *   *

Leigh did not hesitate to return to her bed. She removed Bear's boots and her own shoes, then lay next to him on the crowded bed. As she snuggled closer, her hand found his, fingers entwined, nothing sexual, just two people needing to touch. She pulled his good arm around her.

He squeezed her hand, reassuring and strong.

She pulled deeper against him, and he rolled to hold her more snugly.

Leigh closed her eyes, not expecting to sleep.

She whispered, "You're a lucky guy to have survived this day."

"In more ways than one," he murmured.

Surprisingly, in his arms, she felt herself drifting off to sleep. Hearing a raven's muffled cry, she raised her head, looked out the window across the meadow as the clouds moved to the north exposing the moon's soft light on the bird's ebony feathers.

She lowered her head to Bear's shoulder . . . the denizens of the meadow were at rest.

Chapter 9

Reflection

Startled, Bear opened his eyes to a black face, wet nose, and inquisitive pair of coal black eyes. Clearly, it was not the face he expected. Tough was on one side, The White on the other, Jet standing on the bed. Jet's muzzle was so close his breath had awakened the downed warrior just before the tongue made contact.

He mused, *Didn't I crash with Leigh last night? Where the hell am I?*

He scanned the area and he recalled. His first attempt to move also reminded him of the physical aches and limitations he bore. He screamed in pain. "Aaaw-wwkkk!"

The wolves scampered out through the door, and almost knocked Leigh down as they leaped across the steps, tails between their legs.

"So there you rascals are. Leave Bear alone; you're all like an old coon circling a road kill. Come over here," Leigh commanded the wolves. "I want you to help Windy. Now go!"

He lay back in pain and looked toward the open door when Leigh entered. He noted that even dressed casually she was simply elegant. She wore her favorite zippered sweatshirt with *Michigan* lettered in blue across her bosoms, and her favorite faded Wrangler jeans. Her slicker hung open, revealing a small revolver in her belt. Her sweatshirt was unzipped at the neck but still holding in the swill of her breasts that failed to completely mask the impression of the round disks of her nipples. He marveled at her casual acceptance of her own beauty, but he saw much more. She had breathtaking natural beauty with a wild, colorful radiance around flashing eyes, flaming red hair, bright lips, and a voluptuous figure that not even the casual, rough clothes could conceal. She was a woman for all seasons, all occasions; yet she remained a maverick, unpredictable, with an unrelenting passion to explore Alaska.

"How's our warrior? Are you going to make it? Or, is Manitou readying a place for you?"

"Funny you're not, madam."

"Okay, m'man, let me get these togs off and take a look at you."

She looked around and noticed the wolves had crept back to the door to look at the shrieking soul in Leigh's bed.

"Now," she told them, "get out of here, you sneaky fur balls. Go run with

Windy; I've work to do. The sooner I get started, the sooner Bear will be able to join us. Shoo! Away with you, as Joe would say!"

As the wolves scattered, she doffed her slicker and rain hat, then laid the gun on the table already covered by medical supplies.

Bear noticed. "Why are you packing iron?"

"Oh, I got up last night and took it out to Windy. I was concerned with his safety in case a predator noticed the increased number of horses and wandered too close for comfort. The horses were restless. That's normal, I suppose. The gun gave him a whole lot of insurance. Anyway, he didn't need it flogging him while he worked on the shed and smoker, and while brining the fish. That's a rubber-glove-and-full-boots job. By the way, my friend, between the two of us we're about done with all three projects. We'll be smokin' fish tomorrow. Don't I smell like a salted trout? Don't answer that!"

She mentioned to Bear that she had called Joe at the DNR Headquarters and filled him in on the events of the last twenty-four hours.

"He was not pleased," she explained. "Having one of his COs out of action for a couple of weeks was not good news. Nevertheless, he was glad you had survived both incidents, and that Wind Spirit had risen to the occasion and worked out so well. Off the record, he told me that by pulling some strings he had already successfully placed Wind Spirit on the DNR payroll. He'll be working as an intern in training under his and your tutelage. I asked if it was okay to tell him and said no, partly because he had a couple regulation DNR shirts and hat to give to him next week. He'll be stopping by to check on you, too. Hopefully, he'll use one of the horses to pack out some of the smoked fillets. Before he signed off, he mentioned that Dave and Milt, at Ford's Flight Service in Skagway, will be air-dropping some fodder and grain sometime this week."

Bear responded, "Can you believe all that's happened? Life is often stranger than fiction. There is a balance. True? My loss is balanced with Windy's gain, which equates to *our* gain in the larger sense of risks while living in the Tongass. He'll do well, and we'll survive, too."

"How true," Leigh said. "Just look at him out there. Windy certainly fits into the Native way—dedicated to a peaceful life with the animals of the forest, the spirit of an enduring existence in Manitou's wilderness."

"It would be generous of us to take him under our wing in a tutelary relationship, as guardians. Wouldn't that benefit both of us?"

"The principle of your idea makes sense. Yet, it would change many of my goals and objectives for why I'm living in the Tongass. I'd have to give it some thought. That I could do. I'm flexible. However, you've been using the 'us' pronoun a lot lately, and that won't work until you've completed some unfinished business that must be taken care of *first* before 'us' is an operable option. Do I make myself clear?"

"You're right. And yes, you've been very clear about formally ending my ties to Morning Star. The timing of our discussion couldn't be better."

"So!"

"It's happening as we speak. Through Joe, Morning Star has received my letter, my petition to end our relationship under tribal law. A previous letter confirmed her acceptance due to the inevitability of us moving on, she in town, me in the forest that I love. Joe also informed me last week that Gete Wabiska—Old White—the Tlingit Chief and your spiritual father, will be visiting soon to counsel us. You know what he wants, don't you?"

"Yes, and no. What?"

"Well, the first thing he's going to do is take you aside, away from me, and grill you to ensure you know what you're doing."

"Oh? Don't you think you're overreaching?" she challenged.

"Nope. I just separated for good reasons, I think, and he's going to make sure you have your eyes wide open in what will be a more formal relationship with me. I've seen him in action. He's very humble, but always in charge, and doesn't hesitate to offer his opinion. It will be okay. He'll probably warn you about me. After all, you're his spiritual daughter. He's just being a responsible father, even though you're only twenty years younger than him."

"Great! I can hardly wait. I'm looking forward to his comments, his counsel about you. Give me a break. I'll bet he has some stories to tell. You know, he'll probably ask, indirectly, if I've slept with you. Guess what? I've the right answer. I wonder if he'll believe me."

"Yep, he will. He'll also ask me. Guess what? I cannot tell a lie. I did last night. Yep, with me drugged, clawed by a bear, stomped on by a horse, and wrapped like a mummy. Yes, we slept together in the swooning spoon position, not the forking position. Yes, we even held hands. Babe, we'll pass his test with flying colors. Luckily for you, if I had not been clawed, pawed, and wrapped, hard telling what I might have done last night."

"You'd best leave out all that blarney; Old White doesn't need your subtle humor. My dear friend, do you remember, it takes two to tango."

"That's where you're wrong. He's a guy first, chief second. Seriously, I'll tell him you've kept your distance from me in respect for Morning Star. I'll be honest. That's the best I can do, and I hope he understands there may not be a long-lasting future for us when your work is completed. I'll tell him we'll be a pair, a team, a loving couple living together without a tribal bond. We have common goals of enjoying and preserving life in the Tongass. That said, a tribal ceremonial bond may develop. We'll see."

Leigh responded, "Well done, my friend. The more I step back and examine what's going on in our lives, the more I see Carl Jung's concept of synchronicity in play. That is, a coincidental occurrence of events that seem related but cannot be explained by conventional means of causality.

"Wind Spirit's appearance in our lives triggered a series of positive events leading to this conversation. I have a feeling there's more to come as the five of us meet this week. Can you imagine Old White with his elevated rank in the tribe, sitting around the fire with Joe Bloom and his cup of grog telling hair-raising stories of his past, his spirited opinions in his British accent, typically laced with his bloody profanity? Wind Spirit's ears will probably burn. But, he might as well get used to it, since Joe will be his new boss. Nevertheless, I love to hear him carry on with his outspoken opinions of government misdeeds. I can hardly wait." Leigh snickered.

Bear drank to fulfillment with his eyes as she spoke. It wasn't her beauty so much as the aura—the ambience of absolute control—the ability to win over those around her with a sly glance or the slightest smile. He was smitten, one of the victims, conquered months ago by her charm.

"Say, m'man, it's about time we remove that binding and change your dressing. And yes, I want my shirt back. Come on now, raise your arms so I can get this show on the road. You've got to at least sit up and throw your feet off the bed. Come on."

With a muffled moan he sat up, had his temporary binding removed, and lay down on his chest as she removed Joe's now-bloodied field dressing. She cleaned the claw tears and contusion under the arm with a sponge bath of her homemade Witch Hazel, rinsed, and sprinkled a powdered antiseptic on his wounds. After covering the wounds with gauze, she had him sit up to wrap his chest with a sterile, porous elastic binding.

She warned him as he made a move toward her, "No fooling around, m'man. I'm your nurse, not your geisha. If you've got enough energy to grab, that's good—not the grabbing, but the fact that you're feeling better."

"Maybe I'm just inhaling the poignant pheromones radiating from your suppressed desire for me."

"Wrong. Now stop it," she exclaimed while rapping his noggin with a quick snap. "Here's your breakfast of cold cereal, hot coffee, and some more pain pills. Enjoy. I'm headed back outside to help Windy with his construction projects. He's having a ball. In fact, he's already planning to build a sweatlodge down by the river. You wanna bet with the two of us we'll have everything done by sunset? Yeah, we're good. Okay, I'm out of here. Under no conditions are you to leave this bed today. As I say to the wolves: Stay! One of those pills is a strong barbiturate to help you sleep. Now, don't forget to pee before you go to bed. Bye?"

"Damn," Bear murmured. *I've got to stabilize this old body soon. She's starting to act like a mother. I'd better do as she says, lie low, and let this frame repair itself as quickly as possible.*

*   *   *

Both Leigh and Windy continued working by cleaning up the excess lumber by the smoker and setting aside wood for the smoker's fire pot.

"If I do say so myself," Windy announced, "this smoker looks great. Then again, until it starts smoking, at a distance, it does look like a big outhouse. Oh well, it'll do the job. I've finally finished, Leigh. We're ready for those succulent salmon fillets from the deep. We await Neptune's Locker. Seriously, Leigh, I'll start a fire now, even though the brined fillets won't have fully absorbed the salt until morning. I'll have a chance to ensure the smoker's venting properly: tight, but not too tight. Come on, you want to give me a hand with this kindling, Leigh?"

Wop—Wop—Wop—Wop . . .

"Do you hear that, Leigh? Dang if it doesn't sound like a helicopter. What's up?"

Leigh yelled as she looked to the sound coming from the east, "Well, I'll be darned. Joe said the DNR was air-dropping feed for the horses. I didn't know they'd be here so soon."

Looking to the east, Windy exclaimed, "That's sure a strange-looking rig. They must have piled bales in a harness of sorts slung under the belly of the chopper. It looks like a couple of 'joined' love bugs. Do you think they'll land?"

With the sound growing more intense, Leigh yelled, "Not sure, but I don't think so. They'll hover and drop near the ground with a release arrangement. Say, you'd better tend to the horses. The noise and downdraft are going to raise havoc in a minute."

"Okay, good idea. I'm on the way. By the way, did you notice all the wolves took off?! They wanted no part of that chopper." Windy calmly approached the skittish horses and, much as before, his presence with his hands-on technique and soothing voice assured them they would be protected.

Leigh punched in 121.5 MHz on her transceiver as she looked toward the chopper to see its ID number and who was piloting.

"Chopper, Hotel-three-one-zero, this is Tongass ground station. Over."

"Ground station Tongass, this is chopper Hotel-three-one-zero, I hear you loud and clear. Hi Leigh! I can see you, Queen of the meadow. How the hell are you, my love? Over."

"Hi, Milt. It looks like you and Dave are doing well at Ford's Flight Service. Ford never dreamed of owning a chopper. Business must be good. Over."

Milt answered, "It is. It's been a while, Leigh. Stop in sometime. We'd love to see you and buy you a beer. Dave sends his best. Wait, he says he still loves you, and wants to know if you're still available? Over."

"Now there's a new one, a proposal in flight. Tell him yes, but I love all you fly boys. I can't marry 'em all, but I'll try. And, yes, if I get to town, you'll be my first stop for a cold one, a chaser, some good pizza, and even better tales of the Tongass. I promise to drink and eat 'til giddy, just like the old days. Over."

"You're on. Indeed, you've not forgotten the good old days . . . Well, gotta go. With all this load we've only half a tank of fuel. Stand back. Here's your fodder, courtesy of the DNR. See you, doll, love ya. This is Hotel-three-one-zero. Out."

"This is Tongass ground station. Roger, wilco, out."

*　　*　　*

As the chopper powered up and ascended, Dave opened the door and threw a kiss to Leigh, and hauled up the harness assembly. The pair of old friends headed back to Skagway reflecting on their experiences with Leigh.

Dave mused, *I wonder if she knows how serious my thoughts are. She's always been my first love. Chi Mukwa is a lucky guy. I just hope he does not have the misfortune of her previous relationships. She, too, has been through a lot. She's endured more in the last six months than many women experience in a lifetime.*

*　　*　　*

After gaining altitude to about 2000 feet, the chopper's noise abated and Windy left the now calmed broncos to check out the horse's manna from the sky. He yelled, "Hey, Leigh, the guys also dropped a protective tarp and some grain with the bales! They thought of everything. I'll start stacking 'em up on some wood to keep down the moisture. Okay?"

"Sure, that's great."

In a melancholy mood, she thought to herself, *He doesn't know Dave and Milt are both aerospace engineers from NASA, and are probably two of the most talented guys in Alaska. Yes, Windy, they'd think of everything to care for the horses. They are good. They've saved my life more than once. I love 'em both. They're like brothers to me.*

"Windy, I'm going back in for a minute to 'bark' at Bear and force him to get back in bed. Look, that's him in the window just itching to come out here to help us. That ain't gonna happen. I'll tie him down in bed if necessary. Give him a wave, Windy. It will help to calm his nerves."

"Hi, Bear! Take care. We've got everything under control," Windy exclaimed while gesturing toward the buckets of brine, the smoker, the modified horse shed, and the unique, pyramidal hay stack being shaped by Windy.

⼁⼁　　⼁⼁　　⽊

Bear waved back and slowly returned to finish his breakfast with a warm feeling of gratitude for Leigh and Windy, yet still feeling like a caged bruin. The word "useless" came to mind—"dependent," too. A bruin with ribs wrapped tight enough to help the healing process and prevent doing any work of value, not to mention his torn-up back. Yes, the walls of Leigh's hut were his cage, the cage that would hold him fast for days. His options to escape were few to none. The body heals at its own rate.

*   *   *

At dawn, Gete Wabiska (Old White), and the ever-present raven guide, moved through the big timber of the Tongass with the determination and movement of a man half his age. He was in his element. He embraced the forest as the offspring of Mother Earth. The direct route to Leigh's camp on the meadow involved crossing the Bitterroot River many times as it meandered along the lay of the land. He did not hesitate to cross it when following created too much delay.

He never had the opportunity to visit Leigh on the meadow. The timing of her arrival in camp with Chi Mukwa was coincidental with the Raven Clan's departure from the forest. His memories were all positive of Leigh at the clan's last fireside meeting, the meeting where she accepted her spiritual name, "Runs with Wolves," and later when the elders met to support his move to adopt her as his spiritual daughter. After learning the customs and organization of the Tlingit Nation, she now represented the tribe as the last of the sisterhood to live in the Tongass.

Yes, she had taken in Chi Mukwa, and they were probably going to become more than a twosome. Talking with his first spiritual wife, Morning Star, he learned that she agreed that their union was over. That decision would now allow for Leigh and Bear to become a new couplet. He would have a fireside ceremony as soon as possible to bless their union as tribal custom stipulated. These developments pleased him when Morning Star recognized the reality of her position and gracefully stepped aside, allowing Leigh to lower the barriers to Bear's advances. It also avoided him being cuckolded as Morning Star's life moved on to a new relationship.

He hoped everyone would gain, especially Wind Spirit, since Leigh and Bear had talked of taking him under their wing if things worked out, at least until he was old enough to be on his own. At present, he's a runaway from the tribe.

He planned to discuss all these options, plus one more, as the two moved across the plateau just north of the meadow. He had another proposition, a request for them to consider. A young, desperate girl had come to him for help, pleading for him to take her under his care. She was running from an abusive relationship. Taking her in was not possible for him. However, when Leigh and

Bear heard her story, he was certain they'd help. With two men in camp now, Leigh just may need a little help and some sorely missed feminine companionship. He'd soon find out.

"There's the meadow, Raven Maiden. We're only a couple minutes from Leigh's hut on the river," Old White exclaimed. "It's going to be a big day for you and me. For that matter, all of us. I'm sure they will be delighted to meet you and take you in once they hear your story. Let's think positive."

The sixteen-year-old raven haired beauty turned to Old White as a ballerina might pirouette, a spin of grace, a part of her supple ease, a fragment of her beautiful embodiment of class even after two days and one night on the trail. Her native features included high cheek bones, tapered eyes like cups of smoke, scimitar chin, mouth of a permanent half-pucker. Her ears, china saucers, were multiply pierced. A garnet swung on a gold chain threaded through her right earlobe. Her breasts sat high on her felicitous body draped with long ebony locks. When she moved, everything glittered as though the sun surrounded her being.

"I hope so. I'll never be able to thank you enough for your help, Gete Wabiska. I'm so anxious to meet with my old Raven Clan friends," she exclaimed as her step quickened.

They crossed the plateau and followed the trail to the meadow as the raven preceded them to a large pine on the river.

*   *   *

Five miles to the west, Joe Bloom had just broken camp, finished his last cup of tea, and completed packing his rucksack. He was anxious to get started on his trip to the meadow. A lot had happened since leaving Wind Spirit in charge of taking the injured Chi Mukwa back to the meadow. He'd heard of the horse-stomping and wanted to give Bear a 'cheer up' call and some good Irish Whiskey. He was also eager to appoint Wind Spirit to his new position as intern in the DNR.

"Now, come on feet, get moving; although sore, it's bloody well time to get the move on. I know, I know, but you've got to understand, it's a gozewit, as in 'goze wit da territory.' Tramping through the forest goes wit' the job. At least I'll eat well tonight, maybe some of the smoked or fresh salmon they're working on. I've been eating my own drivel long enough. I need Leigh's cuisine. With any luck these old, sore hooves will be replaced by Old Gal's hooves as I take a load of smoked fillets back to Skagway. Come on, old feet, I'm on my way, and damn tired of talking to ya. I need some of Leigh's charming conversation. Now there's a good job of construction by Manitou. She's a beaut. I understand Gete Wabiska also has a beaut with him as a surprise to both Leigh and Bear. Come on, feet; let's hit the road."

He had followed the river to the meadow many times, and each time a different cast of characters and circumstances faced the denizens of the meadow. This was going to be an especially interesting assortment of humanity.

"Welcome, my raven friend. Nice to see you join this old bullock. What have you been up to lately? If you don't mind me blather, I'll be chatting with you. I'm tired of talking to my tired feet, as they me. 'Tis a beautiful time and place to be alive, right? Is there any spot nicer than the Tongass? Ye answer be no."

Chapter 10

Rendezvous

Full of positive feelings and with elation from having just reached their destination, Gete Wabiska and Raven Maiden moved over the edge of the plateau and down the trail to the meadow—Leigh's meadow. They stopped at the top of the trail that offered a clear view to the scene below.

Old White, looking toward the meadow, commented, "Take a look, my friend. As I've observed similar panoramas for many moons, this vista, too, is truly one of the halcyon views of the Creator's forest. It's not only physically attractive, it reflects the practical use of His creation. This meadow is once again a productive, bustling homestead."

Speechless, Raven Maiden nodded in agreement. The scene below took her breath away. She'd felt equal parts of joy and apprehension since arriving at the meadow. She harbored mixed feelings, wondering if Leigh would sympathize with her plight or not. The anticipation of their meeting made her tingle all over. She would be on her best behavior—passive, tolerant, and clear in answering questions. Old White would take the lead and initially do most of the talking. Without a doubt, she knew she could represent herself. She also knew that her heart would be full of trauma and her eyes flooded with tears, making her plea much too emotional.

*   *   *

Still looking across the meadow toward the river and the mountains to the west, Old White reflected on the past and rekindled the previous pleasure of the clan. He had always tried to avoid being envious. However, the scene below generated a sentimental flashback, reminding him of his youth as warrior and, later, chief of the Raven Clan. Few were aware that "Leigh's Meadow" was located on the grounds of his ancestors, who cleared and established a settlement in this area in the early 1300s. It was a sacred place, a cathedral in the forest to honor the Creator, Manitou.

He smiled as he mentally compared the tableau below to a Norman Rockwell print of busy people engaged in various activities.

He observed a woman, probably Leigh, moving wood from a barn-like structure surrounded by a split-log corral containing a few horses. She moved with a purposeful stride as several wolves followed at her heels. He knew the gray wolf, Tough, that Leigh had brought to camp half dead. Apparently she had nursed it back to health. The white wolf was new to him, as well as the black cub that raced to keep up with the little pack. Chi Mukwa's spiritual name for her was apt. Another person, probably Wind Spirit, was feeding a fire in what appeared to be a smoke house for fish and game.

The woman scurried back and forth, collecting and carrying scattered pieces of wood from the area to a huge rick next to the smokehouse. A dozen or so white plastic pails were also queued nearby. The smokehouse attracted the wolves, which kept the man busy shooing them away. Absent a prevailing wind, the smoker created its own low-hanging clouded mask so dense that it obscured a large portion of the meadow.

Chi Mukwa was nowhere in sight. From what Old White had heard from Joe about Chi Mukwa's life-threatening injuries, it seemed unlikely he would be out and about. He was probably recovering in the hut. Joe had also mentioned that he, too, would be at the meadow midweek. Joe had carried the message concerning Chi Mukwa's wishes to make a formal break from Morning Star and perform a ceremonial blessing of him and Leigh. If possible, Bear would also like the ceremony to be held among his friends at an evening campfire. Old White also had some very important additional business to discuss.

It was indeed going to be an exciting evening, in more ways than one. Old White had to present Leigh with the positive and negative aspects of a spiritual union with Bear. He had been and continued to remain a free spirit, and he'd have to remind her that this was not going to change. And, wasn't she only staying in the Tongass temporarily? Had they talked about the transitory nature of their lovefest? Is that what it was? Or was it companionship only? Not likely, he decided, knowing both as he did. What was their responsibility to each other? To Wind Spirit? They'd just asked permission to be guardians of Windy. No doubt they'd consider the importance of care, spiritual guidance, and discipline in raising a teenager to become a man.

That said, his next request was even more formidable. He would have to fine-tune his persuasive skills for the more difficult task. He could very well fail. He had cautioned Raven Maiden that her request was no sure thing.

He also had to ask Bear and Leigh to be the guardian of a downhearted Tlingit girl, Raven Maiden.

*   *   *

Raven Maiden thought, *I wonder if Leigh will think I'm too much of a burden. Yet, I could be useful. Two men require a lot of care. I would be another pair of hands to help wrangle her herd of two- and four-legged animals. A few are talented, all right, but they can also be very demanding. I've heard Bear often takes off on a moment's notice, as DNR assignments crop up. Leigh is alone by choice, I understand but there's Windy, too. Word is that he, too, may face the same occupational hazards—that is, having to leave suddenly on DNR business. That may be a good thing for me. Although alone by choice, she may welcome my company when the men depart. One thing is certain, I'll know her feelings by sunset. She's a quick study. She'll make a decision swiftly and let me know with candor. She doesn't mince her words. You know where you stand with her. She's tough. I can only hope for Manitou's presence when Leigh makes her decision as one sister in the clan seeks aid from another in need of help.*

"Gete Wabiska, don't you think Leigh, as a writer, will be proud that I've graduated from the tribal high school and excelled in literature? She has told me, 'To be a writer, you must be a reader of good literature.' She'll love the *Journal of Thoreau's Writings* I've brought for her as a gift."

Continuing down the slope, Raven held Old White's hand on the rougher parts of the trail. She told him of her love for Thoreau and asked him to hold up a moment. While he caught his breath, she fingered a bookmark, then opened the book to a selected section.

"Rest while I read one of my favorite passages. It explains, in part, why I must live in the forest. See if you agree. I have a feeling these were once your beliefs, too. Are you comfortable?"

"Yes, my dear. While you're reading, I'll scan the beauty of the meadow below. Go ahead."

Slowly, and with feeling, she quoted, Thoreau.

> "The Indian . . . stands free and unconstrained in
> Nature, is her inhabitant and not her guest, and
> wears her easily and gracefully. But the
> civilized man has the habits of the house.
> His house is a prison."

"This was from page number three-hundred of his Journal dated 1841. He was twenty-four at the time. What do you think? Town was a prison for me, too. Yes, I understand that at your age, and with the clan's needs, a move to town away from subsistence living was better for the clan. But not for me. Doesn't Thoreau have a way with words?"

"Indeed he does, my dear. I, too, remember one line of his that struck me as so very true to the experiences I've had. It goes something like this: 'That man is the richest whose pleasures are the cheapest.' Now, that is not only true, but I've lived it and found it to be gratifying."

"I could find the quote, but I like it the way you spoke it."

Thoreau's writings had brought Raven Maiden to life. It's as though she had been a pupa in a cocoon. His thoughts had drawn her out and shown her that she was truly a butterfly destined to enjoy the solace, the beauty, the love of living in the glades of Manitou's forest. Living in town numbed her senses. Only the forest nourished her soul.

She stopped and waited for her mentor to catch up before entering camp.

Old White joined her. She looked at him in a sentimental way that was clearly tied to their previous relationship. They were permanently locked in a reciprocal bond. They both hoped for success in their mission.

With moist eyes, she embraced him in gratitude for his efforts as the moment of truth came near. Emotionally naked without him, she realized he was indeed more than a father figure; he was her hope of the future. With him in her arms, she felt fully dressed and confident in her preparation to humbly request Leigh's help.

She could not find adequate words to fill the silence. She knew he understood.

To his clan on many occasions similar to this he had said, "Do not worry. Native people do not need to fill all available space with chatter. Your eyes, your heart, your soul speaks clearly to me. I know your thoughts."

Her embrace had served its purpose.

Old White spoke, "Shall we get on with it, as Joe Bloom would say? You'd do well to remember that no one, not a soul on the Creator's earth, has mastered the craft of communicating their wishes and desires to another. Be assured, you will do well. Leigh will read your emotions, your desperation, your needs. She will understand. As I said, if you need me, I'll be there, and as I mentioned earlier, Joe will be there for you, too. He loves you as a daughter, like I do. Remember, Leigh is my spiritual daughter; she does listen to her father's wishes. Let's go."

*   *   *

Joe was hiking in from the west along the floodplain of the Bitterroot. He had been in Skagway and then Yakutat on the Pacific coast on DNR business. In Skagway, he had also met with several members of the Raven Clan to see how their fisheries project was coming along. At that time, Gete Wabiska briefed him on the progress of the clan's wholesale and retail activities from fishing on the mighty Pacific. He also took him to the clan's docks on the Lynn Canal so he could take a look at their new trawler, Windward. Joe was impressed with the fishing operations. They already had a licensed captain, a sharp-looking dock, support buildings, and huge drying racks for their seine nets. Their primary catch was salmon, but they also long-lined for halibut. A motor buff, Joe climbed aboard and went directly to the engine compartment of the boat to examine the engine-room. At his request, Captain Runs Fast fired up the diesel so he could hear the purr and smell the power of the four-hundred horse six. Many men, including Joe, would rather hear and smell a working diesel than a painted lady's incessant chatter and aromatic perfume.

Later, along the Bitterroot, Joe spoke to a breaching hook-jawed male salmon. "That was a bloody good show, me friend. You jumped as high as you are long, that 'tis damn good. 'Tis lucky you escaped the clan's Pacific nets or you'd be in a can or smoked. I guarndamnteeyou, you're a survivor. You made it! Bloody well, away with ye; keep up the good fight to breed and continue against the raging current in your face. Your girlfriend awaits your arrival. Right now, as I speak, she's preparing a sandy bed for both of you. Her roe will soon be there for creation. Godspeed to your union."

He planned to arrive at Leigh's meadow at approximately the same time as Old White and Raven Maiden. The men had discussed their strategy in placing Raven with Leigh. Informally, it was decided to do no more than reintroduce her to Leigh, since they had met earlier at the Raven Camp. Then they would explain her desperate situation and let her take over and request permission to stay until she turned eighteen. They'd be there with her, but silent until called on by her or Leigh. They planned to play it by ear since Leigh did have a lot on her plate. After all, Leigh and Bear had been asked by Old White if they could be guardians for Windy. Raven came with a similar set of problems.

Nevertheless, Joe had said with a wry look, "She's a busy lassie, bloody well, but she can hack it."

"'Tis about noon, 'tis, and I'm about a mile out or a half-hour from camp. I'd best be on me way and not dither any more with the bloody fish. I'll take a moment to mark my territory; you never know when I'm being trailed by a wolf. Ah, that did it. I've marked the tree and made the initial 'J' in the sand. Good shot, Joe."

As Joe broke out of the shadows of the dark green spruce, paper birches, and giant bracken ferns, he scanned the meadow. Sure enough, Windy and Leigh were at the new smoke house surrounded by a pack of curious wolves. Chi Mukwa was nowhere to be seen; he was probably recuperating in the hut. It was indeed a beautiful spot, made even prettier by Leigh.

Upon further examination, his eyes noticed movement to the north on the slope coming down from the plateau.

Smiling, he said, "Bloody well, I'll be buggered; there they are. We've arrived at the same moment. And yes, the meadow blooms with even more beauty as the Raven's radiance spreads through the meadow. I'm here for you, my lassie; just ring me up and I'll come running. Aren't I the romantic old bloke? I didn't know I could be stirred so easily."

*   *   *

The wolves noticed the two entering the meadow from the east, then looked toward Joe in confusion. Their feet went one way and their eyes another. Frustrated, they started howling and spun in place. Leigh and Windy went to the confused wolves.

"What is it?" Leigh said as she glanced in the various directions the wolves were looking.

Joe was sauntering in from the west as Gete Wabiska and a young girl approached from the east.

The wolves held fast, waiting for Leigh's command.

She yelled, "Stay," and then, "Sit." They all responded except Jet. He took off toward Joe and greeted him with licks and a subservient roll to his back. Joe picked him up and carried him as he continued toward the meadow.

Meanwhile, Leigh discovered it was Raven Maiden with Old White. *She probably wants to visit Bear and see how he's feeling since Old White was coming to the meadow. That's nice. She always liked him, and Bear treated her like a daughter.*

Leigh noticed that it looked like Raven Maiden had a book; maybe it's the one she had lent her during her studies. At least it looked like her old dog-eared copy of "Thoreauvian Works" by Henry David. They both loved his writings. Her favorite was from *Walden*. They had memorized the passage that pretty much described her reasons for trying to live on the meadow. She recited it out loud:

> "If a man does not keep pace with his
> companions, perhaps it is because he hears
> a different drummer. Let him step to the
> music which he hears, however measured or
> far away."

She smiled at the perfection of her performance.

Looking to the east, she greeted her tribal friend. "Welcome, father. Welcome, Raven Maiden. We are very happy to see you. I hope your trip was pleasant. Our modest forest glade is enriched by your presence."

Leigh embraced them both as Windy joined them. His embrace was more tentative as he gave Raven a hug. Theirs appeared to be very warm and gratifying to both. He gave Old White a traditional arm-grasping, native greeting.

They all looked to the west as Joe entered the meadow.

Leigh hollered, "Come on in with that furry fellow. Set him down before he licks you do death. He's not your grandson to spoil. Let him go."

They all got together and exchanged their latest experiences until Leigh interceded and asked for their attention. "I can't think of any better therapy for Bear than to have you all visit him bedside. Come on, let's drop in on the good old guy in what he considers his 'detention.' Ha, it's a full-time job, just keeping him down. Come on, let's go."

Of course, Bear was not in bed as they moved toward the hut. With a big smile spread across his face, he waved out the window.

Indeed, this was the treatment he needed: friends.

Chapter 11

Resolution

Drawing near the hut, the gang of five two-leggeds and three four-leggeds were abuzz with the sound of "catch up" rumor and gossip from their own lives or province. The combination of their various speech patterns was music to the ears of Chi Mukwa as they approached. Gete Wabiska's calming speech overlaid by Joe Bloom's louder, raucous British accent competed with the reserved, taciturn pattern of Wind Spirit and Raven Maiden as they renewed their relationship with rapid-fire talk uninhibited by nosy tribal elders. Leigh's pithy voice cut through the background banter in an attempt to calm the aroused wolves. They had never seen this amount of activity or people visiting Leigh on the meadow, and they were noticeably agitated.

The humans' visit with Bear was brief and to the point. They did not want to be the reason to set back his rehabilitation program. Sadly, Raven could not hug him due to his injuries, but she laid a big kiss on him while in a tender, loving wrist hold. Old White's greeting was more formal with an added note that he was praying for a speedy recovery. Joe Bloom's humorous comments implied that a better man, a UK man, could have fared better in a black bear attack and horse-stomping. Their repartee made Raven Maiden blush, especially when Joe implied that Chi Mukwa got his comeuppance getting too romantic with a flirtatious she-bear. As Raven glowed red, Windy chuckled. He was used to Joe's tomfoolery. The frolicsome nature of Joe's workaday habits were legend across the Alaskan frontier. He worked hard and played hard. Some, on the other side of law, thought him to be a barbaric, uncontrollable, enigmatic lawman. Not so by those who knew him. He was simply a big, smart, aggressive, fun-loving, old-time British subject who enforced the law of the land, no matter whose path he crossed. Yes, he celebrated his conquests frequently with a little bit of grog. Many a barkeep got to know him as he drank to his British hero, "Old Grog" Vernon, of the 19th century. 'Twas Admiral Edward "Old Grog" Vernon that he honored with continued scabrous toasts and song, till the bottle was clear.

Without a cue, Joe started singing the song that was familiar to barkeepers across the north:

Some say, Old Grog, the Admiral, 'twas an old fool at the
wheel,
But sailors said he knew how to keep a ship on a straight keel.
Loaded with rum when his lady of ill fame came up the plank,
Trouble started when he tripped and stumbled and gave her a
yank,
His scheme was to hope she'd not notice his hand cop a feel.

*   *   *

As the Admiral took her to his cabin for an erotic greeting,
He yelled at his first mate to get the crew working, As the gig-
gles and squeals echoed from the cabin,
As the laughter grew from his bed . . .

Leigh quickly interrupted Joe, knowing the next verse was a wee bit racy.
"That's probably enough singing for now, Joe. Let's give Ole Grog a rest."

"Me lassie, we were just getting to the good parts."

"Yeah, that's exactly my point, you old provocateur. You can teach us the
words later, maybe tonight by the fire. Deal?"

"'Tis good. You've got yourself a deal, me lassie."

There was work to be done for the evening's ceremonial fire, so they all bid
Bear adieu as Leigh prodded them towards the door.

*   *   *

Gete Wabiska asked Leigh for a few moments of her time—alone. The gang
left to lay a fire by the river as Leigh walked with him to the edge of the meadow.

Leigh scanned the meadow and said, "On this lovely evening, what's on your
mind?"

"My dear, at tonight's ceremonial fire, with you and Chi Mukwa, I am prepared to bless your spiritual union, your bond of love. I heartily embrace your
decision and feel honored to administer our tribal rites."

"We, too, feel honored," Leigh said.

"I will also perform an oath of allegiance as you and Bear join hands with
Wind Spirit and agree to be his guardians. You have made that boy a young man
in just a few weeks of guidance. I'm proud of you, dear—both of you."

"Again, we are honored to be of help. Don't forget Joe. He has been, and
will continue to be, a driving force in developing Windy into a man."

"How true. I will make my appreciation known to that rollicking old Brit.
Now, as your spiritual father, I feel reluctant, but earnest, to ask you to make
another decision tonight. I've debated this request back and forth in my mind for

some time now, and I've always come to the same conclusion. It was presented to me last month by the Native American Council at the county's social service department in Skagway."

Leigh thought, *This must be a whopper. I've never seen him so careful, so hesitant, so measured. I'll bet it's something to do with Raven Maiden. I'll soon know . . .*

"Raven Maiden is sixteen, and she needs a home until she turns eighteen. She ran away from an abusive environment several weeks ago, and if our clan does not place her, she'll be shuttled to foster care for a couple of years. I'll not hear of that. We must do everything in our power to care for our own. The clan is family. We cannot turn our backs on her needs. Do you agree?"

"Yes," Leigh said, anxious to hear more.

"Another part of the problem is that she insists on placement away from town. If possible, she pleads for a return to the forest where she can be closer to her first love, the remoteness and solace of the forest. In town, the noisy crowds, the bright lights, and the endless cement are very unsettling. The poor girl has only known the forest and its tranquility. Life in Skagway is unacceptable for her. Having said, 'I'll help,' I have a problem."

"You certainly do," she said, having pretty much figured out where this conversation was headed.

"With your union tonight, you and Bear qualify for placement of Wind Spirit. For that I'm forever grateful. He, too, was a runaway. Through the generosity of both you and Bear, he has a home until he reaches eighteen when he can stand on his own two feet. Who would ever have imagined that he would have performed so well with Bear and Joe that he was even offered a job in the DNR? He's already close to being independent. He may not realize it now, but he soon will recognize that he owes his good fortune to your commitment and Bear's faith in his skills. Look at him over there, showing Joe how to hang fillets in the smoke house. As Winchester Arms would say: He's a one-in-one-thousand."

"Yes," she agreed with an enigmatic smile.

"With your union and accepting tutelage of Wind Spirit, how can I possibly ask you to do the same for Raven Maiden? I'm in a quandary. This shadow of doubt has been with me for days. She knows failure and rejection. Fortunately, her persona is as hearty as her beauty. I'm at a loss for words."

"Dad, why don't you ask if we'll take her?"

"Leigh . . ."

"Dad, say no more. I see better than I hear. I've read your heart. You've already asked."

"My dear . . ."

"Of course we'll take her. In doing so, I also thank you, and the Creator, Manitou, for the opportunity to be of assistance to his creatures. Especially those who have tasted the sweet milk from the breast of Mother Earth. Look about you, all those you see are living in the Tongass by choice: Bear, Joe, Windy, and me—and now, Raven Maiden. Dear Father, I, too, know where your heart is, where you would be if it weren't for your responsibility as chief."

"I love you," he said as relief washed over him.

Gete Wabiska and Leigh embraced by the edge of the meadow as the sun passed over the tree tops and cast their shadows across the pair in a paternal union.

Another shadow shaded Joe and Windy as they finished loading the smoke house.

Another cast on Raven Maiden and Chi Mukwa as she stacked logs by the fire pit.

"Looks like we've got the key personnel together by the fire pit. Let's mosey over and give her the good news," Leigh whispered with galvanized zeal.

Quietly, Old White said, "Leigh, don't we need to speak to Bear? Don't we have to ask him first? Does he know anything about this?"

"Dear Father, no, he knows nothing. But, when you know a man as I know that loving hunk, you know. I know how he thinks. However, I'll discreetly whisper in his ear and inform him of our discussion. But, be assured, we'll accept both Wind Spirit and Raven Maiden as responsible guardians tonight. It will be a busy night for you. First, blessing the union of Bear and me, then within minutes, giving us the responsibility of two hard-charging sixteen-year-old tribal youths. Are you up to it?"

"My dear, I'm not only up to it, I feel blessed to be a small part of the Creator's plan. Do you feel His presence? Do you sense the calm in your lovely meadow? Tell me, is the atmosphere always this peaceful? I am not so naïve to think people's beliefs affect the Earth's natural or physical laws controlling events. Yes, we have a certain amount of free will, but only within the Earth's nominal cycle. However, when serendipitous events enter our lives—those not sought, but agreeable—I feel blessed. Such an event is occurring tonight. Three of the Creator's two-leggeds have entered your life for their benefit. My wish is for their presence to benefit you, too. Bless you, dear. My faith leads me to believe these events are not happenstance. I feel the presence of Manitou."

They both walked toward the fire pit by the river to greet Raven Maiden and Bear, the latter who shouldn't even be out of bed.

She mused, *Maybe that's why I love him so. He's where he's needed, when it counts. He probably saw her alone by the fire—and came out to be with her. How can I be mad at him? She needed someone to talk to at this critical time of her life, and he was there.*

"Hi! How's the fire coming along?" Leigh asked.

"Bear answered, "Before you say anything, my dear, I'm not doing any work

I'm just keeping Raven company. Go ahead, tell Leigh. I'm just getting some fresh air, right, Raven?"

"I'll come to your defense," Raven said. "Yes, he's behaving very well. He's just keeping me company while everybody's off doing their thing. In fact, here come the fishy pair. I hope they left most of the smoky fish smell at the smoke house."

As the wolves ran to greet Joe and Windy, Leigh sat with Bear and shared her conversation about the chief's request about Raven Maiden. He fell silent, then looked at Leigh with a blank stare. She nodded her head as if to say, *Do you understand?*

He continued his blank stare.

She nodded again with more expression, as if to gain his assent or dissent. A sign in mime. A whisper. A nod. Something.

His final, facial expression was all smiles, a clear smile of approval. She threw an arm around him, carefully. At that, he grimaced in pain.

"Leigh, I can't think of a better solution. But, have you considered the impact of living accommodations in the hut? The tendency of teenagers to act out their interests in the opposite sex? Your goals to live alone, explore the Alaskan frontier, and write your journal. You'd better take a deep breath and see if you are ready to morph into a woman bonded with me and two teens. Have you thought about how to bed, and how they'll be fed?"

Leigh sighed. "Somehow we'll manage, dear. I know it sounds overwhelming, and maybe it is. You are all unique individuals who I know will combine your skills to make it work. More important, I want to be a part of your lives, be it only a couple years. I want to share my life with good people. With you helping me, I know we'll benefit as much as our high-spirited Tlingit pair. When I write of my experiences in Alaska, I'm positive this young pair will enhance my life and their lives, then trickle down to my journal."

Bear commented, "My concern is based on a little guilt. I'm in this with you one-hundred percent, but I'll be gone a lot on DNR assignments. That will leave you with the yeoman's share of the toil. Then again, Windy and I will be together frequently, and Raven will he here to help. That, my dear, is a positive, but that will deny your long-sought solace."

"You're correct. I may not be alone anymore, but with you in my heart, and knowing you're at my side, at my core, the kids will be a mere diversion in the long haul. Besides, I have not yet met a person that I did not learn something from, and these kids will be no different."

Joe and Windy joined them at the fire, so Gete Wabiska and Raven Maiden walked over to Leigh and Bear in a talkative huddle.

The chief said, "Hello there, am I interrupting?"

Bear responded, "Certainly not. We were just talking over the exciting prospects of being guardians of both Wind Spirit and Raven Maiden. We're ready, girl. Are you?"

Raven Maiden appeared to stiffen. She stared at her new guardians in disbelief . . . then at Gete Wabiska. Her eyes flooded with tears.

Bear hurried to her side and embraced her as a father would a daughter.

"Welcome, my dear. Go ahead and ring out those tears of happiness. And yes, you may embrace me, too. The pressure of your arms on my back is truly a healing balm."

Leigh and Gete Wabiska joined Bear and Raven as well as Windy and Joe. They all embraced to share in the joy of Raven's happiness.

Leigh announced, "Let's all join hands and ask for Manitou's blessing."

After Gete Wabiska chanted a short petition, Leigh asked them all to help prepare for the formal ceremony.

"C'mon, dress up and clean up. This is going to be a beautiful ceremony."

She called Bear over to the fire and held his hands. "You know, you big hunk, I'm in this for the long haul. As one of my favorite authors, Robert Frost, wrote, in the last stanza of *Stopping by Woods on a Snowy Evening*:

> "The woods are lovely, dark, and deep,
> But I have promises to keep,
> And miles to go before I sleep,
> And miles to go before I sleep."

"I, too, will keep my promise to you."

As they prepared for the evening's ceremony, a raven croaked to announce its presence in the ceremony.

"Did you hear that, Bear?"

"Indeed, it's nice to have Him with us tonight."

Chapter 12

Resplendent

As the sun moved below the horizon, it left fading shards of light radiating to the indigo ether. It was indeed a beautiful evening for a celebration—a Tlingit ceremonial event. The autumnal mood was enhanced by the splendor of the forest's radiance.

Gete Wabiska, resplendent in his white Chieftain vestments, revealed many icons of the Raven Clan. A warrior's vest had rows of tubular bones arranged in rank and file across his chest. A blue scarf-like head band streamed long tails down his back. The blue sash held a small knife with antler handle sheathed in deerskin. A large silver pendant with a raven icon hung around his neck, symbolizing his status as Chief of the Clan. The Clan's sacred bundle lay at his feet; a ceremonial drum and his Chieftain Staff, with three eagle feathers, to his right. A traditional Chilkat blanket draped his shoulders. He faced the participants and asked Leigh West, also known by her spiritual name Runs with Wolves, and Chi Mukwa, sometimes called Bear, to step forward.

Speaking in laconic eloquence, Gete Wabiska explained how he would be following the ancient laws that were the foundation of the Raven Clan's sovereignty. Since time immemorial, traditional ceremonies have validated identity and culture. Tribal laws provided for large and small potlatches like this one, celebrating birth, marriage, giving a spiritual name, sharing wealth, raising totems, and honoring a leader or the departed. He explained the Tlingit legend of the "The Raven and the First People," expressing how Raven discovered mankind and is responsible for the present order of the universe.

"Since the original subsistence clan has disbanded and moved to town, I am pleased to assign you *Clan status* tonight, for upon completion of tonight's activities, you will be a family of four or more. Your Clan name in the Tlingit language will be *Yeil*, meaning Raven. You'll share moieties with the Eagle Clan, called *Ch'aak*, to the north. You will also have the same rights and privileges of sister tribes: Haida on the Pacific islands, the Tsimshian to the south, and the Athabaskan in the interior.

"Since you are not large enough to have a village headman, I will act as your chief, your arbiter between the two Tlingit clans, Raven and Eagle, plus your sister tribes. I have decided to perform one ceremony for both your formal marital union and guardianship of Raven Maiden and Wind Spirit."

Venus illuminated the meadow as the crescent moon raced her across the sky. Could it be that the goddess of love dominated the evening as the symbolic message of her powers of passion to the parties below?

The chief asked the participants to meditate in silence, to consider the impact their decisions would have on their lives. He also requested they review their judgments leading to the dramatic changes that would surely take place.

They meditated.

Thinking something was wrong, the wolves looked up and around . . . on alert.

The silence was broken when the chief directed Joe to begin the slow beating on the ceremonial drum he had brought. In a syncopated manner, Joe methodically beat a cadence to simulate Earth Mother's heartbeat. Played very slowly and softly, it could sound like her breathing, like the rushing wind; or her circulation, like a slowly running water nourishing her earthen breast.

Drum—drum—drum—drum—drum—drum . . .

As certain as the sun set in the west, a raven appeared from its circling flight and descended slowly while looking for its favorite perch. Flaring like a fighter-jet on a carrier deck, the majestic bird landed in one of the twin pines by the fire pit. Its cry of arrival echoed across the meadow and ridge lines.

"Good evening, my fine feathered friend," said the chief, "welcome to Leigh's meadow. I'm sure by now you know her well—better than I, is certain. We've got quite a bit of activity scheduled for this evening; you'll be busy watching all the action. Hope you can keep up."

The raven looked down on the chief as if the meeting were expected.

Facing west, breathing in a deep rhythmical cadence, he maintained a solemn silence and prepared to repeat the prayer of his father and his father's father, the prayer of thanksgiving repeated by his people over the years to Gitchee Manitou.

He carefully dispensed tobacco to the four points of the compass, then lit a smudge pot of cedar, sweet grass, and sage. Smoke wafted to the participants for cleansing with the eagle's wing while the chief chanted:

> "Atewiopeyata, nawajin yelo, wamayanka yo! Ite, otatya, nawauin yelo.
> (Creator, to the west I am waiting. Behold me.
> The wind is blowing in my face. I am waiting.)
> "Gitchee Manitou, The Creator, Great Spirit, Life Giver, Creator of Earth, Our Island Home, you carried us across the vast expanse of interstellar space on the back of the Great Turtle. All the Earth is Turtle Island. This inland home teems with loving things. The waters teem with fish, the woods with four-leggeds

and crawling beings, and the skies are full of birds, and finally
Anishinabeg, the two-legged arrive.
May the nourishment of the Earth be ours.
May the clarity of light be ours.
May the fluency of the mighty river be ours.
And so, may a slow wind work these words of love around you
and the petitioners here tonight with your invisible cloak of life."

Silence returned to the area as Gete Wabiska personally reflected on the fact that this ceremony had been repeated time and time again by his forefathers on this very spot, centuries ago.

He faced the petitioners.

Leigh wore a beautiful straight line, beaded dress. The bleached, fringed buckskin garment reached to her ankles. Her moccasins were white with gold beading. Her auburn hair was braided into a long cascading strand down her back, fastened with a bleached rawhide tie. A white headband, decorated in gold with Tlingit symbols of Raven, Thunderbird, Wolf, and Bear made her look like a queen, a lady in waiting. Her bodice was dominated by a bright yellow sunburst on a blue background with a forested margin. A mystical black silhouette of a raven with its wings extended hovered over the sunburst. Typically, she did not wear any makeup. Her medicine bag rested on her bodice, and a sheathed knife hung on a rawhide tie around her waist.

At the chief's nod, she stepped toward him, winked, and bowed her head in a respectful manner.

Chi Mukwa wore simple two-piece bucks in trappings beaded in blue, outlining the bear icon. A small headband of red cloth, with a long streaming tie, cascaded down his back. Similarly-beaded moccasins carried the outline of an abstract raven in flight. A red sash was tied at the waist, holding a well-used tomahawk. He also carried a calumet, a symbol of peace. A large medicine bag, decorated with porcupine quills, presented many geometric designs.

The chief nodded again. Bear stepped forward, grasped Leigh's hand, gave it a loving squeeze, and mouthed the word "finally" to the chief.

The drumming continued. *Drum—drum—drum—drum . .*

The chief raised his hands to the evening sky and chanted slowly at the cardinal points. He stopped at north and sang to the creator:

"Pity us! O Sun! O Moon! O Stars!
Mother Earth! Pity us! Pity us!
Give us food and drink.
Bless this couple; may their trails lie straight."

The chief asked the three witnesses—Joe, Windy, and Raven—to join them, stand in a circle, and pray. He retrieved the pipe from Bear and spoke. "In filling the pipe, all space and all things are concentrated within this single point. The bowl or heart of the pipe *is* the universe. It is man. The bowl is the *center* of the six directions. As we smoke the pipe, all of us will be *as one*." He lit it, and passed it around to all members of the circle. Some prayed aloud; others spoke silently. Joe sang a short ditty about a gal needing a man, and Bear was that man. Finally, the pipe came back to the chief, completing the important symbolic circle of life. He then blew his medicine whistle to the four points of the compass and sang:

> "Hear! Above-Spirits and Underground-Spirits, birds and animals, our secret helpers. May they live long and have plenty. Let our couple grow and have a full life and be happy."

The chief brought forth a small pouch of white clay, the sacred paint. "Now is the time for your blessing."

The witnesses stepped back.

He motioned for both to come closer, then painted her cheeks on the right side, his on the left. Then the chief drew a half circle on her right forehead and a half circle on his left forehead. The final paint went on both of their chins. He described the circle, when together, as the sun's daily course through the heavens, and the need for them to be together to enjoy their life as a couple.

He retrieved a beaver skin from his sacred bundle and passed it down both sides of their heads, shoulders, and arms; then ended with an upper sweep, by which he imparted his final blessing. They prayed:

> "Before you, my Father, Gitchee Manitou,
> I present to you my daughter and new son.
> Let the white paint be like the sunlight,
> to protect and bring them health and strength.
> May all my people be kind and help them,
> that they may be happy, as long as they remain among
> Indian brothers and sisters.
> Give them the light of day,
> that their path may be free from danger.
> If they should go into the wrong trail,
> lead them safely back,
> that their path may be firm and downhill to old age."

The drumming continued. *Drum—drum—drum—drum* . . .

"Your union is now blessed in accordance with Tlingit tribal customs. You may kiss the bride and offer her your petition of love."

Bear looked at his beautiful wife, paused, then smothered her with his embrace and kiss. He then told her of his love:

"I bring you a life with me.
At sunrise I will express my love to you.
At sunset I will demonstrate my love for you.
When the thunder rumbles, Manitou has spoken to you.
When the wind whistles, the Spirits have blessed you.
When the sky rains, Mother Nature has blessed you.
When the raven calls, He will guide you.
When the sun shines, the World has accepted you.
When you look at the moon, it will be your Lover's face for you.
Let your soul come to mine so I can love you.
I offer you a new life of Friendship, Admiration, and Love."

Nervously, he held her, lowered his head to hers, found her eyes, sought her tender lips, and touched them with his . . . his expressing passion of a determined lover.

They gazed into each other's eyes.

Leigh paused, looked into the eyes of her lover and spoke from her heart:

"It's fate that we are together.
I'm your mission and you are mine.
When you walk, I am the stones beneath your feet.
When you come home at night, I am your bed.
During the day, I am your air, and when you die,
I will be the earth that enfolds you—I am everywhere."

The drumming continued. *Drum—drum—drum—drum* . . .

They embraced again and turned to their witnesses. With Churchillian grandeur, Joe exclaimed, "Me boy, ye have done it! 'Tis good for us all; godspeed to you. I'll be drinking one or two to seal the deal. Aye, me boy, let's break out the rum!"

The chief calmly informed Joe that in no certain terms the ceremony was not over. He asked Raven Maiden and Wind Spirit to step forward and stand as a pair before him.

She was indeed a beautiful girl, young and broad of mouth and eye and jaw, fresh, solid and airy, as if light rays worked her instead of muscles. She wore a deer-skin dress accented with blue beading and porcupine quill patterns of a wolf, bear, and raven. Her rich long, black, braided hair framed her olive skin. Onyx eyes radiated the intensity of an unapologetic wildness, yet an unrestrained sort of beauty. Her pupils were as rifle bores—shooting what? Was it her skin's luster that enhanced her beauty? Yes, but there was something else . . . Her eyes? Maybe. She looked straight at you as if a target. She, too, had a sheathed knife tucked into her sash. A beaded medicine bag hung around her neck.

Wind Spirit wore a deerskin jacket with fringed sleeves and denim trousers. His boots were western-styled, leather with some sections retaining the animal's hair. A sheathed knife was located in the center of his back Crocodile Dundee-styled, held in place by a diagonal strap across his chest. His head band was of blue denim embossed with a perched raven. A blue medicine bag hung around his neck.

The chief asked each of them key questions in the area of their understanding of relationships of guardianship and the responsibilities of both parties. They affirmed their commitment to Leigh and Bear and their enthusiasm to be part of their united life.

The chief asked them all to come forward and kneel as he blessed "The Partnership of Four" on the meadow. Turning toward the north, he cast tobacco, then to the east, south, and west. Turning he raised his arms to the sky and gave thanks, asking for a blessing:

> "Creator—Manitou—our protector,
> hear my thanks and my plea.
> Bless these youngsters for their courage;
> provide for their future and give them strength.
> We praise your role in our lives, and
> let the spirit of the clan watch over them."

They looked at each other with an overwhelming sense of gratitude. Then with an obvious awkward facial expression, Windy asked if it was all right to kiss her. In his wisdom, the chief gave him the understanding look of affirmation, and they grasped each other in a clinging hug that slowly worked to a brief kiss.

The chief looked at Leigh and Bear's approving smiles and silently felt the blessing of the ceremony.

The moment ended as quickly as it started when Joe yelled out, "Good goin', mate; you've proved to me good one at squeezing the lassie. Bloody well, we'll have to keep close watch on these two."

⁂

The Tlingit party of five celebrated into the evening, led by the United Kingdom's unofficial party animal, Joe Bloom. He was in his glory, directing the festivities by leading songs and offering multiple toasts to the participants, Manitou, the wolves, the ravens, the giant pines, and yes, even the Queen of England. "God bless Elizabeth's sweet royal arse!"

Everyone dined on salmon just out of the new smoke house, freshly killed venison backstrap, tenderloins, and kabobs, plus fine wines from California and ample rum for Joe. He also made certain the wolves got their share of venison.

As the couples paired off to walk-off their merrymaking, Joe and Old White lingered by the fire in a reflective mood. The wolves tagged along with Leigh and Bear as they walked near the river. Raven and Windy strolled across the meadow and up to the plateau. Both pairs had a lot to talk about.

The older couple discussed their new relationship without the previous limitations set down by Leigh. He grabbed her butt to let her know that he was anxious to start their new closer bond. But, she reminded him of their more pressing need. The first task seemed to be rearrangement of the hut to accommodate sleeping two more. Bunk beds should solve part of the problem, but privacy would require some temporary curtains for both male and female. With the younger ones' hormones peaking at this age, they discussed the needs for certain rules of behavior for everyone's benefit.

"Hey, my guy! Speaking of sleeping, I've an idea for tonight's gang that's staying over. It's such a nice evening, let's all sleep outside under the stars, or a canopy for those who don't want to be 'dewed.'"

He looked at her in disbelief.

"You can't be serious. E-gads! Woman, this is our first night together."

Turning to hug him, she said, "I know, my dear, this idea changes our plans to be alone, but guess what? I'll make it up to you—double—I promise."

"Damn, you sure have some hair-brained motherly ideas. Don't you realize I've got such a build-up of testosterone, it's stuck in my throat?"

"If that's the case, I'm feeling better already. Here's the deal: hold your hormones until tomorrow night, and swallow those sex hormones so they can go down to where they will do some good."

"Okay, okay, I guess you're right. Sleeping outside will solve our guests' needs, again at my expense."

"Poor baby, do you think you can possibly survive one more night?"

"No! But my options are limited. I'll take a double dose of pain pills and dream of you until I crash."

He grabbed her butt and held her high on his hips. She wrapped her legs around him and buried her lips in his sulking face. They kissed and petted until Bear's legs gave out, and they fell to the pine needles and rolled around.

"My friend!" she exclaimed. "If you have any plans for a bare-naked roll-around under these pines, forget it! We'll do that and more on the morrow. Now let me up or you'll mess up your already-busted back."

"No way, babe. I'm not moving until you promise to roll in the Tongass with me at a later date."

"I promise. In fact, I'm looking forward to it. Do you think you can handle all that a University of Michigan gal can deliver?"

"If I can't, I'll certainly die trying."

They got up and had a final kiss before heading back to the meadow. The wolves seemed to enjoy their activity as they pounced, jumped, and followed the pair.

*   *   *

On the plateau, the younger pair talked about their previous relationship and the serendipitous events of the last couple of days. Her frank comments about them being careful to remain friends—like a sibling bond—was refreshing to hear. He had no passionate plans towards her . . . at least not for now.

"You know, Windy, it's been a while since we've had a chance to talk. Who would have ever imagined that we'd meet again like this? My life has certainly changed since we played games together in the clan. After the unfortunate events that resulted from my move to town, my perspective on life has been altered for all time. I'll soon have to resolve many options facing me. I know the forest is only a temporary respite. However, it will give me time to think. I'm so thankful for Old White, Leigh and Bear's commitment, and all of your help. Bear has always been like an uncle to me, Old White a grandfather, and Leigh a new aunt. Thankfully, you have always been like a supportive brother to me. I'm so fortunate. Then there's Joe. He's beyond description. He's there whenever a problem needs attention. Look what he's done for you. Although I hear you earned his respect, overnight he has become your mentor, your counselor, your employer. You look mighty fine in your new DNR shirt and hat . . . right handsome, I may add. Some say Joe has too many rough edges. Well, I do not. Those who know him pay no attention to his barroom blather, frisky sexual innuendo, and profanity toward politicians—including, as he would say, 'The Bloody Queen.' In fact, be ready, no one is safe from his jocular verbal attacks. Nonetheless, if you need something, he's the first to show. Yep, he's my buddy, my dependable defender."

"Well," said Windy, "I agree. I'm gonna learn as much as possible from that old rascal—at least what I can understand. I have trouble when he switches to his mirthful British phrases in the modified King's English. I, too, have a once-in-a-lifetime opportunity with Joe. Say, we'd better head back and see how Leigh's gonna handle bedding down this overnight, overfed, and over-served gang of six."

*   *   *

As he and Joe cleaned up the area and stretched a canopy between the trees, Chief mentioned how brilliant Leigh's forethought was to sleep the gang out-of-doors. To him, it was the norm. For that matter, to Joe, too. Along the trail, all hikers and explorers used cedar bows for their bedroll and for cover, too. Tonight's cover, the twelve-foot-square canopy, would keep the dew off and keep everyone close and cozy.

Couples came back to the fire. Leigh got bedrolls for all and laid them on the fresh cedar bows Joe had cut earlier.

"Humm, doesn't this bedroom arboretum smell sweet?" Leigh remarked. "'Tis worth more than a room at the Ritz! It's been a long day's night, as 'da boys from UK said, and a longer night for us; let's hit the sack."

Pairing did not occur for several reasons as Leigh manipulated the bedrolls so the men slept separately. Her action triggered another disgruntled stare from Bear, so she threw a kiss with her hand and mouthed the words: "Tomorrow, dear!"

Sleep came quickly, but before they passed into dreamland, each reflected individually, to themselves, bygone days and their future plans . . .

*   *   *

Joe thought of the pleasures of working with Bear and Windy, and of having found a home away from home, at Leigh's meadow, with the added pleasure of seeing her and Bear together. He had felt for the last quarter of his life as if he had lived it to the fullest, surviving many fateful encounters; he was at peace.

Now is the time, he mused, *to pass on all I've learned to this lovely family that has, by their actions, embraced me as one of their own. I'm grateful to be welcomed to this new clan by the meadow.*

He also thought it may, just may, be time to back away from drink . . . just a little. One reason being that just before he fell into a deep sleep Pan, of Greek Mythology, the god of the woods and fields with a man's torso and head, with goat's legs, horns, and ears, appeared in his dreams. Feeling threatened, he swore off drinking—again.

*   *   *

Gete Wabiska silently praised Manitou for His blessings of the evening's activities. He felt proud of the small role he had played in bringing the group together. He was uncertain of his decision to name Leigh's group a clan, but they were all Tlingits. Although small now, they may grow. Nevertheless, the presence of a clan in the Tongass was important, no matter how small.

His thoughts shifted to the trek back to Skagway, on horseback with Joe and two-hundred pounds of smoked salmon. The trip should be interesting, if not adventurous, for Joe was known for his constant stories of conflict with man and beast at fireside chats, and other stories of a few female conquests thrown in.

He would, no doubt, learn a few new barroom phrases and drinking songs all melodized in the King's English.

*   *   *

Windy reflected on his good fortune being accepted by Leigh and Bear. He also looked forward to his next assignment with the DNR. Joe had made a classy presentation by the fire of his new shirts and hat with an embossed DNR logo. It brought tears to his eyes and warmth to his heart.

He was a little bothered by his feelings for Raven, feelings different from how one regards a sister. While walking on the plateau, he had felt more for her than brotherly love.

He'd have to play that by ear . . . and carefully measure his caring, versus his passion, for his tribal kin.

*   *   *

Raven felt so refreshed and invigorated after the ceremony that she finally managed to relax in her new home with Leigh and Bear.

She smiled at the events of the evening with Joe's bawdy songs, and in Leigh's motherly shushing when his lyrics crossed over what she thought a sixteen-year-old's ears should hear. She smirked; over the years, she'd heard all of Joe's earthy songs. He'd visited the Raven Clan frequently, especially when he ran out of food or drink. She had always treated him in an avuncular way. He was like the father she had never known.

She felt so fortunate to have several men that have been, and continue to be, mentors: Joe, Old White, and now Bear. Windy was also there for her as a brother figure. Then again, she felt like more than a sister during their walk alone tonight . . . She'd have to watch their relationship very carefully.

*   *   *

Bear chuckled as he looked over to where Leigh slept. Although his complaints to Leigh in deferring their "first night" 'til the morrow were in jest, he understood her logic. He felt fortunate to have a second chance at love. His life felt fuller than ever before.

Part of that fullness was the guardianship of two attractive teenagers. Both would, without a doubt, contribute to his and Leigh's bliss. Yes, he was a lucky man.

He also longed for his son Chinodin, and would soon ask him to visit on weekends now that his relationship with Leigh had been blessed.

*   *   *

Leigh reflected on the last six months while living in the Tongass on the meadow's edge. So much had happened.

Many of her close male friends had suffered tragic deaths: Bush pilot Ford, as a result of his plane crashing; Tlingit shaman Walkswithwater, from a grizzly attack; Tlingit warrior Walkswithwind, from a cave-in of the Tlingit's sacred underground chamber . . . And now there was Bear.

Chills ran up her spine as she thought of her bad luck with men. Could it be her? No. Of course not. But? She hoped that with her formal bonding ceremony her chances for peace of mind would be assured.

She whispered, "Please. Please, Manitou, let's pull together to make it work this time."

She rolled over, looked at Bear, and caught his eyes staring at her. She winked and threw a tender kiss to express her love.

He did the same and mouthed "Tomorrow . . ."

*   *   *

As the celebrants slept, the meadow rested. Then suddenly, as if on signal, a White Owl flew across the clearing and perched on the pine, then looked below.

Gratified by the day's activities, the scene pleased Him.

Chapter 13

Rectitude

The evening breeze silently moved the mist across the meadow. The only sound heard was the rattle and prattle of midnight denizens gnawing and nibbling on the ground cover of grass, seeds, and leaves in the fern-canopied moss.

The meadow was once the animals' euphonious habitat. Now, the colonies were stressed by the pack of wolves that ran over the rodent range by day and night and, even worse, horses that clomped over the area with tectonic pressure on the subsurface. It was becoming near impossible to schedule food-gathering due to the potential for constant serial bombardment by hungry hawks, pestering canines, and now the colony is on alert again as two of the celebrants from the fire have decided to take a stroll on the meadow—at midnight. Puzzled, a few of the rodents surfaced to determine how to prepare for this latest intrusion.

*   *   *

As they made their getaway from the fire, Leigh felt the warmth of Bear in the cool evening breeze. Their flesh glowed in the moonlight filtering through the trees as they lay on the soft mattress of ferns. Tranquility returned to the meadow as the incessant scurry of invisible denizens went about their nocturnal routine without agitation.

There on the meadow's carpet of club moss, fern fonds, and fescue grass, Leigh and Bear lay in the buff, wrapped in a blanket. They had accomplished their initial objectives as they panted and exhaled in a satisfying rhythm. They doffed the blanket to cool down after expressing their love to each other. They felt totally exhausted from spending the passionate forces held back over time. She now laid her moist head on his shoulder as he put his leg over hers in an effort to maintain maximal body contact, skin to skin. They searched each other's faces, speaking silent words with their eyes, then turned slowly to search the sky.

Stargazers for years, they looked to the zenith as the sky cleared. Leigh felt like they could see to infinity. They gazed to the heavens while resting . . . until she heard a noise echo from the bonfire area. Concerned they might be discovered, she lifted her head up and held still, as a doe listening for potential detection. Fearing nothing more, she rested her head on his chest.

Bear whispered, "I give thanks, double thanks, triple thanks that we have been united in one form. We've given our bodies through our mouths, our faces, our hands, our words, and our flesh inside and out. We wonder as we speak of love, scarcely knowing, until now, that we have a new life to share with each other."

She rolled over on him and lay so that he felt the fullness of her body. Looking him directly in the eyes, she said, "I will keep your face inside my soul. This autumnal night will be kept in my dreams in whatsoever task I touch, whatever thoughts we utter. I will be there for you until I wither slowly in thine arms."

They sealed their pledges with Act II of their physical expressions of love.

Later they rolled onto their backs, then scanned the sparkling black desert of sky, fixing in their minds the positions of key constellations that would mark this special night in their lives.

Long necked Cygnus stood out from afar, pointed to the water like a spear, and spent the night falling southwest, unflinching. At the breast of Cygnus floated Sadir, with Vega completing the overhead triangle in the star-smeared Milky Way. Meteorites streaked by every minute or so.

Bear pointed at his namesake, Ursa Major (greater bear), which contains the stars that formed the Big Dipper; and its cousin, Ursa Minor (lesser bear), which includes the North Star at the tip of the handle.

She whispered, "My dad and I lay on our back like this frequently when I was in my teens and sometimes with my old boyfriend—clothed, of course. It's unfortunate, due to so much light pollution, that many are blind to the wonders of the heavenly bodies circling the North Star. As for me, I've got a hold on my favorite body—right here."

"You know, woman, I'm anxious to look through the other end of the telescope into your early years on the farm in southern Michigan and your days as a U of M Wolverine."

"As Joe would say, 'Get on with it, laddie.' I know you'd love my dad. He had a way with words. You knew where he stood on any subject and told you what he believed, whether you asked or not." She chuckled. "He argued with many that the Little Dipper looked more like a box store shopping cart and it should be renamed 'Kmart Cart.'" Slightly chilled, she rolled over on him again, seeking only warmth.

He misread her intentions and grabbed her in all the right places. It worked. They raised the curtain on Act III and performed for each other's needs. Their movement did not go unnoticed by the busy field mice.

When the curtain finally came down, she whispered, "We'd better go back before our absence is discovered. At that, it's going to be hard to dash across the meadow bare-assed, and slip into the bedrolls without being detected. C'mon, my Tlingit warrior; c'mon before you mess up your back. I'd forgotten all about your injuries. I guess my mind and body were elsewhere," she added with a wry smile.

"Damn, if that isn't a good sign—love with wanton abandonment. 'Hail to the

Victors,' as you would proclaim in Arbor Town."

"Let me pull you up. Hold on—not to that! Give me your hand. Good, now that you're up, wrap this blanket around us both and we'll make a stealthy amble back to the fire. Here, I'll hold the blanket and you hold me. Not there! Behave! You'll wake the wolves."

As they moved carefully toward the fire, she hoped that her California Chianti had kept everybody in check. They were lucky; not a soul moved as he kissed her and she slipped into her bedroll. The last slap to his hand did not rouse the sleeping celebrants as he tried for one more caress. Her last words, as she slipped under the covers, were, "You animal . . . I love you."

"Hey, gal, that's the nicest thing you've said to me all night. Yep, you bring the bruin out in me."

As he quietly slid into his bedroll, a faint whisper came from the larger bedroll to his left. "Good morning and good going, mate. I knew you'd find a way. I be proud of ye in holding up the DNR tradition of always getting our woman."

"I might have known that you've always slept with one eye open," Bear whispered back. "How are you, mate? Yes, I've had a busy night. Leigh is a wonderful woman. I look forward to our life together. I will always respect her and always love my son. He's the only child I will ever have. In fact, I've asked the chief to let my son know I'd like him to visit us now that Leigh and I are united in a spiritual marriage. It's going to be an interesting relationship. What do you think?"

"You do have a lot on your plate, m'man. Bloody well, but you can hack it. Failure is not an option. 'That dog won't hunt.' Now get on with it. Marriage is complicated and unique; and you've been fortunate to have loved twice. Do not let the loss of Morning Star alter your energetic love toward Leigh and Chinodin. Give 'em both all the love in your heart."

"Thanks, you old sage of the British Isles. Now, I suppose I can't persuade you not to tell the chief that we snuck out earlier?"

"No. 'Cause he saw you, too."

"Damn."

As they both turned over and hit the sack, Leigh, hearing their whispers, couldn't help but smile.

*   *   *

The sun broke over the eastern horizon and crept past tall mountain sides, emerging onto the nets of golden lichens hung from their boughs. The orb lit up the ether in a yellow glow of rebirth, a day for Manitou's creatures to enjoy Earth's bountiful gifts.

The celebrants had just begun to move, chatting about the previous night. All had eaten, drunk, and danced too much. One brave soul got up first to stir the fire and make the requisite wake-up coffee. The four argued good-naturedly about who was the lesser person with subservient status to serve the others. Joe was tagged. Leigh and Bear still slept, which surprised a few—except Joe and the Chief. Joe thought, *The bloody buggers had a good workout last night while most of you slept. 'Twas a good night for love.*

While the four were straightening up around the campfire, Wind Spirit exclaimed, "Joe, there's an incoming message on the radio. See the light flashing! We'd better go check it out. It could be either for us or Leigh. I'll go see what's up."

Leigh always left the telecommunications equipment on standby in case someone wanted to alert her to an emergency, or for the DNR traffic that applied to their needs.

"Okay, Laddie, I'll be right with you. I've lost the battle with this lazy old chief and this young gal. I've been told I'm the one to shepherd them to wake-up brew, a warming fire, and breakfast. We British can handle that, as we've been doing long before you Yanks pushed us back across the big pond. No complaints, now; me cooking hasn't cost anyone their life—yet."

Joe's bluster roused Leigh and Bear to move into the normal wake-up mode of calisthenics in stretching their joints, well exercised from their amorous sojourn on the meadow. Joe stirred the fire, laid the coffee pot near the flames, and headed to the hut to make breakfast as Raven helped Leigh pack up the sleepover gear. Old White sat by the fire with Bear, who had a little twinkle in his eye. They gave each other the arm/wrist clasp and greeting of Tlingit warriors: "Boo-Zhoo, nin-din-iwe-maa-gi--nag." (Greetings, all my relations.)

His final words indicated knowledge of last night's activities: "You did well last night, my son."

Joe ran toward the hut. Bear joined him as they entered. The printout read:

Emergency Emergency

Tsunami Warning

Message from DNR Headquarters, Juneau, 0500 hours, this date.

<u>Attention</u>: Mark Martin, GBNP Manager.

Two significant earthquakes have shaken Alaska's remote Aleutian Islands at 0300 hours this morning. Aftershocks of a magnitude—7.2 quake were recorded seismically along the island chain. Subsequent quakes of magnitude—5.9 and 6.1 struck one minute later. They are centered 100 miles west of Akak according to the

U.S. Geological Survey. The Alaska-Aleutian megathrust zone has created a high tsunami hazard for the adjacent coastal areas. A vertical sea floor displacement of water is expected at the DNR's coastal station on the west shore of Glacier Bay National Park.

*** Wave height could exceed 20 feet. ***

Seismic water waves are anticipated at the DNR station in early morning. Considerable damage is predicted.

*** Additional Action. ***

Messrs: Joe Bloom, Chi Mukwa, Wind Spirit (intern) will depart this noon on an FFS helicopter to assist local personnel at the station in any way in saving lives and property from the water's impact.

You will report to station manager Mark Martin upon arrival, and me, when the damage assessment is complete. Be careful.

By order of the Director, S. Geez, DNR Headquarters, Juneau.

End of message.

Their response was automatic to the call for help. The women helped them pack for an extended mission.

Leigh whispered to Joe, *I've a strange feeling this assignment is going to be hazardous. Bear is already injured. I hope he's careful. I don't want to lose him. He's my hope for the future . . . Please watch over him.*

After giving her a hug of assurance, Joe briefed Bear and Windy on what to expect at the DNR station on the coast. Since Joe was already traveling, his rucksack was packed, so he helped the chief load up the container with smoked salmon, tied it to the travois, and readied Old Gal for the trip to Skagway. Joe also took the liberty to pass a message to Chinodin, Bear's son, to visit them on the meadow. In fact, Joe suggested that he bring Old Gal back while he's at it. With a sly look, he also proposed it be a 'drop-in' visit, and to come even if the DNR mission kept the trio on the coast longer than expected.

Chief agreed; a surprise visit works either way: a nice meeting together with his new stepmother, or alone with her if Bear was still on assignment. People change as relationships change. Chief said, "I'm anxious to see the new family together—

meaning, not only Chinodin, but add Wind Spirit and Raven Maiden. Now, there's an interesting combination, not counting Leigh and Bear: male to male, male to female, and two males to one female . . . It could become very competitive," Chief chuckled.

Then Bear reflected, "Maybe they'll get along great. After all, they'll all cast their souls to the four winds when they're eighteen. It is, what it is."

Chief was ready to leave and anxious to reach Skagway before nightfall. He asked for all six to stand in the sacred circle and join hands before departing. His wishes always carried the weight of a command, so they all joined hands at the river in repose. Without direction, they meditated in silence as he called the Spirits to bless their separate travels and tasks.

He cast tobacco to the cardinal points, thanked Manitou for the previous day's activities, and petitioned for His blessings as the trio prepared to travel to a difficult assignment. He also asked for His assistance for those, if any, that may be victims from the crashing waves of the tsunami. He raised his head to the sky and spoke:

> "Manitou, hear my plea, and protect your people and give them courage against this disaster. As you know, a man's greatest virtue is to aid his own. Please lead them and tell them that when it seems darkest then there shall be light, if only from the pulse of one beating heart of his fellow man."

A raven let his presence be known as the croak echoed across the meadow from its perch in one of the twin pines on the river.

Chief said in an excited voice, "Welcome, my friend. Let me introduce you to the growing family on what used to be Leigh's meadow. It is now the family's meadow, continuing in the Tlingit tradition of years gone by."

They remained standing, holding hands like a family would when a loved one is leaving for the unknown. Chief gave the word, and they dispersed. Leigh and Bear looked at each other with the fire of love in their hearts. Their relationship was unique, not only in the way they met, but in the complexity of their union a mere twelve hours ago.

As if mechanical, a halyard on the main, love drew up something new. It raised an everlasting reach to the wind that captured Leigh and Bear's windward force.

Leigh gave Bear a final hug and reminded him again that he was not to work as strenuously as the others onsite.

Windy awkwardly followed suit and hugged Raven. It seemed as if she appreciated his move and made it worth his effort by giving him a hardy embrace, too.

As the chief headed out on Old Gal, the remaining five discussed all the con-

tingencies that might crop up. Leigh assured the trio that there would be no problem for them in their absence on the coast. She asked for a conformation call upon
arrival, and their assessment of damage. As Joe was about to answer, they all heard
the sound coming from the treetops to the east: *Wop—Wop—Wop.*

Joe was first to speak. "Bloody well, me lassies, we be gone. C'mon mates."

The FFS chopper hovered over the meadow and slowly dropped to the surface.
"Meadow base, this is Hotel three-one-zero, do you copy? Over."

"Roger, Milt, this is Leigh, I hear you loud and clear. How are you? Over."

"Fine. But you look better, remember, this crew still loves you even though
you've 'hooked up' with Bear. Congratulations. Tell da boys this will be a touch-
and-go landing without cutting power, so have 'em get aboard quickly. Over."

The chopper landed in the middle of the meadow. When the PIC signaled, they
walked briskly against the prop wash and debris to the open door where Rob, the
crew chief, helped get them and their gear aboard. The door closed and they buckled in. Milt powered up, and the chopper leaped into the air and slowly gained altitude. At 500 feet the chopper rotated to its designated azimuth of 277 degrees, tilted
to that direction and powered away to a cruising speed of 150 knots at 1000 feet.

"Meadow base, we're on our way. Wish us luck. This is Hotel three-one-zero.
Out."

"This is meadow base. Take good care of my men, you old fly boy. Godspeed
to all of you. This is meadow base. Out."

*　　*　　*

The girls watched until the chopper disappeared over the ridge, then walked
back to the fire, sat on one of the logs, and poured coffee. The wolves, who had
wanted no part of the chopper, returned.

Emotionally drained, eyes wet, Leigh looked directly at Raven and said, "I wonder, are you sure you want to be a part of this extended family? You've joined a
dynamic group. Look what's happened on your first day. Some are at risk, and my
injured mate is gone just after sunrise of our first day together as man and wife. I
hope we soon enjoy a sunset in each other's arms."

Raven Maiden held her tightly and said, "It will happen, they're a team out
there, and I know Joe and Wind Spirit will not let any harm come to Bear . . . for
you, and for themselves. Come on, let's get this place cleaned up, you'd think there
was an all-right party here, or something like that."

"You're right. Thanks, gal. I think this is the start of a first-rate link to a good
life," Leigh sighed.

"Me, too. By the way, I saw you and Bear sneak out last night. I was hoping
you'd do so."

"Dang, are there no secrets in this family?"

"No. Probably not."

At that, Leigh gave her a smack on the shoulder. They got up laughing, then walked to the hut with three wolves wanting to play and two horses wanting to be fed.

Raven stopped before entering the hut. "Hey, I've an idea. While the men are gone, I'll show you the process of tanning that bear hide that Windy and I were going to do."

"Sounds good to me. Let's start this afternoon."

After they closed the door to the hut, the raven perched on its favorite pine croaked.

Leigh looked at Raven. "Did you hear that? He's still with us."

Chapter 14

Rescue

There was no warning of the disaster about to happen. At 0530 hours, both of 'the techies' were asleep and unaware of the danger that lurked to the west. They were in the DNR's research shack that served as kitchen, bedroom, and meeting room, in the center of the coastal clearing.

The first indication of a threat was the roaring noise coming from the ocean to the northwest. It could be a ship cruising close to the shore or a large seaplane flying by on a rare evening flight. Puzzled, John turned in his bedroll and strained to determine the origin of the threatening sound. Unable to do so, he got up and went to the window and had a mystified look on his face. Across the clearing he heard and then saw a flock of puffins flying from their sea cave to the north. That was strange, they rarely flew at night. Stranger yet, they were flying inland . . . at night. Weird.

He stopped and wondered if he should get dressed, but decided it would only take a minute to investigate the sources of the noise. The sound grew louder and seemed to be closer as he grabbed the knob and opened the door—then it happened.

At that instant, a wall of seawater crashed into the shack tossing him back against the table and chairs then the water drove him to the rear wall with crushing force, through the wall. Then, as if in a sluice, both John and Mark were viciously driven out the rear of the collapsing building. Both were tumbled and tossed unceremoniously among the splintered remains of the building and its contents. Within seconds their bodies were jammed against the tree-lined perimeter to the west of the clearing. In the process, a rowboat from the shoreline smashed into Marks's arm with such force that a 'crack' was heard above the tumult of their cries of alarm and pain. As if in a whirlpool, both were driven beneath the seawater and gasped for air as they tried to hang on to anything that would keep their heads above water. They looked for a tree, a branch, a limb—any kind of anchor to keep them secure. Secure from the next force they started to feel—the rip tide—that started dragging them back to briny deep. Luckily finding a small branch, John looked for Mark, knowing that with his injured arm he would have trouble keeping his head above water. Then it happened. The branch he was holding snapped-off and some floating boards drove him back out to sea. He cried in panic for Mark as he tumbled alone toward the briny deep.

Separated now, John looked for Mark, knowing with his injured arm, he was more vulnerable to drowning. Then, after slowing down in the current, about thirty feet from shore, Mark's head popped up and he appeared to be struggling to remain afloat. John made a frantic dash through the flotsam to his side, and grabbed him just in time as he continued to gulp lethal amounts of seawater. No sooner had they started to swim ashore, a secondary wave forced them back to shore like surfboards. They moved with unimaginable force in a more northerly direction toward the rocky shore. As they were driven forward, John embraced Mark, and told him to hold on with his good arm. As the velocity of the wave increased, they were lifted to the crest that reached at least thirty -feet. They hit the outcropping rocks with such force, John was knocked unconscious. Mark was dropped, and they both slid down the face of the rock onto a ledge in front of a sea cave. The sea cave's ledge saved their lives.

While coughing up seawater from their lungs, the waves kept crashing over them, receding for a moment, and crashing over them again . . . and again . . . and again. After gaining some strength and purging his system of seawater, Mark dragged John to the rear of the cave with his good arm. He found a stick and lashed it on his arm with torn cloth. He checked for John's vitals and found him breathing okay, and pulse adequate. He made him as comfortable as possible while on his stomach as he continued to clear his lungs.

Several questions begged an answer . . . How long could they survive? Were the rescuers on the way? They must be; surely many stations would know that the station would be vulnerable to a tsunami of this magnitude. He lay down with John to share their diminishing body temperature and prayed. He repeated a short prayer Joe had taught him:

> "Greetings, all my relations, and
> the Great Spirit.
> Have pity on me, help me
> to walk a straight path
> here on earth.
> Much thanks.
> I am finished."

Broken, bruised, and bleeding, they waited for the rescue team.

*   *   *

Milt and Dave, pilot in command (PIC) and copilot, scanned the horizon to the west as they flew toward the coastline. DNR Crew Chief Rob filled in the trio on what he knew of the mission plan for assisting DNR Coastal Station Bravo. Rob's briefing was quick and to the point due to the roar of the engine, vibration noise from the airframe's constant shaking, and the Wop—Wop—Wop of the knifelike rotor blades angled into and biting the moisture-laden coastal air.

Headquarters' message and Rob's briefing indicated the rescue team would arrive *after* the large wave impacted the shoreline and Bravo station. They had departed the meadow around 1230 hours with an expected ETA of approximately 1300 hours. As such, if the local DNR CO, Mark Martin, and his student intern, John Johnson, had survived, the team's task would primarily involve securing property and helping Mark get the station back to full operation.

As always, the most critical aspect of the team's mission was to discover why neither Mark or John were answering calls from Headquarters Juneau or other stations along the coast. As the noisy flight continued, Joe thanked the crew chief for the update and asked him to take a break. Being heard over the chopper's noise was hard on his voice. Briefing over, they had a chance to check on the landscape below.

*   *   *

Colorful, autumnal trees carpeted the area with intermittent outcrops leading along ridge lines to the coastal mountains. These immense peaks surrounded by glaciers were typical of a rain forest, the Tongass National Forest. It stretched from Yakutat north of Glacier Bay National Park, then sandwiched between the Pacific on the west and British Columbia on the east, and terminated at Prince Rupert in the south. The forest's outcroppings and glaciers were a jumbled mass of four large islands and literally thousands of smaller ones. One-hundred miles wide and five-hundred miles long, the panhandle called Alexander Archipelago contained one of the last stands of Earth's most majestic, old-growth woodlands described as a cathedral-type forest of giant Sitka spruce, red cedar, and western hemlock. By contrast, unseen by air was the not so nice tangled six- to ten-foot secondary growth of downed limbs, ferns, lichens, devil's vine, brambles, and other murk hindering access to only a few hardy four- and two-legged souls.

The federal government safeguarded logging interests in the Tongass Forest's 17-million acres against perennial attacks by local people and outside corporations' logging pressures. Yes, even logging by the Tlingits, who once 'owned' the entire forest, had to be managed by the DNR. Saved from attack from the saw was the one-million acre Glacier Bay National Park.

More accurately called a rain forest, the Tongass has had a research station on the coast since the early 1900s, thanks to our Rough Rider president, Teddy Roosevelt.

*   *   *

The naturalists, known as 'the techies' Mark and John, had been stationed at Bravo for two years. They had both worked with Joe for some time with Joe doing 'ground truth' surveys and data collection as he hiked through the park. Joe loved trekking in every part of the forest, taking samples and collecting data for the pair since he preferred living in the natural Creator's Cathedral. In a strict reading of the DNR's organizational chart, the techies worked for Joe, but he treated them as an autonomous group reporting directly to Juneau. Joe liked being the 'legs' of the boys when they needed the hair of a grizz, a scale from a spawning salmon, or a cone from a giant red cedar. He loved it.

Yes, at times da boys were referred to as "tree huggers" by the self-serving double-digit IQ crowd, but each of their tasks were focused on testing, measuring, and making suggestions for sustainability of the logging, hunting, fishery, and tour-ist industries. Be it animal, vegetable, or mineral, their recommendations would af-fect management's decisions that, at times, rippled down to the 48. It helped that da boys were two of the most knowledgeable and dedicated souls who not only stayed along the beautiful, wave-washed shore in summer; but also in the lonely, desolate, icy outpost in winter. Their clothes, at times, looked like something the cat had dragged in. Their worn pockets, however, frequently contained a satellite radio transceiver in one, a palm pilot in another, and a GPS unit sewn to their hats. Yep, they were geeks.

That's why headquarters' personnel were very concerned why radio traffic was neither sent out from the station nor acknowledged with their frequent radio trans-missions from Juneau. Yes, they could have been injured and unable to respond, but both? Not likely. The rescue team was sent ASAP.

The crew was very conscious of the dynamic events that nature could bring, and were cautious about strangers dropping by with strange ideas. They did not suffer fools gladly.

The crew shared some of their ideas as to what might have happened:

- Extreme flooding could have washed away all communications equipment.
- They were trapped in a below-ground cave, a karst, or a sea cave.
- A riptide had pulled them out to sea with tragic consequences.
- Hostile carnivores, stirred-up by the tsunami, injured the pair.
- Their physical condition was so grave they could not send data, much less receive due to their degraded health. This was the option they hated to consider.

*   *   *

As the chopper flew to the coastline at 1,000 feet, Milt scanned the horizon to the west. He spotted what was left of the DNR station, then looked at Dave and gave him the thumbs-up, sign, saying, "Great work, m'man." With only a direct compass bearing, and no corrections along the way, Dave's skill at charting a flight plan was outstanding. They also arrived within minutes of his predicted ETA in the face of coastal head winds and variant northerly winds along the entire route.

The DNR station had been obliterated. Only flotsam could be seen.

"Dave, I'm going to pass over the station a few times to see if Mark or John are somewhere among all this debris. This is horrible! Dammit! I hope they had enough warning to escape. Tell the crew we're going down for a look, and we'll need their eyes." "Roger that, Milt." On the intercom, Dave told Rob to tell the crew to be heads-up with their eyes as they passed over the station. He then radioed headquarters.

"Juneau tower, this is Hotel three-one-zero. Do you read? Over."

Static, a clear signal, more static, and then a strong, clear signal . . .

"Hotel three-one-zero, this is Juneau tower, hear you loud and clear, send your message. Over."

"Thanks for the comeback. This is Dave of FFS. Would you please call Geez at DNR Headquarters and relay the following message: We've arrived at 1310 hours; there is extensive damage; we've seen no survivors yet; will be landing shortly; will contact you again at 1500 hours with a damage assessment. Did you copy? Over."

"Affirmative, Dave. Say again the time of your next sked? Over."

"Roger. The next transmission will be at 1500 hours with a damage assessment. Over."

"Roger that. Lots of luck—I know those guys. This is Juneau tower. Out."

"This is Hotel three-one-zero, no further traffic. Out."

At 200 feet, while the chopper slowly flew over the station's cleared property in a zig-zag pattern, the crew scanned the area for signs of Mark and John. After the final pass, Milt decided the drainage around the demolished helipad was firm enough to set down. He told the crew to buckle up as he maneuvered the bird towards the sea-soaked pad. The lower he got to the pad, it became very apparent that no one could have survived the tons of water that must have impacted the station's facilities and equipment.

The portable dock, the boat launching ramp, the motor launch, and the stacked smaller boats were all gone. Presumably, all washed out to the sea. None of the antennas were standing . . . nothing survived. What he could see was the debris of miscellaneous equipment, boards, logs, and drowned animals. The devastation was horrible. He feared for the techies. The damage reminded him of a fierce hurricane.

Milt had already briefed the crew that the chopper would be staying on the ground for no more than two hours. His concern was for the potential of additional aftershocks and resulting waves. With a little luck, this flight would provide for immediate medical evacuation, if needed, should the station personnel require extensive medical treatment. He knew that this flight, for them, would be one-way since their return would most likely be by boat, sea conditions permitting.

He also knew very well that they would not depart at 1500 hours, even if the MJ boys were found. Rob could handle their care on the flight back to Skagway, or Juneau if they needed critical medical attention.

As the chopper took its last pass, it was apparent that the MJ boys were not going to be spotted from the air.

"Okay, boys," Dave relayed to Rob and the DNR crew, "buckle up. We're going down."

Heading into the wind, the chopper approached the damaged helipad from the south. Milt nosed her up. He gently tested the sandy pad compactness with the rear portion of the pontoon floats. They touched ever so carefully, and Milt turned to Dave and gave him the okay look for his starboard side with the same nonverbal communications used so often in the cockpit's noisy environs. Dave gave the same okay look for the port. Milt brought the nose down. The pontoon settled into the wet sand. He cut power and told the trio to debark.

Due to the horrific devastation, Milt decided that he and Rob would go with the trio. Dave would stay with the chopper to handle any radio contacts and emergency departure in case of an unforeseen danger . . . Such as a threat from another tsunami.

"Dave, I want you to promise me that you will not hesitate to get the hell out of here if the chopper is compromised by a sea wave. Matter of fact, power up to idle for the next two hours so that if there is an emergency, you can leap into the air in one versus ten minutes. You have enough fuel. Agreed?"

"Okay. You're the PIC. And, yes, it is a good decision."

"Done then. In any event, Rob and I will be back at 1500, with or without the station personnel."

"The crew of five made preliminary plans for their search pattern, synchronized their watches at 1330 hours, and agreed to reassemble at 1400 hours.

As they were ready to take off to their assigned search areas, Joe reminded them, with forced jollity, "We'll find 'em, by God. 'Tis gonna take a wee bit of time, but we will. Keep your eyes open to the most unlikely places for a man to be, and that's where he'll lay. And, bloody well, be careful lads; I no wanna have any more injuries to you blokes. Godspeed. Now away with you."

*   *   *

"Did you hear that?" Mark whispered in John's ear, while straining to speak. I think it's a chopper. Hold on, John. I'm sure it's a rescue crew. Hold on! We'll have you out of here in no time," Mark pleaded. His voice was barely audible in their prison-like sea cave, their captive grotto twenty feet above the Pacific.

*   *   *

Sea caves were formed by the unrelenting impact of wave action against the softer limestone layers in the harder sediments like basalt or granite parent material to those outcrops facing the sea. Over time, the constant erosive action of sea waves crashing on the rock wears away the softer limestone layers.

Some caves are 20 to 30 feet above sea level, over 100 feet deep, and have openings, to the sea, measuring anywhere from 10 by 20 feet. Over the millennia waves have eroded away the depths of many caves to an earthen break through, a blow-hole up to the surface. This hole in the ground is called a karst. A karst resembles a sink-hole on land. However, in this case, the hole is connected to a sea cave. They are very dangerous to both man and animals as the openings are frequently covered with vegetation. This explains why some caves contain skeletons of wolves and wolverines.

Sea caves of Southwest Alaska were spectacular in many ways. During glacial intervals, sea levels varied; the sea caves formed during those times are located randomly above and frequently below the present sea levels. Some that formed during such times are drowned. Conversely, many are elevated above the current sea level. Rich in artifacts, many caves contain examples of life from the past, including animal and human skeletal remains. As such, many sea caves have been explored and named by scientific personnel.

Mark was an example of a research doyen who wore two hats. One as manager of the DNR's coastal station, the second as professor of anthropology at Michigan in Ann Arbor. His graduate assistant and DNR intern, John, was doing his PhD field work with Mark. They had traced some of the cave's artifacts through radiocarbon dating as far back as the Ice Age.

Puffin Grotto was one of these spectacular sea caves on the western side of Glacier Bay National Park and Preserve. Located 100 yards north of the DNR station, both visitors and local workers had climbed up and into the grotto at 20 feet from the current sea level.

Well above normal wave heights, Puffin Grotto had received a torrent of water from the recent tsunami. The crashing waves had tossed many aquatic plants to the edge of its mossy floor near its seaward edge. The seaward opening was an ellipse measuring about 10 by 20 feet. Farther back, through various crawlways, the cave opened up to a room full of wave-rounded boulders. Among the boulders lay various skeletal remains of birds, whale vertebra and more recent otter bones. Farther back, an adventurous explorer would find many land animals such as wolverines and wolves, still residing there.

Besides glacial variants that influence the changes of the Pacific's sea levels, tsunami waves generated by earthquakes eroded the caves several times a year in this area. It was not unusual to have minor tsunamis. Unfortunately, seismic water waves originating in the Alaskan-Aleutian megathrust zone could travel across the Pacific and destroy coastal towns within hours after generation. They also climbed the coastal outcrops and purged the elevated caves. Additionally they deposited modern-day flotsam and jetsam from ships and sometimes, unfortunately, coastal inhabitants. The caves were a gold mine for cultural anthropologists, and naturalists like Mark and John, especially since they were studying the Tlingit culture that lived along the coastline.

In this case, the crew hoped that the techies would be found somewhere near the clearing and had not perished in the sea.

*   *   *

Joe finally said, "Wouldn't it be wonderful if they were found in one of Mother Nature's niches. A place to protect a man before rescue. It's possible. She takes care of her people. Let's be about our business, mates."

Chapter 15

Revival

Behind the rescuers, half mile up, puffy clouds cavorted and crashed into the jagged edge of the coastal mountains. The turbulence reflected the sea's torment of only twelve hours ago. The calmness of the sea now belied its recent past.

Joe had informally assigned the teams to search the station's base area, perimeter, and shore. He left to probe elsewhere, including up shore areas, into the forest to check the several "blow hole" karst locations, and possibly climb up some of the outcroppings to check on the sea caves.

Although Dave was tied to the chopper, he could search much of the area around the base where the structures once stood and still hear the radio with the chopper's engine at idle. He decided to walk a circular pattern around the chopper, slowly expanding the circle until he could no longer hear the radio.

After looking for a probing/walking stick, he found a half buried number-two iron. One of these guys was trying to improve his golf game by banging balls into the Pacific.

He shook his head and mumbled, "More power to 'em."

*   *   *

Milt and Rob paired off in a swing across the base and to the perimeter of the station. Clear of mature growth Sitka Spruce, the three-acre site included a half-circle area that was fairly level, though strewn with small boulders and beach sand. Beyond this area, as if reaching to the sky, towered the gigantic spruce trees at 100- to 200-feet high. The undergrowth was minimal since the old-growth trees' canopy stole all the sun's nurturing rays. However, due to the sun's impact at the forest's edge, a band of secondary growth flourished. With the rain forest's moisture and sun impacting this border, a barricade of flexible shrub stems, spruce saplings, thorn plants and 'bushwhack' plants thrived.

The pair fought their way through the perimeter growth heading due west from the beach to see if Mark and John may have been washed beyond the growth ring, onto the forest's floor beyond. After plunging and ducking through the sapling barrier, they stopped in shock at the scene confronting them.

"Rob, do you believe this? What the hell! Can you figure this out?" Milt exclaimed.

"Damn," Rob answered. "It looks strange to me. Here we are on the west side of the foliage and finding what appears to be a land-locked marina."

What they found was a pile of unceremoniously dumped and demolished boats of various shapes and sizes. The slightly-damaged 18-foot, aluminum I/O motor launch lay on its side. Two half-buried aluminum row boats, one about 14 feet and the other a 16, stood on end as if shrines to some transcendent god. To their surprise, two undamaged kayaks with oars lashed to their bows stared at them as if ready to go—or row.

Milt said, "I can only guess what happened here. I think the first huge wave washed over the boats stored or stacked up at the water's edge, and that wave carried them over this plant barrier. Then when the wave receded with less volume and velocity, they were captured, letting smaller items through but catching these larger ones. See? There's no small stuff on this side of the barrier. What do you think?"

"Sounds possible to me, Milt. I just wish the techies were here, too."

"True. Well, let's plan on retrieving these items later. For now, I suggest we search this side, the forest side of the hedge. Why don't you walk north and I'll go south. Remember Joe's comment: 'Look in the unexpected locations, and that's where a person may have lain.'"

As Rob took off, Milt gave the boats another look by tipping them over a bit and looking under them as much as possible. While poking around, he found one of their water-soaked communicators, a digital camera, and a single tennis shoe.

After looking around and finding nothing more of interest, he, too, headed out, southbound around the perimeter.

*   *   *

Bear and Windy walked slowly along the beach with thick cudgels constantly probing the soft aerated sand along the shore. They turned over every bit of jetsam and flotsam they could reach, looking for any evidence of Mark and John, but dreading what they might find. So far they had not found any clues to help explain their disappearance. That was good news. Having traversed the shoreline several times, they decided to search the surf.

"Bear, let's walk together so in the event that one of us needs help pulling out a large item."

They walked slowly along the beach. When they saw something of interest, or of value, they threw it onto shore. So far, they'd thrown a few oars for the boats, a portion of the rails for launching the bigger boat, a couple of damaged chairs, several pieces of clothing, shoes, pots and pans, and other miscellaneous parts from the facility that had not been carried farther out to sea.

"Look, Bear. Here's a good boot . . . half-laced, and recently worn. I hope it wasn't torn off one of the guys if they were thrown around violently by the waves."

"True, but let's be positive. It may be a spare. Remember, these guys were probably running around the station at night, bare-arsed, to save what they could. That was their mistake. Equipment can be replaced; lives can't."

They continued walking along the beach, throwing miscellaneous items on shore.

*   *   *

Joe had walked south along the beach about one-hundred yards to the small peninsula jutting out in the shape of a scimitar, which captured items floating in southerly current from Prince William Sound. Indeed, he found many items from the station, but, luckily, no bodies.

Finding nothing more of significance, he walked due east into the forest about 100 yards, turned north, and walked carefully along a familiar game trail he had walked for many years.

"Hold up you bugger," he said to his GPS unit. "It's about time to consult me friend to see where the sam hell I be. Come on now, you smart ol' machine; it's about time to tell me how close this ol' bloke be to those karsts that are connected to the sea. I be workin' like a rented mule so far. So do your stuff." He cranked in the coordinates of the karst location from his note pad.

Because he had previously stored the karst location while doing some 'ground truth' exercises with da boys, the unit told him where he was and how far he was from the site with an accuracy of three feet. It told him he was 100 feet south and 30 feet east of the site. With a little processor in the GPS, not unlike the Pythagorean theorem, it computed the hypotenuse, in degrees, that told him he had to walk 104 feet to the north-west to reach the karst.

"Bloody well, my little friend, 'tis to the NW I go. Thank ye. I have to say, 'tis not that you're better than this old bugger; you're just faster. Of course, I've been known to tell a fib or two when pressed by new technology."

He moved out on the compass azimuth provided, with plans to take 35 steps along the route given to the site.

After a short trek of ten minutes, he located the karst. It had changed very little since his visit two years ago.

"Well, this sink hole has not been disturbed. Da boys have not been here voluntarily or involuntarily. That's a good sign. But, in any case, thank you Mr. GPS—or is it Miss? That's what me needs on a cold winter's night."

The next karst was about 600 feet to the north behind Puffin Grotto, so he took off. He knew very well he would have to confirm another GPS location when closer, but he was just obstinate enough to try to hit the bull's-eye without any technical help. Nevertheless, he knew Mother Nature did not like to share all her secrets, and the site may have changed over the last few years. He was pretty pig-headed and would not ask for help until trial and error failed. That's the Brit in him, people used to say.

"Oops, I've got to watch my time. We've a rendezvous at 1400 hours and it's bloody well 1340 now. Come on, feet, pick up the pace. We've got to find that hole before I meet with the search team. I've a feelin' this karst may be the answer to their disappearance. On with you, feet; your arse is grass if I don't make it soon, and I'm the lawnmower. Let's kick butt."

As Joe moved northward he would stop momentarily and listen, then move on and stop again in a non-repeatable pattern. He'd move, stop, pause, move, stop, pause. The pauses were variable, their frequency unpredictable. In the past he'd flushed many animals that were tailing him or just watching from afar. This procedure worried the wary since it copied their own non-rhythmical movements in the wild when stalking their kill. Although he was exploring today, not hunting, wild game still took no chances after their first curious look. They left quickly, ran fast, ran far, and stayed long. Over the years, Joe had learned as much from the forest animals as from the classroom. The animals taught him methods and means of survival in an environment where carnivores kill and devour each other so they can live another day. The laws of survival were simple: kill or be killed.

Joe's objectives today were two-fold. He was listening for John or Mark's voice, or for any unusual activity by the park's animals that would indicate an unnatural event related in some remote way to the tsunami.

After trudging along without any sign, Joe suddenly looked like he was going to get his wish.

He heard a commotion about 100 feet along the azimuth he was following. The sound was like little barks, squealing, rustling, and low pitched growls. He moved forward at a brisk pace, but with stealth, so he could observe the source of the unseen noise.

"Bloody well, you ol' goat, we're on to somethin'. The noise is comin' from the exact area of the karst. Thankfully we're downwind, so be careful feet; don't be settin' off any alarms by steppin' on snappin' branches."

As he walked toward the ruckus ahead, he switched his communicator to vibration versus alarm.

Peering over a small knoll, he discovered what he had expected: a full scale knockdown fight. A vicious wolverine and a sly little fox were in full blow competition for a pile of bleached animal bones strewn all over the edge of the karst. With misguided covetousness and in fear of loss, they thrust and parried at each other, with sword like bones in their mouths. The wolverine, noted for its strength and tenacity, the most feared flesh eater in the northern forest, was ruthless in its defense of the newly found bone yard around the karst opening. The sly fox, known for its cunning and smarts, took off with just the one bone, knowing very well one bite from the wolverine would break many bones in his body.

With utmost respect for the wolverine, Joe approached the cocksure beast as it hissed and spat like the fat in cooking meat. Feeling no personal hostility to the growing beauty in black, yellow, and white fur, he stood and chatted walking-stick at the ready, and started at the aroused terror of the Tongass.

"Okay, me boy. I've no beef with thee. Just take your bones and move a little before we get into a fight. Now, what will it be? You'd be wise to step aside before I take a pop at ye."

Joe advanced toward the opening of the karst very slowly so as not to provoke the unhappy fuzz ball.

In a flash, the cranky animal lurched forward, bit into Joe's walking stick, and pulled it to the side. Just as quickly, Joe raised the hearty stick and brought it down forcefully, smashing the wolverine onto a small boulder. Surprised, it gave a quick yelp, released the stick, and cowered backward while keeping an eye on Joe.

As soon as the petulant animal cleared the karst opening, Joe spoke. "All right, me friend, have you learned anything today? 'Tis not wise to fool with this old Brit. Have ye any more tricks up your sleeve? If so, let's see 'em now, but be wise, 'cause the second time you try somethin' you may not fare as well."

The wolverine seemed to settle down, but maintained an indignant posture about twenty feet from Joe and the bone pile by the karst.

"Okay, me friend. Now that we've got an understanding and we've settled who's boss, you can sit there and grumble while I go 'bout my business. Bloody well, you better stay put while I take a look down this hole."

With one eye on the simmering fur ball, Joe looked down the blowhole and quickly concluded that his suspicions were confirmed: a wave had cleaned out the tunnel all the way from the sea cave, including all the residual bones from years and years of animal deaths, natural and otherwise. He pictured a geyser spewing bones and debris into the air all the way from the cave's opening at the Pacific. This action is the reverse of normally pooling rain flowing into the softer limestone, through tunnels to the sea caves on the Pacific shore.

Joe thought, *If a wave could generate that much force to travel into the cave along the tunnel and spew debris out of the karst—it could also pick up a body in the water and throw it up and into a sea cave.*

"That's it," he said. He knew his next move.

Looking at the growling bundle of furry nerves, he said, "You're the first to know, Mr. Wolverine. I think da boys are in the Puffin Grotto. I'm not certain, but I'm gonna check it out ASAP. I'm feeling better already. Now, me friend, I'll bid you adieu. You've been fine. I'd have taken a bite of some two-legged tryin' to disturb my dinner, too. Now, have a pop at it, enjoy your bone-crushing banquet, and I'll be on me way."

He made a quarter turn to leave, and suddenly thought. *What if the boys were hurt so bad they could not tell us where they were. Maybe I can be a little more certain. I could try yelling down this opening and see if I get a response. It'll be worth a try.*

He turned back.

"Excuse me, Mr. Wolverine, I've one more task."

The animal growled and backed away slowly, keeping his eye on Joe.

Again, Joe leaned over the hole, with one eye on the Tongass terror, and yelled down the hole. He could not see very far since the tunnel took a sharp turn just below the surface.

"Hey, Mark! Hey, John! Are you there? He, you guys, this is Joe. Do you hear me?"

Silence.

Nervous, the Wolverine hissed.

"Hush your mouth."

Silence.

"Dammit, nothing."

He got up to leave, and heard a sound, a strange sound like a rock falling. He dismissed it, but to his dismay he heard it again. It sounded much like the first. Then, another. And another.

"Someone is throwing rocks down there. It's them. I'll bet they can hear me, but cannot holler back. Sonabitch, we've found the bloody blokes."

He bent down to the hole and yelled again. "Hold on, mates. We'll be there soon. Hold on, you yankeepotlickers; the gang of five is on the way. Hold on! I'll be dipped in dung, rolled in flour, and cooked all night."

Before he moved briskly to the beach, Joe thanked his wolverine companion for being a good listener and left him to his bone yard as he moved to the rescue team on the beach.

It was 1410 hours when he informed the team of his discovery.

Within minutes, they had secured additional rescue equipment, and were ready to go.

A raven circled the area and landed on the salvage pile near the shoreline. After finding an elevated perch, so he could be seen, the bird croaked so the crew would know He was there.

All eyes turned to the symbol of the Creator's messenger.

Joe said, "Welcome, my dear friend."

Chapter 16

Respite

Joe called the search teams while he headed back to the beach. They all welcomed the good news, but sounded somewhat languid and depressed from their fruitless search of the debris-laden shoreline, the wave-ravaged station property, and the shadowy perimeter of gnarled limbs, tangled vines, and fractured elements of the station. He told them about the shouting into the karst opening and someone answering by throwing stones, but admitted he could not be certain it was Mark or John until they entered the cave. That was the tricky part. Gaining access to the opening, straight up a vertical wall twenty feet above the Pacific, would be difficult.

Still talking to himself as he walked back to the beach, he said, "I've got to rally the guys to a can-do attitude. We have to get up to me mates quickly. They're probably injured badly; they apparently cannot speak, much less get down under their own power. Yes, it be a daunting task, but I'd better have a solution when I talk to the guys, though I'm overwhelmed with premonitory speculation about their possible life-threatening injuries."

He wondered if they had little voice left after yelling for help for hours, or if salt water had inflamed their throats.

How could they have survived a thrashing by waves with over 75 tons per square foot of force, then submergence in frigid seawater for several minutes? They probably tumbled inland to about the perimeter of the station, then got dragged out to sea by the rip current, and thrown back with the second wave up and into the elevated sea cave. Shouldn't they have drowned? Wouldn't their lungs be full of sea water? How could a mammal survive a watery environment? Gills?

Then Joe remembered Mark's comments about man's innate ability to survive extended immersion. By the station's fire pit one night, he told of a graduate student coming next semester to study that phenomenon. It was called the "mammalian diving response." Apparently, when mammals are submerged in cold water it leads to an automatic redistribution of blood flow. This ensures the brain and heart a constant supply of oxygen, leading to a longer apneic duration without risk of asphyxia. This response is present in aquatic mammals, such as seals; and semiaquatic beavers and otters. Mark and Joe agreed that they were aware of the constriction of blood vessels and reduced oxygen consumption in more tolerant tissue in cold environs. That was the students' thesis leading to the study, namely: The diving response is also present in terrestrial mammals (humans) where apnea through face-chilling—e.g. by immersion and the stimuli for eliciting the response—leads to increased survival rates.

Talking to himself, Joe said, "That will be one of the questions I ask Mark. Little did he know he'd be one of the test subjects for the students' experiment. Maybe Mark could validate the hypothesis presented for testing at the DNR's petri dish on the Pacific. Time will tell, and experimental results are very revealing. Truth has a voice of its own."

*   *   *

Joe met with the crew on the shoreline. He spoke with the hum of the Sikorsky Sea King, SH -3 turbine, idling in the background.

"Okay mates, here's my idea for rescue. I'm open to other suggestions, but this is what works for me. Hear me out, and then we'll do the best we can with the equipment we've got. 'Tis what it is. We can't say, *What if?* We be looking ahead, and quick at that."

He led all five to the shoreline past the salvaged material. Then all briskly walked north on the beach to where it ended at the massive outcrop. There was no beach in front of the rock; in fact, the depth of water at the face was approximately fifteen feet. From this point they could see just the edge of the grotto that was about 100 feet north along the water line, and about twenty feet high on the rocks. Since the opening faced to the northwest, and they could not see it clearly, Joe remembered its opening was about ten feet high and about twenty feet wide, an elliptical shape. A four- to six-foot ledge jutted out from the bottom, covered with moss and puffin droppings.

"Gentlemen, that's our target. You cannot see it all clearly from here, but believe me, mates, I've sailed by that opening many times. Furthermore, I think two injured, near naked, freezing, bruised, and hurting men are waiting for a miracle rescue. Since I do not believe in miracles, I'll tell you what will work: our skill.

"A rescue from that rowboat on the Pacific ain't gonna cut it, nor is scaling the rock from the boat. Maybe Windy could do it, but guess what? We've got to get two injured bods out, too.

Make a ladder? Forget it.

Make a raft? Nope, it would take too long and we'd still need a ladder. Rubbish!"

The crew assessed a few other options and looked at Joe. Milt, said, "I can't see any other options. What did you have in mind?"

"You're the key man in my plan. Milt, you're going to fly that eggbeater of yours over the grotto so we can 'pluck' our mates from the cave."

They looked at each other, the chopper, the salvage material, and back to Joe. Milt and Dave looked at each other. Bear gave the high sign to Windy as they both looked at the salvaged rowboat and ropes on the beach.

Joe spoke. "Well, me boys, I've an idea you've figured it out. That idling chopper over there is gonna pick up that rowboat with a sling, hover by the cave, extract da boys, come back here, and do so quicker than you could say, God save the Queen."

The crew were all bright eyed and bushy-tailed, now—as if they had gotten a mental goose. In fact, they did. The look in their eyes pleased Joe.

"Okay, me boys, we're going to have to move quickly, surely, and safely, following these steps: Milt and Dave, you're going to fly the chopper to the sea cave and hold. Bear and Rob, you're going to rig that rowboat over there under the chopper with those ropes in a strong harness/sling tied to four points on the bow and stern; the four lines will be at least twelve feet long and joined at a bowline with a large loop to engage the chopper's grapple hook; then you'll load the boat with a couple hundred pounds of rocks so it will be stable in the prop wash. You'll also make a forty-foot rope ladder for an alternate exit from the cave.

"Windy, you'll gather all the PFDs and cushions and lay them on the rocks in the boat to give our injured brothers something to lay on.

"The crew, Milt, Dave, and Rob, will lift off and hover while Bear and Windy hook up the boat to the chopper and climb in the boat. I'll assist as required to ensure you've enough weight and the load has the proper CG, and I'll stay on the beach to help when you return.

"You five will fly to the cave, hover, descend to the ledge, touch the boat to the ledge, and hover. Rob will direct operations with hand signals. Bear and Windy will leave the boat, tie off the emergency rope ladder, and then hopefully find our mates, assess their condition, and carefully load them into the boat—no matter what shape they're in—and get aboard—this must all be done in 30 seconds.

"I cannot stress to you how difficult it will be for Milt and Dave to hold the chopper on the ledge and away from the rocks; he may have to abort at any moment in case of a wind gust or down draft of unexpected origin . . . that's why the rope ladder is provided. Yes, if we abort, we'll try again, but we must be prepared for a 'wave off' by Rob. We'll keep trying until we're successful.

"Milt will fly directly to shore and touch the boat on the sand by me, I'll remove the sling from the chopper, and you'll land on the helipad, but do not power down.

"Bear and Windy will escort or carry da boys to the chopper for immediate evacuation to the closest ER. Both of you will board the chopper and help Rob with first-aid on the flight back.

"I will stay here and be available to coordinate, and work with the DNR personnel from the Yakutat station as they reestablish Bravo Station operations. "Any questions."

Milt responded first. "Good plan, m'man. I've been waiting for a difficult assignment . . . and I've just got it! Holding those blades away from the rocks is going to be tough, but we're ready; let's go Dave."

"'Tis good to hear you're up to it, Milt, and it looks like your crew is as anxious as you. Good Bloody Luck, me friend."

"Thank you, you ol' bugger. Let's go, boys."

*   *   *

Everybody moved smartly to their assigned tasks while Joe helped where needed. Within minutes, the boat was rigged with a rope sling, the chopper hovering, rocks loaded and balanced, cushions placed, and Bear and Windy aboard.

As the chopper lifted, Joe felt he had done all he could to motivate the crew, knowing well the real stimulus was the powerful anesthetic of escape. The crew had a single focus now in helping the techies escape their prison-like cave.

As the chopper reached the opening and slowly descended to the ledge, a raven circled. Bear noticed the bird and pointed it out to Windy. "Good medicine," he said toward the bird; "we'll need your help today. Stay close. This rescue is in the hands of fate."

Over the roar of the turbines, Dave relayed, "Okay, Milt, just a little lower and hold . . . a little more . . . okay . . . hold."

Rob was relaying information with hand signals to Dave from the open door as the chopper approached the solid rock above the ledge.

"Okay, move in a little, a little more. You're about two feet off the deck. Okay, just a little to the north. Okay, now down slowly . . . Bingo! We're on the ledge."

Without a cue, Bear and Windy jumped out a second after touch-down and quickly disappeared into the cave's dark interior.

"Did you tell 'em to get out yet?" Milt yelled to Dave.

Dave responded, "Ha! They were out a millisecond after the boat touched. They're gone . . . out of sight. How you doing? Is it hard holding her steady?"

Milt, ringing wet with sweat, responded, "I think so, but not forever. This baby is rising and falling two or three feet every second as it is. I hope I can hold her for thirty seconds."

Dave replied, "If anyone can, it's you. Fifteen seconds left. Hold on."

The chopper was doing anything but holding. It pitched, yawed, rose, fell, and turned like a disco dancer. Milt was using almost all his senses as his sweat-soaked left hand moved the blade-pitch control; his right, the collective pitch control; and his feet, the rudder pedals changing the tail-rotor pitch; all while watching the stand-off of the main rotors to the massive rock to his starboard.

Dave yelled, "Here they come! Bear's carrying one that looks unconscious and loading him on the boat, and here comes Windy. He's walking with Mark. They're all aboard. Let's go!"

The powerful Sikorsky, hardly feeling the load, leaped into the air, rotated, moved away from the cave, and immediately flew over to the beach where Joe was waiting.

Dave and Rob coordinated with Joe as the chopper lowered enough to unhook the sling; then lifted up and landed on the helipad while still maintaining power.

Joe helped Bear carry John to the chopper, and Rob strapped him down on a series of cushions laid on the floor. Rob checked his vital signs and started a 'work-up' to determine what immediate first aid he could administer.

As Windy brought Mark to the chopper, he indicated that he was unable to speak, but ambulatory as they started to board. Mark stopped and hugged Joe with his good arm and gave the crew a high sign, plus many other not-so-clear ASL finger signals that related, even to the untrained eye, that he could not speak, most likely due to the swelling of his throat, probably from the effect of salt water; still, he looked grateful for the risky rescue.

Both Mark and John were suffering from extreme exposure, bruises, muscle tears, and contusions, all framed in swollen black eyes as if they had been keel-hauled, not once but several times. Their breathing was raspy, lips swollen, finger nails torn and bleeding.

"Okay," Joe yelled, "Let's get this show on the road. Give Mark one of your extra flight suits, wrap him in a blanket, and strap him in. Let's get these blokes to the closest emergency room."

Rob gave Mark some pain pills as he seemed to be motioning in some sort of sign language, a dive or diving action, and a high sign as if to say, It worked. He finished by smiling.

Rob looked at Joe and said, "What's that all about?"

As Joe was acknowledging Mark, he answered, "It's a long story. I'll tell you sometime, sometime when I've got an hour and a glass of grog."

Between the two of them it was clear: Mark was indicating that he was living proof of survival due to the "mammalian diving response."

"Away with ye. Enough talk. Be gone, and yes, I owe you all a bottle of the Queen's best whiskey when we meet again. Now, throw out me rucksack before you leave. I've a bottle in there to celebrate your good work."

Bear and Windy gave Joe a warrior's hand grasp before boarding, and also gave him the all-important look of confidence . . . the look that he had led them well, and would join him again, solving difficult tasks.

Just before the deafening roar of the turbines screamed to full power, they threw out his rucksack and the chopper's emergency rescue pack.

Before Rob closed the door, he yelled, "Milt said to give you this pack. It has a tent, raft, food, commo gear, and lot of goodies. You need it more than we do.

Dominus vobiscum.

"The Lord be with you, too."

Joe waved as he backed away from the prop wash. The Sea King leaped from the beach, turned at 500 feet, and headed toward Skagway Memorial Hospital. Inside the cabin, Rob had an IV flowing into John's arm, a BP cuff on, and was preparing a list of his physiological condition to call ahead to ER. Mark, too, was drinking a lot of fluids in hopes of regaining some strength. Unfortunately, he was still trying to communicate as an untrained ASL expert, so the crew humored him. After all, it was only a 45-minute flight. They could play "charade-like" parlor games for a little while.

Milt was on the horn to Skagway.

"Skagway tower, this is Hotel-three-one-zero, FFS. Over."

"This is Skagway tower. We copy. Send your message. Over."

Milt summarized the condition of the two patients he was bringing in, their approximate ETA, and asked for the message to be relayed to the hospital. "Roger, Milt. We'll relay the message. Any additional traffic? Over."

"Negative. Thanks for the service. This is Hotel-three-one-zero. Out."

"This is Skagway tower. Nothing further. Out."

*   *   *

Joe stood on the beach, alone for the first time, reflecting on the day's successful rescue. The satisfaction of the team's skill, under pressure, filled his heart with pride. The FFS boys went beyond their assignment. They were hired to bring Joe's crew to the station, not risk their lives and property. They probably saved Mark and John's lives.

As the chopper faded over the horizon, a nimbus of dread welled in Joe's chest. John's injuries were grave. Still, he felt proud of his crew. Not a single one hesitated to participate in the rescue.

As he pondered the events of the day, he still worried about the condition of Mark and John. Mark's signaling on the chopper, with a marginal attempt at ASL, indicated that, indeed, the apneic diving reaction had merit . . . or they may not have survived their extended immersion. His last thoughts formed a question. Is it plausible that evolutionary pressure during a semiaquatic phase of early evolution favored this adaptation?

"Come on, old man, let's get on with it. You've got to make camp, get a little drink in ye, and be prepared to be here a day or two, at least until the blokes from headquarters decide to send a boat around and set up a temporary camp. I've a mind to set up camp smack dab in the middle of this wave-washed clearing, and gaze at the sea until picked up by me brothers. That's it. Enough of your blither and sentiment; let's get to work."

After setting up camp, starting a fire, and opening a bottle of good Irish whiskey, he sat on an improvised chair and called DNR headquarters to let them know the good news of the rescue and the crew's transit to ER. He knew they would already know, but it gave him a chance to ask when he'd be picked up. Their answer was as expected: As soon as seas permitted, a boat would be down from Yakutat. It could arrive late tomorrow, at least, in 48 hours. He expected as much, and decided he'd enjoy the time on the beach and even do a little exploration, maybe climb up into the Puffin Grotto. After all, the rope ladder was still in place, and the boat was available. Yep, on the 'morrow.

Still overwhelmed with the good fortune of the day's rescue, he decided to offer a prayer of thanks to the Great Spirit, a prayer Gete Wabiska, the Tlingit chief, had taught him. With his English accent, be spoke:

"O' Great Spirit, whose voice I hear in the winds and whose
breath gives life to all the world, hear me. I am weak, I need
strength and wisdom. Let me walk in beauty, and make my eyes
ever behold the red and purple sunset.
Make my hands respect the things you have, make my ears sharp
to hear your voice.
Make me wise so that I may understand the things you have
taught my people.
Let me learn the lessons you have hidden in every leaf and rock.
I seek strength, not to be greater than my brother, but to fight
my greatest enemy—myself—and be blessed with dreams worthy
of your faith in me.
Make me always ready to come to you with clean hands and
straight eyes so when life fades, as the fading sunset, my spirit
may come to you without shame.
This I ask in your name."

Joe gazed upon the sunset and its beauty. His last visitor was a solitary raven that let his presence be known by the echo of a croak across the calming sea. The noise caused the puffins up on the grotto to stir a bit before returning to resting posture. Little did they know, they'd be having a visitor tomorrow.

After an adequate amount of a generic sleeping tonic called whiskey, Joe decided to sleep under the watchful eye of Polaris, the north star. He moved his bedroll and mattress out of the tent and onto a blanket as close as local tidal variants allowed. The lapping of waves had lulled him to sleep many times in his lifetime. It was not unlike a woman's voice, a lover's serenade, a rhythm proven to induce sleep.

Chapter 17
Resiliency

The dawn announced a new day as the shadows of the Sitka Spruce crawled across the wave-scoured campsite. An inventive mind may have seen the tree-line silhouette as a beautiful woven tapestry, an example of nature's skill sans weft and warp. Its only inhabitant was gone, leaving the remains of a smoldering fire by the orange tent.

An early riser, Joe had coaxed flame from the previous evening's glowing coals in the fire pit. A hardy eater, he had already finished his morning workout, vigorously attacking the scones and canned span, followed by a coffee wash. The chopper's survival pack provided ample support for his breakfast needs. He never missed a culinary opportunity—four meals a day when he could swing it. He lived by a simple gastronomical role: Eat anything that won't eat you. Poking around the survival pack revealed nurture for up to a week, pleasing him to no end.

Chops full, he checked in with headquarters in Juneau on his plans for the day, and received a good report on Mark and John's health. They informed him that the FFS chopper had dropped Bear and Windy off at the meadow, and the flight crew were back at the FFS hanger in Skagway. He also was surprised to receive a congratulations from his boss, S. Geez, on the success of their mission. He thanked him and asked that Geez prepare a formal DNR certification of thanks for Milt, Dave, and Rob for their work in rescuing Mark and John. Geez responded in kind saying that the paperwork was already in process and he couldn't agree with him more. He added that Joe, Bear, and Wind Spirit would also receive recognition. Slightly embarrassed, Joe thanked Geez and acknowledged that he would return to headquarters after the personnel in the DNR boat, from Yakutat, reestablished Bravo Station.

"Everything has happened with bewildering rapidity. Bloody lucky, we are all okay, and be God 'tis still not gonna stop me from exploring the Puffin Grotto."

He loaded his fanny pack with some key items from the survival pack, items he might need while exploring the clearing and the grotto. He selected a small electric torch (flashlight), a small framed .38 caliber handgun, mini-binoculars, and a Swiss army knife. He also stuffed in a dozen granola bars, from the pack.

He trudged across the clearing and fought his way through the mangled shrubs, broken limbs, and piles of flotsam trapped along the perimeter. Disappointed, he found very little to salvage. Bear and Windy had already scavenged the area for worthy items. Their footprints were still visible, so he searched elsewhere. He meandered along the torn and tattered jungle of upended trees and root systems, and through the quagmire of man's myriad needs to survive in the 21st century. He wondered if these items were truly needed, or just nice to have. He did find a few more kitchen items, and laboratory glassware which may be less of a necessity now. Man must always be nourished, not always researched. He tied a few pots and pans together and hauled them out to the orange research/kitchen/bedroom tent of Bravo Station's makeshift headquarters. A weathered, plastic-coated pamphlet in the debris caught his eye. It seemed to give instructions in military jargon, and also on converting from Russian to English with most of the equipment picture labels in Russian. Several pages were missing. He put it in his pocket, with plans of looking at it more carefully later.

He stowed the pots, pans, and miscellaneous hardware in a wooden crate, wondering if anyone would ever use the damaged goods again. Then he remembered his mother's counsel, "waste not want not," and secured all the hardware. His mom's words were etched in his hide.

He went way back beyond the perimeter to retrieve both undamaged kayaks. Being lightweight, they were thrust up and over the perimeter hedge and found their way back on the needle-covered ground under the big timber. Oars lashed on their bows, they were ready to go. He cleaned out their hulls and tied them to the logs by the fire so the wind or an accidental high wave would not steal them again. He also salvaged a serviceable, yet rickety, table with three legs, and a chair with two good legs. Lashed into service with broken limbs, the set gave the camp a bit of charm. Yes, with a candle from the survival pack, it could be a 24/7 operation.

Taking a rest on his jury-rigged table and chair, he looked around and wondered if the station had experienced similar destructive waves of various origins. There must have been damage in the past, either by earthquake-generated tsunamis or by other high-wind waves coming directly out of the west. He wondered if the research shack had been replaced once or twice before. The shack that was just destroyed was 200 feet from the shore and only four feet above sea level. Headquarters Juneau would know how long it had been since the last destructive event.

When he leaned back on the chair while taking a swig of whiskey, it broke unceremoniously, and he crashed to the ground. With a few choice words out of the realm of acceptability to the Queen's ears, he quickly rebuilt his prized throne with stronger splints.

A lone fox paraded across the clearing from the northern edge of the perimeter, then walked up to the camp as if a long-lost friend. It held at a safe twenty-foot distance and stared at Joe.

"Bloody well, what have we got here? Welcome, my cunning friend; how's Reynard on this fine day? Did the aroma of me gourmet breakfast tease the air and whet your palate? Is your belly yearning? What would you be wanting, me friend? Getting tired of mice? Well, since you're bashful, here's a scone. We do want to be neighborly now, don't we?"

The fox aggressively attacked the scone at ten feet from Joe.

"Well, you be jumping up and down like a tart's knickers. Ye must be hungry."

The fox chomped and gulped the scone while simultaneously licking up the fragments as if someone was going to steal his treat. Clearly, it was part of its survival mode in not knowing when another predator would appear to thieve. Like a vacuum, the fox cleaned the sand of every last crumb.

Ever so close to Joe, the fox stared at him as if a typical family pet waiting for more treats. As if frozen in place, Joe could not resist the begging eye of the beauty in orange. Lacking more breakfast scones, he broke a granola bar in half and threw it even closer. Now at five feet, the fox hesitated a moment, scanned the area in a typical defensive posture, then crept forward, stopped, crept, stopped . . . and pounced.

"Way to go, m'man. See, it did you no harm, nor did I. See, I've not moved me butt. If you only knew, it would take me a minute to get up, on a good day."

The fox looked around the area again as if to say, Are there others nearby to harm? Apparently there were not, hunger trumped safety, so he lunged forward, grabbed the other half, and retreated to a safer ten-foot separation.

"I'll be damned. I be thinking you're probably the sly old fox that fought off that bossy wolverine by the sinkhole yesterday. I'll bet a hundred pence you are. You certainly look healthy and pleasing to the eye. I've another bet. Methinks you may have previously made rounds of the DNR shack for mice and tidbits to supplement your diet in the forest. Me friend, I've a little good news along with a little bad. I'll be sharing me vittles with you, but there will be no more mousing out here for a while. Then again, you may find a gold mine of little fur balls amongst the flotsam along the perimeter. It harbors a wealth of nook and crannies and chow for rodents. In any case, I'm pleased to be your friend; you're a pleasant guest."

The fox stared as if a student in a lecture hall.

"Besides, if you're the one that gave that ornery old wolverine a challenge I applaud your tenacity. You know, the enemy of one's enemy can be a friend. I'm jolly glad to have you join me. There's an old Native American saying that indicates the same. It goes something like this: 'You are always welcome at my lodge to share a meal and to warm your spirit by the fire.' I embrace that thought for two- or four-legged friends, too."

A little overwhelmed, the orange beauty lay down in a leisurely way as if saying, You're okay with me. Of course, giving a wild or domestic animal food has an indisputable effect on familiarity.

"Well, you ol' bloke, it appears you've made a decision to hang with, me, at least as long as food is part of the relationship. Welcome. For all I know you were a camp friend of Mark and John."

Looking resplendent in the morning sun, the fox curried its comely fur with its tongue. Then a raven, an old companion of Joe's, hovered, dove, flared, and perched on one of the logs by the fireplace. Without its normal announcement of arrival, it started preening feathers silently in the shimmery light.

He felt like the center of an idyllic scene, a man getting ready to make his climb to the grotto as his four-legged and winged companions improved their appearance.

"You're certainly gussying up for the day. Be both of you visiting the Queen? 'Tis me feeling the old gal will pay you no nevermind, but the jolly Prince Charles will. He's an environmentalist who loves the out-of-doors. In any event, I'll not need a pretty face; I'm on the way to the grotto."

Rather than take the aluminum boat, the one they used as an airborne gurney, he decided to inflate the six-man raft from the survival pack. Having everything else jammed into his fanny pack, pockets, and jacket, he was ready to go.

While looking at the sunbathing beauties with a little envy, he commented, "With you blokes lounging around me camp, I suppose I'll have to button up pretty tight or you'll eat anything you can break into, chew into, or snatch and run with. Bottom line on this relationship says 'tis my food you like more than me charm."

He zipped-up the tent, fastened lids, and snapped up his rucksack pouches. He took the last morsels from his frying pan and threw them to the fox and the raven equally.

"That's it; kitchen's closed until noon. You're welcome at that time when I return from the grotto."

He left the frying pan out, knowing very well the fox would lick it clean. He'd clean it in the surf after the fox had a pop at it. As his camp followers were busy cleaning and chomping, Joe inflated the raft by pulling the gas cylinder lanyard. It was pure entertainment to see it unfold automatically in a slow procession from quarter to half to three-quarters and snap at full inflation to a cool-looking boat.

"Bingo! Here's more neat stuff in the side pockets. Dang, some water, another electric torch, signal flares, MREs, first-aid items, fishing gear, a knife, and lots of miscellaneous survival items—everything but a bottle of rum. Rubbish, don't these blokes know we need a bit of the keg to sustain ourselves. Fear not, I'm good for another week if it be necessary."

He moved to the shoreline after loading a little more rope, engaged the oars in the oarlocks, and pushed off from the beach.

Since the sea was calm, he rowed about for a little while scanning the horizon and later the depths of the water for the station's equipment in the shallows. Not much was visible, but he rowed along the shore and out a ways in a box pattern to ensure he had covered an area about the size of a football field in front of the station's shoreline.

Experimenting a little while in the raft, he found out that standing was definitely not advisable. However, he had to do just that at the face of the cliff below the grotto. After some near-turn-over attempts, he decided to grab the ladder rope while kneeling. The lower CG did the trick, so he rowed toward the grotto's rock face.

A clamoring flock of puffin's peeked over the ledge of the opening. One gave an alarm to the flock, and they all flew away as the DNR mariner rowed up to the rock.

As with most startled birds, flying unexpectedly from their roost, the puffins had an offering. At least every other one released a chalk-like white bomb that landed on the water, the raft, or the unwelcome visitor from the UK. He'd been exposed to worse, but smiled in the thought, "I'm like a plumber, in my job; I see a lot of crap."

Joe waited as the small flock of about twenty birds circled once, then again, and finally flew to another rock aviary to the north.

"Me girls, are ye just about done with your show of disgust at me presence? 'Tis away with thee with utmost dispatch. I do not need you buzzing me as I climb Jacob's Ladder, or especially when I'm goin' over the ledge. Ah, good, jolly well; you've left to bother some other bloke."

Joe tied the lines from the raft to the bottom of the escape ladder at two locations, for and aft. He had to be certain the raft was secure and would be there when he returned.

The rope ladder had double-knot handholds every foot, and double-strung foot loops every two feet. Lying against the rock without standoff-backing made the first couple of feet difficult, but once underway the rope came away from the rock. However, under any conditions, it would be an arduous task.

Hand over hand, he engaged his foot, lifted and pushed down, and reached up in a repetitive motion to the ledge. That required a little more effort since the rope ladder was fast to the rock. Once he was at the top, the rope did offer a little more purchase since it was tied higher on the cave wall. With one last pull and belly slide, he slid over the ledge lubricated with kelp, moss, and guano. The seaward ledge was so slick that he had trouble getting solid footing to stand up.

"Bloody well, you've done it, you ol' bloke. Maybe not so pretty or as good as Sir Edwin Hillary, but close. He didn't have to contend with heaving sea from a little raft, dangling lines, seaweed, and dive bombing puffin bombers. Then again, he had ice and snow, temperatures below zero, extreme winds, and thin air in elevations above twenty-nine thousand feet. Okay, me kin, you had it a wee bit tougher, but I had no Sherpa guide."

Other than being roughed up by the basaltic rock and slimy plants, he was no worse for the wear. He was in good shape for an ol' goat. The raft remained upright and his fanny pack in place.

"Okay, me boy, let's have a pop at it. Now, I've got to slide me fanny pack around from me arse so I can get into it. I can't be reaching back like some of these young bucks. Ah, that'll do."

He glanced about the ledge, searched the horizon, and after double checking the raft and rope ladder, moved to the edge of the cave and looked inside to assess its darkness, surprised he felt a crepuscular feeling, an eerie sensation. In broad daylight, he was entering into the darkness of night.

He retrieved his light, glanced about the entrance again, and stepped into the forbidding blackness of the cave.

"Bloody well, this could be dangerous. I wonder if this casual exploration is worth me time. 'Nough of your blather. Get on with it. The techies said they hadn't been up here in years; 'tis about time we took a look. Watch your step, feet; 'tis slippery in here. You'd best pay attention to this stinky, tangled kelp."

He examined the walls with his flashlight as he proceeded deeper into the cave. At about thirty-feet he recognized the outline of a raven profile with wings extended, but with the small light it was hard to see much detail. Nevertheless, he was able to see its beauty up close. Gete Wabiska, the Tlingit shaman, had mentioned the Raven Clan had lived along the coast. Many of their totems were also found along the coast. You never know, maybe I'll find an artifact or two that the tsunami waves tossed up here."

As he moved along the slippery rocks, a strange feeling came over him. It was as if in a tomb. There were small animal skeletons, and a carcass of a rotting bird or two. It was as if hanging there unmentioned, an invisible second traveler lingered. Additionally, the repulsive air seemed to be between him and silence. At forty feet, the air was stale, and the adventure long gone from Joe. He turned to leave and the ghost-like shadows followed as he departed the cave's enigmatic interior.

"Watch your step, feet. There's a lot of debris over here. That wave sure drove some unusual items up the rock and into the opening. Here's an aluminum cooking pan. Damn, I wonder what else is up here."

Kicking aside a lightweight rock that seemed to be attached to something, he fell. While struggling to get up, he looked at the round gray to white rock. Its shape was almost circular, but with many holes throughout. He pointed his light at the rock. Then exclaimed, "Damn! It's an animal's skull! Some kind of big animal, maybe a bear."

It was partly covered with rotting kelp. He pulled some away and moved some debris from the area. Then he looked closer.

"Well I'll be damned. It's a human skull."

He froze for a moment anticipating what to do next. Its location was unusual.

How the heck could a skull suddenly appear here unless it was cast up from the deep and tossed into the grotto much like Mark and John? He removed more of the concealing kelp. Much to his surprise, a full skeleton was revealed, partially clothed in a torn and tattered suit—a flight suit—like pilots wore.

Stunned, he shined his light above the left blouse pocket where identification is generally worn. Above the left blouse pocket was a sea-worn patch, it read: C C C P and a name under it appeared to be in Russian.

"Me God." Joe was stunned with the discovery. He sat a while and contemplated his next move. There were few options. He'd better let his boss know what he had literally stumbled on. "Whoa is me. I'd better copy this name, and inform Geez."

With the flashlight leaning on a rock casting its beam toward the body, Joe copied the Russian characters on the pilot's name tag. Although the flight suit was torn and degraded, Joe noticed there were many items in the zippered pockets. Nevertheless, he did not disturb anything on or near the body.

He piled a few rocks as a marker, and departed at a slower pace due to the difficulty of walking toward the sun's rays emitting from the cave's opening. After reaching the ledge, he scanned the horizon, climbed down the ladder, onto the boat, and rowed to his camp.

Still disturbed with his find, he went over what he was going to say to Geez. He finally called and explained his discovery and gave him the Russian characters from the pilot's name tag. It had not been a good day for Joe.

*   *   *

Headquarters, in Juneau, was busy tripping over itself with Joe's report. The discovery of the Russian's pilot's remains started a series of phone calls so complex that his boss finally called Joe and told him to relax and standby, he'd contact him when the diplomatic dust had settled.

Director Geez didn't need any more problems; he was in the middle of a damage assessment of the tsunami's destruction to DNR stations along the coast.

The command structure started calling each level until it reached the state department. The ambassador for Russian Affairs would get word to Geez ASAP. He told Joe to be patient; diplomatic events move slow.

Geez wished him, "Good luck!"

To which Joe replied, "I make me own good luck. Good night."

Joe was fixing supper about four hours later when he monitored the following messages.

The US Ambassador sent the following message to the Russian Ambassador:

Attention: Ambassador A. Suslov.

The skeletal remains of a Russian Pilot has been discovered on the Pacific shore after the recent tsunami. Preliminary identification indicated it could be Lt. F. Petrolovsk.

We are prepared to recover the remains and ship them to a location you select via armed guard air freight.

The remains are under our protective custody. Please send instructions for disposition.

Signed, U.S. Ambassador, H. King.

At 1600 hours, six hours after Joe's discovery, the following message was received by U.S. Ambassador H. King.

Attention U.S. Ambassador H. King.

We acknowledge your discovery. Our records show pilot Lt. F. Petrolovsk missing after an aircraft malfunction in international waters on the Pacific several years ago. No doubt, the recent tsunami brought forth our gallant son. We will coordinate all aspects of his disposition. That said, to expedite removal, a submarine patrolling in international waters nearby will arrive at the location named at 0600 hours tomorrow. Captain First Rank, Vladimer Kobzar will contact your Officer J. Bloom at that time, and remove the remains.

Contact this office if there are any questions.

Ambassador A. Suslov.

After a flurry of activity between the DOD, the State Dept., and the DNR regarding the sensitivity of a Russian sub at our shores, the objections were set aside and the following message was sent:

Attention Ambassador A. Suslov.

The recommended recovery procedure is approved. Our navy and associated military units have been informed that you will be on station at 0600 to 0700 tomorrow.

U.S. Ambassador, F. King.

Joe received the information on his communicator via a text message at about

1900 hours that evening. He was staring at the fire thinking of the scene the morning would offer. "Bloody well, who would of thunk I'd be giving a cheerio greeting to a Russian submarine commander? I'll see if I can be proper."

He had determined from talking with Geez that the Russians insisted that only *they* handle the body, and the area's remoteness made a sub pick up logical, and the submarine was already in the area. *Unsaid . . . everyone knows where each others' submarines are.*

Joe got up from the fire and walked to the shoreline while pondering the events of the last twenty-four hours. The next twenty-four could be just as tense. He hoped the Russians appreciated the amity shown by our State Dept.

Then he heard the unmistakable sound coming from the treetops to the east . . . *Wop—Wop—Wop—Wop.*

"I'll be darned. Methinks I'll have a little company for the night, and our guests on the 'morrow. Maybe I'll make a little tea for whoever is on the chopper."

The big U.S. Marine, Blackhawk gunship, fully armed, did a flyover, turned at sea, flew back, hovered, and slowly descended to the helipad.

Joe thought, *This is going to be interesting.*

Chapter 18

Resolve

It was a beautiful day. As he looked to the west, the gray basaltic outcrops stood against the blue sky in brilliant contrast, while white puffy clouds drifted along like tall ships.

Joe rekindled the fire for warmth and to heat early-morning coffee. No gourmet, he just threw a handful of ground beans into the water-filled pot and slid it over the grill on the edge of the fire. Few knew his method. Those who savored it were unaware he poured slowly so the grounds remained in the bottom of the pot.

Dawn provided a measure of relief as the cedars slowly cast their shadows across the clearing. They pointed toward the outcrop that contained the sea cave, the Puffin Grotto, which had been polished and hollowed by the action of water over centuries of erosion. Its limestone tunnel, called a karst, connected to a sinkhole landward at two-hundred feet. Yes, he had explored both openings. It was truly an unusual geological formation.

The morning breeze whispered, the waves wopped as they curled back on themselves, and the flock of puffins cooed.

"Be Jesus, the second shoe is about to drop." He sighed in concert with winds flowing through the trees. He looked to the east as the orange light nicked where the highest tree-lined peaks and ridges crept down their flanks like slow-motion gold.

"Bloody well, that climb up, into, and back from the cave made these old bones as stiff as Norman Bate's mother, and now I've got to go up there again. Torpid, that's what I am, stiff and just as numb. The recovery team really don't need me, but it's my duty to be there. Hear that, ol' body? They're bloody lucky, really, damned lucky I'm still in one piece. Bouncin' on and off that raft on the bloody Pacific was not me idea of a good time at the beach. Oh well, the whole lot of 'em will be out of here by noon."

As he wandered to the shoreline sipping coffee, he heard the crew tented by the chopper stir.

"Ah, you be me friend, Mr. Coffee. Aye, me rather have thee than a woman first thing in the morning. Well, on second thought, let's not go overboard, Joe. You need her warmth at times . . . her love all the time. Me coffee will be the first test of these blokes; we'll see what they're made of," he said with a chuckle as he approached the tent. He went over his role in today's operation as formulated last night. He certainly had a new appreciation of Captain Dice's Delta Force and the interwoven aspects of a Russian submarine on our shores. It was neither a simple operation, nor the kind he'd like to be involved with on a daily basis.

"There you are, m'man. Top of the mornin' to you, Captain."

*   *   *

The chopper banked slightly as it approached, then slowed and hovered. Joe protected his eyes from the stinging sand. It leaned back and thumped louder as it settled down, the backwash from its rotor-blades lashing the pad.

With blades still whapping, the side door slid open, and a sergeant in gray fatigues hopped out holding a M4 carbine and sporting a backpack. He looked like a Navy Seal, with blackened face, on a serious mission—no greetings allowed—as he searched the area with his eyes.

"What the bloody hell is this?" Joe muttered to himself.

Four more Seals hopped down, several loaded with packs of electronic and communications gear. Last to jump was a tall man, thin, with black hair and bony face, without face paint, wearing similar, but blue fatigues. After he gave the four men some instructions, two trotted up to the knoll above the cave in single file, the other two split with one checking the northern perimeter, the other to the south. The two that checked the perimeter met at the beach, checked Joe's tent and the fire pit, and returned. The other two signaled from the top of the basalt outcrop that the area was clear and they were setting up the communication link. Likewise, the two that checked the clearing reported.

"The area is secure, sir," barked the taller of the two with chevrons on his arm.

"Very well, take your position by the beach and let me know when you are operational."

"Yes, sir," the man replied. "Is Delta Team #2 operational yet?"

"Affirmative. They just checked in from their position to the north. They'll link headquarters to our communicators as soon as all stations are networked into our server."

"Good. We're on our way. Is there anything else, sir?" He looked at Joe with a curious *Is he all right?* look.

"Negative. I'm okay. Lots of luck."

As the sergeant and the other Seal took off to the beach, the man in the blue fatigues strode over and stepped in front of Joe.

"May I ask you to identify yourself?" he said in a neutral voice of authority.

Joe let a moment pass, paused, and responded, "Conservation Officer, Alaska Department of Natural Resources, Joseph T. Bloom." Joe, too, sounded authoritative. He did not move.

"Very well. I am Captain David Dice, U.S. Navy, Special Ops Group, Washington, D.C. May I be the first to congratulate you for the professional manner you and your department personnel managed the discovery of the Soviet Pilot?

Joe was taken aback. *This is more like it. I may have misjudged these folks. Bloody well, this ol' bloke may be okay.*

"Captain, I'm certainly glad to hear you speak. I wasn't sure what was going on. All I knew is that my boss in Juneau, Geez, said there would be some assistance arriving to help the Soviets recover their downed pilot. This is more than I had planned on. So, welcome. Why all the military presence?"

"You're question is valid. Say, may I get a cup of that java, Joe, and we can chat by the fire?"

"Sure enough. As they say, if you've got a cast iron stomach, I've the coffee for you. Well . . . you decide, others say that, not I."

"Fine, I'll be right there. I need a short word with the flight crew."

The PIC, copilot, and crew chief were getting some fresh air when he asked the senior officer if they'd mind setting up camp and start getting some grub together for tonight. As the request was acknowledged, he turned toward Joe.

"Would you join us tonight? It's not going to be much, but we doctor up standard issue MREs better than anyone else. How 'bout it?"

"Is the Pope Catholic? Bloody well, with bells on. If someone else is cooking, I'll like it, no matter what it is."

"Very well, dinner for ten tonight," he yelled to the Navy pilot/cook. "Now, let's get a cup of your famous killing coffee, Joe."

The captain sat on the log placed around the fire and leveled about what seemed to Joe as an over-reaction to the recovery mission.

"Joe, nothing we do in the military is easy when a non-NATO nation is involved. Sure, we could have returned your call and said, 'Yeah, thanks for the coordination, you can handle it, and keep us informed. But, that's not the way it works once the State Department becomes involved."

He looked around the treeline and out toward the sea.

"You're probably not aware, nor should you be, of what has happened to this simple recovery mission. Did you notice my men checked the area to ensure it was clear? Clear of any civilian personnel. That was no accident. The surfacing of an armed Soviet nuclear sub, one mile off our coast, is Top Secret, need-to-know-only information. No one knows we're here from the DNR, except your supervisor, Geez. To be perfectly candid, if—and I repeat, if—there were any civilians in the area, they would have been detained. Let's just leave it at that. Our mission is to assist the Soviets in recovering the body of their pilot as quickly as possible; that's why you are key to the mission's success. You're the only one who has seen the body and knows its exact location. That's key to a quick timeline. This is not a typical mission—it's strictly off the books. Do you understand?"

"Now that you put it that way, yes. But, what do you mean by other support groups? Don't you think the Soviet captain will feel we're showing an excessive amount of force?"

"Yes, and no. He's used to the games we both play in and out of the Cold War tomfoolery. They do it, too. He knows how nervous our government would be with a nuclear sub knocking at the door, even if on a mission of mercy. We both know how 'tight' the political animals are. Can't you just hear the theatrical senator from the South, 'Can you believe the opposition has allowed a missile-bearing sub at our shores?'"

"Yeah, you're right . . . I've heard my share of opportunistic blow-hards at the capitol. But I'm uncertain of what other support groups are involved. What's their mission?"

"On the diplomatic level, the Soviets felt that due to the remoteness of the find, their ballistic Submarine number four-twenty-seven, out of their base in Rybatchiy Naval Station, on the Kamchatka Peninsula, would be the best recovery means available. It happened to be cruising in international waters at fifty-five degrees north latitude and one-hundred forty-five degrees east longitude. That's close. As you can imagine, that got the attention of the State Department. To make a long story short, common sense prevailed, and I was directed to pick a team to support the DNR and ensure U.S. interests were protected. Not so much for fear of life and limb, but security. That's about it. Questions?"

"Bloody well, not! I love the intrigue of nations relating to each other in the age of Detente. Or as some have said, Carry an olive branch at the end of your spear . . . and watch your arse!"

"Okay. I formed a Special Delta Force, a portion of which you see here. I have a similar unit at your Yakutat Station to the north, and at Pelican Bay Station to the south. We are in communication with them as we speak. Furthermore, all airspace inside a triangle from those two stations and Juneau are closed by the FAA, from 0100 to 1000 hours tomorrow. No commercial or general aviation flights will be allowed. A loitering AWAC command and control plane will be airborne tomorrow at 0400 hours. Two submarines from our Pacific fleet are 'informally escorting' four-two-seven to our coast: the USS Los Angeles SSN-579, and USS Dallas, SSN-587. Yes, the Soviet Captain in the Golf II, Foxtrot four-two-seven knows he's being watched. There's not much in the silent service that goes unnoticed. A Predator, unmanned aerial vehicle UAV, MQ-1A will be airborne this evening, controlled from Fort Greely, south of Fairbanks. The men on the knoll above the cave will coordinate all communications with our support group, the men on the beach with the Soviet sub.

"That's where you come in. Your prime responsibility, and a very important part of this mission, is to tell the four-two-seven crew what they need to recover the body. Records show they have four 24-man life rafts for their crew of 88. Assuming they launch one of the rafts, you need to tell them what other equipment they'll need to extract the body from the cave. Let's get to that list before another cup of your 'killer coffee,' which does live up to his name. However, be aware, we in the military can match this death defying brew. That was a long-winded briefing, but necessary. Are you ready? Any questions?"

"Damn, I'll be pickled in rum. This has turned into a massive operation. Thanks for the rundown. Who would have thunk?"

"A pleasure. If you don't mind, I'll get a clipboard and we can write down your directions for the Soviet sailors so our linguists can relate clearly your words—with few British terms, if you will. Ha! Just kidding. Be at ease, and just talk as if you're telling me what to do. They'll have sailors that speak English, so relax. Have a drink if you wish. I've never met an Englishman or Irishman who wasn't better with a little sip of the Queen's whiskey. Kidding aside, I'll go get Sgt. Marks, who will be relating data to the sub, and we'll wrap this up in no time flat."

Joe went to his tent for his bottle, thinking, *Who would have imagined an effort of this magnitude happening at old Bravo Station? And I'm right in the center of the action. Damn.*

He took a quick swig to calm his nerves, since the Captain told him to—*and that's an order*, he thought with a wry smile.

The Captain came back with Sgt. Marks, and they buckled down to work with Marks taking notes, which he'd later rewrite into brief radio-telephone jargon, clear but to the point to keep air time to a minimum.

Here were Joe's key points, some which the Soviets would be aware of, but for clarity, were repeated:

* They need a body bag and body board.

* They should bring the sub's boarding ladder. The emergency rope, now in place was inadequate for passing the body board down.

* They would need at least six men, two to remain on the raft for stability; two to remain on the ladder to hand the body down; two to enter the cave, locate the body, bag it and lash it to the board, and carry it back to the ladder. This group will need flashlights. Officer Bloom would join the group.

Joe suggested they pick him up on shore. He would direct them to the cave and join the group that enters. Upon successful retrieval, they would drop Officer Bloom on the beach and return to the sub.

"This sounds good to me, Joe. I'll condense it a little, and pass it by you and the Captain, and we'll be good to go," said Marks.

"Good show, guys. I think we're ready to go. Let's remember this is not a social call. Be ready for the unexpected, and let me know if you see anything unusual. Sgt. Marks will establish the guard watch between the seven of you for tonight. Joe, with a chuckle, you're excluded. We'll be on station at 0400 hours tomorrow, and with any luck the Soviet crew will be on time at 0600 hours and be out of here by 0700 hours. Joe, you're a key part of this mission. Be aware, there will be a sailor on the raft that speaks English. I suggest you stay focused on the mission and not chat about unrelated non-mission subjects. In other words, button up. Their so-called sailor may be a major in the KGB acting friendly, and inquisitive in a manner to get you to speak. Be just a little quieter than normal and maybe just a little rude if someone is too probative. In fairness to the Soviets though, it may not happen.

"Any question? If not, let's get some grub. I could eat a horse."

At chow, everyone had a good time trying to 'match' Joe's stories in and out of taverns across the land. None succeeded; Joe had lived too long and too fast in the UK and North America.

Later in the evening, the Captain stood, saying, "Well done, men. I feel as if we've been entertained by the Crown itself. I bid you good night, and wish you well."

As the Delta Force men retreated to their tent, Sgt. Marks took the first two-hour guard duty.

Just before entering his tent, Joe looked to the sea and tried to picture the beautiful sight he'd see in the morning: The periscope first, the conning tower second, and finally the Soviet Sub four-two-seven surfacing with its deck awash in the rolling sea.

He thought, *Isn't it wonderful that fighting men—yes nations, too—can lay down their arms in respect for one of their fallen warriors? Maybe, just maybe, mankind will soon live in harmony, sans a fallen comrade in arms.*

A raven croaked from its perch in a cedar, flapped up from the tree, and glided through the clearing, cutting the air with another rusty croak. It landed on the log by the fire pit, croaked again, and preened its feathers.

"Good night, my feathered friend. Stick around. The 'morrow will be rather interesting. Bloody well, you can count on it."

The clearing's silence returned to its normal midnight whisper of wind blowing through the cedars. The fire pit turned to glowing coals, and all the two- and four-legged slept with only the waves wop and the puffins' cooing—except for a new sound: a Predator drone turned at the coastline and headed west on its mission to track the Soviet mass below the surface of the Pacific.

Chapter 19

Recoup

All shoreline personnel were on-station at 0600 hours as the 427 raised its periscope. Shortly thereafter the conning tower slowly emerged from the depths of the Pacific. The imagery was truly surreal, an unnatural juxtaposition of the norm. Absent the small shore party, few would believe that a Russian sub was surfacing a couple of thousand feet from the western shores of the U.S. A beautiful yet menacing ship, its dull black hull contrasted with the froth and foam washing over the tower in the aquamarine sea. Unseen, but known to all, were its nuclear missiles stowed in launch silos aft.

With its antenna deployed, Captain. First Rank Vladimir Kabzar wasted no time in establishing a communications link to the shore party. By prearrangement, the U.S. Navy had directed the crew to a specific frequency of 121.5 kHz. Not surprising to either party, a COMINT team from NSA would most likely be monitoring. They all waited anxiously for the first contact.

At 0600 hours, Sergeant L. Marks gave a high-sign to Captain Dice as the first transmission came from the sub. "Shore based U.S. Command, this is four-two-seven. Over."

With a smile on his face and a whole lot of anticipation, Marks responded, "Four-two-seven, this is U.S. Command. I hear you loud and clear; send your traffic. Over."

In clear English with a midwestern flair, the sub answered, "This is four-two-seven. Roger your transmission. We await your message detailing recovery-operations procedures and equipment needed. Over."

With another grin, Marks felt relaxed. This guy Kobzar was a pro. The transmission of recovery plans should proceed without any hang-ups. He immediately relayed Joe's suggested procedures at a measured pace to ensure clarity. Upon completion, he asked if there were any questions. A short period of silence followed.

"This is four-two-seven. All items are available. We will bring our boarding ladder to climb the rock face. It should work very well. A twenty-man raft will be launched immediately. Ten men and myself will be at the shore in short order to rendezvous with Officer Bloom, who will direct our team to the cave. Agreed. Over."

"Affirmative. Bloom awaits your arrival. Over."

"This is four-two-seven. Roger. Out."

Marks and Dice watched through binoculars from shore as the sub's front hatch opened. Several sailors emerged, inflated a raft, and tossed the boarding ladder down the hull. Several men got into the raft with a body board. As they cast-off, a sailor on deck threw the ladder to them at the last moment.

The entire team was dressed in black with black knit hats, and IO/PFDs. Kobzar could not be identified among the team members.

Captain Dice contacted the team on the knoll and told them to relay to headquarters that the sub 427 was on station. The crew, along with Captain Kobzar, were on the way to shore, and would soon leave with Bloom to recover the pilot's body. Although encrypted, this message would be monitored by all military support groups, U.S. and Russian.

All shore station personnel were nervously anticipating the raft's arrival as it came closer and closer to shore. This assignment was indeed a new experience—one they would surely never forget. Working this close with the Russian sailors would be a once-in-a-lifetime opportunity.

As they approached the breaking waves near shore, one of the men hailed. "Hello, may we come ashore?"

Joe, in a bit of spontaneity, answered, "Permission granted. Welcome." Dice had filled him in on naval jargon/procedures. He was anxious to use it, and did well. Seeing "The Search for Red October," five times, helped.

In similar naval fashion, Kobzar responded, "Very well," and the raft slid ashore.

As Kobzar got out of the raft, Dice stepped forward, greeted him, and immediately introduced Joe.

"'Tis a pleasure to meet you," Joe replied while shaking hands.

"The pleasure is mine," Kobzar responded in perfect English. "Shall we get underway?"

Dice thought, with a chuckle, *Kobzar's speech is clearer than Joe's thick British accent intermixed with his Irish brogue.*

"Yes, sir. I've got everything I need in me fanny pack, and me PFD on. Let's be off. Let's go have a look," he said as he stepped aboard, saying hello to the crew in his best English.

Captain Kobzar held fast for a moment and addressed Captain Dice as the senior officer present. "In the event that we do not meet again, please pass on to your superiors Mother Russia's gratitude for the contacts that led to the recovery of our down pilot. Your Country's spirit of cooperation regarding the loss of our brave soldier is appreciated. Thank you."

Dice gave him a snappy salute, which Kobzar returned, and each gave a respectful perfunctory nod. Kobzar boarded the raft.

They moved away quickly to the north and the outcrop.

The Captain introduced team leader Chief N. Pikulik to Joe, and they briefly reviewed the recovery procedures. He also directed Joe to shadow him during the operation for two reasons: to ensure he was not put in harm's way, and to be of help to each other as they searched the cave.

As they approached the outcrop, the puffins nervously waddled to the ledge and peeked over, then launched vertically, banked toward the west, circled the raft, made a bombing run, and flew to the north.

"Bloody buggers. I'll be eating one of you for dinner—count on that," Joe hollered. The sailors who spoke English had a good laugh at Joe's comment.

A Charles Atlas type, about thirty years old, Chief Pikulik stood six feet tall. At two-hundred pounds, he was built like a brick. He grabbed the emergency rope ladder dangling from the cave and secured it to the raft. Before anyone knew, he was up the rope with the boarding ladder on his back. He secured the upper end and threw the unfolding ladder down to the raft. Within seconds, Kobzar climbed the ladder, and passed up the body board and bag to the chief.

With everyone in position, Joe hesitated. He looked down to the raft, and to the sub heaving in moderate sea swells. The horizon was dotted with white specks like clouds of corsairs watching the activity on shore. He wondered who would have thought a DNR Officer would participate in a cadaver detail with a foreign country. This was not a part of the usual career path.

The three stood at the edge of the cave's entrance for another moment before Kobzar asked, "Are you okay, Joe?"

"Yeah, I'm just easily affected emotionally by the delightful Puffin Grotto turning into a near tomb for two of me friends after the tsunami, and now a sepulcher for your pilot. I'll be all right, I guess . . . You're trained for this, and are supposed to set all emotions aside because you're military. It's almost impossible for me . . . it is emotional. I know it's kinda weird; I can look at a dead person, but I look beyond the body and think of the violence, the actual violence that caused death. I be okay. Let's go." They moved into the umbra of the cave's entrance and turned on their flashlights. Joe stopped again and reminded them that there was no path, and that they'd have to follow a switchback pattern. The captain moved in on his own. Chief followed Joe, carrying the board and bag.

They moved slowly and silently for a minute or two. Joe was first to speak. "Me friends, ye best be careful as the cave narrows. The rotting kelp is more slippery as we go deeper, and the flotsam thicker."

"How far back is the body?" Kobzar asked.

"It has to be within the next ten feet. I left a cairne—one stone piled on three. We're at about thirty feet now. Watch your step!"

"Ah, what's this? I think . . . no, it's a dead seal."

As the cave started to narrow, Joe shined his light on the wall where he had noticed an Indian raven icon earlier. After finding it, he mentioned to Kobzar that the body is near the icon. All three slowed and searched more carefully in pitch-black surroundings.

Joe yelled, "Hold it. We've gone too far. Let's turn and circle back slowly."

Joe thought, *I'm puzzled, although highly improbable it appears as if someone has been in here after me. Nah, couldn't be, it would have been last night. Still, some areas appear disturbed, perhaps an animal?*

Kobzar was separated by about ten feet, chief nearby, as they retraced their steps with more precision. At times Pikulik looked like a ghostly winged raven with the body board strapped across his back. It was no wonder; the eerie shadows darted back and forth across the cave walls as each one or the searchers wheeled his light around the debris plugged floor.

Then it happened; the silence turned to a roar of alarm.

"Over here! Here he is!" Kobzar yelled.

As quickly as possible they moved through the debris toward the captain. In an unusual move, the chief stepped in front of him. He could still see the captain, who was already leaning over the body.

Closer now, Joe noticed him doing a search of the pilot's breast pockets. He was positive he saw him remove a small white module from his flight suit.

They locked eyes and exchanged looks . . . but nothing was said. As Pikulik moved closer, the captain gave instructions on the best way to bag the fragile body. He was all business. He did not mention the discovery or removal of the module from the body.

After the torso was enclosed in the body bag, zipped up, and lashed on the body board, they moved out quickly. Joe led the pair carrying the pilot.

They had been in the cave less than thirty minutes.

At the ladder, the two sailors quickly lowered the body to the raft. Joe descended the ladder, followed by the captain, and then the chief, and said, "Wait. Would you do me a favor? I'd like you to cut off the last half of the Emergency role ladder. Would you mind?"

No sooner had the words left his mouth than Pikulik was up the rope ladder. He cut the rope halfway up the rock, then slid back down to the raft.

"A collectible?"

Joe responded, "Yes and no. I just wanted to preserve the cave as a haven for our winged creatures—it should be free of two-leggeds. This makes it a little more difficult to explore and, yes, to exploit. Don't you agree?"

The captain said, "You have a point. Yes, as you indicate, it's the Puffins' Grotto. There's no sense in enticing passing recreational boats with easy access to the cave. Good decision."

The sailors sat in silence as they rowed away from the cave. The respect for their fallen comrade was shared among all nations, all military, and all those under arms. Whether or not they are from the same country, branch or unit; fighting men honor their brothers that have fallen in the line or duty. They all know—it could be them, they could just as well be in the bag. Be it at war or during peacetime, all men and women are treated with respect at life's end.

As they approached shore, Kobzar called the sub's watch officer, Captain Second Rank Alex Zhurarin, OIC, and reported the team's status and ETA. He also gave orders directing the crew to ready the sub for immediate departure. He also mentioned that, when underway, he would personally inform headquarters at Rybachiy Naval Base about the status of their mission.

As they beached, Captain Dice held the raft while Joe deboarded.

"I presume your mission has been successful?" Dice asked.

"Right you are," Kobzar said. "As I mentioned earlier, pass my appreciation to your superiors for allowing our fallen comrade to be recovered; especially in allowing our submarine command to expedite retrieval. A special thanks to Office Bloom for his discovery and assistance.

"Lastly, I suppose we owe a debt to Mother Nature for her tectonic shift causing a deep-sea earthquake that, in turn, triggered a tsunami wave of a magnitude that yielded our lost airman from the depths of her watery breast."

"Indeed," said Dice, "we have a lot to be thankful for. Regardless of our varied beliefs, there appears to be spiritual presence in our lives that provided a special ability to survive the hazards of life's trauma. Have a good return trip."

"Very well," replied Kobzar.

"Bloody good sailing!" Joe yelled.

They watched from the beach as the fore hatch opened. Several sailors emerged. As the raft approached, someone threw the boarding ladder out. It was secured before the body was loaded. The sailors deflated the raft and followed, clearing the deck.

Minutes later the brass bell sounded on the conning tower, and the sub silently submerged to head west.

At 0700 hours Captain Dice relayed the following message.

> CINPAC Command:
> The Russian shore party has successfully retrieved the remains of their pilot without incident.
> Submarine 427 departed our shores at 0730 hours.
> All support activity can be terminated.
> Our team will report upon departure today.
> Nothing further.
> Captain D. Dice, USN

Dice reassembled the team at Joe's fire by the tent for a debriefing prior to departure.

"Thanks, guys; it looks like a pretty clean operation. Any comments?"

The communications team on the knoll had none.

Sgt. Marks reported that all commo to the sub worked very well. He was grateful that several of the sailors spoke English.

Silence followed. Then Joe noticed that the helicopter crew, the four Seals, and Dice were staring at him.

"Joe?" Dice said, breaking the silence.

"Me not being one of you blokes, I was keeping me thoughts to meself. 'Tis mine you crave, too? Here they be. First, I had the emergency rope ladder at the cave cut in half to discourage casual passersby from nosing around. "Second, and the most revealing, I now understand why the Russian's did not want us to retrieve and ship the body to a local airport for their pickup."

Dice inquired, "Why?"

"Well, I could be wrong on his purpose, but I think Kobzar intentionally concealed the fact that he retrieved a white module from the pilot's uniform as I approached the body. It could have been an innocent act, or deception. I think the latter. Something classified? An electronic state-of-the-art prototype? A cryptologic code device? Whatever. Am I full of intrigue? Am I too suspicious? Bloody well, maybe . . . what do you think?"

"No, you're not too suspicious, and yes, you should report everything observed. Others will decide if it's pertinent. For example, the pilot could have been flying an experimental plane that had a developmental module of some sort inserted in the weapons system . . . or whatever. We'll let NSA decide if your comments fit in with other intelligence-gathering activities at the time of the aircraft's fate. Like a crossword puzzle, a little information here and a word there and a sighting elsewhere—seemingly unrelated—sometimes are very significant. Get the picture, Joe."

"When you put it that way, yes. I'll be darned."

"One last item. I could swear, it appeared that someone or an animal was in the cave after me, and before the team arrived. It looked as if the debris had been shifted . . . rearranged a little. I can't explain it. You?"

"There was a lot more going on during this recovery, but you do not have the, 'need to know' and are not cleared TS/Crypto, so what I'll do is share with you what I can. Here's one humorous item. Ready?"

"Sure."

"Do you really want to know the Russian view of your participation in the team?"

"What do you mean?"

"You'll get a kick out of this. Better grab your arse. Our COMINT monitors picked up a conversation that indicated that you were really an undercover intelligence agent posing as a DNR officer to divert their attention. Your British accent contrived and your pedestrian manner another distraction. How do you like those marbles?"

"Ha, I'll be damned. I'll be tellin' this one to me drinking buddies."

The captain's demeanor suddenly changed. "Correction. You'll be unable to tell anyone about the operation that you were in. You'll tell no one. To the world outside this group, this team, this action did not happen. Understand?" More importantly, do you understand why it is classified TS?"

"Yes. I understand. Damn there go me bragging rights. You bloody buggers, you take all the fun out of me storytelling by shutting me up."

"Yes, and no. Be aware you can share your tales with your boss, Geez. He's been on board from the start; he can be your drinking partner."

"Bloody well, maybe I can get him 'in his cups' and ask for a raise."

"Off the record, I think you're in line for deserved recognition and a nice raise."

"Thanks for the compliment. After a pint, maybe he'll reach for his checkbook."

The team had a good chuckle at Joe's quandary. They, too, experienced tight lips about their work to their families or a weekly basis.

They all shook hands, walked back to the chopper, loaded, their gear, and prepared to leave. In a moment of deep respect, each man saluted Joe in recognition of his contribution, then got aboard. Another assignment awaited.

The blackhawk powered up, leaped into the air, and thudded across the treetops to the east.

After requisite coordination to headquarters, Dice made a short statement to the team. "As you're well aware, without a need-to-know, and the requisite clearance, I could not tell Joe what we did last night. That is, that two of you rappelled down the rock from the knoll and entered the cave last night. And that, our search of the pilot's garment did not turn up anything of significance. The module was a simple add on for his on-board computer for navigational operations. We're well aware of this technology. So we left it in place. There was nothing else of value. Good ol' Joe has enough stories to tell, he doesn't need this one. I dislike being less than frank about the operation . . . but that's the nature of our business. He did notice someone had been in cave . . . bugger. He's a good one, I've known some field men who *couldn't run a bordello in a gold rush*. Yep, Joe's a keeper."

*   *   *

Joe was alone again. He looked around for some of his animal companions, and sure enough raven was perched on his log pile, preening.

"Welcome, me friend. Would you mind if I took leave and had a noontime nap? I've had a busy couple days."

By twelve-thirty the only sounds altering the silence of the clearing were the pulsating nasal noise from Joe's deep sleep, the wop of the waves curling on themselves, the cooing of puffins in the grotto, and the ever-present whispering pines.

Silently, Reynard the fox slipped into camp searching for a snack.

Chapter 20

Repose

Horses whinnied, ravens croaked, birds sang, and wolves yawned as the eastern sky brightened, turning from blue to pale yellow. The planet Venus stood twenty degrees above the horizon, a point of light dying in the brilliance of the approaching sunrise over the meadow.

A cell phone buzzed at the hut.

"Hello," Leigh answered in her less-than-enthusiastic morning voice.

"Bear, is that you? This is Geez at the office."

"Do I sound *that bad?* No, it's Leigh, the faithful, understanding wife of the husband you so arbitrarily filched from me the day of our honeymoon . . . without regard for *my feelings.*"

"Damn, that's a good one. Wait a sec, I've got to write that down."

"What's up, skunkboss?"

"You sure know how to hurt a guy. I'm really a loveable old guy. I'm damned if I do and damned if I don't. With you, I'm just trying to give your hubby as many opportunities as possible," Geez pleaded. "You may, or may not, like this one. I'll be as nice as I can, sweetie-heart-baby," he groaned. "I'm afraid to ask if he's around. You probably would not let me talk to him."

"Matter of fact, he's not. He's been fishing since dawn. And yes, since you've a probative mind, as I imagine, we've already had our morning BNR."

"Sweetheart, give me a break."

"Stop it! Don't call me sweetheart! Get on with your business."

"Okay . . . w-o-m-a-n, you asked for it. Here it is, unadulterated. As you know, Bear has finished the FAA part-one ground school for his private pilot's license, passed his physical, and his injured back appears to be repaired. As such, he's scheduled to start flight training at FFS in Skagway tomorrow. Milt and Dave, his instructors, are flying by the meadow from a freight flight to the coast, and will pick him up at around 1400 hours. That's it. Are you upset, or thankful?"

"You know, I'm not answering the phone anymore when you call. You're affecting my pleasant personality. How long will he be gone?"

"About five to six days, depending on weather. He could be back before you know he's left."

"Would you stop it! Don't try to butter me up, you've done enough damage to this marriage."

"Pooo babbbee . . . boo hoo hoo hoo. I don't believe a word of it."

"Okay. Now you're in for it. You'd better put up your dukes next time we meet. Better yet, I may kick you in your big arse!"

"Hey, that gives me an idea. I have not seen you in a while, nor all your expanded family. Why don't we all meet for dinner in Skagway on the day Bear graduates. We'll make it a big deal, and you can kick me in the arse, too. I'll buy. Yep, bring the whole gang. I owe you that at least. I'll see if Joe can break away, too. He's still at Bravo station."

"Sounds good. I'll pass the message to the fisherman, who will take a break. I'm not about to share him with a trout when he's leaving this afternoon. Anything else?"

"Nope. Good talking to you. I'll see you in Skagway next week with bells on. Bye."

"Get ready. I might ring your bell if you rob me of my man too often. Bye."

*   *   *

Leigh strolled out to the stream with her rod, net, and creel while still upset. The truth of the matter was that she was just annoyed. Long-range plans were difficult to keep when you worked for the DNR. One thing was certain, she was not about to let him be alone today—fish or no fish.

She worked her way silently downstream to his favorite rainbow hole. Sure enough, there he was enjoying the solace of a quiet stream on Earth Mother's breast.

The idyllic setting and Bear's silent casts whipping back and forth looked too perfect to disturb. His fly rod snapped, and the line launched its fly over the deep hole for a grandpa rainbow. Again and again he snapped his wrist and pulled line to coax the fly across various spots to tease the fish to rise. At times he'd cast upstream from the hole and let the dry fly float across the hole like room service at the Ritz.

She settled down on a mat of pine needles and watched the ballet of man, rod, and nimble fly. It was too good a show to disturb as he continued his quest for "the big one."

After a while, she rose up from her vantage point when he was changing flies, and waded to the sand bar where he stood, her presence, still unknown.

"Hey, guy, try fishing for *me*. Put on a 'catch Leigh' fly."

"Hi! How are you, girl? Nice to see you. Yep, I might as well try to catch you; the fish aren't biting."

As she closed in on his part of the stream, she telegraphed the radiance of desire he had witnessed many times before. Before he knew what to do with his fly rod, she laid one on him in the middle of the glistening stream. The kiss led to a vertical lovefest of arms entangled with each other's, legs rising and finally wrapping. Physical laws of off-center gravity caused them to tilt, lean, and struggle to maintain their position, and finally yield to the pull of earth, falling ass-over-teakettle into the stream. As the rod, net, and creel washed downstream, they struggled to gain their footing.

"Are you okay?" Bear chuckled, "It appears we've chosen the wrong place to enjoy each other."

"You can say that again. Come on. Get your stuff and meet me over there where my stuff lies. Come on, it's got a nice pine needle bed exposed to the sun. Let's go, we've got to get these clothes off and sunbathe."

"Aren't you worried what might happen if we get naked?"

"Hell no! Worried? The opposite. I'm hoping something happens beyond the sun bathing in the nude. I can do that alone."

Bear chuckled, and said, "That's why I love you, woman, you always surprise me with some intriguing experiences." As they reached the pine-needle bed, he said, "Okay gal, I'll help you out of your soaked jeans if you help me do the same."

"Deal!"

Sunbathing was second on their list of tasks after they removed their clothes and lay bare-arsed to the bears in the sun.

They both expressed their heart-felt emotions to each other, making enough noise to gather a crowd. Several squirrels, a dozen winged friends, and a few mice observed the loving pair as if having seats on the fifty yard line at the Big House in Ann Arbor. As they slowly disengaged their bodies from their oneness, Bear startled Leigh, jumped up quickly, put his arms under her body, lifted her up, carried her into the stream, and plunged.

"You rat!" Leigh yelled as she wrestled him down and under the water.

"Well, consider this: I did you a favor. Someone had to wash all the pheromonal bouquet from your bod."

"Oh yeah, take this!" She tackled him hard enough to cause both to tumble downstream out of control.

They surfaced as two tired puppies, ready to call it quits, then dressed with just enough on to sneak back into camp without Raven knowing that they'd had an impassioned lovefest in the copse. Windy never paid attention to this type of thing, and seemed not to care. Conversely, Raven had a keen eye for sexual mischief, and could generally tell when the two were "messing around." No surprise—women know.

As they walked back to the hut, Leigh gave him the message from Geez. "You bugger, is that what you came out to see be me about?"

"Yes, among other things. I notice you didn't mind," Leigh said with a wry smile.

"Love you, babe," Bear said as he grabbed her butt.

"Feelings mutual, fisherman. You leave in four hours. Get ready, and hurry back. By the way, someday I'll show you the bruises on my arse from your obsession to pinch."

"I'm all eyes."

She thought, *I won't tell him that Geez had arranged to have them all come to Skagway when he graduates. He's enough on his mind . . . including me.*

*   *   *

Bear considered the J-3 Cub the most beautiful machine ever built. At distance, out on the flight-line, it looked like a yellow butterfly basking in the sun.

C.G. Taylor's early-1930s icon was simply a cool airplane to fly. Of course, this was the whole idea behind Light Sport Aircraft, LSA. It was not only cool to fly, it was a forgiving plane for learning to fly. The goal was to make it easier, faster, and a lot cheaper to teach beginners.

DNR's aim was to have Bear obtain an Airplane Single Engine Land, ASEL, pilot's license, with a tail-wheel, ski, and pontoon endorsement. At 100-bp the plane was ideal for economical training, and it had two options for seating: side by side, or inline. An added factor was its forgiving stall speed of thirty-three knots. Pilots understand this forgiving feature. Meaning, it won't stall easily (due to not enough lift on the wings) and fall out of the air.

Bear left FFS flight operations, the building where Milt and Dave instructed new students and briefed other pilots on flight operations. In one week of concentrated instructional classes on the ground and in the air he would complete his training, and live in the transient rooms at FFS, too. Weather permitting, they would fly every day and at least two nights. At the end of the week's instruction he would fly solo, and if successful, would complete his cross country-flight, first in daylight, then at night.

After receiving his ASEL license, he could advance to higher performance aircraft such as the C-150, C-172, and all-weather C-180 since the DNR operates these planes at FFS and elsewhere. After at least one-hundred hours of fixed-winged aircraft, he could apply to helicopter school.

Bear started with Dave's instructional module on FAA flight rules, cockpit orientation, and airport rules and regulations.

When he was released to Milt for actual flying, he walked out to the flight line. The weather was fine with a gentle breeze as other general aviation aircraft stood eager to take off.

Milt met him at a beautiful J-3 Cub he called an American Legend. He looked at the Cub with a little reverence, calling it the vintage tail-dragger that has introduced thousands to flight certification. Including himself. "Let's do a preflight,"

Milt told Bear, "as I explain key aspects of just why a plane flies. As shown by diagrams in class, notice the wings are flat underneath, but curved above." He asked Bear to rub his hands over the surface. "When the aircraft is moving, the air traveling over the top of the wing is forced to move faster than the air passing underneath. It creates a pressure difference, providing lift. A Swiss physicist, Bernoulli, in 1782 determined that the pressure in a stream of air is reduced as the speed of the flow is increased. So, my friend, Bernoulli's principle explained *why* a wing flies, and *why* a sail moves a boat forward, and *why* a propeller moves the J-3 through the air. That's enough science.

"The hinged surfaces here on the lower wing are called ailerons. The yoke, or joystick, moves one upward and the other downward to tilt the aircraft, which we call turning or banking."

As they walked around to the rear of the plane, Bear couldn't help but absorb the dynamics of the airport. Engines roared as planes took-off and others softly whistled in their power-off landing.

"You'll notice the rear half of the tail is also hinged. This is called the elevator. It points the aircraft up or down. Go ahead, pull the yoke back and forth and you'll see the movement.

"The vertical tail is also hinged; it's called a rudder, controlled by a pair of pedals in the footwell. They work like a rudder on a boat."

Milt asked an open-ended question. "Why do you think we need both ailerons and a rudder to turn?"

Silence.

Bear looked around the flight line and at the taxiing planes.

"I think I've got it. You can't use ailerons on the ground to turn; the wing would hit the ground. You use the rudder to steer while taxiing on the runway. True?"

"Quite true, my friend. We also use the rudder in the air to correct for sideways movement, which is called yaw."

They both walked around to the cockpit.

"Since Dave gave you instruction on the instrument panel for flight and engine controls, why don't you hop in and I'll give you a quick review? Now, don't you think it's about time for your first flight? We've already completed most of the preflight inspection. I'll do a few additional things and we'll be good to go." Milt checked a few more preflight items and rejoined Bear and asked, "Ready to fly?"

"Front or back?"

"The trainee always sits in the back."

Bear climbed in, having a difficult time easing himself through the opening. The cockpit was so narrow that he wondered how fat pilots managed, and then realized he had never seen a fat pilot. He also remembered the slogan above the flight operations door that addressed the reckless pilot:

There are a lot of bold pilots, but there are no old bold pilots.

Because of the nose-up angle at which the aircraft sat on the grass, he could see nothing in front of him but the clear blue sky. He had to lean out to the side to see the ground.

Milt showed Bear how to adjust his safety harness.

"These aircraft were designed for training, so they have dual controls. While I'm flying, rest your hands and feet lightly on the controls and feel how I'm moving them. I'll tell you when to take over.

"Take another look at the control panel. For now, let's concentrate on the six most important avionics while we're up this time. The others are important, too; we'll get to them later.

"The *air speed indicator* tells us our speed through the air via a pitot tube.

"The *turn-slip-indicator* combined with the horizon indicator tells us the position of the plane when we cannot see the ground.

"The *altimeter* gives us our height above ground based on barometric pressure.

"The *vertical speed indicator* tells if we're diverting from level flight.

"The *tachometer* provides engine/prop rpm in planning flight times/distance.

"The *magnetic compass* keeps on course in directional routes to sites/VORs.

"As I said, Bear, all the instruments are critical to a safe flight, but I'd like you to pay attention to these today. Ready to go? Let's do it! Put your headsets on and swing the mic to your lips."

Bear could hear Milt flicking some switches in the cockpit, then in an instant the engine fired up and the propeller turned.

The plane's engine roared, trembled, and vibrated.

Milt seemed to be letting the engine warm up. Then the engine note rose, and Milt turned the magneto switch to the left, both, and to the right, and back to both as a way to test if the dual ignition was working.

"Here we go," Milt said as he taxied to the runway, turned into the wind and stopped. "A few more checks, and we'll be off."

For the first time, it occurred to Bear that what he was about to do was dangerous. Both Milt and Dave had been flying for years without a serious accident, but their former boss, Ford, had crashed and died. He told himself that people died in cars, on motorcycles, and aboard boats—but somehow this felt different.

He placed his hands on the controls. Suddenly the throttle lever beneath his hand moved smoothly forward, the engine roared, and the J-3 eagerly moved along the runway. After only a few seconds, the control stick eased away from Bear's knees, and he felt himself tip forward slightly as the tail lifted behind him. The little aircraft gathered speed, rattling and shaking over the grass. Bear's blood seemed to thrill with excitement. Then the stick eased back under his hand, the aircraft seemed to jump from the ground, and they were airborne.

It was exhilarating. They climbed steadily. Milt banked right. Feeling himself tipped sideways, Bear fought the panicky notion that he was going to fall out of the cockpit.

To calm himself, he looked at the instruments. The rev counter showed two-thousand rpm, the speed sixty mph. They were at an altitude of one-thousand feet already. The needle on the turn-slip indicator pointed straight up.

The aircraft straightened out and leveled off. The throttle lever moved back, the engine note dipped, and the revs slipped to nineteen hundred. Milt said, "Are you holding the stick?"

"Yep."

"Check the line of the horizon. It probably goes through my head."

"Yep. In one ear and out the other."

"When I release the controls, I want you to simply keep the wings level and the horizon in the same place relative to my ears."

Feeling a little nervous, Bear said, "Okay."

"You have control."

Bear felt the aircraft come alive in his hands, as every slight movement he made affected its flight.

As if a seasoned pilot, he, too, came alive and gained confidence as the temporary PIC.

Milt gave him instructions on a coordinated turn using the ailerons and the rudder to prevent a slipping motion, and how to keep altitude during turns.

Then things got a little more hairy. Milt told him to fly a fixed compass course of one-hundred seventy degrees, at ninety knots, an elevation of six-thousand feet—to the Juneau VOR station—then turn, and fly back at three-hundred fifty degrees (the back azimuth of 170), at eighty knots, and five-thousand feet.

Upon completion, he was soaking wet from the stress.

As you may have guessed, Milt was not very forgiving on any large variances. Bear had to keep all parameters within his range of forgiveness: little to none. As hard as it was, Bear passed muster.

It got worse. Milt insisted that Bear do a "Power Off Stall." Bear said, no. Milt said, yes. Being PIC, he won. So, after a short refresher of the "how-to" that Dave had covered in class, Bear went for it.

At level flight, 2250 rpm, he reduced rpm to 700-800, placed the yoke to his chest, kept his feet on rudder pedals, at 5 knots the horn sounded, the Cub shuddered, the nose slowly dropped into a dive, he held the Cub straight with the rudder while losing altitude, then slowly pushed the yoke forward, pushed the throttle full to 2250, when ASI was at 80-90 knots, held the Cub level, throttled back to cruise, and level flight.

Milt warned Bear earlier that this maneuver had to he performed within 100 feet. It had taken 150 feet, so he said they'd have to do it again until he got it right. No problem, practice makes perfect.

"Can you see the airfield?" Milt said. "It's a row of buildings beside a bright green field. Look to the left of the propeller."

"I see it."

"Head that way, keeping the airfield on the left off our nose."

Until now, Bear had not thought about the course they were following. It had been all he could manage to keep the aircraft steady. There was always one thing too many to think about.

"You're climbing," Milt said. "Throttle back an inch and drop down to a thousand feet as we approach the airport."

Bear felt a little guilty; he must have been relaxing too much.

"Okay, let's take her down, Bear. We've been up for forty-five minutes. I'll take her from here."

"Good, I'd be afraid to land her."

"No problem. That comes soon enough. You'll be ready.

"The old-timers have been known to say:

Any landing that you can walk away from is a good landing."

"Ha, that's a good one. Yeah, sounds like me," Bear groaned.

Bear savored the flight time and the ground school as much as any new activity he had ever learned. He was going to embrace flight.

He had found another love.

Chapter 21

Resurgent

Bear flew cross-country solo from Skagway to Juneau to Haines and back to Skagway. At each airport, as part of the FAA rules, he came to a full stop and took off again.

He thought a lot about his next solo cross-country flight, which would be at night. He had fallen for flying in a big way, the Taylor J-3 his newfound love. He loved the evenings in Skagway shared with Milt and Dave exchanging "war stories," and his nightly call to Leigh. She never mentioned the whereabouts of Windy and Raven.

* * *

Joe kept busy helping the DNR personnel from Yakutat rebuild Bravo Station. The new living/research/dining shack would be on stilts to avoid damage from high-wave action and minor tsunami events.

The station's mascots, the noisy raven and begging fox, remained. They came in nightly for a treat by the fire. Their soft-touch? Joe. He was always good for a snack while telling tales to his DNR buddies by the fire.

* * *

Wind Spirit and Raven Maiden worked very well as a team, helping Leigh prepare for the additional people in camp. They built permanent bunk beds, a larger dinner table, and more chairs; and they talked nightly of plans to put an addition to the existing octagonal floor plan, a plan based on one person—Leigh. The new plan had merit since the young pair would be with Leigh for at least a year or two. The addition of Bear was no problem, but, two more made living conditions, especially during the Alaska winter, a mite uncomfortable. Yes, the men were gone a lot, but they would rather be at the hut on the meadow.

Wind Spirit and Raven Maiden walked frequently along the Bitterroot and the plateau to the north. Windy shared with Raven the heroic and stressful stories of Leigh's survival in the face of several bear and wolf attacks, and the loss of her dear friends and lovers, Ford, Jack, and Andrew. Her arrival at the Raven Clan Camp with Chi Mukwa was shared by both. Their meeting at camp and his recognition of her compassionate ways endeared her to him. It had been love at first sight.

He explained the reasons for escaping from Skagway after the clan left the subsistence life in the forest. Gete Wabioka viewed Windy's departure as a vision quest to manhood due to the rigors of the cross-country journey to the meadow. He did not discipline or defame; he let him go and even went so far as to suggest Leigh and Bear take him in until on his own.

He explained how his life finally had meaning, a future with the DNR, and the unrequited love of both Leigh and Bear. An epiphany? Most likely. He stopped and looked in her eyes. His watered, and he said, "Raven, then you came along and completed the picture. I'm so glad you entered my life."

Raven reached for his hands, held them tightly, and smiled in an understanding way. "Our lives have traveled parallel paths. I, too, share the need to be on my own. As you know, it was difficult to leave Gete Wabiska's care after he helped me with a troubled life in Skagway, but he did it for me. He let me go, knowing very well our love for each other would never lapse, never weaken, never fail. I love him as I now love Leigh and Bear. How fortunate we are to be together and together with them. An epiphany for me? Absolutely."

She stepped forward and embraced him in a manner that seemed so natural he wrapped his arms around her and froze.

He said, "It's happened, hasn't it?"

"Yes, I knew sooner or later our hearts would share . . . share the caring they had for each other. We had no choice. It was in the stars . . . in Manitou's realm?" He pulled away from the embrace. Their eyes locked on each other's.

It seemed like an eternity as they examined each other's emotions through their eyes.

It happened again.

Their lips met in a soft union of unknowing expectation, the determined reverie of a dream come true.

Windy came up for air, saying, "Well, dear. I'm not sure what to say. I'm not accustomed to intense feelings like this; I'd better just kiss you again."

With subtle kindheartedness, she thought, *Men! They can talk all day about hunting and fishing, but when it comes to affairs of the heart, they're mute.*

"Did you enjoy?" Raven cooed.

"Like nothing I have ever experienced before."

"Let's tell Leigh," Raven said as they walked back to camp along the river.

"Tell her what?"

"Tell her we're attracted to each other."

"I think not! She'll worry too much. Plus, knowing her, she probably already knows. In any case, let's keep our affection, our attraction to each other, under the radar. Maybe a diversion."

Raven stopped. "A diversion? What do you mean?"

"Here's the deal. I've been discussing hut addition plans with both Leigh and Bear for days. I've shown Bear the detailed plan for a small hexagon add-on, in a

KD package. Leigh always says to show it to Bear; I've done that. He likes the idea, so we've got a preliminary go-ahead. The diversion is *us*."

"What?"

"I'll tell both of them that you and me will handle everything. She's already done one. Bear's always gone. We'll be the construction managers. Do you like it?"

"Sure. But what's the twist—the gimmick—for us?"

"Right on, my dear. The operative word you used was correct: us. I'm going to suggest you and me take the plans to FFS, who fabricated the octagon, and get some cost estimates, schedule, and integration data. For speed of construction, I'm going to suggest another KD or partially assembled package delivered by helicopter. This way we can kill two birds with one stone. What do you think?"

"What do you mean, two birds?"

"As you know, we're invited to Bear's graduation this weekend. I'm going to suggest to Leigh that we ride ahead and meet with FFS and get this project underway before the north winds blow cold. Then we'll meet with them at the airfield."

"Sounds good to me. I love to ride. The horses need the exercise and we'll be snowed in soon. Plus, the sooner the better to get the addition in place. It would be a lovely trip," Raven answered with excitement in her voice. She gave Windy a peck on the lips. He tried for more, but she motioned no, there's plenty of time for that. "Let's go back and see what she says. Come on!"

"Wait up, gal. We've got to plan our strategy to make this deal a *sure thing* for Leigh."

After a little more planning, Raven and Windy presented their proposal. The "kicker" was in allowing them to ride ahead, help FFS in the planning, and join her at Bear's graduation. Geez had offered to bring everyone to graduation and the party.

They asked her to think about it, and they went out to the horse shed . . . being careful not to hold hands.

*   *   *

Leigh noticed how anxious the couple appeared to be, and their oneness in the excitement of a cross-country sojourn on horseback. It was fairly obvious. In the new layout, Windy and Raven would be taking over her and Bear's bedroom section of the hut, and she and Bear would move into a private combination bedroom/study for her writing.

Logic was on their side. Winter storms were a month away, and they needed more room for all their personal needs. Smiling, she again noticed the oneness of their plan—it was no longer Windy's. Yep, Raven had a new sparkle in her eyes when looking at Windy, and a new skip in her step as the two busily helped her around the hut.

I like Windy's assertiveness, and Raven's attitude. They are great kids, and, quite frankly, would make a lovely couple. I'm going to give them a chance to prove themselves and take the trip. After all, It's in my interests. It's got to be done, and those two can pull it off just as well as Bear and me. Yep, it's about time to turn 'em loose.

She went to the porch, saw the couple by the horses, and said, "Hey, you two, got a minute? I'll be right out." She walked out to the stable with the wolves in tow.

Raven was grooming the buckskin by the corral.

"What are you guys up to?"

"Not much. Windy is giving grain to the horses, and I'm giving them a good currying."

Windy appeared at the stable door, "Hi, Leigh."

"Hi. Say, with Raven currying, and you giving grain to the horses, and saying you're doing 'not much,' I say you're doing a lot. I'd say you're getting ready for a trail ride. You stinkers." Leigh chuckled.

"Well," Windy said.

"Don't 'well' me. You know what's up. Do you two think I was born yesterday? Chicanery wasn't either. It looks to me like you two are planning a long trail ride. Maybe to Skagway? Maybe tomorrow? Just maybe?"

Smiling, Windy responded, "What makes you think that?"

"Listen, fella, I'm not going to give that comment any credence." She laughed.

The silence was deafening as Leigh looked at Raven, smiled, and looked back at Windy with a smirk. Leigh broke the ice. "If you did go, may I ask, as your guardian, who's the chaperone for this overnighter?"

They both blurted out, as if rehearsed in a chorale, "G-e-t-e W-a-b-i-s-k-a."

"Oh, sounds like you've done a little planning." Leigh paused and let the silence speak for itself. She let 'em hang, then finally said, "In that case, it looks like we've got ourselves a project. You'd better wrap up your work here, pack a bedroll and saddlebags, and get a good night's sleep."

Raven looked at Windy and smiled. They looked at Leigh. Then spontaneity of youth emerged as both jumped over the corral. They gave Leigh a double-barreled hug and words of gratitude. Unfortunately, all three went down and rolled while Leigh accused them of being ne'er-do-wells, and crafty manipulators.

When the wolves joined in, she called a truce and told them to get on with it.

*   *   *

Chinoodin (Big Wind), generally called BW as Morning Star and Bear's boy, agreed to return Old Gal to the meadow for Gete Wabiska. The chief had successfully returned to Skagway with the smoked fish for social services to distribute. He had planned to have BW return Old Gal as an excellent way for him to be with the meadow gang—especially Leigh now that Leigh was in a spiritual tie to his dad. BW was anxious to do so. He had a short break from the local community college, and was looking forward to a leisurely cross-county ride and seeing Raven Maiden. He'd always had a crush on her in their younger years. At sixteen, he had heard she was a real beauty. The chief had arranged for him to be picked up by FFS and returned with the others to Skagway.

Slender and wiry, BW had a dark cast to his face that many thought came just short of being handsome. His black hat worn at a rakish angle, matching boots, and dark blue silk handkerchief around his neck put him in a wrangler class—at least by dress, if not in fact. A thin scar from the corner of his left eye to the middle of his cheek increased, to some, his good looks, if anything adding a suggestion of sinister dash to the sculpted features.

In a hurry to get on the trail, he left before getting word that all of the gang was planning on attending Bear's graduation. The chief had just learned himself of the rendezvous and party at the airport.

Halfway to the meadow there was an old trapper's shack where the trail split. The more difficult foot-trail over the ridgelines was shorter, but not necessarily faster, unless the hiker was in excellent physical condition. The other trail, along the river, was longer, but faster on horseback. Few locals owned horses. Regardless, it was used extensively since it provided less stress to navigate in inclement weather and at night. Needless to say, it was safer, too, except for the danger of attacks by fishing bears during the salmon run. Then again, it was a rare bear that took a break from fishing to bother a two-legged passing by. They were much like devoted fishermen; they'd rather fish than eat.

BW was enjoying the scenic river route that he had taken many times, on foot, as a boy, often with his dad or his border collie, Sitka. It always amazed him that the trails converged at the plateau near the meadow—not so much amazed, but surprised, more astounded that he was on the same trail that his forefathers walked centuries ago. Artifacts of the Tlingits' altar and spiritual symbols could still be found there. Of course, by accident, Leigh had placed her camp in the meadow next to the sacred plateau. He would visit the vestiges of the altar again, and give thanks to Manitou.

Wanting to enjoy the solitude of a ride alone over Earth Mother's breast, he switched his cell phone to vibrate, hoping he would not feel any calls. In, fact, he had decided earlier not to bring the phone, but wisely changed his mind. Traveling alone, he needed this modern commo to civilization in case something went astray.

Truthfully or not, his dad had told him many times that he rode as well as any man who had forked a saddle. He loved the out-of-doors, and upon graduation from the Tech Center he would live as close to nature as possible, even have a horse or two.

Fall had come early to the park this year. Aspens were starting to turn a bright yellow to orange, soon to turn brown. The air was brisk yet comfortable. Many animals were scampering about with prehibernation food-gathering activities. Mountains loomed in the northwest. Calving glaciers to the west echoed their fall as they dropped to the sea. The grayish waters of the river wound ahead as if to infinity, but in reality, the sea and along the meadow to Leigh's camp. His bliss was not only in riding in Earth Mother's domain, but to see Raven Maiden again. He rode on in the solitude of the Tongass.

*   *   *

The fog hanging over the meadow added an eerie dimension to the three as they left the hut at dawn.

Leigh helped the pair with curry and tack as saddle bags and bed rolls were tied to the saddle's rear.

Windy took a moment to inspect the horses' hooves, showing Raven how to inspect in and around the frog for stones or other irritants.

The wolves added a carnival atmosphere, most unusual for a typical dawn on the tranquil meadow. They were normally very lethargic till chow time at seven.

Before mounting up, Raven hugged Leigh and whispered in her ear, "Thanks, Mom. Know that I'm in love with that guy, but have no worry, we've a lot to discuss before being serious or—what may worry you—intimate; know that we've kissed for the first time last night; and know that your trust means the world to me. Love you, bye."

"Are you gals going to hug and whisper until the sun breaks the horizon? Daylight is a-burnin'. Come on, Raven," Windy urged his saddlemate.

"Okay, I'm corning," she said as Leigh gave her a parting kiss on the cheek.

As they rode away it was as if there was another presence with them, an invisible third traveler in the air, hanging between them and silence.

Leigh looked to the north along the river as the pair disappeared in the early-morning fog. It enveloped them more completely as they rode around the familiar aspen trees brightening to their true fall coat of yellow. Leigh called the wolves back from their playful chase, knowing very well where they belonged.

She walked back to the hut, talking to the wolves. "Now there goes a unique couple. They've been playing patty-cake with their emotions for weeks now. It's about time they recognized their attraction to each other. I envy the excitement of the days ahead for both them and me. What a grand time it will be watching them fall in love right under my hopeful eyes. She's probably right; there's nothing she can do to stop it now. She's got all the right reasons for falling hard. Good for her. Wind Spirit is a good man. If I was in her shoes, I'd be interested, also. He has all the right stuff, plus a fine future with the DNR. He's already proven himself to Bear, Joe, Geez, and me.

"Come on, you four-legged fur balls. Your mother Leigh has returned to her solitary life that I had started months ago—no man, no kids, no horses—just my loving wolves. Come on, let's muck out the stable and go skinny dippin'. It's been a while, with having all this company."

*   *   *

Windy and Raven rode along the Bitterroot to the east on the well-worn game trail shared now with two-legged hunters, explorers, and romantics.

Sharing events of their extraordinary lives dominated their ride. It was as if no one else existed as they exchanged positive and negative stories, each accounting of a similar trauma or, in Raven's case, disparaging encounters with men. Their anecdotes, however wretched, did not diminish the majestic Tongass scenery passing by. Nevertheless, it was lost as each was looking into the other's eyes in their animated talk.

He couldn't keep his mind off her presence as they rode side-by-side and in single file. In the face of all her earlier problems with a foster-care family, someone had done a great job in introducing her to important aspects of real-life experiences. She proffered cultural graciousness and elegance, yet, embraced the mundane and down-to-earth aspects of any group she's with. Her common place in the presence of her grace was an enigmatic shield that protected her from those who she chose to keep at bay. He had successfully penetrated that shield with a thrust and parry until he got her attention.

All shades of men had dreamed of girls like Raven. Yes, the world was full of women, thousands of them, good women, fine women, and many cluttered with charm, but there was only one woman like Raven.

She had been riding all morning and she still locked elegant in her wool riding skirt and soft gauntlet gloves. Her blouse was open on a throat smoother than fall's sunshine and firm as the look she gave him.

The turquoise depths of the fall sky above was no bluer than the blue in the gray silk handkerchief about the collar of her blouse. All were complimented by the rich olive on her face.

Wind Spirit spoke. "We'll have a chance to rest and water the horses ahead. There's an old trapper's shack ahead."

"Good. My butt needs a rest, too."

*   *   *

Big Wind dismounted at the old trapper's shack by the river. It was at the junction of the river trail's separation from the foot trail over the ridges to the south. He knew he was soft. The first day in the saddle had taken its toll on his body. The saddle brought out aching protest from muscles he was unaware he had. Then, as the warm rays of the sun fell on his face, he felt just a little lazy. Life, which had slowed while in school, returned to its vigorous past while riding into the Tongass. He felt sore, yes, but good in the way exercise offers.

He loosened the saddle's cinch on Old Gal, then let her feed on the grass by the river while he rested.

His dad, Bear, and he had traversed this area many times when he was younger and still learning the ways of the forest. They had run trap lines, hunted deer, and occasionally stalked the menacing grizzly. His vision quest took place just over the mountains to the west. Yes, he embraced the Tongass as his second mother. Earth Mother had taken care of him many times.

He felt confident that his parents had provided a rich experience in the subsistence lifestyle of the past, likewise urging him to go on to technical school. Although separated, they were still very supportive. His mother, Morning Star, was dating now and still provided not only continued nurture and support, but still allowed him to live with her to save money. With any luck, he would graduate in the spring, interview in Juneau, get a job, live on his own, and still be able to visit family and friends periodically in and around Skagway.

Holding Old Gal's lead rope, he rested his sore muscles on the river bank and fantasized about his future, and seeing Raven again, and telling her about school and his plans to move to Juneau. The sun bathed his face. Moments later, he slipped away to a dreamy sleep.

A short period of time later, or was it hours, he had an illusion in his dream. Was it a figment of his imagination or real? He pictured Raven Maiden standing in front of him—saying something to him. A phantom image? An apparition? What was it? He grew restless.

*   *   *

"Look ahead, Windy," Raven said. "There's the shack. Wait, there's someone at the shack. See the horse? I'll be darned, it's Old Gal. Old White must be bringing her back."

"Could be. Let's ride up and find out."

Windy anticipated a joyous reunion with Old White as they approached the shack. As they got closer, it proved not to be.

"Windy, it's not the chief; it's BW. Look, he's over there zonked out."

"I'll be darned. He must be bringing her back for the chief. Why don't you go and wake him up, and I'll take Old Gal for a drink?

Raven approached him carefully, and said, "BW! Wake up. It's Raven and Windy. H-e-l-1-o!" Nothing. "Hey! It's me," Raven hollered. Nothing.

Windy approached. "Here, take Old Gal. I'll give it a try."

After Raven left, BW rose, looked as if to see where he was, and said, "Hi, guys!

Fancy meeting you here." With a big grin on his face, he said, "Looks like you caught me napping. How the heck are ya? Strange, I would swear that I was dreaming of Raven, but it was no dream, no illusion . . . she is here."

Windy quickly spoke, not liking the line at which his comments were going, and said, "Yep, she's the one that woke you up, it was no vagary. She's down by the river watering your horse."

BW said in a cocky way, "That's great. I'd love to see our Tlingit Eye Candy. Yep, that's good news. Thankfully, I'm not hallucinating. I'd like to get to know her better. What are you guys doing out here?"

Not quick to answer, Windy sensed trouble with his presence. He thought, *They do know each other quite well. He's two years older, soon to graduate from tech school, and, worse yet, seems to have his eyes on her in an impassioned way. That's not going to happen while I'm around.*

BW wandered down to the river where Raven was giving Old Gal a drink. Windy followed with vengeance on his mind. BW's Eye Candy term for Raven did not set well with him. If BW made a move on her, and did not heed Windy's warning, violence would follow. He shook it off for the moment.

"Hey, guys," Windy yelled. "Let's take a snack break and see who's going where and when."

Raven yelled back, "Good idea; I'll break out our snack. Come on, BW, join us. Let's hear what you've been up to."

Chapter 22

Reaction

"Windy, when you're hurting, I bleed," Raven whispered.

"Yeah," Windy sighed, "but it's his attitude that bothers me. He's become a little elitist, quick to judge, and a little too gregarious for me."

"That's just a little overstated, don't you think? You're jealous, as you should be. That I like. Yes, he's a little too forward. But, I think you're overreacting a little. Settle down. I've given him the indirect signals that you and I are close. He's just a little dense to my cues. Why? 'Cause he doesn't want to be rejected, but he knows. All of us use the same avoidance technique against rejection. Our egos demand it. Believe me, he knows. Okay?" Raven pleaded.

"I guess you're right. I have never trusted—nor wish to be with—one who acts like a bigwig or portrays himself in a high-minded fashion. Going to college has changed BW. I'm not sure I like the new model."

"Please, put your concerns to rest. He is just a storm cloud passing through. He's gone now. Take it easy."

"Okay. Know I care for you," Windy responded.

Raven had sensed BW's aggressive nature at their first meeting by the river, and again when they had a quick snack together and chatted. They had decided BW should continue on to the meadow, return Old Gal, meet with Leigh, and fly back for Bear's graduation. They knew Leigh was anxious to see her new stepson. As BW mounted and waved goodbye, Windy gave him a perfunctory wave.

Hoping it was not just an ephemeral thing, a mystical path to happiness, Raven rode through the majestic rainforest as if it were a hidden valley, a niche in her life to share with Windy. Could it be just a once in a lifetime experience with her new parents, her new love? Could it be that she had finally found her love of life—her home?

It could, of course, be a lovely illusion, the lush Tongass river bed, shielded by giant Sitka spruce and golden cedar titans soon yielding to the fringe of civilization. She knew it would end as they approached Skagway and the Lynn Canal; but for now, the jungle-like glens of fallen timber, dancing ferns interlaced with spider webs, and moss-covered rocks presented a verdant blanket on Earth Mother.

She smiled at Windy.

He returned the look, and asked if she was okay.

She nodded an unspoken gesture of gratification.

As expected, the inspired trek's pleasure ended on the outskirts of Skagway. Several people were ahead, probably on one-day trips along the river. Some looked like serious hikers. A few college kids wore bathing suits and sandals, and one or two were obviously Alaskan tramps, bearded men in ragged clothes, furtive looks. They were probably living in the forest, but close enough to town to walk in for their food stamps and welfare allotment of subsistent items.

They rode past half-naked kids with boomboxes blaring through the solitude of the timber as some bathed naked in the river. Next to them, apparently unseen, were piles of garbage, waste paper, and discarded boxes.

Yes, they were back to civilization where many people do not respect Earth Mother's gifts.

They continued riding west, close to the salt water in the Lynn Canal. Seagulls appeared in the sky, circling and crying. The air took on fragrances of the sea along with the not-so-pleasant stench of brackish pools of stagnant tidal water. Waves crashed against shoreline rocks. There were very few natural beaches along the canal. As was the case on most of Alaska's shores, the water generally joined the shear face of vertical at the water's edge. Where a sandy beach existed, it was man- or stream-made. Other limited beaches were full of boulders, broken and busted trimmings from lumbering, and flotsam.

They rode on the northern trail around Skagway and the tip of the canal to the eastern side where FFS had a significant corporate presence. By the time they reached the airport, a considerable parade of barking dogs and curious kids were under tow.

They had called ahead, so Milt had made arrangements for them to stay in one of the transient rooms next to Bear's. Milt and Dave had horses, also, so theirs were taken care of by a young boy who worked for them.

The evening was going to be somewhat dramatic, as Bear was flying his last cross-country leg—at night. While he was flying, Windy and Raven, the newly formed construction team, would be going over building plans. Better yet, they'd be in Flight Ops where they could also listen in on the progress of Bear's flight.

Bear was not there when they arrived, but his directions on sleeping arrangements had changed from what Milt had made. Raven would be staying alone in one of the rooms—Windy with Milt. He had given Milt "the business" for thinking it was okay for them to share a room. The term "knuckleheaded" was used by Bear to describe Milt's decision. Of course he claimed he didn't know how they slept at the meadow. Weren't they in the same room in separate beds there? Bear told him in no uncertain terms that he and Leigh are in the same room, too.

Bear was out on the flight line when Dave went out to greet him and Milt. Dave and Milt returned after checking in, taking care of the horses, and watching Bear take off.

They went over the plans while listening to Bear report to the FFS the required completion of key points along the route, or any anomalies. The radio was his only backup; its presence gave him a shadow copilot—an aide when in need of advice—especially when getting out of jam.

As they poured over Wendy's drawings, sketches, and plan view of the hex addition, they started running the numbers. Milt called out various construction materials as Dave entered the price estimate into a calculator with a tape print out. Upon completion of what seemed to be an endless list of lumber, aluminum sheets, and exotic epoxies, Milt stopped. "That's it!"

Raven said, "I'm afraid to see the total."

Dave asked again, "Are you sure you want to do all the integration work? I won't figure any on-site labor if you say so. There's no plumbing, but there is electrical power and telecommunications wiring. Can you do that, too?"

Windy said, "No sweat, Dave. All we're doing is adding a junction box for both power and a speaker in the bedroom. The solar battery-pack and transceiver do not move. Right?"

"True," Dave responded. "We'll prewire both lines and give you a connector for the two wires. Okay, we're good to go, if you say so."

"All right, Dave," said Milt. "Hit the little red total key. They're ready to go."

As Dave filled in the worksheet, Milt explained to Raven what Bear was doing in the J-3. The radio/telephone chatter from the tower provided background noise.

"The field is about to close to tower-assisted take off and landing—TO&L—and switch to an automatic broadcast system of weather conditions. Operations will continue, but pilots will have to use visual- or instrument-flight rules for TO&L."

He explained how Bear would be evaluated on several new aspects of flight:

* Under VFRs by landing without tower assist on a lighted runway, coming to a complete stop, checking for clearance, and flying to the next airport in a prescribed manner.

* Knowing when to scrub the flight due to a low ceiling, fog, or excessive cloud cover.

* Knowing when to fly to the alternate field when the instructor closes the primary one he had planned for in his flight. The problem could be ground fog or a mechanical problem, etc.

He added that he and Dave had decided not to throw any contingencies into his flight; Bear was nervous enough.

"Bingo. I've got a number," Dave hollered. "Wanna know?"

Windy answered, "Nope, that's for Leigh. We'll see her tomorrow. How 'bout a schedule?"

"Two weeks," Dave said. "If you can complete the foundation by then, we'll decide how much of the hex will be KD or totally assembled, and be there one way or the other."

Milt told them of the difficulty Leigh had in building the octagon, saying the hut was built KD and air-dropped on four separate pallets over two weeks, with Leigh assembling the entire hut by herself. It seemed like years ago, but in fact was only last year. The chopper made things a lot easier. In the old-days, Ford delivered everything with his old 1970 Cessna C-190, which he called Big Red.

Dave added, "In any event, we've got all the materials and time in the shop to start immediately."

Windy and Raven looked at each other with big grins. She was eager to tell Leigh. With any luck they could wrap up the deal tomorrow. She would run it by Bear, but she was pretty sure he'd go for it, too. If around, he'd even be there to help.

"Listen," Milt said. "Bear's landing at Juneau on the end of his first leg . . ." All strained to hear, looking at the speaker as he was asked for clearance, received it, and landed. "His commo skills have improved, crisp and to the point."

He did get a little jocular with the tower when he stopped at the end of the runway R-27, and said, "Juneau tower, this is N-37. The landing was on the wheels, and right side up. Request permission to depart. Over."

"N-37, Roger. Have a good flight. This is Juneau Tower. Out."

*   *   *

Bear did a nominal preflight on the taxiway, then powered onto the runway, set the brakes, did a run up, and checked the critical instruments. He released the brakes and powered down the runway, lifting the tail. At 80 mph, he pulled the yoke back and cleared the deck.

After gaining altitude and turning away from the main, he headed to Yakutat at 280 degrees and reported to the tower when he cleared Juneau airspace. This was the longest leg at 250 miles over Lynn Canal, Glacier Bay, and the big timber of Glacier Bay National Park.

He cut power to 80 percent and watched his instruments. After passing over Glacier Bay, there was nothing but darkness ahead—no towns, no coast, no beacons, no landing site for all 100 miles. The J-3 purred like a kitten as he kept referring to his trusty altimeter. He didn't want to be 'goosed' in the butt by big timber. Fairweather Mountain at 15,300 feet came into view on the horizon, to the port side, as he cruised by at 5,000 feet.

As the Cub cruised through the night air, he fell in love with the sound of that beautiful engine. He thought to himself, *I've never heard a more pleasing sound than your purr, baby. Keep it up.*

He continued to fly west-northwest without any reference to where he was, except by his instruments and the stars above. Alone, yes, but for the J-3.

*   *   *

BW approached the meadow in the afternoon, anticipating meeting Leigh after so many months and wanting to make a good impression. He also desperately wanted out of the saddle to rest his sore butt.

He rode out of the shaded path where the gurgling river and scampering marmots had kept him company. He entered the sunlit silence of the meadow. Normally the wolves would be out and about to greet strangers. He wondered where they were. Old Gal found her own way to the stable. She knew where the grain and good rest resided.

As he dismounted, the horse's ears perked up and her head swung toward the east end of the meadow. "What is it, Gal? Is something out there? Let's get this tack off you and give you some well-earned rest."

After giving her a good rubdown and grain he gave her a pat and looked around.

There was no noticeable sound, yet the silence felt eerie. It was too quiet. *Where is everybody?* he thought. He walked toward the hut, still looking eastward—and it happened!

"Yipe!" A roar! "Yipe!" Echoed across the meadow.

"What the hell!"

He ran in the direction of the noise. Halfway across the meadow, he strained to see what was going on. There was a thrashing sound in the thicket at the edge of the meadow near the tree line, then a hissing-like sound, then a grunt followed by a huffing and puffing growl.

Bear, he said to himself. *What the hell!*

He heard the howl of a wolf, followed by a "Yipe."

"God damn! The wolves have a bear cornered, and here I am unarmed."

Gotta think. What to do?

Then he heard a strained voice.

"BW!" Leigh shouted. "I'm in the tree over here! The bear drove me up here and the wolves are holding him off!"

"Leigh!"

"The hut! Run to the hut and get my 9mm from the bed stand. Hurry! One wolf is already down!"

"I hear ya; I'm gone!" BW yelled as he dashed back toward the hut. The sounds grew louder. The bear seemed to be increasing the tempo of his bloodcurdling roar. The slobbering chomp of his teeth was followed by another yipe. BW found the 9mm and ran back through the meadow as fast as his legs would carry him to the center of the thrashing. He slowed to a quick walk, holding the gun up in two hands, ready to shoot. They had moved to another location, so he searched at a fast walk, looking for the black beast.

From the tree, she shouted, "Over here! Go to your right! Yes, that's the way. Do you see him yet? Another wolf is down. Shoot that sonofabitch before he gets another one—or us. Shoot him!"

BW moved to his right through some brush and tall grass.

"I see him."

He moved forward aggressively, and found the black mass just as he swiped Tough across the belly and tossed him in the air. The bear spotted him, and while coming to his hind feet and snapping his teeth, he lunged forward.

Ka-pow! Ka-pow! Ka-pow! the 9 barked.

The black mass did not seem to be distressed by the first shot, nor the second to the heart, but the third to the throat dropped him. He got up, again, spun, and punched at his wounds, then came at BW swinging his paws wildly. His last act was to lunge in BW's direction with one last ounce of energy. It was the lunge of a warrior in his death throes. The gallant last attempt at conquest, a fight to the death found in all carnivores—man included.

Ka-pow! Ka-pow!

Even with the bear seconds from death, the shots were for self-preservation, just in case . . . they are tough bastards.

He took his eyes off the bear and looked for Leigh in the tree. She was not there. Panicked, he yelled, "Leigh, where are you? Leigh!"

"Over here! By Tough! He's been hurt."

Seeing Tough thrown by the bear, she had shimmed down the tree—quickly. Both Tough and Jet were down. The White was at her side as BW forged through the tall grass.

She stood and gave BW a hug, then quickly checked Tough's injuries. "It looks like he has some cracked ribs. Here, you stay with him and I'll check on Jet. He got bit first. He knew no better. He charged the bear with courage, all alone, not knowing the pack strategy. He's learned his lesson. He'll be okay. Another case of a torn pelt and cracked ribs. You're gonna make it, won't you, babe?" She kissed his scared little muzzle. "This is the second attack and broken ribs for Tough. He's turning out to be a real survivor."

BW thought, *I wonder if she knows she has lost the top of her bathing suit?*

She carried Tough over to him, then finally got her breath as The White attended to her pup, Jet, by licking his muzzle.

"Okay, what's next?" BW asked.

"Let's carry the wolves back to the hut, do what we can for them, and clean up. You carry Tough. I'll carry Jet."

"Okay, let's go."

"We'll come back later to check on that black bastard. I'll bet you he's got a physical problem of some sort that made him hostile. It's generally the case. Black bears are not violent. I've chased many away with a broom."

As they walked back across the meadow, she thanked him for not saying anything about her bare chest. She explained that the pine tree took her top when she made her quick exit. "Some damn branch wanted it, and I wasn't about to go get it while you and the wolves were risking your lives to kill that bastard. Hey, I'm sure you've seen a couple of conical pairs by now—in fact, probably several pairs. I wasn't concerned about you—the plumber, maybe, but not my stepson."

They cleaned up the injured wolves, wrapped their rib cages, and gave them each a knock-out pill so they'd sleep. Finally, Leigh threw on a T-shirt.

"Well, let's go for a swim. You're full of trail dust, and now wolf hair and blood. Me, the same, and add pine pitch and bark scrapes. Come on, doff your shirt and pants. I've got to wash them anyhow. When we're both clean we can relax a little. Come on."

As they walked to the river, she thanked him again for coming along when he did and putting his life on the line for her and the wolves. "I'll never forget your act of bravery. I'm proud to be your stepmother."

She told him how they had all gone swimming and the bear came out of nowhere to attack them in the water. The bear had blocked her route to the hut and chased her across the meadow. She hoped to circle back to the hut and get her gun, but it was not to be. She mentioned that the spirit of Manitou must have been with both of them today, her for the temporary escape and BW's arrival, him for his success in killing the inordinately mean bear without injury to himself.

Their thankfulness was offered to Manitou with a short prayer.

"On a less serious note, tell me what you've been doing, my son."

They jumped into the Bitterroot and washed the day off their backs. The White followed, and the three continued the wrestling . . . where she had left off earlier. Perched above was their guardian . . . a beautiful raven.

Chapter 23

Rapture

Bear talked to the phantom or shadow copilot. "At two-hundred fifty nautical miles, this leg to Yakutat is kinda tight. Tight on fuel, the maximum range on this gal is two-hundred fifty-nine. I hope Lady Luck is with me. At least there is no apparent headwind, and she's holding at sixty-six knots at eighty-percent lower."

He had acclimated his eyes to night vision soon after leaving Juneau, but still had no definition to the front. The blackness continued from all directions, save vertical. There was no reference except the distant meeting of the horizon's blend to the stars.

No lights shined from the park below. If there were an isolated cabin or two with outdoor lights, they would not be seen at 5,000 feet. Yes, Leigh's camp was below, but the only light there would be supplied by the moon. She did not believe in yard lights. There would be no vehicle lights, since there were no roads in the park. An alternate landing site was nowhere to be found. With or without lights, any break in the canopy was minimal. Leigh's meadow, or the plateau to the north, was open for about 300 feet, but almost impossible to land on. The openings were surrounded by 100-foot titans, and the surface would certainly try to snag the cub's oversized tires—yep, an upside-down landing possible.

Bear was reminded of his ground-school instructions by Dave at FFS, *When ditching over timber, enter the treetops at a forty-five degree angle and hope the shearing effect of the tree limbs lets the fuselage penetrate sans wings, landing gear, and tail slowing the impact of the cockpit.* Dave's words were not that comforting. What if the canopy turned the fuselage into an accordion? Bottom line: survival by ditching in big timber, at best, gives the pilot a 50/50 chance to live.

He noticed the plane tended to climb as fuel was expended, and then remembered Dave's comments. *The aircraft's CG changes during fuel burn to compensate for the constant pulling on the yoke; to keep level flight, the elevator trim tab lever must be adjusted. It is set forward during takeoff and must be adjusted to the center to retrim the aircraft.* He moved the lever until the plane flew level without any pressure on the yoke. He could relax a little more now.

Bear was thankful that Dave also upgraded the J-3 Cubs at FFS with a transponder. The Garmin GTX 320 added another safety factor to flying. It's a radio that upon receiving a certain signal emits a radio signal and that is used to locate and identify the aircraft. With this equipment, all airports with towers would know who is flying into their airspace, including speed, direction, and altitude—all without contacting the pilot. For example, the tower at Juneau knew exactly where he was flying at the present time.

Since Alaskan general aviation had the highest incidence of accidents, knowing where a plane was prior to a crash was valuable. The ground school presented some shocking data. Both the sky and terrain were hazardous. FAA data indicated there were a total of 1,665 aviation accidents in Alaska for the 10-year period of 1990-1999, an average of an accident every other day, with a fatality every nine days, making aviation the most dangerous profession in Alaska; 11% would die in accidents compared with 2.5% average in the other 49 states combined.

Bear was concerned about this data, to be sure, so besides this upgrade he carried his handheld GPS in the cockpit. It was invaluable on the ground as well as the cockpit. It, too, would be added to the avionics suite soon.

FFS had as a corporate goal to improve flight safety by decreasing Controlled Flight Into Terrain (CFIT)—pronounced "see-fit"—also known as "Wings and Smoke in a Hole." The description was just as imagined. The pilot could not see due to fog, rain, or a snow-induced "white out" and flew into the side of a mountain, unenlightened or ignoring flight instruments.

Thump

The plane shuttered and dipped suddenly, and leveled off.

"Oh my God! What was that?"

He looked to the port and saw a flock of Canada Geese in a line, looking quickly to the starboard, the same.

"God damn, I just took-out the lead bird—I think, I hope that's all it was."

He opened the port window very carefully and looked out to the wings and the tail. Nothing. He leaned out a little further, and looked down to the landing gear. There it was, goose liver "pate" spread all over the landing gear struts.

"Holy cow! Am I lucky, or what? That's the strongest part of the plane. Hitting any other surface . . . and I'd be spiraling into the trees below. Thank you my fine feathered friend. No, life is not fair to migrating birds either."

He whispered a prayer of thanks to Manitou for his life.

As he flew on, he remembered Dave mentioning that NASA had lost one of their astronauts when a goose crashed through the canopy of his T-38 at 500 mph.

Bear knew the risks associated with flying as just another aspect of an aggressive lifestyle living in, and now flying over, the Tongass. He embraced adventure, did not fear the unknown, much like one of his favorite essayists, French philosopher Michel Montaigne, who wrote of life's challenges:

> Whenever your life ends, it is all there. The advantages of living
> is not measured in length, but by use; some have lived long, and

lived little; attend to it while you are in it.
It lies in you, in your will, not in the number of years, for you to
have lived enough.

He had been "bear bait" and "wolf bait" more than once, and survived; attacked with knives, guns, and all sorts of weapons by poachers and survived; had prevailed after several perilous helicopter flights over water and the forest and survived. This flight, although hazardous, was like a walk in the park compared with some of the predicaments he'd been in both with two- and four-legged animals. So far, he'd escaped the grim reaper.

After looking at his GPS, his watch, and fuel consumption, he said to his girl, "Okay, Babe, my figures indicate we're about twenty miles out from the YUK/VOR navigational aid. At thirteen miles per gallon, and having only two gallons left, I'm at 234 miles, or enough gas for about 25 more miles. I hope I'm figuring correctly. I'll maintain this elevation until five miles out, descend to 2,500, swing over the shoreline, and approach the runway from the west. That way I can fly over the airport, turn on the landing lights, and check for a clear runway. I don't need a moose welcoming party in the center of the runway. Let's see, it says here the 'light-on' freq is 121.9 KHz. I'll also call ATIS first and check for local weather and wind direction since there is no tower and base ops is sure to be closed."

He banked to the portside, diverting from 260 degrees, descended to 2,500, and leveled off.

An odd noise distracted him. At first he could not figure out what it was. The engine note had been steady for so many hours that he had ceased to hear it. Then it came again, and he realized the engine had misfired. He felt his heart had stopped. He was about to fly over the Pacific for his final. If the engine failed him now, he would have to ditch in the ocean.

It coughed again.

The engine continued to misfire and sputter.

He thought, *What the hell was the condition that occurred when descending from altitude? What the devil was it?* He was instantly bathed in sweat. *What to do? Then he remembered: carburetor icing.*

At lower altitudes the air is more dense and full of moisture, especially along the coast. The tapered venturi tube in the carburetor lowers the air temperature, and the intake fills up with ice, narrowing the opening and restricting air flow.

He immediately turned on the Carburetor Heat switch and waited. Within 10 seconds the ice melted, and the engine seemed to catch and roar back to its previous purring note. The revs also returned to 1,900 without missing a beat.

He looked to the port side to see if he had crossed the shoreline. No such luck. He then banked to the starboard, and to his delight he saw what appeared to be the night lights of Yakutat. He quickly checked his GPS . . .

Ah, he was right on the correct lat/long. He banked to the port and headed west. Finally he noted the stark change from the deep blackness of the ground to the luminescence of the water and its crashing shoreline waves.

Bear was happy to arrive at the coastline for several reasons; his fuel usage had been nominal in having one gallon left, just enough to fly over the field, turn on the landing lights, and make his final approach.

While on the westerly down-leg flight, parallel with the runway, *it happened.*

A red flare burst in the sky about two or three miles due west in the Pacific.

"What the hell!"

Then another flare burst in the same location.

"Damn. What the hell's going on out there?"

As he switched to channel nine, the emergency station, he pulled back on the yoke, to gain altitude.

Sure enough, he was right on top of the Mayday call of a boat sinking just off Yakutat Bay.

He thought, *What to do? I've only got a gallon of fuel.*

The decision came fast. He flew over the coast-line at 500 feet and headed for the source of the flares. Another one exploded about a mile away. He lowered the nose and leveled off at 100 feet.

On the first pass over the sinking boat he saw four persons sitting on the bow just barely out of the water. About three quarters of the stern was below the water-line. One person was holding a red hand flare.

He banked and turned again, dropped to 50 feet off the deck, and passed over them again.

He wondered why they were not in their onboard life raft by now. That boat was about to disappear. Then he suddenly noticed one of the crew drifting away.

He banked, turned again, and dropped to 25 feet. While doing so, he held onto the yoke with his right hand, and reaching behind the seat with his left, he grabbed the plane's two PFDs, opened the window, banked to port, and threw them out.

He banked, turned again, and dropped to a dangerous 15 feet. As he passed over again he noticed the crew was struggling to remain afloat . . . or seemed to be bobbing under.

He banked, turned again, and dropped to 10 feet. Holding the yoke with his right hand, he reached further behind the seat with his left, grabbed the pouch con-taining the onboard life raft, pulled it up and over his shoulder, held it on his lap, banked to port, and pushed the pouch out.

He gasped!

The stall horn bellowed, the stall light flashed, and the plane shook. Bear hol-lered, "Oh no, get that nose up, boy!"

Throttle forward, yoke back, he powered up and slowly gained altitude, he counted his blessings for a second, turned, and flew over the crew at 100 feet.

"Damn! I must have made a direct hit. That sucker is already inflated, and they're in it. That was quick. Come to think, the alternative was unacceptable. That water will kill ya."

Still holding a flare, the rescued crew waved as Bear headed for the airfield with his gas gauge showing *empty*.

There would be no time or fuel to have a typical landing with a nominal glide path and descent from 1000 feet.

He made plans to ditch. Plans that excluded use of the onboard PFDs and life raft. He still had a mile to go to the airfield, and safety from the freezing Pacific.

Still monitoring channel 9, he heard the Coast Guard was on the way. At least they'd be able to find his body quickly. Nevertheless, it would be frozen much like Sam McGee, the McGee who wanted cremation to thaw the ice from his blood.

He was going to try to clear the coast at 10 feet and hit the end of the runway with the negative visual feedback of an extremely acute angle of descent.

He hoped the runway lights would turn on with the first click as he passed over the coastline. He turned the radio to 121.9 kHz, clicked the send button, and waited . . .

Thankfully the lights went on.

Runway #87 was about one-half mile dead ahead.

Then it happened . . . again.

The engine coughed. It misfired. Then the sound, the note, that had been steady for so many hours ceased.

It coughed again.

The runway was 100 yards ahead.

"Bear, you're not going to make it!"

He slammed in the throttle control, but it was already full-forward. Nothing happened. He hit the prime button. Nothing.

It coughed again . . . sputtered, and backfired.

Between staccato roars it continued coughing and backfiring like a bruin in its death throes.

The plane coughed across the outer marker. Bear went into an immediate nose-up flare as he pulled the yoke back and dropped from the sky in a perfect three-point landing while the Cub barked all the way to Mother Earth. Thinking that the constant backfiring of a fuel starved engine was not good for the combustion chambers, he turned the mags off and rolled to a silent stop half-way down the main runway.

Motionless in quiet stillness he wiped the sweat from his brow, hands, and eyes. He was bathed in fluids of triumph.

He got out of the Cub, thanked her for her courage, looked to the sky, thanked Manitou, and kissed Mother Earth.

He cleaned the remains of the unfortunate goose from the bloody strut.

Taxiing to the Ops Ctr for fuel was not an option, so he picked up the tail and dragged the 850-pound plane down the concrete runway to the closest taxiway. The roar of a helicopter approached from the south, most likely the Coast Guard flying along the coastline toward the survivors he just left. *Good*, he thought. Their timing was excellent. Due to the frigid conditions and waves, they'd probably lift them in their rescue basket and bring them to the airport. They would need medical attention.

Bear was pleased to find someone at Ops when he arrived with his plane in tow. "Good evening," Bear hollered. "Good to see someone, anyone. The name's, Bear. I've been in the air awhile, and had started talking to myself."

"Hi," said the good looking elderly man in coveralls. He looked more like an executive than maintenance man. "Let me give you a hand. That old bird must be getting heavy by now."

"Naw. I owe her anyway. She just gave me the ride of my life. Say, you wouldn't happen to know how to get a hold of the airport manager so I could get some fuel and be on my way. I'm on a cross-country training flight and need to get on my last leg to Skagway."

"You bet. That's me. Chuck's the name. Let's swing that bird around, and I'll go in and turn on the pumps and the main landing lights. The Guard will be landing here soon. From what I hear, there'll be a few ambulances, police, a reporter from the paper, too; who knows who else? Want to come in? Take a pee break? Coffee? Whatever?"

They walked into Flight Ops, the manager checked on the Guard's progress, turned on all the lights, played back messages, and got the preflight briefing room ready for visitors. Bear chowed on his favorite bar as he refueled the plane. He smiled when paying for the 20 gallons. He mentioned to Chuck that the next leg was only 150 miles, so he should not have the same problem as flying into Yakutat.

He told Chuck that the J-3 had a range of 259 miles; Juneau to Yakutat was 250 miles, which did not allow for the rescue mission in the Pacific.

"I'd better not drink anything. I've got another three hours ahead of me."

Chuck said, "Aren't you going to stick around—meet the crew you helped save? Celebrate?"

"Nope, gotta go. Thanks again for your cooperation. Bye."

*   *   *

Absolutely surprised at Bear's casual attitude and humble response, he watched as Bear taxied to the runway, performed his run up, and took off to the west. The next sound he heard was Bear calling that he had cleared Yakutat airspace and was climbing to 1000 feet, and the gal around him was purring like a kitten. He also added, give the survivors my best.

The manager thought, as the little yellow plane's lights disappeared into the night cloaked mantle on earth, *With men like that flying for the DNR, we're in good hands.*

No sooner had Bear signed off than the Guard's chopper flew in from the west, hovered, and landed in the footprint left by the little J-3.

A couple of ambulances drove in with lights flashing. Likewise, the local sheriff raced in, his car blinking like a Christmas tree at Wal-mart. They were followed by the local reporter from The Yakutat Daily News. Then half of the town showed up to witness what seemed to be one of the biggest events of the year.

The local press was all over the Coast Guard personnel and the survivors. The reporter went looking for the small plane pilot; likewise just before the four were directed to the waiting ambulances, they asked to see the pilot that had saved their lives. After a short search it was discovered that he was gone but had talked to the airport manager. His departure for Skagway was more than an hour ago.

Joined by the police, the Guard, the reporter, and the survivors, they cornered the airport manager for some answers about the mysterious pilot.

He explained how they had met at the field, had helped him fuel, and how anxious he was to continue on the last leg of his training flight. The reporter pressed for more information.

Chuck answered, "I can tell you this much; he filed a flight plan for Skagway at 2 a.m. and signed it, Chi Mukwa, private pilot, in training, for the DNR. The plane is registered to the DNR and maintained by Ford Flight Service, FFS, in Skagway. He introduced himself as Bear; apparently that's English for Mukwa. I happen to know he's a Tlingit Indian, and in their language Chi is Big, so his English name is Big Bear.

"Until you folks came, I had no idea he played the major part in the rescue. He was so grateful for me being here to fuel his little J-3 . . . the story of the night, to him, was that he must have landed on fumes. In other words, he must have used his two gallon reserve flying over the Pacific to rescue you guys. It sounds to me like he risked his life to find you, drop the plane's PFDs, life raft, and make it back here. You can print this. He risked his life to save that crew.

"One final comment, he asked me to send him a text message when it was learned how the survivors came through the trauma of their dunk in the Pacific. He gave me a simple address: FFS, Skagway, attention Bear.

"That's it. A name. A sweet little J 3 Cub. A heroic act. A humble man. An Indian. His last request: Asking how the survivors came out of it.

"Now that's the kind of guy you'd want on your team . . . I'll still never forget the look on his face when he said,

'Twenty gallons! That's all she holds. I landed with fumes.'"

*   *   *

The out of town paper rack, in front of FFS, held the *Yakutat Daily News*, Morning Edition, *The Skagway News*, and *The Juneau Gazette*. The lead story on the front page of The Yakutat Daily News would be of interest to the FFS owners, and their guests. It read:

Yakutat Daily News,   No. 41937 Morning Edition

Four Rescued as Boat Sinks

Survivors abandoned their 31-foot Tiara Slickcraft boat, Windward, while fishing several miles off Yakutat Bay, north of Glacier Bay N.P. "All four were recovered safely," said Chief Petty Officer Allen Ray. The vessel suddenly started sinking after taking on water before 1 a.m. The owner said a bushing on the main drive prop fractured several miles off shore. Yakutat is 200 miles northwest of Juneau.

Plucked from a life raft, the victims were taken to the local airport aboard a helicopter dispatched from the C.G. Station in Sitka.

Coast Guard Lt. T. Lamb said it was a team effort.

A novice Native American pilot heard the emergency Mayday call while training in the area. He diverted his flight after seeing the aerial flares, and dropped his emergency PFDs and life raft during some tricky maneuvers. Windward's raft had been damaged beyond use; consequently, the timely and accurate drop by the pilot saved the boaters' lives. Survival time in these waters is less than 15 minutes.

The pilot, Chi Mukwa (Big Bear), a Tlingit Indian from Skagway who works for the DNR, said, "Anyone else would have done the same . . . by coming to the aid of our fellow man in trouble." Because he had been low on fuel, he said, "This plane must be able to fly on fumes."

Sconie, the harbor master on duty, said his office had several ambulances at the airport, anticipating hypothermia and other possible injuries. The boaters were treated at Yakutat Hospital and released.

Lt. T. Lamb summarized the rescue saying, the fact there was not loss of life is a tribute to the quick actions of the Indian Chi Mukwa who did not choose to stay and meet the crew he helped save. After refueling, he continued on the last leg of his cross-country training flight to Skagway.

by reporter, J. Curo

Chapter 24

Risible

"Wake up! Windy, wake up," Dave said as he shook Windy's shoulder. "It's two in the morning."

Windy and Raven were staying in Ops with Dave after figuring costs of the hut's addition. Milt hit the sack earlier, knowing Bear was on his way back. The teens were anxious to stay up and listen to the rescue activities over the Pacific, off Yakutat Bay. Even though Bear's communications were limited, they could still hear some of his efforts before he landed. The last message they heard in Ops was his report that he was clearing Yakutat air space and heading home on the last leg of his flight.

Then there was the late night call from J. Curo with the Yakutat Daily News who wanted to interview Bear. The reporter was going to drive all night so she could be there when he was available. Dave tried to wave her off, without success, and gave no assurances that Bear would even see her, much less talk to him about the rescue. Dave knew Bear would not give her the time of day. The U.S. Coast Guard, yes, the press, no. He could just hear it now. Curo would ask him why and he'd simply say . . . because I choose not to, and that would end the conversation.

"Come on, you guys. Let's get a little shut-eye." Dave shook Windy again, thinking *If I leave them here on the couch, leaning on each other like love-birds, Bear's liable to walk in, see 'em, and accuse me of being a poor chaperone. No way.*

H-O-N-K! Dave blew the air horn used for emergencies.

"What's up?" Windy exclaimed.

"What's that?" Raven yelled.

"As concierge of FFS," Dave answered, "I'm authorized to wake you up from sleep, so you can go back to sleep—*in separate beds?*"

"What's happening?" Windy asked, rubbing his eyes. "Is Bear okay?"

"Well, at two-thirty Bear announced that his gal was purring like a kitten, and if the Spirits of the Wind were riding with him, he'd probably touch down at about five-thirty. He added that his body was looking forward to a good eight hours of sleep. I told him you guys were it the sack, separately, and I'd meet him on the flight line at dawn to tie his girl down."

"Thanks. That kind of good news will help me sleep. Promise to wake us up when Bear arrives?" Raven asked.

"No!" Dave answered.

"P-U-U-L-E-E-A-S-E? Please, Dave, my sweetie-heart baby?" Raven pleaded.

Damn women, Dave thought, *their words are so sexually poetic and suggestive.*

"Okay. Only if you're in bed in the next five minutes . . . you in your room and Windy in Bear's. Now get!"

Raven kissed Dave on the cheek, the same to Windy, and scrambled into her room and closed the door. "Then she opened it and yelled, "Ha! There's no lock on my door. Ha!" She closed it again.

Dave looked at Windy and said, "Get!"

Windy left with a smile on his face, knowing very well Raven was teasing him. Her pledge to Leigh carried too much weight to be violated.

Watching after these two must be a full-time job for Leigh, Dave thought. *They do make an interesting couple. Raven certainly knows how to get under my skin with her burlesque jocularity.* "Remember, buddy, I can see both doors from here, and I'll be awake."

Windy turned in the hall at Raven's room, knocked, smiled, and quickly ducked into Bear's room.

Raven yelled, "Get away from my door, lover boy! Go to sleep before Dave and me tie you up and feed you to the wolves."

A welcome silence.

"Night, Dave," Raven hollered, "love you."

"Night, Dave," Windy yelled, "I don't love you. Like you. Yes."

"It's about time. Good night. Don't make me come in there and tie you guys to your beds."

He turned to the console and activated the transceiver to access the transponder on the J-3. He logged the alphanumeric code that indicated Bear's location, speed, altitude, and azimuth. Satisfied that Bear was on course, he estimated his ETA and turned to the latest Playboy—hoping the photos were interesting enough to keep him awake, and, of course, the articles . . .

They were.

*   *   *

Joe was having his last night around the campfire with DNR personnel at Bravo Station. He shared a few of his bawdy stories, but was more interested in the expanded research activities along the coast.

The crew from Yakutat motored down with a lot of material, much of it prefabricated, to help in getting the station going ASAP.

Mark and John, the original researchers, were on the mend and soon to return. In the meantime, two students would be in residence, their supervision remaining in Yakutat.

FFS would be bringing the last load of supplies in the morning and picking up Joe, and later Leigh and BW, to join the gang at Skagway for Bear's graduation.

The two young graduates would be working at one of the three field stations reporting to the Department of Natural Resources through a contract awarded to The University of Michigan. Their research focused on measuring the various possibilities contributing to the decline of the salmon being caught during the fall spawning run. They explained to Joe that they were initially directed to measure the biological and physical aspects affecting the fish food chain.

Passing around another round of ale, Joe chuckled, "Speaking of biological aspects of life, me dad once introduced me to his friends, saying, 'Yes, he raised three children, two of whom were fairly normal—this is the other one.'" The wolverines chuckled at Bear's self deprecation, knowing very well, with all his experience, when he spoke to Alaska's environmental issues . . . people listened.

They also mentioned that upon completion of their fisheries study, others, in Juneau, were interested in the effects of increased carbon content in the air and water in Prince William Sound, south of Alaska's largest city, Anchorage.

With the recent permafrost thaw, and subsequent outgassing of methane, they will be studying this problem, also.

Joe felt he could leave Bravo Station now since the major elements were replaced or rebuilt. The motor launch and its rails to the shoreline were operational, the shack complete, and communications re-established. A generator was on site, and a large solar panel was in place for 90% of the station's needs.

FFS benefited from the three station research teams. The northern station, Alpha, in Yakutat, was 100 miles from the most southern station, Charlie, in Pelican. Bravo was in the center, 50 miles between the two, providing the DNR with "blanket" coverage for sampling along the shoreline. FFS providing shuttle service to the DNR was a nice contract to have, and part of the reason for Bear to get his pilot's license.

Joe and the staff walked to the shoreline to stretch their legs and listen to the swooshing waves as they wopped, and flopped onto themselves and slid back to the next. As they looked out to sea the boys told him that the buoys bobbing on the horizon here, and along the study area, did indeed send data to satellites automatically. Nevertheless, actual sample collection was still a back-breaking, dangerous job. Whether gathering zooplankton or phytoplankton, a person had to be there to collect the sample regardless of the weather. Since these critters are at the bottom of the food chain, that's where they started their work.

"Ah, there's other critters," Joe added, "I've just learned how to be civil to the Irish crew at Charlie Station, in Pelican . . . me thinks they're Democrats . . . who as you know, dwell at the bottom of the food chain, too." One of the boys reflected that he'd heard that Bear had a few words with one of the Irish contractors there.

As they walked back to the fire, the staff commented that the results of their recommendations frequently affected the entire fisheries industry. A one-year ban of catching the tasty salmon could bankrupt many fishermen. More often the DNR choose a more moderated approach such as the one-time three-hour time limit at an assigned location near the mouth of the river that was under limited catch restrictions.

"Me boys, 'tis tine this old man turned in. 'Tis been a pleasure working with ye Wolverines. I hope Mark's arrival will give you all a mental goose. He's a tough old bird, and ye know broken arm will not keep him down for long. I've always said my skills are with me back, his with the brain—and his the bigger. At that, good night, I'll he off in the morn."

He turned toward his tent, then stopped and asked, "Did you fellas hear any more about the rescue off Yakutat Bay?"

"Yes, and no," a student answered, "but it appears from what little commo we heard that a novice pilot on a training flight was key to the four surviving. We'll know more tomorrow."

"Thanks. Night," Joe answered. He thought, *I'll bet me week's pay it was Bear.*

Joe slid into his bedroll like he had just successfully bowled the ball into the wickets . . . leaving the batsman aghast. He knew Bear had scored, too. He was proud to be counted as a friend of the novice pilot in his little yellow bird.

*   *   *

The night by the fire was pleasant for BW and Leigh; going over events of the day and planning for the next was gratifying. BW insisted that he stay and care for the injured wolves. He could also finish dressing out the bear and tie up some loose ends around the meadow.

Bear would understand; it was the right thing to do, especially during the pre-hibernation season when bruins were out and about fattening up for winter's sleep and the sows' birthing.

Jet required a few stitches and wrap around his chest area, Tough pretty much the same. They were lucky as warriors defending their mistress was gratifying. They all knew very well that it was hard to avoid a tear or bruise when you're attacking a bear's throat or groin. Both wolves were sedated and resting as The White comforted them, too.

The fireside chat with BW provided the perfect venue to discuss Bear's background. She asked about his tribal life, relationship with and how he met Morning Star, and BW's experiences with his dad. Probative but not rude, Leigh had many questions about the Raven Clan, Bear's role in tribal affairs, and his youthful personality quirk's that BW had heard from his mom. It was a splendid night. Leigh's head was spinning at the very notion of a son who was still in love with both parents, and his new stepmother.

As they left the midnight fire, Leigh gave him a hug of thanks.

When they walked to the hut, The White joined them to receive the obligatory pat and attention. Her role as nursemaid was more than she probably expected. They gave her the added attention she needed, and she returned to the zonked out patients by the stairs.

BW aggressively urged Leigh to consider staying a day or two in Skagway to relax with Bear. He was going to go after Dolly Vardens, now in the river, and skin out the bear and salt down the hide for tanning later. He'd be busy and certain to enjoy the solitude of the meadow's peace . . . her Walden. Leigh thanked him for the offer indicating she'd probably do it if Bear agreed.

As they crashed for the night, Leigh was overcome with a strange feeling, a tension, a stressful discomfort . . . an unaccustomed sense of concern. What could it be?

She thought to herself, *Could it be Bear's cross-country flight at night? What else could it be? I'm safe here with BW. The wolves will be okay.*

With hesitation, she asked BW, "Did you say the boys at FFS indicated Bear's flight was going okay?"

Just getting into Windy's bed, BW answered, "Yeah, they talked to him when he was about ten miles east of Yakutat—on the way back—and the flight was nominal, as planned. Do you want me to call FFS?"

"No, as you say it will probably be routine: land, fuel up, pee, eat, and take off. I'm such a worry-wart."

"No, you're not. You're in love with a man, and like any person with similar feelings, when you're flying, you're at risk. Bear is flying, and you both know there's an inherent risk in doing so. You're not alone; I hope for a safe flight, too."

"Thanks, love you, son. Night."

"Night, Mom."

"One more thing: would you get my bathing suit top from the tree tomorrow? I'd rather not have Bear find it someday and try to explain to him what happened."

"Will do, first thing in the morning," he said with a chuckle.

"You can just stop that chuckle, Mister. Remember, that unplanned stripping incident in the tree is our story—only ours—you dig?"

"I dig. My lips are sealed. But damn, may I add, you're a beautiful woman. Bear's a fortunate man."

"Okay, that's enough, young man. Night."

"Night, Playboy girl."

"Stop it, or I'll sic the wolves on you."

"Night, mom."

"Night, you scoundrel."

*   *   *

The chopper stopped by the meadow at 0800 hours as planned. Leigh jumped aboard, Joe waved to BW, and they were on their way to Skagway.

BW attended to the injured wolves with his nurse's aide in white watching his every move. Both of the bear fighters were doing very well and undoubtedly would be up and around later in the day. The White had finally trusted him enough to give a positive nuzzle for the first time. However, she was a little confused when BW returned to the scene, of the bear attack, climbed a tree, and returned to the hut with a "tie" around his neck.

After getting a skinning knife from the hut, he sharpened it by the corral so Old Gal could receive a little attention, too.

He doffed his clothes, hung then by the corral, and dragged the bear to the river bank. He noticed how lightweight the bear was even though he had gutted it out earlier.

The skinning and butchering was indeed going to be a bloodbath, but the river would be his wilderness shower. As he separated the hide from the carcass with the skinning knife, it became evident that the bear must have been sick. The body was emaciated. He chopped off each paw from the bone with an axe so they remained with the hide. He did the same with the head, rolling it aside and severing the last neck vertebra, allowing him to separate the carcass from the hide. Then he noticed another reason for the bear's hostile actions. There was a large-caliber bullet hole in the shoulder—not life- threatening, but certainly injurious to mobility for food-gathering and infection. The bear's mouth answered the rest of the story for his aggressive behavior; he had very few teeth, and those were almost flush to the gums. Chewing plants and meat would be, at best, difficult, typical problems of old age and dying in the wilderness.

"Sorry, old chap, but one way or the other, your days were numbered. Interest-ing, this bullet hole is fairly fresh. I wonder who could be lurking nearby?"

With a precise stroke of the axe he opened the lower portion of the skull, then removed the fragments and the brain. He set it in a covered pail of saltwater. It would be used later as a natural preservative in the tanning process.

Several roasts were carved from the hind legs, backstrap taken from the top of the spinal column, and tenderloins from the bottom. With the flashing knife slash-ing through the meat, he had extracted a bucket of flesh and blood in no time flat.

"Damn, I'm blood and guts from head to toe. So be it. I've a lot of roasts to show for it. I might as well stake out this hide, too."

He dragged the hide over to the corral area, laid it in a circular pattern, fur down, tied string to loops of skin and staked the beautiful skin to the ground. Using a moose antler scraping awl, he cleaned most of the flesh and fat from the hide and fed it to the pesky wolves.

"You two are certainly feeling better. Looks like your nursing has paid off, girl.

A reminder to all three, the way you're chomping down this raw meat, be aware sometime in the next twelve hours, you'll be totally cleaned out . . . whether you want to or not," he chuckled.

"The sun is just right here, and still near the building, and the other hide Raven and Leigh had prepared last week. Good job, BW! I'll throw a little salt on the old bear and get cleaned up."

Suddenly he heard the capering noise of hooves. He looked at Old Gal, and sure enough, the bear smell was very offensive to her.

"Hold on, girl. The bear smell will soon be gone," BW said, talking to the troubled horse; she did not like bears.

He left the covered brain by the root cellar, and took the other buckets of meat to the river. While rinsing the meat, he trimmed some pieces and cut others into individual portions. The rest would be ground up as Tongass Bear Burgers, courtesy of Runs with Wolves. After placing the buckets in the 40 degree root cellar, he ran to the river and jumped. He swore a few Dolly Vardens slithered from him as he frolicked with The White. He had sedated the other two so they'd rest and not get too active before healing was complete.

He just knew with the right tackle, he'd pull one out and make him a "surf and turf" for dinner. At home, unfortunately, he had all the lures he needed. Sometimes the Dollys would bite on almost anything jiggled below water, he used: Purple egg sucking leeches. Royal coachmen. Mickey Finn bucktails. Sockeye Johns. Egg Patterns. Alaska Mary Anns. Marabou girdle bugs, and many others.

"These fish would bite on paper clips."

He lived for the challenge of rods arched into parabolas, in the gin-clear waters of the Bitterroot.

The White had fun chasing the soap as it slipped down the current, and retrieved waiting for another chance. While full of suds and going down for the last time, he heard an unusual growl from The White.

Clearing his eyes, he said, "What is it, girl? What's up?"

She was looking down river, so he said, "What did you do, lose the soap in the current? Here, I'll help you. Hold on."

As BW cleared his eyes and heard the growling continuing, he, too, looked down river. Disheveled and wearing black chest waders, a rain hat, reflective silver-like sunglasses, a couple of days' growth on his face, and a filthy rain parka, he looked like a dirty hornet. More troubling, since many fishermen looked good-for-nothing, was the Winchester 94 carbine at his side. Not really at his side, it was leveled at BW. This chap looked anything but friendly. As he got closer, a feather showed in his hat.

BW thought, *I hope this isn't one of the rogue Indians Bear had mentioned.*

Caught in his shorts, he had few to no options other than asking what this questionable character wanted. While restraining The White and asking her to heel, he said, "Good morning."

No answer. The stranger walked closer with the rifle still aimed at BW.

"Can I help, you?" I have my wolf at heel. She will not bother you."

No answer.

At 10 feet, the stranger stopped and raised his rifle to his chest. "What's your name?" he asked.

"First, put that gun down, and I'll tell you. I have no dispute with you. You're welcome to stay and rest here, have a drink of water, and continue on; I have no offense against you."

The stranger threw a rope at BW saying, "Shut up, tie that mutt up, and make it tight; do it now."

BW welcomed the task. If she broke loose, she'd be shot. Making certain the rope did not have a choking slip-knot, he said, "Done. Now may I ask you who or what put a burr up your ass?"

"Oh, you think you're kinda smart, huh? I can tell you're the educated type with your fancy comments, so why don't you just shut up? Now throw me the end of that rope."

BW hesitated, trying to figure out an escape plan . . . but to no avail. The stranger held the leverage with the lever-action 94, and he'd likely shoot the wolf in a second if tested. In the face of these odds . . . *wait for the right moment . . . it will come. This guy is not dealing with a full deck.*

"Hurry up. Throw me that rope."

BW threw the looped end so hard the stranger almost fell over in the water.

"Don't try any fancy stuff, my boy, or you'll be sorry."

The stranger pulled on the rope. The White growled.

"You behave, white one, or you'll end up getting a little of that growl beaten out of you."

BW pleaded, "Please, what do you want. I don't have much money, but what I have is yours. I just butchered a bear; you're welcome to some of it."

"Ha! That's our bear, anyway. We shot it last night. We saw you cleaning it. We know."

"We?"

The stranger looked over his shoulder. "Red Dog, come in. I've got a drop on the boy and the wolf on a rope. Come on in."

A voice answered from across the river and down a few yards. "Okay, Yellow Knife, if you're certain. I don't want that wolf at my throat ."

Shorter, with a big nose and pony-tail, he waded over in the same type of hip boots, almost falling as he stumbled in the riverbed. His gait looked more like that of a drunk struggling with the current. He, too, carried a rifle that looked like an old

45-70 with a trap-door breech. His rain hat and parka were also filthy. Upon reaching his villainous partner, he said, "You told me they'd be gone, there would be no one here. Who's this?"

"Shut up, you bum. I didn't expect anyone to be here, either! It looks like we'll have to tie him up, get the stuff we want, and see what else looks good."

BW countered, "You'll be making a mistake. No one violates the trust that Leigh and Bear represent here on the meadow. If you harm me or any of the animals or property, they'll hunt you down and make you pay. You're making a mistake. I understand, "first-blood," the hot pursuit of the first shot, so take the bear meat and the hide. Let me remind you again: don't do this."

"Shut up, punk!" Yellow Knife yelled.

Red Dog lamented, "Maybe he has a point. Bear and Leigh are well liked in the Tongass, the DNR, Skagway—everywhere."

"Shut up, you dummy. We're only going to take what's ours and a few paybacks that we owe him."

BW yelled, "What the hell's wrong with you guys? You know you can't get away with this. Think—if you've got any brains! Don't do this!"

Yellow Knife screamed at Red Dog, "That's it. Tie his hands and let's get out of this river. Hop to it. We don't have all day."

As Red Dog tied BW's hands behind his back, he mumbled to BW, "He told me no one would be here, they'd all be gone . . . to Skagway. I don't like this. I don't like this at all.

"Quit talking to that pretty-boy, and bring him over to one of these trees. Tie him so he can't move for a while."

They also tied The White to a tree by the river, along their escape route.

As the two scoundrels moved toward the stable, BW thought, *Be cool. Wait to make your move at the right time. Red Dog does not want any part of this and he's two-sheets to the wind. It's about time someone stops these renegade Indians from tarnishing the good reputation of the majority. These bastards are the ones Joe and Bear have been after for years. I know it's them.*

As the odd couple entered the root cellar, a raven perched above BW and croaked its arrival on the meadow.

BW looked to the bird and said, "Welcome! Good timing."

Chapter 25

Riven

The sun rose on a warm late-fall morning with clear skies and a fine southwesterly breeze.

The group waiting on the flight line, with coffee, doughnuts, and a well-read copy of the *Yakutat Daily News* anxiously scanned the sky.

"He'll be coming in low, just over the treetops to the west, if I know that guy," said Dave. "He'll fly over the field, turn, fly his downleg, and land into the wind from the east."

Everyone looked to the northwest while they continued drinking their coffee, munching fat food, and scanning many of the local morning papers in the chilly crack of dawn. Fluffy cauliflower-shaped clouds hung in the bright-blue western sky. A gentle breeze nudged the trees. They all strained to see the fiery yellow Cub appear and glow like gold in the sunlight.

"One thing is certain," Dave said. "He'll be bushed and want to eat a horse—cooked or raw—drink a gallon of water, clean the night off his stinky body, and sleep. Of course, Leigh, you'll get your shot at him for a little kissyface, but you won't linger. Unless you've a respirator, he'll smell!"

Leigh responded, "Is that so? Well, don't think you know so much, my man. We're used to each other's musk. You're right about one thing: he'll not be interested in loving and a-kissing. He'll kiss the ground first, then me. True, there will be no BNR. We'll eat, shower, and crash."

Dave reminded everyone, "Remember, we're planning on a two-o'clock party and presentation of wings in ops. Someone needs to get him up from dreamland."

Leigh answered, "No problem. We're all going to town for a while, and plan to be back at noon. Wanna come with us?"

"Sure, as long as someone stays is ops. It's Milt's turn anyway."

He looked at the crowd and smiled. It was as if Lindbergh was arriving in the Spirit of St Louis. Leigh, Joe, Raven, Windy, Gete Wabiska, several student pilots, and newspaper reporter Janet Curo, a foxy lady, all waited in the early-morning mist. Milt was in ops, covering the console since he was "pulling" the 0600 to 1800-hour watch.

Dave was trying to be polite to the reporter, but kept her at distance and did not go out of his way to introduce her to FFS personnel or Leigh's throng. The reporter was just a little too forward for his liking, but understood it was inherent in the mindset of their work to be aggressive. They had headlines and editors on their backs to get the story and make it sound interesting. If necessary, she would embellish the facts to catch the reader's eye . . . and push the subject being interviewed to get the last scrap of information, more than he or she had planned on revealing. Little did she know, her fine article in the morning paper would probably be the only story she'd report. His guess was that Bear would not talk to her or the public about the rescue at Yakutat Bay.

Dave reminded her that the story was told very well by the airport manager, Chuck, and several U.S. Coast Guard personnel on the scene. She was not listening to anything he was saying. *She wanted* a follow-up human interest story with quotes from Bear—a wrap-up story—one that would humanize Bear, the missing link in the original story.

"All I want is a quick moment with him," she pleaded.

"I'll do my best, but let me warn you again, he is just not the type to talk about personal aspects of his life, whether tribal, DNR activities, or in this case his flight last night. He does not want recognition for what he considers nominal aspects of life's events."

"Okay, are you willing to introduce me if I promise to only ask a few questions?"

"No, you're on your own. I don't want to be on the receiving end of a wicked look I'd get for the introduction."

"Okay, I'll only ask one question."

"No!" Dave replied, "what; part of *no* do you not understand?"

"But . . ."

Leigh yelled, "There he is! Look, he's coming over the trees to the west."

Everyone spread out to see and started walking in the direction of the taxiway exit by the apron, in front of ops near the hangar. Curo was left alone, staring at the little yellow J-3 on its downwind leg. Dave noticed her plight as the others were long gone to ops. She turned and tried to catch the crowd.

She was a looker. Her long red hair, blue-green eyes, and fair complexion turned the head of many men . . . and she knew it. A touch of English accent gave her an advantage in the diaspora of mixed accents of Alaska's mingling rhetoric. On the *Playboy* scale of libidinous qualities, she was a strong 9.

However, Dave felt her spirited solo reporting of recent events could be a cover for other investigative probes she may have on her mind. She asked too many questions unrelated to the rescue at Yakutat Bay. Was she a tree hugger? A whale lover? A Native American sympathizer? What else? He wanted no part of her sensual ways. He'd been cuckolded once and learned to be very careful when getting too close to attractive, aggressive women. There seemed to be more to her than meets the eye. Her agenda broader than she let on. "I could be wrong, but don't think so. In any event, I'm going to put some distance between that woman and me. I smell trouble."

*   *   *

"Dave! You didn't answer me. Dave! Dave!" Janet yelled.

Running after him to try one more time seemed futile. Thwarted by Dave's reluctance to bother Bear, she'd now try to get Milt to help. She'd heard they were both single. As the crowd headed for the hangar where Bear would park the J-3, she headed toward ops and Milt.

She wasn't going to let Dave deter her quest to meet Bear.

On the way over to ops, she unbuttoned the top of her blouse, removed her glasses, and let her hair down from its pony tail. The feminine trick had worked before, so she was going to try it again.

She trudged along the flight-line behind the parked trainers and slipped into the front door of ops. She found Milt at the control console chatting with the field's training traffic and others in FFS airspace. He had just signed-off from talking to Bear, who was on his final approach. She heard him welcome him back and remind him that any landing is a good landing—that you can walk away from in one piece.

They enjoyed a little chuckle, and Bear finally made his last radio contact: "Thanks for the comeback. I'll see if I can land this girl in one piece—wheels down, wings horizontal, and tail dragging, right side up. By the way, my tail's dragging, too. Seriously, I appreciated the help both you and Dave have given me. This flight would *not* have been successful without the contingency plans you guys hammered into this thick head. See you in a bit. This is N-27 signing off."

"This is FFS control. Out."

"Hi!" Janet yelled, "I enjoyed hearing that chatter or the speaker. It sounds like Bear thinks a lot of you guys. How you doing?"

"Hi . . . Janet, right? The reporter from Yakutat? Welcome. We met briefly when you arrived and went to the airfield with Dave."

Janet thought, *It's working. He's going out of his way to be nice. It's time to get down to business. He's also a neat-looking guy.* She commented, "This is certainly an attractive operation. Our airfield, in Yakutat, is not as big or new as what you have here."

"Thank you. Let me compliment you on the fine article in this morning's paper. Nice job. As you've heard, he's landing now. It's been a long cross-country flight for him . . . twelve hours of air time."

Janet said, "I agree, but as I heard, he said he couldn't have done it without you and Dave. He apparently thinks you guys were the key factor in his successful flight."

She thought, *Everybody likes flattery, whether man or beast.*

She tucked her blouse in tighter, moved closer, leaned over him at the console, and asked several questions about the controls, which he was only too accommodating to explain. Then she sat next to him, crossing her legs, showing an ample amount of leg to get his attention.

"Are those the log sheets for Bear's flight?"

"Yep. You're logged-in here, too."

"Really? May I see?" She leaned over his shoulder, making contact for a moment. "So you also log-in visitors.?"

"See here, I've also noted a 'wings party' for early afternoon."

"Wings party?" she queried.

"It's just a graduation-type party where we give him his general aviation private pilot's license, ASEL, Aircraft Single Engine Land, with tail dragger endorsement. He has passed all the FAA requirements. The last of which you are familiar—cross-country at night. Your article sounds like he's done much more than the minimum prerequisites, don't you think?"

"I agree. Say, do you think I could meet him? I already feel I know the pilot I wrote about . . . through the eyes of others. I would not be intrusive. Please?" she pleaded, with shoulders back to expand her chest.

Milt thought, *She is certainly an aggressive type; she's trying every feminine trick in the book. I should tell her she need not display herself. She's about to slip her slip . . . I guess it would not hurt to introduce her.* "Okay, you can stay here in ops and meet him. He'll be by and check with me before he hits the sack. I have to stay here. Remember now, it will be a short 'Hello' and 'Good-night.'"

Janet gave him a big hug, thanking him with her arms and body.

"Remember, he's a man of few words. Native Americans do not feel a need to speak unless it's necessary. Plus, the gang will be with him. By the way, had you thought of being out on the flight-line with the gang and meeting him there?"

She replied curtly, "It would have been too crowded out there."

Milt responded, as if a Doubting Thomas, "Oh."

Milt heard a call from the console, moved to his chair, and chatted with a few pilots, some just checking in, others asking for weather conditions and local information about Skagway.

"He's down, as he said, right side up, and mentioned he'll be by in a couple of minutes. Get this! His one request was for a peanut butter and jelly sandwich, a glass of cold milk, and a bed. Now how's that for an All American snack? Here they come!"

She moved away from the console area and drifted over to the bulletin board across the room. She shifted from her seductive face, for Milt, and put on her all-business look as the gang burst into ops.

Cups in hand, as someone had brought a bottle of champagne, they were all abuzz over Bear's successful flight. Raven was kidding Leigh for her jumping on

Bear as he literally kneeled and kissed Earth Mother; they yelled at her: "Can't you wait?" Bear got the better of her and laid a big one on her prone lips. It was indeed a jolly gang.

"Welcome!" Milt said as Bear gave him a big hug. They chatted a bit, and Milt said, "I'll take care of all this stuff later. Here's your sandwich and milk, a notable culinary delight made here by the one and only Pierre of FFS, the best in the west—west of the flight-line.

"Hey. Some things never change. You guys always have a zinger for me about my favorite food and drink. What can I say, but thanks? Thanks to all of you."

Gete Wabiska stepped forward. "Being thankful is also my business. Shall we take a moment to thank the Great Spirit, Manitou, for his guidance, his witness during your flight?"

"Absolutely," Bear answered.

The group formed the circle of life, the circle unbroken, to show unity and strength. To ensure completeness, Leigh urged Janet to enter, and she did, between Milt and Bear.

Gete Wabiska raised his arms to the zenith, and a silence grew over the room. The only sound was the background communications plane-to-plane and plane to other airport sectors. Gete Wabiska spoke:

> "As we grow up and learn new things, some learn to fly. We will
> be tested by the elements and man. There will be failures but
> likewise many successes in life, no matter the course we choose.
> Embrace the people and things you love in your work. Laugh too
> much, and love like it's your last day. But don't be afraid that it
> will end; be afraid that it will never begin. Live simply. Love gen-
> erously. Care deeply. Speak kindly. Leave the rest to the Great
> Spirit."

Gete Wabiska lowered his arms, approached Bear, and gave him his left arm. Bear gave his left, too, and they clasped each other's forearms in the warrior's greeting of a job well done.

He also asked Leigh to step forward, embrace Bear, and look at each other. He spoke to the new couple:

> "Our lives are our own; they belong to us. Savor the moment."

Bear grabbed his favorite sandwich and slowly devoured every bite as if it were his last.

Milt shouted, "How 'bout another round of champagne while the new pilot is chomping, and include me this time?"

Leigh, who brought the sparkly, poured another round and noticed Janet in the background. Speaking to her, she said, "Why don't you join us? You earned membership here with the fine article."

"Thank you, don't mind if I do. What a wonderful group. You're so supportive of Bear."

Janet made the move toward Bear.

Dave looked at Milt in a disparaging way.

Milt looked back and shrugged his shoulders as if to say . . . no harm done.

"Bear," she said, " I missed you at Yakutat's airfield, but pieced together a story of your action last night. I hope you'll like it. I'm Janet Curo. You can call me JC. It's a pleasure to meet you."

"The pleasure is mine. They told me about your article while walking in from the flight-line. It's always good to give credit to the Coast Guard; they do a great job under extremely hazardous conditions, generally on rough seas and high winds. My role in the rescue was minor. The Guard was on the way—as always. Remember, it was an FFS plane and a DNR employee that was on the scene. I heard the Mayday and responded. It was DNR wages and FFS equipment that put me there."

"Ah, Bear, aren't you deflecting to others just a little too much?"

Bear's head snapped around. He stared at JC. "No, and that's the way you're going to write it. Do I make myself clear? It's been a pleasure meeting you. Now if you'll excuse me, I'm going to thank the crew again, kiss my wife, and disappear. Have a safe trip home."

"But I have a few more questions," she pleaded.

"Fine. Ask the crew, or the gang. I choose not to answer any more. Good Bye." Bear grabbed Leigh and headed for one of the guest rooms.

*   *   *

Milt looked at Dave and smiled, then shrugged his shoulders as if to say, *No harm done; he was more polite than they'd expected.*

Dave got the crowd's attention. "Hey, let's get ready for our trip downtown. I'll take you all in the van. Skagway is hosting the twenty-fifth annual World Ice-Sculpting Championships. Many sculptors from around the world have more than one hundred works of ice during this event. This year's theme is 'Celebrating our Native Heritage,' and several Tlingit Indians are competing. Let's go and give 'em our support. Plus, I'm buying a round at the new bar, The Garden of Eden."

Leigh rejoined the gang. They all took a restroom break and headed to the van.

As the group left, Dave noticed that JC elected to stay. She had gotten some coffee, made a sandwich for Milt, and was now engrossed in flight operations. Just as he was about to close the door to ops, he turned and asked to speak to Milt.

Milt excused himself and lent him an ear.

"Did he tell you?" Dave asked Milt.

"You mean about the plane?"

"Yes, he wants to take Leigh up around fifteen-hundred hours, just after the party. He wants to show her around the park and fly over the meadow. What do you think?"

"It's okay by me. I told him I'd check with you. I kinda said it was okay with me if he flew *only* during daylight and did not stay out *too long*."

"Since he will have had only six-hours of sleep by then, I cautioned him that his judgment could be affected. I was pretty clear that he was at risk. I also repeated the *Privileges and Limitations* of his new license:

> A private pilot *may not* act as PIC of a plane for hire. The excep-
> tions: He can take business flights, demonstrate planes to a
> buyer, and fly charitable trips. That's all, until he gets at least 200
> hours of flight time.

Milt commented, "I agree, you're absolutely right. FAA makes the rules, not FFS."

"Okay then, see ya." Dave headed out with the gang.

"Have a good time," Milt yelled as the gang took off.

As he returned to ops, he thought, *Bear's certainly like a bird anxious to leave the nest and stretch its wings in flight. I'd better have someone get the J-3 ready. Leigh may be his true love, but she'll be sharing him with that little yellow bird for a while.*

As he returned to the console and JC, she was cleaning up the mess and putting dishes in the sink.

"Here, I'll help you," Milt said as he dried while she washed—an event, a division of labor that repeats itself with couples across the land. "Say, I've got to ready one of the planes. Wanna help?"

"Of course. Let's go," JC responded with lots of energy.

They walked back to the maintenance area, and donned coveralls. He serviced the little Cub with her help. She kept offering to do more than she was allowed. He reminded her that the FAA is very specific on who can do what to certified aircraft for hire. FFS was responsible for this little bird being readied by a certified mechanic. No one else.

They were getting along very well; there was no act now.

She carried the empty gas can, he the tool kit, as they walked back to the hangar chatting like jaybirds. He hadn't felt so relaxed with a woman in ages. She was easy to be around. They talked about taking a flight the next day, since she was staying over in Skagway. She would write on her laptop and transmit a file, by phone, a short story on meeting Bear, later that day. As he helped her out of her coveralls, he sensed a look, that look of warmth, a look of comfort and trust by being with him. He wondered if he was reading too much into her eyes, until she gave him a hug of thanks for letting her help him and helping her feel welcome with the gang.

*　　*　　*

The gang returned all wound up after voting on what they were sure was the winning ice sculpture.

Bear was awakened by the raucous gang of celebrants and joined in as they drained the last bottle of champagne.

It did not go unnoticed by Leigh that Milt and JC were very close at the console while Milt managed the early-afternoon flight patterns in FFS airspace. Something was going on there, a lot more than newspaper reporting.

As the gang settled down, Gete Wabiska, in his own inimitable way, needed to perform one more ceremony.

He had Bear stand on his left, then Leigh on his right, and present the flight certificate and symbolic wings. Milt shot a photo of the three, and then with the gang . . . JC included.

Gete Wabiska told the gang, "My presence in the ceremony was as a representative of Manitou. For, as I hear, the flight may not have been successful without His wings in the cockpit."

Bear responded, "It is so." Then Bear asked for their attention so he could announce that his present to Leigh was a quick trip above the park so she could see her beloved meadow from the air. "I'm going to show my woman the giant trees of the Tongass from the top down while dancing in the clouds and floating on the wind provided by the Great Spirit."

Leigh replied, "This is a real surprise. When are we going?"

"My dear bride, we'll be aloft as soon as we get into some flying duds, and wrap that little jewel around our bodies. Let's go!"

As they walked to the flight line, Leigh said, "Bear, did you notice that Milt was holding hands with JC as they walked with us to the hanger? I rarely miss a move between people of the opposite sex."

"I know. He'll be holding more than her hand . . . soon," Bear whispered.

"Men! Is that all you think about . . . is sex?"

"Kinda, after flying."

"You'll pay for that comment, fella."

He grabbed her butt, kissed her quick, and off they went.

*　　*　　*

Bear chatted endlessly with Leigh about the J-3's characteristics as they flew southwesterly over the park toward her meadow. He also gave her the task of keeping him on an accurate compass heading of 260 degrees. When he strayed, she was to bring him back on the correct heading.

"Bear, you're drifting, moving to port at two-fifty-five. Bring her around about five degrees," she would shout.

"Roger dodger, you ol' codger. Will do. How's that?"

"Good, you're almost there . . . that's it; hold that mark, m'man. Am I doing pretty good as a copilot?"

"The best, since I've never had one before."

"Don't, get smart, wise guy. Anyway, you'll never have one as sexy as me!"

"Probably not. You are a provocative broad."

"That's enough, watch where you're going."

As they flew over the wonders of the Great Spirit's forest, Bear checked his GPS and found he was a mile from the meadow.

"Hey, gal, the meadow's to the port, right ahead. Hold on; I'm banking and going down to five-hundred feet."

"Hear you, babe. Let's go."

As they banked and nosed down to treetop level, the beautiful Bitterroot seemed to wrap around the meadow on two sides and run off to the west and disappear into the Pacific.

He banked to starboard and turned to the north.

She was first to see it.

"Bear, look. By the corral. Old Gal is out, and there are two men loading something on her. No, it's on a travois. Bear! What's going on? Where's BW? Where are the wolves? Bear!"

"Hold on. I see."

"What the hell is going on?"

"Something is terribly wrong. I'm going down, hold on."

"Be careful. You're already at treetop level."

They banked and turned over the plateau and dropped to 300 feet on another pass over the meadow.

"Bear, look! There's BW. He's tied up to a tree, and the men are hustling to leave. They've seen us. BW's in danger . . . everything is in jeopardy down there. Bear!"

"I've got to land; BW needs our help!"

"Bear, you can't land here; it's too rough!"

"Yes, and no, but I can try to land on the plateau. I've got to try. I'm going down. Hold on!"

Bear swore to himself. *Damn it, I can't take off from the plateau, but I can set this baby down. I'll worry about gettin' out later.*

Bear positioned the little yellow bird for a very unusual approach to the longest leg of the plateau, not from a normal glide slope . . . since the tall trees would not allow it. He approached the longest leg of the plateau at a 90° angle.

"I hope the hell this works. Dave said it would under some conditions. I hope those conditions are riding with me now," Bear shouted to Leigh.

"Bear, are you sure you want to do this?"

"Absolutely! Tighten your seat belt, dear. It's going to be a little rough."

Chapter 26

Redemption

What was it that Dave warned about for a short field landing? Bear thought. *I think it has to do with side-slipping.*

"What? Bear, what are you going to do?" Leigh bellowed as she tightened her seat belt.

"I'm going to buzz 'em one more time, hoping to scare the hell out of the bastards. I've just figured out the maneuver I need."

"What?"

"I'll let you know in a minute. I'm going to make one more pass over the meadow to set up my idea. Hang on!"

"Bear, be careful. Are you sure you want to do this? Those bastards are already on the run."

"Absolutely! Doesn't matter. Yellow Knife and Red Dog have to go down; I've had enough of their felonious behavior to last a lifetime."

The Cub banked and dove to the deck at 100 feet, flew over the meadow, and dropped to 50 feet with the plane pointed directly at the fleeing pair.

At the last second he climbed up and over the treetops, then banked north over the plateau.

"Hold on, gal. We're going down. I just figured out how to do it."

"Bear, be careful."

Okay, here's the drill, he said to himself. *Approach the landing at a ninety-degree angle, power back, keep the nose down to maintain lift, slide down until a couple-hundred feet off the deck, then hard left rudder, and bank to horizontal to level the wings. Power to idle, glide down to flare, and hit all three points at once. A three point landing.*

"I've got it, gal. Grab your knees and lower your head."

The plane approached the go/no-go point of the turn, and Bear committed to the maneuver. There was no turning back now as the plane banked, slid, and dropped to the surface . . . turning to the horizontal at the last moment and hitting the ground hard.

They bounced in the air and hit again as Bear killed power and crossed his fingers that the rollout was short of the tree-line. "You okay?"

"Yep!" she shouted as the plane tipped and rocked, bouncing across the rough terrain of the plateau. "Except for a flatter ass than before we hit. Are we okay?"

"I think so. Lean back like this to keep the tail down. Our worst enemy is the forward CG and a tendency for this girl to tip forward on the prop. Stretch back as far as possible. Good. That's it." He could hear the elevators being torn up and the landing gear acting as a brush-hog, but thankfully the wings did not touch the ground.

As the plane slowed short of the tree-line, Bear reminded Leigh to get the emergency rescue kit from behind her seat, and throw it out before she deplaned. He wanted the knife and aerial flare gun from the kit.

The Cub came to a rocking soundless stop about 100 feet from the pines. Silence.

"Babe, we've made it!" Bear exclaimed.

"Wow ! Good flying, but I have a feeling we were not supposed to land here."

"What makes you say that? It looked like an airfield to me."

"Ah . . . yeah. Try to sell that line to the boys at FFS."

He thought, *Wait 'til I ask the boys at FFS to pick up their J-3 from the plateau with their helicopter. They're going to run my tit through the ringer, saying "You did what?" I'll have to be at my best to explain this one.* "Okay, let's get out of here and down to the meadow."

They both deplaned, secured the knife and flare gun, and started to head for the meadow.

Leigh stopped and spoke to Bear. "I know we're in a hurry, but we should thank the Great Spirit for being with us as we landed."

"You're right."

Bear embraced her and whispered a prayer of thanks to Manitou, and asked for his blessings as they continued their difficult tasks ahead.

"Okay. What are you going to do?" Leigh asked.

Bear explained, "With luck, and our quick descent without power, the scalawags most likely did not hear us land. They probably think we returned to Skagway, so we may have a chance to sneak up on them. Then we'll determine how to rescue BW and the wolves, and apprehend the rascals.

"We're going to do all that with only a flare gun and a knife?"

"Yep, because we're smart and they're dumber than a box of rocks. My dear, be aware that I would not hesitate to shoot a flare up the arse of either one of those bastards."

"You're right. I just hate violence."

"Hon, so do I. I'll do anything in my power to apprehend them peacefully. It's kinda up to them, right? If you live by the sword . . . you die by the sword. Remember, we didn't start this. Are you okay?"

"Yeah."

They quickly ran to the edge of the plateau and listened, heard nothing, then jogged down to a wooded section behind the hut.

The good news followed. They heard a man talking to the restless wolves. It sounded like BW, who appeared to be okay. They moved a little closer, then rushed in with no delay, Leigh first with flare gun at the ready, Bear with a wood club and knife.

Three wolves jumped at their tethers as BW greeted them, saying, "How the hell did you guys get here?" As Bear removed his ties, BW told them the rogue Indians had rigged a travois on Old Girl and taken both bear hides with food from the root cellar.

"Did they take anything from the hut?" Leigh asked.

"No. I kept threatening them that if they did they'd really be sorry. Strange, they had some dimwitted idea that if they only took what Nature had provided Native People, it would be okay. I told them it didn't work that way, and to my recollection never had. Anyway, the leader, Yellow Knife, is our problem. His partner, Red Dog, was half drunk and apologetic for their actions."

Bear asked, "Are you all right?"

"Sure, I'm ready for some paybacks. I'd like to kick the ass of Yellow Knife. So, you must have landed on the meadow."

"Yes, a very dangerous maneuver. Did they hear us?"

"Hell no, I didn't, so they sure have no idea you're here."

"Good. Leigh, here's the plan: go get your 9mm for BW and my 94. I'll still use the flare gun with its four cartridges. BW and I will leave immediately, since they've only got a thirty-minute jump on us, and they're encumbered by the travois. Are you ready, BW?"

"Chomping at the bit."

"I want to go, too. I'd like a piece of those bastards."

"Hon, we'll bring a piece of them back. You're needed here more. Not only to keep the wolves from, following us, you need to let Joe know what I'm doing. Call FFS and tell them they have a helicopter pick-up of their beloved Cub Trainer. I'll suffer the harassment later."

"Okay, you've got a point, but be careful. BW, look after him. Don't let him take too many risks."

"Okay, Mom."

"Another favor, babe: go back to the plane, check for damage, and tie her down. You'll figure how. There's some windy weather coming down from the north this afternoon. Thanks, loads."

"Will do. Now, get your butt back here and give me a kiss."

A little embarrassed in front of BW, he did as he was told.

"That's more like it. You be careful out there."

They took off along the river. Bear figured they'd catch up with them in about 20 minutes.

*   *   *

"There he goes again," Leigh said. "Another hazardous event in our life. When will it ever end? Probably never."

The contrasting experiences of life and death that were a part of Bear's lifestyle never ceased to amaze her. It was part of hers now, too. How long could they live on the edge? When was his—and now her—luck going to run out? The hug at the plane should have ended her fear of death, but within minutes he left her arms and put his life in jeopardy again. Would it ever end? He was forgiving of others' mistakes. He'd always said, "Those who do, err. Those who never do, never err." It was wanton destruction of others, or their property that he could not forgive. At least until a penalty is paid. No doubt BW would mirror many of his dad's traits, too. He was certainly a part of that quality as he pursues those who violated the common rules of acceptable behavior.

"Come on, let's go," she said to the wolves. She moved to the stable, got the axe and some rope, and headed to the plateau.

Tough and Jet were about 90% recovered as they all trudged up the bank to work on the plane.

When they reached the top, she stopped and rubbed the wolves' necks. They showed signs of rope burns and a partial loss of hair. Luckily they'd all heal. Hair grows back, and the stiffness from fighting the tether would abate. She chuckled to herself. BW had said that when Red Dog slipped a noose over Tough's head, he almost took his hand off, despite being sedated. Leigh giggled when all the wolves stopped and growled at the Cub. The big yellow bird was indeed a strange intrusion to their pristine plateau.

"Come on, you disheartened wolves, it's not a wolf-eating god from the sky. At least you can come with me into the timber as I cut more stakes."

They finally followed her, with a casual glance and growl at the yellow bird. She cut four stakes from fallen limbs, sharpened the ends, and returned to the Cub alone. The wolves stayed at distance, again.

She laid down the stakes and did a damage assessment first.

The tail wheel was bent 90 degrees into the body of the tail. The elevators were full of small saplings and brush, with several tears in the fabric. The wings, being high profile, were clean and clear of damage, but their struts were full of brush and leaves. The landing gear was a mass of grass, brush, and dead birds probably thrown back from the prop, and many varieties of flowers. She looked again as something moved. Moving closer, she found a meadowlark trapped and entangled, but alive in the mass of grass wound around the landing gear. Carefully, she removed the little creature, stroked its head, felt its frail body and, before she could react . . . it flew away. Now that was a good feeling. *Enjoy your freedom, little bird. Sorry to harm your meadow home.*

She tied down the plane at each wing strut, the tail, and the landing gear. "That should keep you from flying away."

With. two of her tasks complete, she dialed FFS and asked for Joe. Milt was having none or that. He immediately asked where she and Bear were, why she needed to talk to Joe, and a zillion other questions he didn't want to hear answered. She explained what happened.

"You did what?" Milt yelled into the mike. In the background he told Dave and Joe to come into ops.

Milt and Dave asked about the plane.

"Yes, it's buttoned up so rain will not get into the electronics," she finished after a lengthy interrogation.

Then Joe got on the line, for the battery of DNR questions. "Bear made it clear," she cautioned amid the barrage, "that they want no additional help. He added that, being a deputy now, he could not cut them any slack, It would be hard to give then a second chance . . . again."

Milt came back on line with a little more relaxed attitude, saying, "Well, co-pilot, how can we help you?" She heard laughter in the background.

"You buggers, you know damn well what Bear wants. When, I'm not sure, but you rascals know."

"We'll see what can be done," he said, followed by laughter . "This pilot . . . a friend of yours, is he? What's his name again? Is it Fearless Flying Bruin of the DNR? Yeah, that's right?"

"Stop it, you rascals."

"Oh, we're not done. It's goin' to cost him dearly. First, a five-course dinner at Skagway's best for the pick-up. A large bottle of Irish Whiskey, for Joe, to keep this landing quiet. And finally, a pig roast, by you, on the meadow to top off all paybacks you two owe us."

"You rats. Give us a break!"

"Negative. No way. We've got him by the escroto, and we're goin' to keep the harassment at full tilt."

"Just wait, that's my territory, you bums, there will be paybacks."

"Okay, babe. Seriously, when he's finished rounding up those rogues, let us know, and we'll be there in less than an hour. We've got a sling, and the Cub only weighs nine-hundred pounds. Maybe we can fly out everyone who needs a lift. Is there anything else we can do?"

"No, I'm ready with my 94 if the bastards double back."

"Sorry for all the harassment, but you'll have to admit—it's a good story. Luckily, Windy and Raven have taken Janet downtown, so we're shielded from the press for the time being. Then again, she shoots straight. If I ask her not to report something, she won't."

"Fine, I noticed you two were in each other's eyes. Good show. Milt, it's about time you linked up and landed with something other than an airplane."

"That's enough, girl . . . so you noticed."

"Yes. Dave wouldn't, but we women are trained to know when passion is in the air. That's about it. Tell the kids I said hi, and I'm okay. Bye."

Being assured the Cub was resting well, she gathered her reluctant wolves and returned to the meadow. As they followed the trail down, a raven silently glided to one of the twin pines by the river and settled on its favorite perch.

After returning to the hut, she noticed someone had been working at her desk. She looked at the paper, and much to her delight, it was a draft of a short story BW was writing for school. As a stepmother, she read with interest this curious find. She thought, *This sounds fascinating. I wonder how it ends.* She sat with a mother's pride and continued reading . . .

*   *   *

English 101: A satirical short story.   by Chinodin, (Big Wind)
Professor L. Jones   Fall Semester

A Water Rescue

It was a dark and stormy night when Big Wind's bar of soap floated down the Bitterroot River, under the Tongass Memorial Bridge, through the Lynn Canal, into the Gulf of Alaska, and finally into the blue waters of the Pacific Ocean.

Due to "climate change," the melting iceberg waters of the Arctic gently pushed the bar southward toward the warmer California Current.

Hugging the coastline, the bar drifted leisurely along the loosely connected archipelago that comprised the inside passage of Canada's Northwest Territories, past picturesque British Columbia, and into the Strait of Juan de Fuca. The gradually shrinking bar traveled through the fog-shrouded San Juan Islands and rode the peaceful surf to shore, landing in the shadow of a resort known as The Rendezvous, where college students had gathered during spring break.

He thanked the Great Spirit for a safe voyage and rested . . . but not for long. As the waves gently inched him farther up the beach, two gorgeous women approached, a blond and a brunette. They wore revealing bikinis and white tank tops emblazoned with the challenge: *TRY ME!*

As the curvaceous brunette reached down to pick up the itinerant traveler, she said, "Look Shirl, a tiny bar of soap. It looks like it's been on a voyage . . . from Alaska, perhaps."

"I think you're right," said her buxom friend as she knelt in the sand and allowed the surf's bubbles to caress her toes, her toned calves, her athletic thighs, and her petite bikini bottom.

While cleaning the flotsam from the bar's body, the two foxes admired its determination. When they carried their rescued soap toward Shirl's red Jaguar, an ebony raven landed on a nearby Sitka spruce and croaked its arrival.

"We're goin' to take you home," said the brunette.

"And use you in the shower," finished the blond.

And to that, the little bar of soap thought, *Ah, life is good.*

—The End—

*   *   *

That's cute," Leigh said, "He's a clever writer. Like all men that age, he has pretty girls on his mind. He is a lot like his father."

With a smile on her face, she bustled around the hut and straightened up the area designed for one, now shared by four.

Chapter 27

Revenge

"I told you!" Red Dog shouted to Yellow Knife. "There he is. Dammit! See what you've got us into? There's two of 'em. Look, they're armed to the teeth. Bear's got some sort of police grenade gun in his belt and rifle at the ready. The other guy, hanging back, has a rifle, too. Worse yet, he looks like the boy we tied up. What are we gonna' do? They're gonna' blister our asses. I told you not to mess with him. Let's leave everything and run! Come on, you arse hole!"

"Shut up, you fool!" Yellow Knife yelled. "I'll figure somethin' out. Get rid of that bottle and drop behind the log over there."

"I'd rather run."

"I know. Be quiet. I'll find a way to talk us out of this jam. Maybe I can say we were just taking what was ours in the first place."

"Forget it. He'd never buy that. Think. Look, he's walking towards us just like Cooper in *High Noon*."

"Shut up. He must have crashed the airplane. Maybe he's hurt and unable to fight."

"Don't count on it. He's as tough as they come. Look, he's stopped about a hundred feet away by that dead pine. Damn, here comes the rain. It's gonna' get harder to see anyttin', much less those two."

"Would you shut up. I'm thinkin'. We're protected here; they're in the open. We'd win in a firefight."

"I think you're forgettin' he's now a conservation officer in the DNR; you don't want his blood on your hands. Let's get out of here."

Yellow Knife glared at him. "You simpleton. The police will never know who killed them; we could get away to one of the tribe's islands. They'd never know."

Red Dog yelled, "You dumb arse, there was another person in the plane . . . remember? Have you got your arse where the sun don't shine? They'd know."

"Damn, I forgot. But, maybe that person died in the plane crash. Yeah, that's it."

"You're a real piece of work, a piece of crap. That dog won't hunt. I'll show him right now. I'm not goin' back to the pen! Those five years felt like fifty." He racked a shell in the chamber.

"Don't do that, you fool. Settle down. You're half-drunk, anyway; you couldn't hit the broad side of a barn from the inside. Get that round out of the chamber!

You're liable to shoot that old blunderbuss accidentally."

Red Dog spoke in an incoherent manner. "Don't you realize? I'd be a three-time loser in the pen."

"Calm down, Dog. I'll get us out from under this!"

Bear moved to a better vantage point about 50 feet from the pair, checked on BW's location, and faced them hidden behind a couple of logs under the ledge. Without the travois, the horse wandered away to graze on tender fern fronds nearby.

"Okay, you bastard," Red Dog mumbled while looking at Bear. "You're in my sights."

*   *   *

Typical of the Tongass, rain started to pour. Bear stopped, checked on BW again, and motioned for him to get down.

He loaded the flare gun.

All he could see under the ledge, with the rain falling harder, was two shapes behind a couple of logs, their bodies leaning over what appeared to be guns. With rain dripping off his cap, his rifle, and his hands, he decided it was time to speak. They were not going to come out.

"Yellow Knife, this is Chi Mukwa, an officer in the DNR! I'd like you to put down your weapons, and come out so we can resolve your problem peacefully! I have to put you under arrest, but with luck, you may do local jail time versus prison in Juneau. Please! This doesn't have to end in bloodshed!"

"See? We're done!" Red Dog yelled. "No way! I'm not goin' back." In a fit of misguided passion, he leaped up, leaned into a firing position, aimed his old rifle . . . and fired.

Ka-Pow!

Bear groaned as he spun around and dropped into pooled water.

"Take that!" Red Dog shouted. "I'm not goin' back!"

"You fool! Get down," Yellow Knife yelled at Red Dog.

The slug had penetrated the left side just below Bear's rib cage. Gasping in pain, he grabbed for the flare gun at his fingertips, rolled over in anguish, looked toward the ledge. Red Dog was starting to run away. Bear aimed and fired. The ignited propellant blinded him temporarily. When the smoke cleared, he felt BW at his side.

"Get down, Dad. Stay down. The other one is up and aiming this way. As Red Dog screamed in agony, Bear saw the flare eating into his chest cavity.

Ka-Pow! Ka-Pow!

A round splintered the tree overhead, and the other tore into a log at their front. Lying on his side, BW yelled, "That's it! Drop your gun!"

Ka-Pow!

A round splashed in the water near BW's feet.

"You dumb sonabitch," BW yelled while moving to his knees.

As the rain obscured their vision, BW stood and pointed at the mass now running out from under the ledge, and fired two quick rounds at the blurred figure.

Ka-Pow! Ka-Pow!

A cry came from the area near the overhanging ledge. "I'm hit! God, I'm hit!" He fell to the ground, then got up and ran toward BW. "Don't shoot! Help me. I'm bleeding. Donnnn'tttt . . ." He fell into a pool of clear water that started turning red. He rolled over, threw his gun at BW, and moaned, "U-U-G-G-HHHH . . ."

Quiet embraced the river-side killing scene. Only the drenching rain cascading off the leaves and needles penetrated the hushed tone of the forest. Both men were silent for a moment, too. Bear tried to comprehend the carnage, and what they could have done differently to minimize the loss of life. They looked at each other but found no good answer.

"Thanks, son. Those last two shots were too damn close for comfort. I owe you."

"You owe me nothing. Let's take a look at your wound."

Bear rolled over on his right side.

BW cut away the shirt and examined the damage. "Damn! The slug went clear through and took a little of your side with it. Or, as Leigh would say, 'A little of her love handles.'"

"Is that right? Careful, boy," Bear chuckled.

"Bear, let me make a poultice."

"You don't have to do that."

"Yes, I do. Stay down. Who do you think showed me how to do this? You know who. You taught me in the Indian Guides program." BW removed his slicker, laid it aside, and removed his flannel shirt. He rolled it into a belt-like dressing, laid the sphagnum moss on the wound, and secured it. "There, that should hold you until we get back," BW said as he donned his slicker. "Now, do me a favor and take it easy. The bleeding has stopped, but if you start your typically energetic moves, it'll start again. You'll soon feel like you've been hit by a baseball bat, any way you cut it. So, please stay here; I'll go get the bodies."

"Son, would you talk seriously with me a moment? I've got to ask you a critical question."

"What?"

Bear spoke very seriously. "There will be investigation related to the shooting. Why don't you let me say that I shot Yellow Knife? It would make things a lot easier on you that way. Understand? It's between you and me. You will be pressed when you're questioned. It's just the way the law works. It's not right, but prosecutors always doubt younger men."

"Thanks, but no thanks. Our testimony will stand up to the judicial process. I did what anyone else would do under similar circumstances. If we tell the truth, we do not have to rehearse what to say. You gave them a chance. Do you think I was going to stand by while they were shooting at you like you were a duck in a carnival shooting gallery? No! Dad, coming out with you, I did hope the sword would not be drawn. However, it's clear to see once drawn, one may fall on his own—cliché, yes, but it's the truth, as we saw it unfold this afternoon. Now, hold still. As I said earlier, I'll go check the bodies."

Bear thought, *Now there's a son to be proud of. I'm a fortunate man, a blessed father of a son becoming a self-assured adult.*

BW returned to his dad and reported on the lethal wounds of both. He suggested the bodies be laid on the travois, wrapped in the hides, and that Bear ride Old Gal back to camp. That way he would not aggravate his wound.

"Riding Old Gal won't be necessary; I'm feeling better already," Bear said.

"Yeah, that's what I thought you'd say. In any case, I found the horse chewing down on a juniper, got her hitched up, loaded the bodies, and have her tied down by the trail. Now, I know you'll want to look over the area around the overhang for evidence. Let me help you up."

As Bear checked where the bodies fell, he once again felt sorry. He had to keep reminding himself that lethal force was not his way; it was their way. Certainly, part of their problem was alcohol. Red Dog's shot was probably triggered by whiskey. He could have just as easily done another five.

BW joined him as he examined where Red Dog had fallen. Part of his seared flesh remained. The flare had turned through his rib cage, into his lungs, and out his chest cavity. Voles were already nibbling on the burnt tissue.

BW mentioned that Yellow Knife's wounds were to the heart and lungs. The shock power of the .30 caliber most likely exploded his lungs and heart. He was probably dead before he hit the ground. "I threw the food away and collected the weapons and whiskey. They're on the travois, as evidence. Anything else?"

"Yeah. Let's sit a minute, and I'll call Joe at FFS with our report. It will only take us an hour to walk to the meadow."

"Good. Make your call. I'll check the travois on Old Gal. It needs a little reinforcement."

As his son departed, Bear made his call to FFS and told Joe everything that happened. "Why don't you leave now and you can pick us up, the bodies, and the plane in the same trip? Call Leigh for me, will ya? Tell her what happened, but don't tell her I'm wounded. BW and I plan to go with you to the State Police to make a report after I go to ER."

"We're on our way. Take it easy with that wound. You've certainly had a *full* day."

"Right there, Joe."

Bear thought, *An unscheduled and unauthorized landing, plus unwanted bloodshed is enough for a lifetime . . . actually, it all happened in less than four hours.*

Bear walked slowly toward the river trail where BW was waiting with the bier draped in black. "Well, BW, at least the Native Americans' good reputation in tribal affairs will no longer be tainted by these unsavory Haida rascals. It's too bad it had to end like this."

"Dad, give yourself a break. You did everything possible, including offering your body to avoid bloodshed. You gave them a chance, and what you got was a bullet that just missed killing you, more likely than not, only due to the pouring rain. You probably learned something, too. You learned not to be so trusting with your safety. This experience will help you on what to do in future situations. True?"

"You're right. I just did not want to appear a threat. The faith I had in them being able to reason was just not warranted. Yep, live and learn."

"Are you ready? Let's try that side. You may not be able to walk."

"Say, BW, could we take a minute to thank Manitou?"

"Of course. He's been with us a lot lately."

They held each other's left arms in the warrior's grip and spoke in the direction of the grandeur and beauty of the valley formed over thousands of years by the Bitterroot River.

"Dad, may I?"

"Certainly, son."

> "As long as the moon shall rise,
> As long as the river shall flow,
> As long as the sun shall rise,
> As long as the timber shall grow,
> As long as the birds shall fly,
> As long as the fish shall swim,
> I shall honor the Creator."

"I give thanks for the shield you provide against the perils of life," Bear said in response.

"Are you ready?"

"Yes."

Without a word, they slowly followed the river trail back to the meadow.

Due to BW's insistence, Bear was forced to rest several times along the way. As the afternoon sun slid from its zenith to the west, they sighted the meadow's resplendence. They stopped and looked at each other with expressions of gratitude. They'd made it home. It was as if returning from warfare with some gains offset by losses.

*   *   *

"Well, that's what he said we should do!" Joe explained.

"I don't care," Milt said. "We'll land, pick both of 'em, up, and immediately get the bodies to the police or coroner, then get Bear to the hospital. We can pick up the Cub anytime. She's tied down. In fact, I'll call Skagway ER right now and tell them we'll bring in Bear within the hour. He'll need surgery."

"Okay," Joe responded. "Dave's out warming up the chopper. Looks like we've got ourselves a road show. Let's be off."

"Joe, when you call the police, tell 'em to bring a couple of body bags, too."

"Right you are, Miltie. I'll do so from the chopper."

Joe had explained to the gang—Raven, Windy, and now Janet—what was going on. He also told then, much to their displeasure, that it would be better for them to stay at FFS during the first flight. The flight back would be crowded. He mentioned that if Milt and Dave approved, they could all go on the second flight to pick up the Cub. That would allow for Janet to visit the meadow, too. She was anxious to see the beauty of Leigh's retreat. Leigh had given her approval to visit, and was going to check with Bear, too.

Milt and Joe jumped aboard. Milt gave the go-ahead to Dave, he powered up the 1,000 HP turbine. They leaped into the air.

As they flew west, Joe checked the on-board first-aid kit for pain relievers and put a handful in his pocket for Bear.

Joe thought, *What have I forgotten? This ol' brain is close to overloading. We've got the hospital and police covered. I'd be remiss if I didn't brief me father and son on some of the unpleasant grilling the police frequently use, like good cop versus bad cop, or asking the same question five different ways to see if their stories hold up. I be takin' care of that. No problem.*

Joe got on the intercom to speak to Milt. "Milt, did Bear tell you anything about who shot the Indians?"

"No. I thought he may have told you. I was wondering, also. Maybe Bear did all the shooting. Then again, BW would have to be armed while in pursuit. Maybe BW was just a witness. But, Bear said BW saved his life. The way I see it, BW did some shooting, too. Had to, the way Bear talked."

"Right you are, m'man. We'll find out soon enough. I just want to make certain their confrontation, their shooting story is clear and to the point so the police don't have any doubts as to the veracity of their comments."

Milt answered, "Soon enough. We're fifteen minutes from the meadow. I'm starting down."

Joe answered, "Thankie. I'll call Leigh and let her know we're on the way."

*   *   *

Leigh yelled, "That stinker. He could have called me, too. Wait till I get a hold of him. I'll wring his neck."

Leigh heard the news, then hung up the phone and thought, *Has fate dealt me another blow? Please, Manitou, don't let me lose another.*

No sooner had she reached the renowned bench by the twin pines on the river than BW appeared. He was leading Old Gal along the path, her traces lashed around her with the travois dragging behind. Bringing up the rear was Bear. They looked soaked to the bone.

Not knowing of a unique greeting for the two men with conflicted thoughts displayed on their faces, Leigh gave the universal greeting.

"Hi! Guys, welcome back. I've missed you."

Chapter 28

Reprisal

A raven's call echoed across the meadow as the pair emerged from the trail.

Leigh sighed. *Look at them, beat-up physically, and I'll bet mentally, too. They survived, true, but the deaths of those Indians is going to be hard for them to forget. I hope Bear understands their tribal elders had no kindred relationship for the pair. They had been causing problems to law-abiding citizens along the Lynn Canal for years. There will be no regrets.*

"Hi, Mom!" BW shouted.

Leigh's heart skipped a beat hearing those words, that sound. In an instant tears came to her eyes. She loved that boy. "Hi, guy. I hear it's been a tough trip. How are you?"

"Fine, but I'll feel much better in dry clothes and drinking some Irish coffee."

"That, I can take care of. How 'bout that guy bringing up the rear?"

With an attempt at humor, BW said, "Oh, that guy. I picked him up along the river. He, too, will be looking for some dry clothes, smooth whiskey, warm food, and a hot woman."

"That, I can handle."

"Hi, dear," Bear whispered. "How the hell are you?"

"Fine, now that you're here."

"The feeling's mutual, dear."

As BW walked Old Gal to the stable, Leigh and Bear held each other, their emotions blending the two as one. Words were unnecessary to communicate the feelings lovers experience when one had been close to being lost.

Leigh's sense of relief proved a poignant contrast to the anguish of her past, the lovers she had lost.

Was it seconds or minutes? They held tight without a beginning or end, an embrace by lovers with absolute fidelity to each other.

A sound suddenly caught their attention.

They looked to the east as the hum turned to a rumble and then to a thumping sound and then to a *Wop—Wop—Wop*.

"Good timing, dear," Leigh said. "Milt and Dave want to get the bodies and you out now, and return for the Cub later."

"But . . ." Bear whispered. "I thought . . ."

"No buts. It's their decision. They're not worried about the Cub; getting you to ER is what's important. Taking the Cub now would slow them down."

"Okay, I understand. But, is she tied down good?"

"Listen, you shot-up-hunk, I was like a Lilliputian tying down Gulliver; the Cub ain't going anywhere. In fact, Milt's coming back tomorrow to pick her up. Satisfied?"

"Yes, dear. Thank you. You must understand my reasons for safekeeping the Cub. They're two-fold: I'm the one who put her down where she's not supposed to be; and in a violent wind she'd be in a hangar, not up there exposed to the elements. Understand? Chasing bandits is no excuse for exposing an FFS plane to the elements."

"All that is true, but isn't hindsight twenty-twenty? You did what you felt was right at that time. Didn't Yellow Knife try to kill you at the fish weir? The answer: Yes! Was our home and son threatened? The answer: Yes! Haven't you preached that you can always replace property, but never a person's life?"

"Yeah, but . . ." He reluctantly yielded to her logic.

"Now, let's have a look at that wound."

"How do you know . . . I suppose I can answer that. Joe, that old blabber-mouth, told you. Right?"

"Does it matter? Do you think I didn't notice your left side swollen? Are you pregnant? Can I have a look?"

"You know—I think not. No offense. Let's not disturb BW's moss-pack. The bleeding has stopped, and with luck, I'll be at the hospital within the hour."

"Okay. I'll take a look when we get there."

"You don't have to go," he said. "Who's going to stay here? The wolves? The plane? The horse?"

"You know, you're not the only one figuring things out. Windy and Raven are riding the big buckskin and the sorrel back as we speak. They'll be here in an hour or two. Any more questions?"

"No, I should have known you'd have everything figured out."

"Well, the great warrior of the northwest has given his simple wife some credit. Hear hear! He's just realized he did not marry just any old broad."

"Okay, you're a keeper. If I threw you back, you'd jump right back into my creel, anyway. Hey, it's stopped raining. Before the chopper lands, let's get us some dry clothes."

Milt brought the chopper down near the stable, flared, and cut power to idle. Joe slid the door open, jumped down, and joined BW, who had dragged the travois to the edge of the meadow where they landed.

Joe laid some old FFS blankets on the ground, and the pair retrieved the Indians' bodies from the hides, wrapped them in the blankets, and respectfully transported them to the chopper. After Joe secured the bodies, he signaled for Bear and Leigh to get aboard.

Bear told Leigh, "Forget the clothes. Mine have dried on me." Double-checking the wolves and Old Gal, BW told the animals that Windy and Raven would be here soon, not to worry.

Leigh whispered to Bear, "You'd think the animals were kids and understood what he was saying. He's such a dear."

Bear gave her a scolding look. "We natives believe the four-legged do understand. You newcomers to the forest have yet to be aware of this. He knows."

She knew enough not to argue with him, and said, "Yes, I had overlooked native skills as 'whisperers.'"

BW jumped aboard, buckled up, and the big bird lifted up and over the plateau, seeing the Cub below, and heading toward ER and the inquisition by police in Skagway.

*   *   *

Joe used the flight time to everyone's advantage by explaining how the interrogation by police generally worked. Joe had been through many sessions in the past, both as an armed officer of the DNR, and as a Canadian Mountie. His concern was not so much for Bear, an officer in the DNR, but for BW. Some of the "old bulls" in the detective unit were pretty pushy toward youth. They tried harder to break a youngster's sworn testimony. In this case, it would soon be revealed that BW killed Yellow Knife to save his dad's life. Bear's testimony would match BW's, but their job was to be certain the conclusion was self-defense.

Joe asked each of them to tell his story to him, and do it again until it was crystal clear what had transpired. Joe was satisfied with their continuity, but he reminded BW that some old bulls would hammer on his inexperience as short-tempered, immature, and with hippie culture liberalism. All this was to get them mad and maybe, just maybe, contradict the story. Nevertheless, Joe thought him ready for a grilling. He was a very mature eighteen.

He told Bear that once Geez heard what had happened, he flew in to show his support in Skagway.

Joe reminded Leigh that she might also be called, as his wife, to address Bear's stability under pressure. He gave her a few tips. The most important, do not volunteer information that is not asked for. In other words, zip it. Be as quiet as a little church mouse. Also, remember KISS: Keep It Simple Stupid.

Bear could not hold in his chuckle.

"Hush up," Leigh said. "I can be quiet when I want to."

Bear mumbled, "That will be the day Niagara stops falling."

"I know you said something under your breath."

"Gee, give me a break."

"No."

Joe went on. "Milt and Dave may also be called. They pose no problem—except if asked if it is normal for a pilot to land on such a hazardous surface as the plateau. I asked them to tell a little white lie, meaning, yeah, it was not that unusual, considering the circumstances. They may try to infer you're a little loony."

"Leigh, don't you say a word," Bear said.

"Why, the thought."

"Stop it, you two. I've got you covered anyway. Tell them the PIC can make decisions based on the situation at hand. He's in charge of the aircraft and passengers."

Leigh said, "Do you mean, when he's flying, I have no input as to our next move?"

"That's about it, Leigh." Joe sighed.

"Bummer."

"I've asked Morning Star to be there," Joe said. "As BW's mom, she may be of value to explain his level-headedness. After all, he is chairman of the Writer's Club at the college. She was happy to help, and not a problem, having parted with Bear in an amicable fashion. Also, she's a Tlingit. A few of the police here are of mixed blood. Generally, Haida, or Tlingit. That's it, me friends. Ready or not, here we go."

As the chopper descended over the crowd, he could pick out Geez, Morning Star, Janet, and "the bulls" in their forty-dollar Sears suits, the swelling below their armpits provided by Smith & Wesson. The attendants stood by the ambulance. There were no onlookers. It appeared that the local police had closed down the airfield, probably until the bodies were removed.

As the bird smoothly touched down, Joe requested a moment with Milt before deplaning.

As the rotors came to a silent halt, Milt and Dave entered the passenger compartment.

"Thanks, Milt. Me friends, no matter who we are, what we've done in our lives, or the beliefs we hold dear, I believe we have an obligation to ourselves to say a little something for the deceased men before us. Shall we take that moment?"

They all nodded.

A surprise to Joe, BW spoke. "May I lead the petition for our lost brothers?"

"By all means."

BW cleared his throat, inhaled, and began,

> "Great Spirit, lover of all plants and animals in your Kin(g)dom,
> I petition you to accept and forgive the souls of these deceased
> Native Americans, of the Haida tribe, Yellow Knife and Red
> Dog. We ask that their souls be set free to live again. Have pity

on them and hear our voice of sorrow for their families. Bless
our brothers as we humbly continue to serve your Kin(g)dom."

"Be Jesus, m'man," Joe said. "Ye'd make a good man of the cloth."

"Thank you," BW said, "but I'm more of a man of reason than sightless faith.
I've been influenced by Jesus; The Buddha; and Native American Spirituality. But
I am not a trinitarian. I believe Jesus was the greatest prophet of kindness to walk
this earth; The Buddha, the greatest teacher of the four noble truths for awakening
our loving kindness toward each other; and Manitou, the Great Spirit, the Creator,
who teaches us to appreciate nature and our environment, be it Earth Mother, Father Sky, or all the creatures herein.

"No," BW continued, "not a man of the cloth; a man of reason still learning
how to live with others in this complex world of varied plants and animals. We
indeed need each other, two- and four-leggeds, to survive. I've always said, the
Kin(g)dom, of the Creator is spread upon the earth for all to see, and we must hold
dear and respect the treasures of our universe. I will attempt to do just that—to
spread the word that we'd better learn to appreciate nature before we lose it."

"Any who," Joe said, "thank ye, BW. We be proud of ye."

"You're welcome."

"Remember what I told ye," Joe said. "Zip it up after you've told 'em your
story. As they say in the military, don't volunteer for anything."

*   *   *

Joe watched the ambulance back up to the open door of the chopper. The
medical attendants placed the bodies in the body bags, loaded them, and quietly
departed.

Friends waiting on the apron for the crew greeted each other. Bear thanked
Geez for coming. Then, while Milt and Dave were talking with Morning Star, Bear
hugged her, followed by BW, and then Geez. Milt and Dave left with Janet at Milt's
side.

Shortly thereafter the two detectives approached from their cruisers. Those remaining, Bear and BW, plus Leigh, Morning Star, and Joe were introduced, and the
detectives asked for Bear to ride in one car, BW in the other on the way to the
hospital. They wisely indicated that Bear's treatment was the number-one priority.
So, without further delay, they left. Joe drove a FFS truck with Leigh and Morning
Star.

"See you later," Bear shouted to his friends.

As BW got into the cruiser, he said, "Cogito, ergo sum."

Joe glanced at Morning Star with a puzzled look, "What the heck does that
mean?"

"Oh, he's such a character. It's his way of telling me that he'll be okay. Things are working out. He feels confident in the situation he's in. In Latin, it means: 'I think, therefore I exist.' It's one of Decartes' favorite sayings. BW learned it at school while studying the language."

"I'm glad you're here. Tell him next time to speak in a way this ol' Brit will understand."

"My dear, there will be no next time."

Joe followed the two vehicles in one splashed with *FFS-Flight School, Your first introductory flight—only $10.* Call Milt or Dave.

After ten minutes at a snail's pace, Joe complained, "They're certainly driving slow enough. They also seem to be yammerin' at each other animatedly. Don't you think? You can see, too?"

Morning Star answered, "I'm not sure if that's good or bad. We Natives do not fill up all available space with chatter. It's our way . . . to become good listeners. If they're talking as much as it appears, they're either trying hard to prove a point or have done so and are gabbing. Men do gab, you know. I hope it's the latter."

Leigh chimed in, "You can say that again. Bear can gab, if he feels like it. Then again, at other times he's great for one-word answers. Yes. No. Yeah. Maybe. That's right, he thinks that's talking. He can be a real clunkhead at times."

"Believe us, Joe," Star said. "We know. Things must be going well or both would be in the 'Yes' and 'No' profile. It even looks like they're speaking into a recorder. See that mike in Bear's hand."

As they pulled into the hospital parking lot, Joe suggested that he join the four and see how things went during the in-car interrogation. "Then we'll meet them in the visiting room as soon as we know something."

Already in the room, Geez was delighted to meet Bear's wives. Within minutes, Milt and Dave showed up with Janet. Owing to her profession, when introduced to Geez her conversation was more like an interview. He didn't seem to mind since she was asking about the DNR, his second love.

At the nursing station Joe learned Bear was being examined. His next surprise was when he walked in on the animated conversation between BW and the two detectives. It sounded like a high-school reunion.

"Is that right? You, too? Well, I'll be darned."

What's going on here? he thought. He approached the three, who were engrossed in describing tales of past exploits around Alaska's vast frontier. "How we doin', BW?"

"Oh, there you are. Fine. May I have the pleasure of introducing detectives Lt. Anderson and Sgt. Gnodtke. Then again, you probably already know them."

"No, I have not had the pleasure. Joe Bloom. Pleased to meet you."

"Indeed. We're new to this area along the canal. So we finally meet the former

Canadian Mountie, and now USA's terror of the Tongass. Yes, we've heard of you via reputation and deeds from Barrow to Kitchikan. Pleased to meet you," Anderson said as both shook Joe's hand.

"May I help you with the background information of the deceased? I've been in this area for a while and have quite a file on their activities."

"Thank you, but that won't be necessary. The files at the office provided quite a bit along with their extensive rap sheet. We're closing our investigation with the interviews on the way over. We'll attach the results of the autopsies, which is being performed as we speak, and file the report in the morning. This investigation is closed. BW and Bear are free to go. Bear is a lucky man. BW tells us that if the rain had not affected sighting accuracy, he may have been hit worse. Don't you love his son's joke about the hit 'right through Bear's love handles'?" Anderson chuckled.

"Mr. Bloom," said Gnodtke, "the office tells us many agencies have been after these rascals for years. Even their tribal elders did not like them slinking back to the reservation for protection. Sadly, for you in the DNR, many of the crimes involved fish and game violations, unfortunately fueled by meat hunters from the lower 48 who hired them so they did not go home without a trophy. Yes, Mr. Bloom, the lethal force needed to stop all these misdeeds was unfortunate, but necessary when you're in the sights of a violator. I'll bid you and your friends good-bye and hope to see you again under more favorable circumstance. Good day."

"BW, it's been a pleasure," said Anderson. "Lots of luck in school with your studies. Give my regards to your dad."

The detectives departed through the visiting room, tipped their hats, and left the building. The gals hustled to the nursing station where Joe and BW were waiting for Bear.

Leigh was first: "What did they say? Will they arrest them? Will they have to go to jail? What's next?"

Morning Star followed: "Are the men going to be allowed to leave tonight?"

With a smile, Joe told them what happened.

"Few in law enforcement are weeping over the fate of those rogue Indians. Their elders are probably sad but likely knew that this day would come. They'll still be buried with some respect. The elders will pick up their bodies tomorrow."

BW got a couple of hugs from his mother and stepmother. Luckily, Joe received a couple, too, since he was in the cross-fire of motherly love. As the others joined, they also got a hug. Geez was also enjoying the hugs and kisses.

Bear was finally wheeled out of ER with the doctor pushing. Although able to walk, regulations required that he be in a wheelchair when released. He had convinced the doctor to come out with him to meet his friends since they were such a cool group. They bumped into Leigh and Joe first.

She ran to him and gave him a careful kiss, hugs to be deferred for a later date.

The doctor got his share, too. "Welcome back to a normal life, my dear—as normal as you'll let it be. Let's get you to FFS so you can rest." Then she whispered, "We've got to figure a way to make. love on your right side without hurting your left."

"Believe me, dear, we'll find a way," he chuckled.

Joe grinned, knowingly, then said, "Say, me friend, there's a few people out there who would like to greet you."

In the next few minutes, Bear was inundated again with thank you's until he escaped to the pharmacy to get his Rx for the night.

Finally, it was over; people started leaving and going their separate ways.

*   *   *

After Bear reached the visiting room, he stopped and slowly got up from the wheelchair. He tested his legs, which seemed to work quite well, and for good measure held on to Leigh as he departed. Leigh nudged Bear on the good side. "Look at that. Morning Star is sitting with Dave over a cup of coffee. They are sitting very close. Would you believe? BW said she was dating. Who would have guessed it was Morning Star."

"I think you're jumping to conclusions. Maybe they're just friends."

"Ah . . . yeah. And what do you think that leads to? They're both single. Believe me, I can tell they have been together before tonight."

"You sure seem to match people up with little evidence."

"Wrong you are. This is exciting. First Windy and Raven, then Milt and Janet, now Dave and Morning Star. The Tongass is on a lover's roll!"

"By the way, did you remember that Windy and Raven are alone at the hut tonight?"

"Don't remind me."

"How 'bout Joe? No woman is rolling with him under the sheets."

"He doesn't count. He's a loner, a wanderer, an explorer. The Tongass is his bride. No one will ever have his shoes under her bed . . . no way!"

"You think you know so much. I hope he drops in one night and presents his woman for your approval."

"No way, Jose."

"Let's get out of here and try the right side."

"We must be careful, dear . . . but be assured, my lips and hips are at your service."

Chapter 29

Repertoire

As the sun broke over the tree-tops, Windy nailed the last set of planks. With Raven's help, the pentagon was almost finished. The design change from a hexagon was based on air-lift weight, architectural enhancement, and sizing needs.

Old Gal helped them haul the 24-inch boulders to the site. At each corner, the half-buried stones gave the foundation's sill plate the necessary stability for the 3-ton addition. The most critical aspect of the planking was to ensure levelness and that each angle was at an exact 36 degrees on each of the five corners.

Unbeknownst to Leigh and Bear, FFS personnel had dropped off the foundation planking earlier, and had been working on the addition for the last week. The good news was that if the foundations were complete by early morn, the pentagon would be flown out in the afternoon, weather permitting.

They finished in the early morning.

"Hon, we'd better get on the horn to Milt," Raven said. "We've made it! We've finished!"

It was hard work, but they achieved their goal earlier than planned due to Raven's focused work ethic and no-nonsense attitude. Windy had developed an enhanced opinion of her. She knew how to play hard and work hard and, better yet, when to do each. The project's short timeline also gave him a chance to see them both working under stress and sweat.

"You're right, Babe," said Windy. "We're ready to mate the prefab to the foundation's sillplate, and it looks great. We'll certainly need Milt's skill to drop her close, and our hands to guide her onto the anchor bolts."

"How true," Windy said as he started raking a kindling pile at the fire-pit. "It's going to be a tight fit, but we'll manage. We make an unbeatable team. Why don't you call Milt while I do some cleanup and feed the horses."

"Milt? Hi. It's Raven. Yep, we're still bright-eyed and bushy-tailed and ready to go. Today! Yes. No, we were in separate beds, as always, my friend. Why do you ask? Just curious, is that it? Could you be the 'front man' for Leigh? My, but you're inquisitive. No. No, not even a BNR . . . now I know you're asking for Bear, that's his term. Yes, we behaved. *Milt!* Stop it. What kind of a gal do you think I am? You stinker. I hear you and Dave laughing. This harassment is goin' to cost you, big time. Okay, I figured they were behind the questions. You're forgiven. Okay, see you in about an hour or so. Yes, with you and Dave helping we will get it done before nightfall, and be ready for Leigh and Bear tomorrow. See you. You're still a stinker."

They worked on the octagon's modifications next. An opening for the entry door from the old to the new was cut; the overhang on the mating section was torn off. Their final mod was to mark holes for cable routing.

Windy gave a Tarzan yell and grabbed Raven with the gusto of an ape man. "Me Tarzan, you Jane. We go wash. You wash me. I wash you, no?"

She answered, "No."

"Okay! Here's my more suave, debonair approach. Madam, may we bathe?"

"Well, here's my answer: Monsieur, to be sure, if your character is virtuous."

They ran to the river with the wolves in the lead. They knew what was coming down and were ready for a water fight.

"Isn't it great? We're done!" Raven boasted. "Then again, we've just started. I guess it's that the hard part here is finished. I'm excited since this is the first project I've seen grow from concept and design to costing, fabrication, and now to final assembly . . . and with you and I as Project Managers. Cool huh?"

"Ditto, Kiddo! I agree. Say, rather than just washing up, let's swim," Windy suggested.

"Sure, but you've got to behave yourself. Do you realize we've been pushin' it since the trail ride from Skagway yesterday, hauling boulders last night, setting the sill plates this morning, and getting ready for mating this morning? I'm ready for a good dunking, and a good night's sleep. First things first: You're gonna have to get the soap back from the wolves; it's like a floating ball to them."

"Yeah, I'll get it in a minute. Babe, I've enjoyed every minute being with you. Working together has been a privilege. Isn't it great to feel we've played a small part in getting the addition ready for Bear's healing time, his convalescence, even though it may only be a few days? Just think, in a manner of speaking, his son saved his life. How good do you think that makes both father and son feel? Yep, I may have misjudged BW."

"True, his only mistake with you was in not knowing that I was not up to involvement with another man. You know, it's in your loins. You're always looking; it's the primitive man coming to the surface . . . with words versus a club."

"I guess, in any case, he's earned my respect."

Her next comment made his jaw drop, "If you behave yourself, let's go skinny-dipping, then I can wash *all* my clothes. You've probably noticed, I haven't changed clothes for the last forty-eight hours."

"I wouldn't have noticed. I only look at your beautiful, blue-green eyes."

"Aren't you the romantic? Flattery will get you . . . me—or something like that. I'm not as good at slogans as performance. Did I say that? Whoa, girl."

He thought for a second. *Pinch me, self. Is this really happening to me?* "Sounds good to me." He started doffing his clothes before she changed her mind.

"You know, the crew will he here soon," she said as she turned, dropping her well worn denims and pulling off her Michigan sweatshirt. "Now, you've promised *not* to get frisky. I'm holding you to that, m'man."

With her back to Windy, she released the clasp in the front of the lacy, blue bra, and while standing on one foot removed her matching blue panties. She then grabbed her clothes, turned, and jumped into the water with the bundle covering only half of her sexuality. She shooed the wolves away, then washed and rinsed her clothes, very carefully, since the wolves and current wanted them.

He thought, *Just look at her, it's as if the splendor of her womanhood is unfolding before my eyes.*

She yelled, "Are you gonna just stand there and stare, or come in, and wash up, and get these wolves away from me?"

At her prodding, he lost all his earlier sense of modesty, stripped, and jumped into the river with all appendages flailing. "Woo! This is invigorating!"

"Me, or the water?"

"Both, for sure. You're a beautiful woman, Raven. Better throw me the soap before I blow a gasket. Maybe I can wash away my feelings."

"I doubt it. Could you call the wolves away from me? I've already lost a bra in the current. Shoo, wolves, shoo!"

"Over here, you guys. Come on, Tough. Get over here!" Windy yelled. As the wolves came over to wrestle with him a while, he chuckled to himself. *Losing a bra is not so bad for me. I may be in for a swinging time.* "You know, you've been pretty good to me, yet pretty hard on me, too. Being young and restless, it's like grilling a man his favorite steak, putting it in front of him, and saying he can't eat."

"Poor boy. Do I have to review the rules we agreed on? Here's the soap; wash some of the sexual urge from your body." She threw the soap. The wolves followed, leaving her standing alone in only three feet of water.

At that sight, he was beside himself with lust. The wolves aside, the totality of her erotic beauty was beyond measure. *Why me, Lord?* he thought. *And I promised to behave. Rats. You fool, try something before the opportunity is lost. Try anything.*

He yelled, "I'm clean! Do you need the soap? Can I wash your back? Rinse you off? Rinse your clothes?"

"Whoa, big boy. Rules are rules. No, I'm all squeaky-clean and rinsed, and I feel invigorated, too. This cold water could wake up the dead."

He whispered to himself, "Maybe for me it's what's *in* the water that has awakened my loins."

"What did you say?"

"I said, I'm awake, too."

She gave him a skeptical look.

"Okay," he continued, "a compromise: How 'bout a kiss? We've done that before!"

"Excuse me, but not when I'm naked as a jaybird!"

"Okay, just a little kiss with my hands tied behind by back, no BNR—ITR."

"BNR, I know," she said. "BNR—ITR? What?"

"Simple: No Bare Naked Rollaround—In The River."

"You're hopeless," she said.

"I p-r-o-m-i-s-e to keep my hands to myself."

"You're a real pain in the arse. You men! Okay, get over here in the deep water so *I* don't get any ideas from *your* arousal."

"Deal."

He followed her to a deep hole in the river and gave her a healthy kiss, which she returned in kind. Excited by her suggestive lips, he reached around her waist and held her whole body tight. Her arms followed to his back, and they enjoyed the wet splendor of mutual passion. He felt her whole body . . . but she quickly broke away and dunked him.

"That," she said, "should take care of you—for a while—but, my dear Windy, don't lose that thought. We can use it later."

As he surfaced from the dunking, he saw her exit the river, clothes in hand.

She turned and yelled, "Come on, m'man. We've got to get dressed; they'll be here any minute." She disappeared up the trail and into the hut.

Reluctantly, he trudged out of the water, put his clothes back on, and sauntered back to the hut. He was happy that they had taken the first step in showing their mutual love, yet a little frustrated that he could not linger longer. Nevertheless, she had made the rules, and he had pushed her to the limits. He knew very well she was right in cutting him off when she did, that he needed his libido dunked. If she hadn't, there would have been no Dolly Vardens for days.

Wop—Wop—Wop

As he approached the hut, she ran out, looking beautiful without makeup, a shiny look of youthful vigor in a ponytail.

"Quick," she said, "dry your hair and straighten up. I'll go out to the site. Love ya." She gave him a quick peck on the cheek and ran out to greet the chopper that looked like a mother with a baby hut dangling from its umbilical.

He joined her in less than two minutes and contacted the pilot, Milt. "This is meadow base. Welcome, FFS. You're a sight for sore eyes. You look like you've just given birth to a little house. Do you read? Over."

"This is FFS," Milt responded. "Read you loud and clear. We've had a good flight, and are ready to deliver this bouncing baby house. You ready? Over."

Windy said, "As they say, ready, willing, and able. I'm excited to link up these two geometric forms, then stand back and admire your work. We just finished a few hours ago, and we're ready. Over."

"Okay", Milt said, "here's the deal. See those two lanyards hanging down from the base plate? There's one on each corner of the pie shape that attaches to the existing hut. When I lower the unit, use the lanyards to pull/position the new module to the existing unit. Don't worry about a couple of inches of error. We can force the module square with a sledge. Got it? Here we come."

"Got it! Bring her down. Over."

"One more thing: Joe will be releasing the sling when we're in place—not me—so be sure of your signals to him. Here we come."

Windy and Raven caught the lanyards. It became more stable. All the signals worked well as Joe lay in the open door, relaying information to Milt.

As planned, the module nestled on the sill plates. Windy and Raven pulled it snug to the parent octagon unit. Joe released the eye-hook, and the sling fell harmlessly on the module's roof. The chopper lifted to the cheers of the ground crew.

Milt came back on the air. "How'd it go? Is it down, snug, and level?"

"It is, Milt. It looks damn good from here. How's she look from up there? We're ready to close her in. See you in a bit," Windy said excitedly.

"I've got a little surprise for you. I'm going to set down here and help you before we pick up the Cub. The five of us will be at your service in one minute."

Windy told Raven.

She looked puzzled, too. "I wonder who the other two are? We planned on Joe, Milt, and Dave—Wait, I bet I know. It'll be the gals."

The chopper landed and, sure enough, Janet and Morning Star, the flyers' gal friends, got out with the aid of Joe. After power-down and shut-down of the flight systems, Milt and Dave joined the gals, and they came over to the hut, jabbering a mile-a-minute.

Raven spoke first. "Isn't this a pleasant surprise? Would you believe that we'd see you so soon? Welcome to the meadow, gals. It's about time I got a chance to kick it with you. Windy's been working me like a dog. Just kidding; we've made a lot of progress, more than planned. I kinda like acting as hostess while Leigh stays with Bear another day. They'll be here tomorrow. I'd better warn you gals, there's never a dull moment at the meadow. Why don't you guys show the gals around, and Joe can help us button this baby up."

The couples liked that idea. Milt took Janet to the river. Dave and Morning Star climbed to the plateau. It was very noticeable that holding hands was not needed for stability, in both cases.

*   *   *

Raven whispered to Joe as they moved to the hut. "Will wonders never cease? Look at 'em, both of those fly boys are talking an ear off the gals. Their hearts are in it. Little do they know how many couples have given their hearts to each other on these sacred, communal tribal grounds. It looks to me, Joe, like there's going to be more."

"Me lassie, 'tis no doubt you be noticin' the same as I. Da boys are smitten. Be aware, the look I see in your eyes indicates the same. You and Windy do make a fine couple. You two have also given Leigh and Bear a mental goose, a stimulus of sorts, to make their life more excitin'. I be proud of ye. Keep up the good work."

"Love you, Joe. Thanks for noticing," she said as she gave him a good kiss on the cheek.

*   *   *

"Okay, folks," Joe said, "here's the plan. I'm goin' to take over this bloody hut-assembly operation. As soon as Dave and Milt get back, they'll connect the power and commo lines, since that's their area of expertise. Windy and I are goin' to join the units with the necessary fillers and shims at the external walls, then patch the roof lines together, and chalk the joint, and shingles. When finished with that, we're goin' to trim the bloody doorway openin'.

"Raven, you can start now, or when the gals return. The whole layout has to be altered to move Leigh and Bear into the addition as a sleeping area and place for Leigh to write—her getaway. You know more about that than I, so have at it, gal.

"If those fly boys get in your way solderin' connections, or whatever, just give 'em a kick in the arse. Come on, Windy, let's hop to it."

As they started working, the couples came back and joined the closing-in activities. No doubt the sounds indicated it was indeed a labor of love. It was not unlike a scene from Habitat for Humanity, sans Jimmy Carter.

Finished by noon, they all sat by the river chewing on smoked salmon and French bread and drinking California dry white chardonnay, with a chorus of wolves singing their begging song of the Tongass.

Joe brought Windy and Raven up-to-date on the incident with the Haida Indians and the surprising decision by the police at the hospital. They also looked at the two couples with the same surprising resolve. Milt and Janet's togetherness happened in the open. Joe had seen it coming from the first day at ops. On the other hand, Dave's move to Morning Star happened under the radar.

Joe added, "It was probably out of respect for Bear. Although they split amicably, when love moves in uncharted waters, frequently unknown hazards appear. Until certain about a relationship, it's best to keep its presence known only between the two involved. That's what Dave did at FFS. Me is the only bloke safe from the overnight woman."

Raven questioned, "Overnight woman? What?"

"'Tis easily explained, my dear. I may be with a woman some night, but she would not be stayin' overnight. Off she goes before morn."

Raven sternly chided him. "That's not very nice, Joe."

"Me lassie, I do not care if I'm nice; I'm not interested in the long term. No one would want me anyhow."

"Don't be so sure of that. She's out there. She has yet to find you, or you her," Raven said in a nicer tone.

"I'm not so sure of that. I'll leave all the lovin' and kissin' to you and Windy."

"I'm not sure what you mean. Yes, we're close friends."

"Yes, apparently so . . . as I observed through my binoculars just clearing the tree tops earlier. I spotted some interestin' activities on the meadow."

Raven quickly responded, "What activity?"

"Well, at distance, and with all the vibration of the chopper, I was still anxious to look ahead and see if you guys had finished buildin' the foundations."

"Did you see that we were ready?"

"Sure did. I also saw a lovely girl run from the river, au naturel—starkers, as we Brits say. Do you have any idea who that lovely lady could have been?"

Windy was visibly attuned to the conversation now. She studied his facial features for an answer, and finding none, she said, "No. Do you think it could have been The White, the white wolf, running by, and you could have been mistaken?"

"My dear friend, you know I love you as a daughter, but between you and I, that was probably not the case. I don't know of many four-leggeds which run on their hind feet. Be that as it may, I'll say no more to anyone about the athletic wolf, my altered vision, and my blurred sighting. That will be our agreement . . . to each other. After all, me thinks an animal must take a bath. True?"

"Thanks, Joe," Raven said as she gave him a big hug.

"Thank you dearie. It looks like you've got a winner there, Windy. Shall we round up the loungin' lovers and get on with our next task? Carrying our little yellow bird back to the nest? Where did those blokes go?"

Raven chimed in. "I think they're still by the river and the plateau. I'll go get 'em."

Joe got up and said to Windy, "Let's go and get that bird rigged up. Milt and Dave have other fish to fry. Come on, me boy. Do take good care of me little girl; I can tell you're both in love. Treat her with the respect Manitou would wish, and be very happy."

"Deal. Thanks for not pressing on Raven's exposure."

"Don't mention it. I've been skinny-dipping with a gal or two over time, too. I hope you enjoyed the swim."

"Indeed, I did . . . for only five seconds. She is tough. I have a feeling I'll not be interlocked with her until Gete Wabiska blesses us. That's okay; she's worth the wait, and we plan to talk to him very soon."

Raven joined them as they walked up to the plateau, everyone focused on flying out with the Cub in tow.

"There you are, Milt. Let's get this show on the road," Joe kidded.

*   *   *

Milt answered, "Indeed. The gals would like to stay longer, but I promised to bring them back, and they agreed to leave . . . but only under those terms. Okay, it looks like Joe has the bird ready by attaching the sling the two pick-up points above the cabin. Fortunately, all planes have this hoisting or pick-up lugs at their CG for times like this or for maintenance. Here's the deal. We'll load up and fly over the bird. Raven, you get on Windy's shoulders like you did as kids, as if you were in a water fight. Okay? Then, when I descend, hook the safety clasp in the loop from tie chopper. After you give a sign to Joe, I'll slowly lift our little bird up. You two will move away to avoid any side-slipping by the plane. Got it?"

"Got it. Let's go!" Windy shouted.

*   *   *

The gals gave Raven a hug as they departed. The crew gave Windy a thumbs up, and Raven gave Joe a bear hug tight enough to last a week. As she released him, he whispered in her ear, "Do you think that white wolf that I saw could have been running from an aggressive alpha male? Just wondering. Love ya."

"You stinker. Get!"

Windy asked, "What was that about?"

"Nothing."

As the crew walked down to the chopper, someone yelled, "Remember to take pictures!"

Raven yelled back, "All set. I wouldn't miss recording this flight."

Much to her surprise, Raven saw Morning Star running back to her. Out of breath, she whispered, "Raven, will you be okay? Will you be safe staying another night? Alone?"

Catching the inference of her sexual safety, Raven answered, "Yes, Windy is good protection against roving bears and is a trusted dear friend. I'll be fine. You can pass that on to Leigh, too."

"That is comforting to hear. Please try to understand, we ask questions as a mother to her daughter. We think of you as one. Love you, and thanks for one of the most wonderful afternoons I've had in years. Between us girls, it looks like all three of us have some mighty nice men in our sights . . . now to bag 'em. Doesn't that sound terrible?" Star chuckled.

"Naw, women have been doing so since the beginning of time. Have at it, girl.

Remember to mention my request to Gete Wabiska."

"Will do, with pleasure." Morning Star yelled as she ran to catch up.

The chopper descended. The bird hooked up to the mother ship. The hooking pair cleared the area, and the little yellow bird flew.

"Meadow base, this is FFS chopper. We are underway without any problems except for a restless bird below that is telling us, through her oscillations, that she'd rather be under her own power. That I can understand. See you soon. Thanks for being a great pair . . . A couple? I'm bringing Bear and Leigh tomorrow. Let's give 'em a good welcoming. They're gonna love the new hut. FFS out."

Raven answered, "Will do. As you know, she's planning a party. I'll see you then. Meadow base out."

Windy and Raven held each other close as the mother and baby bird flew over the tree tops and disappeared.

As they walked down to the hut, Windy got a little frisky while wrapping his arm around her. Raven reminded him, "Careful, big fella, just 'cause everybody has departed, the rules have not changed. Don't get too frisky, yet. Need I remind you, it's still separate beds."

"Yes, dear, I know. I'll behave."

"Good," she said. "If you do, we can go skinny-dipping in the morning."

"That's music to my ears, my dear. I'll sleep on that tune."

Several hours later, nestled in the new hut, she whispered, "Good night, dear. Sleep tight. If you conduct yourself properly tonight, you can wash my back tomorrow."

"Deal. Good night, Raven Maiden of the Meadow."

As the moon replaced the sun in the sky, a raven landed in its favorite pine and announced its presence.

Later on, a Dream Catcher's shadow moved across the room. It traveled from Raven to Windy as if uniting their dreams as one.

Chapter 30

Reunion

The late afternoon sun shined in their eyes as the thumping sound drew their attention. Dangling below the mother ship, the little yellow bird revealed herself in the setting sun of the western sky.

"Would you look at that, Bear? We'll live a lifetime and never see anything quite like this," Leigh commented as she and Bear walked along the flight line.

"You're right, dear. No one at FFS could even imagine this type of what Milt calls extraction. To extricate a perfectly good aircraft that's able to fly is unusual, to say the least."

"Dear, are you yammering just a little?" Leigh said. "There was some damage. You saw the plane, albeit for just a moment. The tail wheel was rendered a skid. There were tears in the elevators. Nevertheless, it was clear that your benefactors, directly or indirectly, still tip their hats to you. Many are grateful. Need I also remind you, dearie, if you've said it once you've said it a thousand times: property can be replaced, people cannot."

As the restrained Cub moved closer it appeared to come alive, struggling to fly away from its captive sling.

Bear spoke to her. "Sorry, girl, we'll go up again soon on a normal flight—I promise."

Leigh asked, "Did you call the kids at the meadow this morning?"

"Yes, dear. This morning at eight. They're fine, just as they were last night at eight." Jabbing her a little verbally and now physically with a little playful punch, he said, "Do you wish, mother, to have me call again at ten? You can ask if their dishes are washed, or better yet . . . behind the ears."

"Stop it! You know I'm just a little concerned; we are their guardians. It's the first time they've been left alone overnight. Just think if some scoundrel or a rogue bear wandered into camp . . ."

Bear interrupted, "—Or an aggressive two-legged alpha male, unnamed of course. Perish the thought that he may have romance on his mind, and there's my innocent little Raven Maiden pleading to retain her chastity against all odds. I do believe that's her voice I hear echoing across the Tongass: "Save me! Save me! Rescue me from this Tlingit warrior's wants and desires!' That's why the calls, true?"

"Stop. Would you stop it!"

"Well, isn't that the truth?"

"You know that's only part of my concern."

"Yeah, ninety percent. The other ten is probably focused on where they're sleeping."

"Kinda?"

"Dear, let me give you some advice from a couple of old timers who have loved and lost once or twice. Both Joe and I know women, and we know Raven Maiden through her words, deeds, and body language from an avuncular point of view. Now, if she told you she was not going to sleep with Windy while you're gone, she won't. For Christ's sake, give her a little credit. She's probably proud of the fact that you trust her. She sure does not need our absence to yield to passion. Dig down on your list of the most important human traits and pull out the word trust. Then use it."

"I'm sorry; you're right. I'm just a little embarrassed. Quite frankly, I'm just not sure I could behave under similar circumstances. Don't call again."

"Woman, where has *your* memory gone?! You're absolutely wrong. Do you remember who you held at bay, no matter how hard he tried? You submitted only after being blessed by Gete Wabiska. I do. It was me."

"Oh yeah. I forgot, poor baby." She gave him a big suck-face kiss.

"Wait, I'm not done. I didn't like it when you held me off, as Windy's not going to like being set aside, but sooner or later, he'll appreciate her more—and wait. Like me. You, dear, were worth the wait."

"Thank you, my dear." She asked, "How's the side feel after walking out here?"

"As I was told you earlier, it feels like someone hit me with a Louisville Slugger, and not just anyone; more like Ted Williams swinging for the bleachers. It hurts like hell!"

"Remember, doctor's orders are for two days bed rest and restricted activities for three. That's gonna happen, dear; I'm the enforcer. We've got a brand new bedroom suite where you can recuperate, with a huge window looking out to the meadow. The boys here tell me everyone hustled to have it completed for our arrival this afternoon. In fact, the most strenuous part of the next four days, for you, will be the vibration of the chopper ride to the meadow."

"Okay, okay. I'll behave. It's in my best interest, you know. I'm scheduled for chopper school in Juneau as soon as the Doc clears me, and I'm anxious to start."

"Gone again . . ." Leigh sighed.

"What?"

"Oh, I'm just complaining to myself. It seems you're gone more than home with me. If you recall, my dear, you went on your last DNR emergency the day of our honeymoon . . . with a torn-up back."

"I'll make it up to you, I promise."

"By the way, the administration of Skagway schools has approved my proposal for home-schooling Raven and Windy. They'll be anxious to hear the good news. They both need only eight more credits to graduate. I'll be able to teach that in one year."

"Excellent! You'll probably make those kids into University of Michigan wolverines, if I know your style. I can hear it now. Soon, when we receive a blessing from our Creator, we'll have to stand and sing, Hail to the victors valiant, hail to the conquering heroes . . ."

Leigh answered, "Sounds good to me."

Bear announced, "Look! Here she comes. She cleaned up pretty well in the rain and prop wash. Last time I saw her, she looked like a brush hog."

"All we women clean up pretty well for our men, no matter how badly we look at first."

"How true."

"Should I go over and help put her down?"

"Nope. Stay here. Joe's already leaning out the door ready to release her. She'll be dancing too much in the downdraft to get near her. She'll be rockin' and rollin' for awhile, and land hard, but she'll survive."

No sooner had Joe released her and Milt pulled away than the FFS repair crew converged on the little bird and rolled her into the maintenance hangar. Bear and Leigh followed her. The crew put her on blocks to do the necessary repairs, then stripped her of the engine cowling, propeller, landing gear boots, tail wheel, and huge "bush" tires.

Bear looked at her in shock and said to himself, *She looks naked.*

Rob, the foreman, stepped forward and explained the reason for the major overhaul. Simply put—she was due. The rough landing and at 90 hours since the last overhaul triggered the maintenance. He added that all planes are required to have an FAA-mandated 100-hour inspection and renewed certification. She was ready.

Then casually but surely, Rob gave the maintenance crew a subtle nod and Bear and Leigh found themselves surrounded.

Leigh whispered to Bear, "What's going on? What are they doing?"

"Don't know, but I think I'm about to lose a little arse, or additional scathing words of repudiation for the unauthorized landing and the torn-up Cub. They're angry." Bear thought, *Rob's body language disallows anger. What's goin' on?*

Rob finally spoke, "It's my understanding that you were the PIC of the J-3 Cub yesterday. Is that a correct statement?"

Bear thought, *What the hell? What the hell's goin' on?*

"Ah . . . yes . . . but . . . let me explain."

"Just answer the question," Rob said with some sternness.

"Yes."

"Was this woman your copilot?"

"Yes . . . but."

"No matter, it's *you* we're after."

"Did you or did you not land on an unauthorized runway?"

"Yes, but . . ."

"That's all this FFS crew wanted to know."

"But."

"No buts."

The FFS crew, with tools in hand, closed in the circle. Rob continued, "I have been designated by the BPA, Bush Pilot's Association, to award you a certificate of accomplishment and membership in the newly formed TG&BPA, Tall Grass and Brush Pilot's Association, with all rights and privileges. Allow me to read the commendation:"

Bear thought, *I'll bet Milt and Dave are behind all this.*

"On this day of our Lord, the TG&BPA awards Chi Mukwa the honor of being one of Alaska's finest. Finest, because he has no regard for normal runway landings and a total disregard for take-off requirements. He landed on a field of choice that appears to be an elevated plateau, called a *mesa*, a mesa so small a take-off was not part of the plan. We at FFS give Chi Mukwa his new handle: *Mesa Man.* This name is appropriate, since without FFS, he would still be on the *mesa!* Presented this day by the DPA, Daredevils' Pilot Association. Sponsored by FFS owners and maintenance personnel.

"As the old timers say: Any landing you can walk away from is a good landing."

Bear bit his lip while thinking of an appropriate response to these characters. Before he could speak, the FFS crew broke out in laughter and gathered around him to shake his hand, with Milt and Dave leading the pack.

As Bear shook Milt's hand, he said, "You bugger, I'll *get* you for this."

"Correction: don't you remember? I'm the one who *got* you from the mesa, Mesa Man. The crew came up with that handle. It's better than Plateau Pilot."

"Those stinkers," said Leigh as she looked over Bear's shoulder at the certificate.

Bear said, "My dad once told me, when you've got very little to add to the conversation, it's best to remain quiet. That's my choice to all you FFS scoundrels. Nevertheless, thank you. I'll hang it in an area where the FAA cannot see. Now that you've all got my infamous flight off your chest, Leigh has an announcement."

Leigh stepped forward with her smile still lingering from the joshing Bear had just received from FFS, and said, "We owe so much to our friends and those here at FFS, Bear and I are inviting you all to a pig roast at the meadow tomorrow at noon."

Bear added, "Yes, partly due to the Cub's retrieval and repair, but mostly for just being the kind of people we can count on when help is needed. The hut's addition needs an open house, too."

Leigh told Milt and Dave, "Make sure you're at the chopper at eleven tomorrow. Gete Wabiska will be blessing the addition and whatever else needs his spiritual grace."

The crew hollered, "Hip-Hip-Hurray!" and shook hands with Bear, all with a big grin, then returned to the Yellow Bird, the Cub's new name.

Leigh had arranged for a caterer to deliver a roasted pig, foodstuffs, and refreshments for twenty to FFS at ten; the gang would leave at eleven. Six maintenance men and nine friends would be a large group, fifteen in the chopper. Milt indicated that number would not be a problem, if Bear held the pig. They were still picking on him.

Geez, at DNR Headquarters, was also invited.

Bear was hustled back to bed in the guest room behind ops since Doc was coming to change the dressing and check for infection. Bear played by the rules and slipped into bed. Urging Leigh to join him did not work. "Later, dear. We'll catch up in our new pentagonal suite," Leigh begrudgingly said.

Before leaving Bear, Leigh turned back to take his temperature, a good indication of whether the antibiotics were fighting infection. "Bear, open your mouth."

The reading was good, at 99. While she wrote it down for the doctor, he grabbed her by surprise in a place only a married woman should be . . .

"Stop that, you horny old man. You're not supposed to get excited!"

He responded, "Well, dear, you'd better get out of the room because your pheromones have just crashed into my hormones. You'd better run for your life."

"I'm out of here. See you later . . . if you can behave yourself."

"No guarantees."

*   *   *

Windy received a call on the plans for a house warming party. He busied himself laying firewood in the pit and cleaning up. One unusual request from Gete Wabiska was to lay some wood for a fire at the old altar site on the plateau. Windy did not ask why; rank has its privileges.

As he came down from laying the fire, Raven asked, "Are you finished? I can help, if not. I'm done, in the hut. Wait 'til you see how neat it looks. I've moved all their personal stuff into the Penta from the Octa, set up her desk, and put all Bear's stuff on the opposite side of the room. It looks great. They'll have to finish the details. Your and my areas are neat, also. Our beds are about five feet apart; that should satisfy our 'keepers.'"

Windy answered, "Five miles is the only distance that would satisfy Leigh."

"Don't he so hard on her; she'll calm down."

"Say," Windy asked, "did you contact Gete Wabiska about our request?"
 "I did. It will not be a problem."
Windy said, "Let's hit the sack. It's goin' to be a long day tomorrow."
"To the sack it is. Come on." Windy led her to his.
"To our separate beds, my dear friend."
After their normal passionate jousting, with Raven keeping him at bay, she gave him a kiss and they settled down to the business at hand: sleep.
Silence.
Ten minutes later . . . "Raven, are you sure you want to do this? What does Gete Wabiska think?"
Raven got up in her revealing Univ of Mich XX-size T-shirt, walked through the buffer zone, gave him a quick kiss, and said, "*I'm* absolutely sure."
She ran back to bed before he could grab her, "See you at the river at six. If you behave, you can wash my back, again. Night."
He groaned, "Night. I'm supposed to sleep while thinking of that?"

*   *   *

Everyone arrived at the meadow by noon. The athletic FFS gang had fashioned a ball field and were playing a wicked pick-up game of baseball. That meant anyone who could pick up the ball could play. Adding to the spirit of the game was a pitcher of beer at each base, to encourage runners to stop and enjoy the game rather than worry about scoring runs.
The FFS pilot and copilot, predictably, had each taken long walks with their newfound loves, Janet and Star. Leigh and Bear showed others the results of construction managers Raven and Windy's work with FFS. Then they joined in the ball game.
Thump—Thump—Thump came the sound of the lightweight Bell-10 chopper Geez flew from DNR headquarters in Juneau. As he descended, Leigh and Bear walked out to meet him. Geez had brought two passengers: Mark, the manager of DNR's Bravo station, and John, his student intern. As Geez powered down and the wolves returned cautiously from the bush, tears welled up in Bear's eyes. He waved hello to the survivors of the Bravo station tsunami. They trotted out to him and Leigh, looking fit as fiddles.
Being from the U of M, too, she immediately dominated the conversation until they got to the fire and some beer. They all retold their own particular angle of their experiences in the tsunami and the ripple effects of the Soviet pilot washing up and into the grotto. Chinodin joined in with countless questions about this international incident . . . heretofore kept very quiet. Soon they were out of yarns and starting to talk about their new assignment from The U.S. Department of the Interior, in measuring the effects of global warming on Alaska's food chain, so Leigh called for

chow.

She noted, "How the heck can I call all these people? They're scattered. I haven't seen the pilots and their women for the longest time."

Geez volunteered to help.

"What are you going to do?"

He went to his chopper, reached under the seat, pulled out a bugle, and blew "Assembly." He hoped the hungry crowd would remember the sound when John Wayne barked the command to his bugler to assemble the troops.

It worked. Everyone knew the sound of the U.S. Cavalry on the move.

As the evening wore on and everyone filled up on pig or beer, Leigh noticed the conversations becoming softer and more mellow. It was time to make her announcement. She stood up, asked for everyone's attention, and proclaimed, "We are honored by your presence at our house warming on the people's meadow. Bear and I have more wealth from the Creator and your caring ways than any possessions bought with gold. Your vigilance is priceless.

"You are all welcome to stay over," she continued. "Windy and Raven have a canopy strung over some spruce boughs near the hut. Sleeping out-of-doors is a wonderful experience you should enjoy. Stay with us. Fall asleep as the Tongass shares with you the movements of all the plants and animals of the forest. I'll swear you can hear life as you've never heard it before. Be our guest. I'll make breakfast in the morning.

"Finally," she concluded, "Gete Wabiska has chosen the site of the collapsed altar over the sacred cavern of our Tlingit ancestors to ask for Manitou's blessings. He feels this location draws on the Songs of the Earth. Please follow him to the fire pit on the plateau. Its warmth awaits you."

While walking up the path, the crew from FFS looked at each other and said to Leigh, "We're definitely staying. We're in no condition to do anything but crawl into the sack."

Geez spoke next. "Is there a doubt? I'm not flying out while overfed and overserved. I didn't intend to drink *that* much." He chuckled.

Milt smiled, put his arm around Janet, and told Leigh, "Your questions on staying are rather deceptive. I wasn't flying back tonight, anyway."

Janet smiled, too. "Don't worry. We won't let on and spoil your story." Leigh winked at them both as all eighteen two- and four-legged celebrants headed up to the fire.

*   *   *

Gete Wabiska raised his arms to the sky, "Friends, we gather on Earth Mother's bosom to thank the Creator, Gitchie Manitou, for His blessings on our lives. We are here as His people to honor the gift He provides in good and bad times. Tonight is one of the many good times He provided as we enjoy the fellowship of each other in His Kin(g)dom. I chose this site of the former altar of our forefathers who reside below. Beneath us is the sacred cavern of our past—the vestige of the Tlingit nation."

He continued, "My father, Golden Bear, explained to me many moons ago that this is 'The Place Where You Go To Listen.' According to legend, this is the spiritually-attuned place where we can hear the voices of the spirits—the unseen things around us. This is the place where you can hear the pulsating patterns of the earth's drums, the seismic events that abound in Alaska. My children, lend your ears to the quiet, the solitude of the earth. You will hear the drums, the shimmering sounds of the sun setting, the chorus of the dancing solar wind, and yes, the abyssal tone associated with the rotation of the earth. Listen to the ambient sounds, the music of the earth working below. Shall we listen?"

Silence enveloped the group. They listened in wonder of the sounds.

He continued, "I have been asked to have our hostess, Leigh West, speak to you on a very important announcement. They are all yours, my daughter."

Leigh hugged Gete Wabiska, turned to the group and said, "As we plan for changes in seasonal activities, let us remember the winter's snow restricts our movements, but it is also the time in the white silence when the bear and the deer develop their young in the womb.

"Now, my friends, if you're with the one you love, hold each other close, feel the double dose of the love of this earth and the erotic love of your mate. Tell your lover what he or she wants to hear. Tell your lover what he or she has never heard before—go ahead. If he or she is not with you tonight, let your lover know later. Then thank the Creator for the glorious day we've had on the meadow.

"Have you noticed, as I, the development of our two youngsters on the meadow? They have changed from teenagers to young adults. Part of their success is due to living in the forest and their caring friends. They truly are a model of a couple that respect the spirit of Manitou's grace.

"I introduce to you Raven Maiden and Wind Spirit, who have asked me to announce their engagement tonight to their special friends—their very special friends gathered in the forest."

The group buzzed.

Leigh, with tears in her eyes, smiled at Bear.

"Would you step forward?" asked Leigh.

Holding hands, Raven Maiden and Wind Spirit stood before Leigh.

"This beautiful pair has asked me to read what they wrote of their feelings they have for each other:

"I cannot turn away. I cannot leave the rich life and experience

we've shared. I want you more than life itself. I wouldn't trade
you for anything on this earth. I cannot live without you. My former life does not exist—it is our life now. I humbly ask you to be
my soul mate. Will you marry me?"

Leigh asked Gete Wabiska to bless the couple.

He raised his arms. "It is indeed a pleasure to be a part of your decision. May
the Creator be with you as you show your love for each other. Bless you, my children."

Leigh proclaimed: "It appears to me that a new generation of Tlingits will
continue its presence in the Tongass as we elders move on. Tonight marks the beginning of a new chapter of life on the meadow."

Raven Maiden and Wind Spirit turned to face the group. They thanked their
friends for being present on this special night. They asked Chi Mukwa and Runs
with Wolves to join them.

Raven Maiden spoke. "You both have given us the clarity of life, you have
removed the clouds of *unknowing* and made our future known to us. We love you."

As the four embraced each other, and the sun reached the horizon, chanting
pulsated patterns with the drums below.

They were, as the chief said, in The Place We Go to Listen—to listen to the
Songs of the Earth, where the spirits are pleased with man's fulfillment.

As the assemblage moved to the meadow, a white owl flew silently above the
throng for all to see. It circled the meadow as if to join the celebrants, and perched
in one of the twin pines by the bench.

Leigh looked up and said, "He's here; we are truly blessed. Thank you Manitou.
You have guided us on a journey to greater heights than I could have hoped. I have
a new family, a place in life, an understanding of myself and my world like I never
imagined."

Chi Mukwa and Runs with Wolves joined Raven Maiden and Wind Spirit. They
stood facing the setting sun as the rhythmical drums and songs of the earth filled
the air. The Great Spirit was pleased as another generation of Tlingits had decided
to live in the Tongass.

The Fresh Ink Group

Publishing
Memberships
Share & Read Free Stories, Essays, Articles
Free-Story Newsletter
Writing Contests

Books
E-books
Amazon Bookstore

Authors
Editors
Artists
Professionals
Publishing Services
Publisher Resources

Members' Websites
Members' Blogs
Social Media

www.FreshInkGroup.com

Email: info@FreshInkGroup.com

Twitter: @FreshInkGroup

Google+: Fresh Ink Group

Facebook.com/FreshInkGroup

LinkedIn: Fresh Ink Group

About.me/FreshInkGroup

COURAGEOUS LADY:

A Woman's Alaskan Quest for Native American Spirituality

By Mark Allen North

In the first novel of *The Lady Trilogy*, auburn-haired Leigh West travels to Alaska's majestic and mysterious Tongass National Forest in search of self-discovery and harmony with nature. In her journal, she chronicles all she learns from native Tlingit tribesmen and nature: the cunning wolves, belligerent brown bears, and those transforming seasons of the region's glorious landscape. It is through Native American spirituality that she sparks new passion within herself, a new appreciation for the physical world, and a life filled with love.

www.FreshInkGroup.com
ISBN: 978-1-936442-12-6

VALIANT LADY:

A Woman's Alaskan Quest for Native American Spirituality

By Mark Allen North

In the third novel of *The Lady Trilogy,* auburn-haired Leigh West continues her adventures in Alaska's majestic and mysterious Tongass National Forest in search of self-discovery and harmony with nature. In her journal, she chronicles all she learns from native Tlingit tribesmen. She marries one and adopts two, fights a devastating fire, and promotes environmental concerns all in those transforming seasons of the region's glorious landscape. It is through Native American spirituality that she sparks new passion within herself, a new appreciation for the physical world, and a life filled with love.

www.FreshInkGroup.com
ISBN: 978-1-936442-14-0

PAPALA SKIES

By Stephen Geez

Chicago native Rochelle DuFortier likes to imagine the future, her world a series of picture postcards so vivid they sometimes seem real. When a foolish mistake at thirteen causes her mother's death, she's sent to a secluded Hawaiian valley, an outsider "haole-girl" among pidgin-speaking boys who hurl flaming papala spears under the full moon to summon her mother's spirit. After boarding school and a prestigious university back east, the ambitious young woman is torn between chasing new career opportunities, discovering her mother's heritage in a remote French village, and meeting obligations pulling her back to Hawaii.

On this island steeped in ancient mythology and modern superstition, Rochelle tests the possibility of sharing pieces of her life with those whose beliefs she barely understands and never intends to embrace. She dives the depths of a pristine coral lagoon, conceals bodies in a subterranean lava tube, and challenges the eruptions of a living volcano, even as she deciphers the truth about her mother's death and struggles to satisfy new debts born of old betrayals.

Papala Skies is the story of a young woman who makes all the right choices, only to find herself living an unexpected life. It is about the need to belong, and seeking one's own version of truth amid such differing cultures' responses to wrenching loss and abiding grief. It is about yearning for a sense of place, yet having to confront new ways to honor the love of family and friends.

Will Rochelle lose what matters most, or might she learn what the smart octopus already knows?

www.FreshInkGroup.com

ISBN: 978-1-936442-07-2

JAZZ BABY

By Beem Weeks

While all Mississippi bakes in the scorching summer of 1925, sudden orphanhood casts its icy shadow across Emily Ann Teegarten, a very pretty young teen.

Taken in by an aunt bent on ridding herself of this unexpected burden, "Baby" Teegarten plots her escape using the only means at her disposal: a voice that makes church ladies cry and angels take notice. "I'm gonna sing jazz up to New York City," she brags to anybody who'll listen. 'Cept that Big Apple—well, it's an awful long way from that dry patch of earth she used to call home.

So when the smoky stages of New Orleans speakeasies give a whistle, offering all kinda shortcuts, Emily soon learns it's the whorehouses and drug joints promising to tickle more than just a young girl's fancy that can dim a spotlight . . . and knowing the wrong people can snuff it out.

Jazz Baby just wants to sing—not fight to stay alive.

www.FreshInkGroup.com
ISBN: 978-1-936442-10-2

BEEN THERE, NOTED THAT:

Essays In Tribute To Life

Observations, Inspiration, Remembrance, & Noteworthies To Share

By Stephen Geez

The simple lives of everyday people in a mundane world prove extraordinary in this collection of 54 personal-experience essays by novelist Stephen Geez. The eclectic mix of memoir, commentary, humor, and appreciation covers a wide range of topics, each beautifully illustrated by artists and photographers from the Fresh Ink Group. Geez catches what many of us miss, then considers how we might all share the most poignant of lessons. *Been There, Noted That* aims to reveal who we are, examine where we've been, and discover what we dare strive to become.

www.FreshInkGroup.com
ISBN: 978-1-936442-05-8

WHAT SARA SAW

By Stephen Geez

The boy looked back.

A simple pencil drawing, this depiction of a child watching from the reeds of a country pond frustrates and angers Geoffrey, unexpected reactions that stir Phrekka's lifelong passion for understanding the elusive power artists infuse in their creations.

Their only clue a "Sara" signature, the unemployed graphic designer persuades the enchanting Korean-American curator to help him discover more images by this enigmatic artist. From her world of privilege and mystical spiritualism to his of heartland farms and fundamentalist values, they will cross the country in search of the meaning in Sara's sketches, an odyssey to divine one extraordinary person's singular secret for touching people's souls.

Staggering revelations entangle them with issues of mortality and faith, sexuality and family violence, obligation and responsibility, deception and truth. Only by looking close at the dark and profane will they have any chance of coming together to create a legacy more beautiful than either ever imagined.

What Sara Saw paints exquisitely vivid portraits of two young people who must follow their hearts to recapture that innocent grace long lost to the whims of circumstance and fate.

www.FreshInkGroup.com

ISBN: 978-1-936442-03-4